Wartime for the Chocolate Girls

ANNIE MURRAY

Wartime for the Chocolate Girls

MACMILLAN

First published 2023 by Macmillan
an imprint of Pan Macmillan
The Smithson, 6 Briset Street, London EC1M 5NR
EU representative: Macmillan Publishers Ireland Ltd, 1st Floor,
The Liffey Trust Centre, 117–126 Sheriff Street Upper,
Dublin 1, D01 YC43
Associated companies throughout the world
www.panmacmillan.com

ISBN 978-1-5290-6499-5

1 3 5 7 9 8 6 4 2

A CIP catalogue record for this book is available from the British Library.

Typeset in Stempel Garamond by Jouve (UK), Milton Keynes
Printed and bound by CPI Group (UK) Ltd, Croydon, CR0 4YY

Visit **www.panmacmillan.com** to read more about all our books
and to buy them. You will also find features, author interviews and
news of any author events, and you can sign up for e-newsletters
so that you're always first to hear about our new releases.

. . . they are wrapped first in metal foil, then in an airtight wrapping gummed at the edge, then in a purple and gold wrapper. The machine on which I work wraps 80 of these blocks every minute . . . People often ask me 'do you find it monotonous doing the same job all the time?' Well no, because although you might think that every day appears to be the same, the same noise of the machines, the same miles and miles of chocolate bars and blocks from the Moulding Department, I've got so used to it that I can talk and joke with my friends as I work. That makes every day different and I enjoy it.

Food Factory: The Story of One of the World's Largest Food Factories, Told by Some of its Workers, c.1938

It has been my aim and that of the other directors – and I don't think it is a low aim – to make the business profitable. My second aim has been to try to make Bournville a happy place. The provision of amenities, of good buildings, is of course a help, but a spirit of justice, of fellowship, of give-and-take, an atmosphere of cheerfulness, are more important than material surroundings . . . My – our – third aim, has been to serve the community as a whole, but always giving the public a high standard of quality at a reasonable price, striving to be efficient and enterprising in our policy. We have also tried to make Bournville an asset to the neighbourhood.

Edward Cadbury, *Bournville Works Magazine*, December 1953

Bournville: the Cadbury village. What was once farmland, four miles to the south-west of Birmingham's industrial heart, the Cadbury family transformed into a garden chocolate factory, a green suburb with gardens and playing fields, with specially designed housing for the workers in the tree-lined streets around it. A small brook, the Bourn, trickled past nearby. The railway ran sinuously at the edge of the works. And one of the intricate networks of the city's canals threaded its way to the wharf at Cadbury's. The barges glided in to moor up, laden with sacks of cocoa and sugar, with churns containing gallons and gallons of milk from condensing factories close to farms in the countryside, to manufacture the chocolate that was enjoyed in many countries of the world. That was a picture that could be painted in peacetime. But now, in the early 1940s, trade routes were endangered and supplies of milk, sugar and everything else were running short.

These were just some of the changes brought about by the war. Night bombing had battered and terrorized the city since August 1940, leaving old landmarks destroyed and streets with smashed, missing sections cracked open to the dirty sky; and leaving loss, leaving people sick with fear and exhaustion. Families were doing their best to stay cheerful for the kids, for each other – simply hoping to reach the next morning, and loving and clinging to what and who they had.

I

1941

One

Someone was banging on the front door. Six-thirty on Holy Thursday morning in their quiet Bournville street. The early morning after a night of one of the worst air raids of the war . . . Bang-bang, knock-knock. *Oh Lord, no, please no . . .*

Ann Gilby limped along the hall, wincing at the pain in her ankle, and stopped in dread on the mat, her hand raised to unlock the door. She still had a blanket round her from the shelter, trying to thaw out after last night. Whoever was on the other side, it could not be good news. If she left the door closed, just didn't answer . . .

None of them were home yet. Martin, her son, was out with the ARP. Her daughter Joy and husband Len were both at the nearby Cadbury works – he in the Home Guard, she on the night shift. All of them out, as bomb after bomb had fallen, smashing the city. With an effort, Ann forced her hand to the latch. The door swung open to reveal a familiar face.

'Annie? You all right, all of you?'

'Oh my . . . For heaven's sake, Hilda!' Ann sagged against the door frame, feeling as if her legs might give way. 'What time d'you call this? We're not long out of the shelter! And Martin's not back yet – nor the others . . .'

'Sorry.' Hilda had obviously not thought through the effect it might have, her turning up like that. Ann was still recovering from being injured in the bombing herself, without needing any unexpected callers. 'What a night!

3

Sorry for frightening you. I don't know why, but I had to come.'

Hilda stepped closer and looked into Ann's eyes.

'You are all right? It's just, lately – I don't know. I've had the feeling something's wrong.'

'We're all right.' Ann tried to brush this off. Where could she even begin, talking about all that was going on in her family? 'There's only me and Sheila here – and little 'un. They've gone up to bed, at last.'

Her eldest daughter, Sheila, had come home before Christmas, after Ann was caught in a bomb blast when out on the streets with a WVS canteen. Sheila had been living in a village down south, to get herself and little Elaine away from the bombing.

'Come in for a minute, Hilda. You got time?'

'I could do with another cuppa before I get to work, if you can spare it.'

'It'll take my mind off waiting . . . Is Roy home?' Ann asked, hurrying to the stove. Hilda's husband, like all of them, worked at Cadbury's, but he was also a fireman.

'No, but Fred called round to say he's all right,' Hilda said, seating herself by the table. She was handsome and dark-eyed; a strong, upstanding woman. She and Ann, now both in their forties, had been the best of friends since starting work at Cadbury's, aged fourteen.

'That was one of the worst.' Ann sat. It had sounded like some of the heaviest bombing over Birmingham so far, for hour after hour. It was a shock. All through the autumn there had been continual raids: so much destruction in the city, so much tragedy and fear and exhaustion – and bravery as well. Since Christmas though, it had tailed off a bit and they had been able to sleep in their own beds of a night.

'In Holy Week too,' Hilda sniffed, folding her arms. 'Barbarians!'

Ann found herself suddenly about to cry. Her broken ribs and scars from being caught in the bomb blast were healing, but her ankle, which had been smashed up, still gave her pain and she could not walk far or fast. And then there was the strain at home – all the things she had not told even Hilda, her best friend.

'You all right?' Hilda peered at her.

'It's just nice to see you,' Ann said, struggling with her wobbling voice. 'We don't get together enough these days.'

'Well, you'll have to come back to work then, won't you?' Hilda said.

Parts of the factory still looked as they always had – turning out chocolate bars, albeit chocolate made with powdered milk. A lot of it was parcelled up and sent to lads in the forces. But other sections of the factory were changed completely: the Metals Department was making parts for aeroplanes, as was the Chocolate Moulding Department. This was all part of a new firm, Bournville Utilities, which had been set up for the duration of the war, producing parts for companies like Lucas's and Austin.

Ann's and Hilda's daughters, Joy and Norma, were two of the minority of women in a sea of men already doing this work, producing parts for aeroplanes. Cadbury's was also producing gas masks – Hilda was working on these – and jerrycans, and filling anti-aircraft rockets. The buildings were draped with camouflage netting, and there were signs all over the place: 'Help to save materials!', 'Don't waste gas and electricity!', 'Avoid Waste!'

For a moment Ann ached with longing at the thought of Cadbury's. She had always been so happy working there. Even the air-raid shelters there – reinforced basements under the factory departments – felt safer than being in a little garden air-raid shelter, with only a strip of corrugated iron and some soil over your head. And there was more company when you were at work. She missed the WVS women she had worked with, but she knew she wasn't going back to that – not after what had happened. But everything at home was such a strain. She was so tired . . . And, faced by her friend's sympathy, she put her hands over her face and her shoulders shook with sobs.

'Annie?' Hilda leaned across the table. 'What ails you?'

It all came welling up – all the strain and sadness of the past months, the war going on inside her, and the tumult of emotions they had been through over the past few months. Ann longed to lay it all out in front of her old pal, to have one person she could truly confide in.

'Oh, Hilda,' she sobbed. 'Everything's such a mess and it's all my fault . . .'

Normally Hilda would have said, 'What in heaven's name are you talking about?' or some such, but for once she was silent in the face of so much emotion. It wasn't like Ann.

'Come on, Annie,' she tried. 'It can't be that bad. Let's hear it.'

Ann sat up, wiping her cheeks, but more tears welled up. She couldn't start talking, however much she longed to – not now, when the others might walk in at any minute. Even though all of it kept storming around in her head, she could not say it. It was all so laden with shame . . .

Martin is not Len's son. His father is someone I fell in love with before we were married, during the last war, but I couldn't marry him when I was engaged to Len and he was away fighting for his country. And then, years later, my lovely Tom came back, and I don't know what came over me but . . . We just had one afternoon together – that's all, in that whole time. And then I found I was expecting

Martin . . . And Len has been having an affair with a woman called Marianne, and now they have a little boy called George. But she was bombed out of her house and I don't know where she's gone, but I know he must be going to see her somewhere . . .

How could she come out with all that tangled reality? Not to solid, straight Hilda, who thought she and Len were exactly as they had ever been, all these years. Because both of them were trying their very hardest to keep up appearances, to act normal for the rest of the family and to rub along as they always had.

It's terrible and shameful, and it's all my fault, Ann wanted to wail to her friend. *I know Len must have felt all these years that part of me was never his . . . And the only people who know everything are Margaret and Cyril, and they're the last people in the world I ever wanted to hurt, because Len's mom has been a better mother to me than my own . . .*

Hilda was staring at her, and all Ann could do was burst into sobs once more.

'Annie?' Hilda said cautiously, as if her friend might be a bomb that was about to explode.

'Don't take any notice of me.' Ann made herself look up. 'It's since what happened, after that night, and being injured – it's made me so nervy . . .' Hilda's face was all concern and Ann tried to smile. 'Honestly, I'm all right.'

'Well, if you say so,' Hilda replied, but she did not look convinced.

There was a sound out at the back and Ann jerked herself upright, frantically wiping her face and craning her neck to look out of the window.

'Oh, thank heaven: it's Martin – he's putting his bike away.'

Two

'All right, Mrs Baines?' Martin greeted Hilda as he came in, unwinding his scarf from round his neck. He was a friendly lad with nutmeg-brown hair and grey eyes. Everyone liked him, though these days he was quieter than before, seeming more turned in on himself. Ann put it down to the war and all that had happened, and these tiring nights. Not to mention his age, the 'in-between stage' of fifteen – neither quite man nor child.

'Hello, Martin,' Hilda said fondly. 'You're taller every time I see you.'

'Eats like a horse,' Ann remarked. 'Given half a chance, anyway.'

'Is everything all right?' Martin looked from one to the other.

'Yes, course, love,' she laughed. 'It's just been a bit of a night, that's all. What about you?'

'It was bad,' he said. 'But much worse in town. Someone said they've hit St Martin's.'

'What – in the Bull Ring?' Hilda gasped. The church, with its tall spire rising above the market stalls, was known and loved by everyone.

'Apparently, and New Street. And a great big bugger came down in Steelhouse Lane . . .'

'Martin!' Ann got up, finally remembering to make tea. 'Language!'

Hilda and Martin exchanged grins. 'Getting out into real life's rubbing off on him, I can see,' she said.

'Oh, Hilda – I'm sorry, the tea'll take a while.' She set the kettle on the stove.

Hilda waved this away. 'I'd best be off. I hope the others get back all right. Ta-ra, Martin. Don't worry about seeing me out . . .'

Ann heard the front door open.

'That was good timing,' Hilda exclaimed. 'All right, Joy?'

Ann's heart thudded with relief. Her children were safe! Now there was only Len to come home. Blood rushed to her face as she thought of how close she had come to spilling out all her secrets to Hilda. Thank heaven Martin had come home when he did.

Sheila and Joy both knew about Tom. While searching for some of her things to take to the hospital after she was injured, they had found Tom's letter; just that one, so full of love that Ann had kept it, out of all the others, and could not bear to part with. But they did not know about their father's carry-on with that woman – not so far. And Martin, she would have to find the right time to tell him about his father. Every time she thought about it she shrank inside with dread.

But as for anyone outside the family, she and Len had managed to keep their shameful problems to themselves without causing any tittle-tattle, and that was how it had to stay, however great a strain it was.

Later that morning Ann was baking some little cakes, from a recipe she'd found in the factory's works magazine. She was spooning Bournvita powder into the bowl when she heard the rattle of the letterbox and the quiet slap of letters falling on to the mat. Immediately she hurried into the hall, her heart rate picking up speed. Before she had even picked them up, she knew one of the letters was from Tom.

9

She smiled at the writing on the other one – Alan, Joy's lad. She was glad they had made things up before he went away into the Army. Joy seemed really chirpy these days. She'd be happy to see it, when she woke up.

She went into the kitchen, poured a stewed cup of tea and sat at the table. Len had come in from his night with the Cadbury's Home Guard, washed and shaved, eaten his bacon ration with an egg and some wedges of bread and gone off to work again.

Ann had sat with him as he ate, feeling sorry for him. He was getting even less sleep than the rest of them. She often looked at him, this sturdy, blue-eyed husband of hers with his strong, wavy hair, and wondered where the man she married had slowly disappeared to. The light-hearted Len who loved football and cracked jokes. That Len surfaced now and again, when he was not so tired, but he was so quiet now, so ground down by everything. Guilt gnawed at her.

'Go easy,' she said as he got up to leave. She didn't really know what this meant, but it was an attempt at sympathy. Len gave a wan smile and left, hardly having said a word.

Sheila and little Elaine were still asleep, but it couldn't be long before Elaine would wake. Ann hurriedly slit the envelope with a knife. She read the brief note – Tom's dear voice speaking to her from the page:

Southampton, 9 April '41

My dear Ann,

As ever, I can't say I have a lot of news. We all just keep carrying on, as I dare say you do as well. There have been a few bad nights – not as heavy as in the autumn, but still bad enough. No point in dwelling on it, as I know things are exactly the same where you are. My

father has not been well this week, so I have been taking
up the slack in the business, but he seems to be on the
mend . . .

Ann read the short note. Tom's letters were, on the face
of it, disappointing. He often wrote about his work –
which, after all, was much of his life. Before the Great War,
Tom had been a marine engineer, but the loss of an arm and
an eye had reduced him to more of a stock-keeper and
salesman in his father's chandlery business. He bore the
frustration of this without complaint – what was there to
say?

Tom was such a decent man, who would rein in his feelings and would not say much to her, a married woman. She
was grateful to him for it and yet . . . The very existence of
this letter, of him, glowed in her life, an inner flame of love
and hope that – wrong and shocking as it seemed – kept
her going through everything. It was the last line she
always looked for, the feeling behind his few restrained
words: *'My love to you, as ever.'*

She slid the paper back into the envelope and sipped her
tepid tea. From the way Tom wrote, anyone might think
she was a sister, a friend, nothing more. This man whom
she loved, had shared passion with, had a child with. The
older Martin grew, the more he looked like Tom. For a
second, panic almost choked her. Was she mad, thinking
they could go on like this? All trying to get by, pretending? She and Len struggling to live on their past love, on
the familiar routine of each day, when often she felt like a
car rolling downhill with no brakes and precious little fuel.

'Just get on with it,' she grumbled to herself, getting up
and pushing the letter into her apron pocket. What else
could she do, but keep on trying to do the right thing?

'Is Nanna talking to herself again?' Sheila said, carrying Elaine into the kitchen.

'Hello!' Ann beamed, going to Elaine and stroking her cheek, pink from sleep.

Elaine, now nearly fourteen months, bounced with excitement – 'Nanna!' – and almost threw herself into Ann's arms.

Sheila, Ann and Len's eldest, was the more staid one of their daughters. She was a bonny girl with long, sandy brown hair and was big-boned, like her father and grandmother. But before the war she had been a timid, rather plaintive young woman. Ann was surprised every time she realized how much stronger and sure of herself Sheila had become. She was married to Kenneth, who was on the east coast in Air-Sea Rescue. Sheila had spent a difficult time there with him in Grimsby when she first had Elaine, before deciding to come back home to Birmingham. But her time evacuated to Goring-on-Thames, a village in the south, also really seemed to have toughened her up. The woman who had hosted her, Audrey Vellacott, sounded a good sort – but the husband had been a different matter. Sheila had really had to learn to stand on her own two feet.

'You all right?' Ann asked, as Sheila bent over the table.

Sheila shook her head, then looked round. Their eyes met, meaningfully.

'You sure?'

'I've missed this month.' Sheila stood up and a smile broke across her face. She had not seen Kenneth since Christmas, when he had been home on leave. 'We said if it was going to happen, it would happen.'

Ann swallowed her immediate worry. Here was her daughter, expecting a second child in the middle of a war – what if Kenneth was one of those who never came home?

But it was no good thinking like that. She returned the delighted smile.

'A brother or sister for you, little Lainy,' she said, kissing her granddaughter. 'You sit there, Sheila – I'll get you both some breakfast.'

Three

'You'll all come to church with me tomorrow, won't you, Annie?' Margaret said, on Easter Saturday.

'Yes, course we will,' Ann said eagerly. Anything she could do to please her mother-in-law, she would do.

'All right, bab – we'll call for you on the way.'

Ann's heart buckled. Margaret had not called her 'bab' these last months. Not once had she used that casual, fond way of speaking to her. Not since the day Margaret had walked on to the hospital ward and seen her with Tom. Now, she realized, Margaret had momentarily forgotten and was talking to the old Ann – the trustworthy daughter-in-law she had loved as her own – but she would be unlikely to do so again. She knew that something had been lost for ever.

Ann was not a regular churchgoer, but they always went at Easter. The family gathered down in the back room that Sunday morning. Ann had hard-boiled a few of their hens' eggs to paint with food-colouring for Elaine. She had come into the kitchen to find Len doodling Hitler cartoon-moustaches on them with a pencil.

'Oi!' she exclaimed. 'Those were supposed to look pretty for Elaine!'

Len grinned. 'Sorry – couldn't resist. They'll rub off.'

But she was heartened to see his mischief. He had been acting strangely for the past couple of days, hardly seeming to be with them, even when he was there. She wondered what had made him so cheerful all of a sudden.

14

Ann had on her best navy dress as they gathered to set off for church. Sheila, in a maroon skirt and cream blouse, had put Elaine in a pretty little frock in pale yellow. Joy, darker-haired liked Ann, pretty and vivacious, was in her Sunday best, a wool dress in a soft moss green. Martin wore his school trousers and jacket, which were getting short in the leg and sleeves, as he was growing so fast. Ann straightened his tie, patted his shoulders and grinned up at him.

'There – perfect!'

'Yes, Mother.' He smiled back tolerantly.

'You all look very nice. Oh, there's the door. Go and let Nanna and Grandad in, will you, Joy?'

Margaret and Cyril were also togged up their best. Margaret's steel-coloured hair, caught up loosely in a bun as she invariably wore it, was tucked under a brown velveteen hat, which matched her coat. Cyril looked very dapper, wearing a tie with his Sunday best.

'All right, all of you?' he said cheerfully.

Sheila, Joy and Martin all greeted them fondly and they both made a fuss of Elaine. Ann ached inside as she watched, seeing the toll that the last few months had taken on both of them. Margaret was a big-boned woman, kindly faced and, though now nearly seventy-three, she had always been active and strong. Suddenly she seemed stooped, her face more lined. Even Cyril, scarcely taller than his wife and with a chirpy, cheerful personality, was more bent, his face thinner and fragile-looking. But everyone was doing their best to hold it together, and Ann managed to keep up a smile.

'Where's Len?' Margaret said.

'Len?' Ann went to the hall to call up the stairs. 'Everyone's here!'

No reply came and she hurried upstairs. As she walked

into their bedroom Len was rummaging in the chest of drawers. What on earth had come over him now?

'What're you looking for?'

'Nothing.' He closed the drawer. He really wasn't looking for anything – it had just been a way of not meeting her eyes.

'You ready?'

'I'm going to give it a miss this morning. Bit tired.'

'What – the communion service? Your mother'll be ever so upset.'

The nights since the terrible Holy Week raids had been quiet, and Len had managed to catch up on some sleep, so why now? Ann felt suspicion burn in her.

Len looked away, uncomfortable. 'Well, I'm not, you know – religion, and all that. I think I'll just rest up, like.'

He was a truly terrible liar. He was going to see *her*. For a moment Ann stared at him, at his blushing cheeks and shamefaced manner.

'All right.' She went back downstairs, rearranged her face, determined to look cheerful as she went into the back room. 'Come on then, everyone.'

'What about Dad?' Joy said.

'He's staying here. Says he's worn out. Come on, we'll be late – let's get moving.'

Her mind was not on the service at all. The church of St Francis of Assisi was close to Bournville Green, the open space in the middle of the village, with the circular Rest House in the middle. Ann stood at the aisle end of a pew, between the pale, arched colonnades inside, amid the smell of wood polish and candle wax, her lips moving mechanically through the words 'Christ the Lord is risen today.'

Sheila was at the other end of the pew with her grandparents, Margaret helping to keep Elaine amused. Joy was

16

to her right, then Martin in the middle. Ann could hear Martin's tuneful voice, below Joy's sweet soprano. Did Martin sound like Tom when he sang? she wondered. She realized with a pang that she had never heard Tom sing.

Ann was burning inside. Should she even be here, in church? She had been unfaithful. A fallen woman, some would say. And so had Len, and now there was his son George, another child to bring up. God knew, Len had brought up another man's child. He had only discovered Martin was not his own a few years ago. How could she even begin to reproach him, given all she had done? Even so, his going off today, of all days, in the face of the whole family, his parents . . . What in heaven's name was he thinking?

She glanced at Joy, singing beside her, so fresh and lovely-looking, her voice soaring. Ann's lips turned up for a second. At least Joy was happy. She had her beloved Alan and she was on cloud nine.

Ann swelled with love for her daughters. Sheila and Joy had found out about Tom while Ann was in hospital. At first, when she was brought into the General, shattered by the bomb blast, everyone had thought her close to death. Maybe that was why Sheila and Joy had been so understanding when they found Tom's letter. They had even found Martin's birth certificate. Both of them had been so sweet, so tender with her and understanding – miraculously so, she realized. But then they had been overwhelmingly relieved that she was alive, after all that had happened; that she was going to be all right and they hadn't lost her.

Now though, did she imagine there was an edge to the way they looked at her and spoke to her sometimes? And who could blame them? Their mother was someone they did not really know. Shameful, unfaithful. Their brother was only half their brother, after all. It was Sheila whom Ann especially felt was silently reproachful. Good, solid Sheila, married to Kenneth and completely unable to imagine that she could ever love anyone else, or that he could, either.

Martin knew nothing of this. Not yet. And none of them knew about their father's unfaithfulness – about Marianne and little George. Margaret and Cyril knew, but they had not told the children: why load more on to them than they needed to know, the poor loves? It meant that Ann would always be the wicked one. The woman who had gone astray. But there was a part of her that wanted to be the one who was a sinner. After all, she sinned first and that, surely, had caused Len to turn to someone else?

Glancing along the pew as they sat after the hymn, Ann saw her in-laws taking a seat, with Margaret offering to take Elaine on her lap and Sheila handing her over.

Dear Margaret. Ann would never forget the look on her mother-in-law's face the afternoon that Tom came to the hospital when Ann was still recovering from her injuries. Margaret had walked on to the ward to find Tom there. Ann and Tom, who until then had not seen each other for fifteen years. Who, for a few seconds, had not seen Margaret come in and were too slow to hide from her what they were to each other. Ann, the betrayer of everything Margaret held dear. Once she was home from hospital she insisted that Len tell his parents about Marianne – about his child with this other woman.

Margaret had taken time to digest all this. She had returned in silent shock to her own house along the street. Later she came back to tell them what was what.

'I could knock your heads together, that I could,' she announced furiously. 'But your job is to carry on and look after this family. Cyril and I'll give you all the help we can, as we always have. You're married, and that's that. So pull yourselves together and keep your troubles to yourselves, because they're no one else's but your own.' Speech delivered, she got up to leave. 'Just get on with it, the pair of yer.'

As the vicar talked on above her head, Ann picked at the bobbly bits at the end of her navy coat sleeves, feeling as if she was going to explode. *Tom, Tom . . .* None of this was fair on him, either. It was madness, all of it. And it was all very well them trying to go on like this, with the children not knowing the half of what was going on – but if Len kept disappearing? She raged inwardly. *How could he?*

Margaret had insisted on cooking dinner for them all for Easter, even though Ann had tried to argue that she would do it.

'I'm easing up on the WVS work and you've got enough to do, Annie,' Margaret said. 'Specially with that gammy foot of yours. Anyway, I like to have a houseful. We can pool our rations.'

They all crowded into Margaret and Cyril's cosy back room, further along Beaumont Road. Mouth-watering smells of roasting beef and potatoes wafted from the kitchen. Martin groaned with pleasure.

'I could eat a horse. Two horses!'

'Horse is off today,' Cyril grinned. 'Watch out, babby,' he warned Elaine. 'Sinbad doesn't like his tail pulled about. Let's find you summat else to play with.'

They all managed to separate small child and cat. Sinbad, a solid black-and-white fellow, retired to the back of a chair and sat watching Elaine resentfully, his tail twitching.

Sheila sank back into a chair, glad of a rest as Martin and

Cyril played with Elaine. It was hard work, looking after one child while expecting another.

Ann and Joy helped Margaret with lunch. Ann hurried to obey every instruction, anxious, always anxious to do everything she could to show her mother-in-law that, despite all her sins and wickedness, she loved her and always would.

'Well, where on earth has Len got to?' Cyril called through. His voice was accompanied by a little *phuuch!* noise as the top came off a beer bottle.

'Run and get him, will yer, love?' Margaret said to Joy. 'He's probably asleep and forgotten the time.'

Ann felt her pulse start to hammer as the front door closed behind Joy. She just knew Joy was not going to find Len at home. What was he thinking, not coming to his mom's for Easter dinner? As she put a jug of water on the table, her mind was racing. Was this it? Was Len ever coming back? Or was this going to be the day he left home for good? Left all of them?

The front door opened again: Joy's steps on the hall lino, then the dark line of her brows, frowning.

'He's not there.'

Margaret came in from the kitchen. Her eyes met Ann's for a split second. Ann knew she was thinking the very same thing as her.

'That's odd,' Ann said, her voice light. 'He was going to have a nap. Perhaps he's gone out for a breath of fresh air. He'll be along in a minute.'

'Well,' Margaret said calmly. 'It'll spoil if I don't serve up now.'

'The lad'll be along,' Cyril said, lifting Elaine off the floor. 'Come along, young lady – let's get you into your high-chair.'

*

They were most of the way through the meal of beef and potatoes, parsnips and cabbage, all soaked in Margaret's delicious gravy, all chatting cheerfully, laughing at Elaine, saying 'Happy Easter' and trying to pretend there was nothing odd about their husband or son or father vanishing on such a day.

'Here's to peace and the end of that so-and-so Hitler,' Cyril said, raising his glass of ale.

'And to Ken coming home,' Sheila, feeling queasy, was not managing to eat much.

'And Alan,' Joy added. 'And dancing – and no raids!'

'And no rationing.' Martin was drinking ale as well, his voice a fraction louder than usual. All of them had pink cheeks.

They kept toasting, adding their own versions, to quiet nights and no more blackouts or shelters or U-boats . . . Ann heard the door amid the hubbub. Then Margaret heard it and looked at her questioningly.

'Dad!' Joy said as Len appeared at the door.

'Come on then, Son – better late than never . . .' Cyril was saying, when they all took in that Len was not alone. Blonde hair was visible at his shoulder. A slender woman, carrying a little lad. Ann saw that her husband's face was aflame: utterly ashamed, but aggressively defiant.

'This is Marianne,' he said, touching her shoulder and bringing her into the room. 'And little George. They've got nowhere to go, and I said they could come and stop with us for a bit.' There was a pause before he added, like a bomb dropping into the room, 'George is . . . my son.'

Four

Everyone froze. Ann's eyes searched the faces of her children, all stunned, unable to take any of this in. Joy opened her mouth as if she wanted to say something, but could not bring out any words. Ann's gaze found Marianne, standing beside Len but slightly behind him, as if she wanted to disappear. She clung to George, looking down, absolutely mortified.

Margaret got to her feet, Martin managing to find the presence of mind to grab the chair before it tipped over behind her. A lock of her grizzled hair fell over her right eye and she pushed it away impatiently. Her eyes were fixed, burning, on her son.

'Get out of my house!' She did not even raise her voice. 'Go on – get out.'

Len stared back at her, as if he could not believe what he was hearing, his face and ears aflame. Ann found herself feeling sorry for him. In all the years they had been together, she had never once heard Margaret speak to her son in that tone before.

'Margaret . . .' Cyril laid a hand on her arm, but she shook it off, quivering with emotion.

'No, love. I'm not having it. Not when we've all sat down to eat a meal on Easter Day. I'm not having . . . *this*' – she flicked an arm in their direction – 'spoiling a decent celebration. You can go down the road and sort yourselves out, but you're not coming in here – not now.'

'Come on,' Len, speaking very quietly, turned and took

Marianne's arm. No one else said anything as they left the room, and they all heard them go along the hall. The door closed behind them.

Margaret sat down as if her legs had given way. Everyone looked at one another, and no one knew where to start or what to say. In the end Sheila, after seeing the stunned faces of her brother and sister, said, 'Did you know anything about this, Mom?'

Ann nodded. For some reason her own face was burning, as if that shame also belonged to her.

'Yes. I did know.' She looked round at them all, eyes swimming with tears. She felt a sudden sharp pain in her injured ankle, as if all her agonies were confusing themselves with each other. 'Nanna and Grandad knew as well. But we thought . . . There's been so much happening and — We just didn't want you three to have to . . . We thought we could manage.'

It all sounded so ridiculous now. She looked round at them, tears running down her cheeks.

'It's all a mess. A terrible mess – your dad and me. We've hurt everyone . . .' She broke down, pushing her chair back, hands over her face as sobs broke out of her. 'And we're sorry – we're both so very sorry.'

She heard a movement and raised her head to see Margaret walking out of the room as if she could not stand any more. Cyril got up. As he walked past Ann, he pressed his hand on her shoulder for a second. 'Eh now, bab,' he said, so very awkwardly, wanting to give comfort, but then hurried out after his wife.

'Dear Lord, I think I'm going to be sick,' Sheila said and dashed from the room.

'Oh, Mom.' It was Joy who got up and came to her, put an arm round her shoulders. She couldn't think of anything else to say, but it meant the world to Ann, that touch of sympathy. She looked up to see Martin wiping his face and a wave of anguish went through her. Her beloved Martin – and he didn't even know the half of it.

'I'm sorry,' Ann kept saying. 'I'm just so sorry . . .' It was the only thing she could think of to say, because the two of them were so upset and awkward.

In the end, after a long silence, Martin said, 'So does this mean pudding's off?'

'Mart!' Joy whacked him on the shoulder, but it broke the tension and all of them managed a laugh through their tears.

Sheila came back, looking utterly wrung out. She sat down in a chair and said nothing. She was followed by Margaret and Cyril, with Margaret walking very upright, as if she had resolved something in her mind. Finding the three of them laughing, she looked very put out until Joy explained.

'Martin's worried about pudding.'

Margaret's face softened. 'Don't you worry, my lad – jam roly-poly is on the way – no one's going to get in the way of that.'

'Dead man's leg,' Martin cheered. 'My favourite! Oh, Nanna, you're the best ever.'

'And custard, even though it's powdered milk.' Margaret sank down at the table. 'Joy, go and bring it in, will you? And, Martin, you can help, since you're so keen. And after we've had it, we're going to get Len and that woman back up here and have things out.'

She eyed the dish as Joy set it on the table, with the long, amputated-looking pudding on it. 'I've never known a carry-on like this before, that I haven't.'

Elaine and George sat on the floor, looking at each other across a heap of wooden bricks, as bewildered as anyone else. It was blindingly obvious how alike they were:

George's father was Elaine's grandfather. George looked most like Sheila had done as a baby. Elaine was fairer, favouring her father Kenneth's colouring. What was even more startling was that the two children were clearly almost exactly the same age.

In this strange, fraught situation, the little ones made things easier.

'When's his birthday?' Sheila asked, as if Marianne was merely an acquaintance she had met at a baby clinic. Because what else was there to say?

'February the second.' Marianne spoke hardly above a whisper.

'Elaine was born on February the twelfth,' Sheila said.

Everyone let this sink in. Len was leaning forward, arms resting on his thighs and his shoulders hunched. At this, they seemed to hunch even more.

Ten days between the two children. So when his first grandchild was being born, Len's mistress's illegitimate child was already in the world, Ann thought savagely. She could see, from Margaret's face, that she was thinking the same. But at this moment even her anger felt unreal – just as everything else did. It was all like a dream.

Seeing Marianne sitting here now, with her fair hair and freckles, she seemed to Ann younger than when she had first met her. She also began to take in that Marianne was clearly not in a good way. She was wearing a limp, grey dress that looked as if she had had it on for days, a soiled black cardigan and some old-fashioned boots, black and cracked at the edges, which reached halfway up her shins. Ann remembered her as a pretty girl, but now her hair was oily and unkempt. She looked exhausted and beaten down and frightened. In a resigned sort of way, Ann found herself feeling sorry for her. She decided someone had to take charge of this situation, as Len looked like a fish that had already been lying gasping on a river bank for far too long.

'What's happened, Len?' she asked. 'Marianne?'

'We were bombed out,' Marianne said, her voice breaking, and she burst into tears.

'What – again?' Ann looked at Len, who nodded.

'After the last lot, she went to her nan's – in Highgate. Terrible place, on a yard, but she's got no one else. It were smashed up in the raid, Thursday night.'

'We went in the shelter at the back,' Marianne managed to say. 'We thought we were going to die. And then, in the morning . . .' She shook and sobbed again.

'I went over there and I thought . . .' Len put his head in his hands. 'It's taken me a while to find her – she's been in one of them rescue places for days.'

'What about your grandmother?' Ann asked.

Marianne seemed overcome, as if all the shock and horror of the past days were shaking themselves out of her.

'Oh dear,' Sheila said. She managed to sound horrified and sad and angry all at once.

'The old lady's been taken in by some neighbours a few streets away.'

'They've no room for me,' Marianne sobbed. 'And no one wants a baby in the house.'

'So you thought you'd bring her to live with your wife and family, did you?' Margaret said, glowering at Len.

'Margaret . . .' Cyril said. 'Lay off her.'

'I haven't even started on *her*,' Margaret erupted. 'Carrying on with a married man and then expecting his family to take her in!'

'I didn't,' Marianne sobbed. 'Don't, I mean . . . It was Len said we should come here, and I said it was wrong, but I've got nowhere else to go. It was terrible there: hardly any food and toilets, and I haven't had a proper wash for days – or George. He's red-raw underneath . . .'

Everyone looked at George, who seemed a placid soul despite the afflictions in his nether regions. He was still gazing in fascination at Elaine.

'I just thought,' Len said hesitantly. 'I mean, I couldn't leave them both there. I thought maybe if one or two of us could stop here with you . . . ?'

'Oh, did you now?' Margaret said. 'One or two? And which one or two did you have in mind? You and your mistress? Your children? Or is your wife supposed to give up her home to you both, while you carry on together as if nothing has happened?'

'It might be best,' Cyril ventured, 'if Len and . . . the young lady stopped here for a while—'

'Oh no!' Margaret erupted. 'I'm not having her in my house. If anyone's coming to live here, it's Martin and Joy – and Ann, if you want . . .'

'I'm not moving out of my own house!' Ann protested. Had Len gone completely mad? 'Why the hell should I? And nor should any of the children have to, either.'

'I could stop here for a bit, I suppose,' Martin said uncertainly. Ann felt her heart buckle.

Marianne was shaking her head. 'No – you don't need to move out for me. Look, we'll go . . .'

But Len stopped her getting up, murmuring something reassuring to her.

'No offence, Nanna,' Joy said. 'But when we get the chance to sleep in our beds, I want it to be in my own room.'

Sheila sat forward, looking furious. 'I tell you what: I've had quite enough of all this. I'm going back down to stay with Audrey. I don't want to be killed in my bed, and I certainly don't want Elaine living surrounded by all this . . .'

She waved a hand over all of them, her face full of disgust and seemingly unable to find the right word for 'all this'.

'I don't know what you've been thinking, Mom, Dad – either of you. I've never been so disgusted in my life.' Sheila got up, swept Elaine from the floor and headed for the door. 'I'll leave you to sort yourselves out, the lot of you.'

As she went out, finally, little George started to cry.

Five

'How are you today? How's the tummy? Firm and steady or a little wobbly?'

The Radio Doctor's teddy-bear tones came growling from the wireless. Ann clicked it off.

'Your tummy'd be feeling wobbly, if you were in my shoes,' she muttered, going back into the kitchen to start on the washing-up. At least she had missed the eight o'clock news – another dirge, no doubt.

It was Friday of Easter week, the end of what had definitely been the most difficult few days of her marriage. On top of that, the Germans seemed to be taking over everywhere: Greece, the Balkans, as well as North Africa. It was frightening to listen to. Sometimes it felt better just to stick your head in the sand and leave it there.

Martin came running down the stairs in football shorts.

'See you later . . .'

'Martin?' She tried to stop him, wanted something from him. *I'm sorry, I'm sorry . . .* Reassurance: do you still love me, in spite of everything? But then he didn't know about 'everything'.

'I'm late – gotta go. I'm meeting Ian and some of the others for a kick-about.'

The door closed. Ann went back and sank down at the kitchen table. Len had already left for work, and Joy was home in bed, after her night shift on munitions at Cadbury's. *She*, Marianne, was upstairs in the attic with George and hardly ever came down. When she did, she crept about like an apologetic little mouse. Even so, Ann felt as if her house was no longer her own.

Sheila had gone. Her anger and contempt, and the fact that she had taken Elaine away, had left Ann with a heavy, anguished feeling that she could not shake off. They would be safer, that was one compensation, but her little grand-daughter going away again felt worse almost than anything else.

'I couldn't be more appalled,' Sheila had raged at her, early on Easter Monday. She had had a night to think, still in her own bed; Marianne and George slept in the front room until she left.

'How old is Marianne, anyway – she can't be much older than me!'

'Twenty-five,' Ann said. This she had got out of Len last night.

Sheila glared at her.

'She doesn't even look that old. God, I thought you and Dad were decent people. I don't even know who you are any more – I've no idea! You're both as bad as each other. It's shaming. It's disgusting.'

'Sheila, stop it – calm down.' Joy had come in and was drinking a cup of Bournvita before taking herself off to bed. She got up and shut the kitchen door. 'Why're you going on at Mom? It's not her fault what Dad's done, is it?'

'Isn't it? Isn't she just as bad?' Sheila leaned queasily against the kitchen cupboard, arms folded. For a moment she looked like a little girl who has not won the prize at a party: sulky and disappointed. Ann wanted to go and put her arms around her. *I'm sorry* . . . It was the only thing she could think of to say, all the time. But then Sheila started off again. 'And while we're at it, what about' – she mouthed silently – 'Martin? When're you going to tell him your dirty little secret?'

30

'Right, that's enough.' Ann rounded on her. 'When I'm ready, and when I think it's the right time, I'll talk to Martin. When I think he needs to know – which is not now, so don't you go shooting your mouth off!'

'It's not our secret to tell, Mom,' Joy said. Ann was quite surprised by Joy's calmness in the face of all this. And as for Sheila – life had been easier when she wouldn't say boo to a goose.

'No, it's not,' Ann went on heatedly. 'Both your father and I have made mistakes, make no bones about it.'

'Mistakes!' Sheila folded her arms, shaking her head as if she could not believe what she was hearing. 'You call all this a "mistake"? Both of you carrying on, for years, the way you have. It's not like . . . I don't know, dropping a hammer on your toe or something. *That's* a mistake.'

'No,' Joy contradicted. 'That's an accident.'

'Oh, *shut up*!'

'We have *both* made terrible mistakes. And I'm sorry any of it has involved any of you children – I never meant it to. But then I never expected anyone to go rifling through my private things . . .' She eyed them both. They both looked set to argue, but Ann held her hand up to silence them. 'But what's done is done, and it's for your Dad and I to sort out. And however much I wish things had gone differently, I don't need you bossing me about, Sheila, thanks very much.'

'Well, that's all right – I shan't be here much longer,' Sheila said. 'I'm going back down to Audrey's tomorrow.'

Ann was startled. 'You're really going? Does she know?'

'I rang her. She said any time. She's on her own with the boys, so she'll be glad of the company. At least we won't be in the way *there*.'

You're not in the way here, Ann was about to say, but

it wasn't true now. She had had the wind taken out of her sails, and suddenly she felt like weeping again.

'Oh, Sheila. I'm sorry. With you expecting and everything. I wish you wouldn't go – and take Elaine.'

'Yes, well . . .' Sheila started to soften, tearful herself now. 'After that to-do the other night, I was thinking about it anyway. And if Her Majesty there has really got nowhere to go, at least she can have the attic for a bit.'

The three of them looked at each other, taking in the crazed strangeness of the situation. Only two days ago they would never have dreamt of this conversation.

'God, Mom,' Joy said, stirring her tea, 'I'd never've thought either of you had it in you.'

They all said tearful goodbyes to Sheila and Elaine the next day, and off she went. Ann walked her to Bournville station. She held back her tears until she was on the way home, the imprint of Elaine's baby-soft cheek on her lips. Looking across at Cadbury's as she walked back, she ached for the past. Those carefree days, herself and Hilda working side by side in the fillings department, all jokes and laughter, sitting out by the lily pool in the girls' garden at dinner time, the kindness of the Cadbury family. What a blissful time that had been – so uncomplicated by feelings and responsibilities . . . She yearned for those days.

She had met Len at Cadbury's and he had fallen in love with her. Many times in recent years she realized that his keenness on her had made her think she was just as keen on him. And she had been fond of Len – very. But she had also fallen for his parents, Margaret and Cyril, who were kindness itself, treating her as one of their own. If only she had known, innocent young thing that she was, that love could be so much more . . . Tears rose in her eyes again. That was what she had discovered, in wonder, when she met Tom, wounded in the campaign at Gallipoli, when she was already engaged to Len.

A feeling rose in her, a hunger. A great big bar of chocolate – that was what she felt like now; that would sweeten everything. Fat chance of that, these days!

Arriving back at the house, she pulled herself into the present, wiped her eyes and braced herself as she opened the front door. There was Joy home, asleep in bed – and Marianne.

Marianne was downstairs when Ann came back into the house, no doubt hoping to make the most of her being out. She was holding George and spooning porridge into his mouth. Hearing Ann come in, she turned, with a hunted look. All she had on was an old peach-coloured nightdress that Joy had given to her, her grey cardigan and some socks. Her blonde hair was hanging down, all tousled. She looked like a little child who had climbed out of bed after a nightmare. Ann was touched by the sight of her.

I don't have to hate her, she thought. What's the point?

'Why don't you put him in Elaine's high-chair?' she suggested. She brought it in from the back room. Marianne looked at her, amazed. They had seen very little of each other during the days since she had come to stay with them and, Ann suddenly realized, they had never been on their own together.

'You don't mind?'

Ann indicated for her to sit George in it. 'She's not going to be using it for a while.'

'She's gone because of me, hasn't she?' Marianne turned and looked at her. She was youthful, pretty and Ann could also see a firmness in her – a pride, of sorts. None of this was really her fault. She would have continued soldiering on in Katie Road, if things had been different.

'Partly,' Ann said, filling the kettle. She overwhelmingly

33

needed a cup of tea. Sitting it on the gas, she said, 'Well, you don't have much luck, do you?'

Marianne's lips twitched upwards for a second. She slid another spoonful into George's mouth. 'Falling for a married man and being bombed out, twice? You could say that.'

'Did you know?' Ann folded her arms.

'That he was married? Not at first, no. But him being older – I asked, after a bit. Len said no, to start, then yes, in the end. But it was too late by then.'

'Maybe you should have asked sooner.' Ann couldn't keep the bitterness out of her voice. 'Or didn't you want to know?'

Marianne hung her head so that her face was almost hidden between the curtains of hair. But Ann caught sight of her peering out, and there was something sly about it that made her uneasy. Had Len told Marianne about Ann herself – about Tom, about Martin? Had he poured out everything in some hour of need, making this young woman a party to all her secrets as well? Ann certainly wasn't going to ask. She went to wash the old grouts out of the teapot and tipped water from the heating kettle to warm it.

'We don't want everyone knowing.' She had to force the words out, her pride hurting her. 'The only people who know what's what are Len's mom and dad. So we'll keep it that way, all right?'

Marianne nodded. 'I've got no one to tell, anyway.'

Her desolate tone made Ann look round.

'What, no one? You must have some friends – and what about your grandmother?'

'Oh, that old crow.' She almost spat out the words. 'My best friends, two of them, joined up. Both in the ATS. I

34

was thinking about going as well, but I had a good job. And then I met . . .' She held back from saying Len's name.

Steam started to gush from the kettle and Ann filled the pot. She didn't take to Marianne especially, but she couldn't find it in her to dislike her too much, either. It just felt like having another child in the house. And what a fix Marianne was in – even though it was with her own husband, Ann couldn't help feeling sorry for her. It was Len she was furious with.

'Well, we'll have to muddle on for a bit,' Ann said. 'Unless you can find somewhere better to live. See how it goes.'

There was a pause, then she heard, 'Thank you' from under Marianne's hair, although truth be told, she did not sound all that grateful.

Six

Joy hurried up Linden Road that afternoon towards Hilda and Roy's house. Hilda had been her mother's almost-lifelong friend since they started working at Cadbury's before the Great War and, when they had daughters of almost the same age, the girls grew up together and both joined the Cadbury firm in their turn. Norma was Joy's best friend and the family had lived in Sycamore Road for as long as Joy could remember.

At least some things don't change, she thought sadly.

It was a relief to be out of the house with all the carry-on with Mom and Dad. It had all been a terrible shock, but most of the time she put it out of her mind. She had her own life to think about. And at the time when she and Sheila had found out about their mother, coming across Tom's letter during those dark, frightening days when Mom was in hospital, then they had simply been relieved that Mom was still alive. That was all that seemed to matter.

But one shock had followed another. She knew Sheila was appalled and so angry that she could hardly look at Mom and Dad. Joy felt differently. Disappointed, with the let-down feeling of finding out that people are not quite who you think they are. But after what happened with Lawrence Dayton, and coming so close to giving in to her feelings – her fear and inexperience being the only things that had stopped her, in truth – she had more understanding. About powerful emotions. About being drawn in, tempted.

And, though she could hardly admit it, she felt relief. Everyone should be faithful and in love 'til death do us part – that was the ideal. Of course. But did it mean that you had to stay trapped, if that was not how it was? Because she could see that Mom and Dad were just going through the motions. Could there not be a way out that did not bring such shame and disgrace? Could things not be more honest?

'That's not going to happen to me,' she muttered, hurrying up the road. Alan's face, his smile, appeared in her mind. His boyish happiness when they whirled around a dance floor together. Now she knew for sure who was the man she loved and that he loved her back. And she was going to make sure she lived without piling up regrets.

Norma opened the door and grinned, seeing Joy, her hair vivid ginger in the bright afternoon sunlight. Norma, freckly and flame-haired, very much took after her father Roy, a gentle giant, carrot-topped when young, though his hair was now faded.

'All right, kid? Come on in – Danny's here.'

Joy stepped inside gratefully. Everything felt normal and familiar here. Norma's parents Hilda and Roy were both at work. Since Joy and Norma were both on night shifts at the moment, they sometimes met up in the afternoon once they had had a sleep. Joy and Danny had been walking out almost since they were children, as he lived only two doors away.

'All right, Joy?' he called through as they came in.

'Hello, Danny!'

His cheerful grin met her in the back room. Danny was a slender, pale lad with brown eyes and a dry sense of humour, and Joy had always got along easily with him. Danny was apprenticed as an engineer at Cadbury's and even though he was still young enough to be called up, so far the call had not come. He had just started a stint of nights as well.

'How's everyone?' Danny sat back at the table in his shirtsleeves, as comfortable as if he was in his own home.

'Oh, all right – going along as usual, thanks,' Joy said. Then, realizing what an enormous fib this was, she felt her face blush red. Quickly she added, 'You?'

'Yeah, all right, ta,' he said easily.

'Danny – move, you lazy lump, and let Joy sit down,' Norma said.

'Sorry!' Danny shifted, letting Joy through to the table. 'You been dancing lately?' he asked as she sat.

'No. Not really. Working nights has really cramped my style. I think I'm going to ask if I can switch to days again. Anyway, it's a bit difficult when there's no one much to dance with!'

'You'd always find someone, wouldn't you?'

Joy laughed, feeling herself relax, settling into their company. 'Yes. Someone – but there's not many really good dancers. Not now Alan's gone.'

A soft, tender feeling stirred in her. Alan and she had had such difficulties, misunderstandings. But now she knew more of the truth about his family and the struggles they had had, she loved him through and through.

'Here.' Norma, looking stately and upstanding like her mother, swept in bearing a plate of chocolate biscuits that had been through some mishap or other. As Cadbury's staff, they could get reject products from the factory shop. 'Tea's coming.'

'Want a hand?' Joy asked.

'No, you're all right. You just sit on your backsides, the pair of you – you and Prince Danny. I'll do all the work.'

Joy and Danny grimaced at each other, but it was all good-natured. Norma never acted the true martyr. Danny was one of three brothers and the other two were now away, one in the Navy, the other in the RAF. Danny's mom was very glad that at least one of them was at home to be spoilt. 'She'd put the food in their mouths, if they'd let her,' Norma would sometimes say. 'I'm training him – I'm not having that!'

'You seen the new sheds they're putting up by the cut?' Danny asked. 'Nissen huts, sort of thing.'

'No – what for?' Joy seldom had reason to go near the canal.

'More war work, I think,' Danny replied.

'Maybe we could get moved over?' Norma said, coming in with the teapot. 'I wouldn't mind a change.'

'It'd be cold in there, wouldn't it?' Joy said. 'Just think, in the middle of winter!'

'Oh, I 'spect they'll look after us,' Norma said. 'They usually do.' She poured the tea, then looked at Joy. 'Mom says you've got someone staying with you?'

Joy felt a jolt go through her. She wasn't sure if they noticed. How in hell did Hilda already know that anyone was in the house? Surely Mom hadn't told her? They hadn't even seen Hilda since the morning after the raid. It was incredible how word got around about things.

'Oh yes,' Joy said, trying to sound as casual as possible. 'She's a sort of cousin of our dad's: she got bombed out. Won't be for long, I don't think. She's got Sheila's room – Sheila's back with Audrey. That last raid really shook her up.'

'Cousin?'

Joy felt as if Norma's blue eyes were piercing through her over the edge of her teacup. It was a bad feeling, having to hide things from her friend, but this was the story her mother had asked her to tell.

'Yeah, they've never been close,' Joy said. 'But she's got

a baby – needed somewhere to go.' Desperate to change the subject, she said quickly, 'Danny was asking me about a dance. Fancy coming out again?'

'Count me out,' Danny said quickly. He always claimed he had two left feet, and Norma was quick to agree.

Joy and Norma had been assigned to what, before the war, was the Chocolate Moulding Department, now tooled up to produce cases for aeroplane flares and parts for Stirlings and Spitfires. She had finally found out that the small metal component that she was stamping out was for the gun doors of a Spitfire.

During the earlier part of the Blitz, in a shelter during a raid, Joy had met a man called Lawrence Dayton. Lawrence was a wonderful dancer like herself and for a time they had gone dancing together and had an affair of sorts, even though he was quite a bit older than she was. Lawrence had been sent from Southampton after the Supermarine Works there, producing Spitfires, was bombed, to work at the Spitfire works at Castle Bromwich. Joy had got pretty keen on him, but eventually he had confessed that he was married.

'Just think,' Lawrence had laughed when she told him about her work, 'you are making something for us to use!'

It had seemed romantic at the time – still did, in a way. Joy had known she had to get away from Lawrence, with his dancing eyes and feet. Her feelings had already been too involved, and this relationship could not go anywhere. It was true that everyone wanted to seize every moment of happiness, that they could be killed at any time – but it was still also true that Lawrence had a wife and child . . . But she looked back on that time with great fondness. He was not a con man or a trickster; he was a nice man, lonely for female company, living in a strange city that was being bombed night after night. And he had been honest with her – eventually. In some ways she still missed him.

That night, as she worked away on her machine, the time raced past because she was so caught up in her thoughts. She hardly even heard the chat and singing going on around her.

'There's an ENSA group coming in the break tonight,' the girl next to her called to Joy over the racket. 'Should be nice! Joy . . . Jo-oy! You're a dreamboat tonight, aren't you?'

'Sorry!' Joy flashed a smile.

'Thinking about your feller?'

'Something like that.' She blushed, caught out in reminiscing about Lawrence – but 'her feller' was definitely Alan.

Alan had worked at Cadbury's, in the Box Making Department. They had started dancing together and were a fantastic team on the dance floor. Alan was a blue-eyed, clean-cut, good-looking lad, light on his feet and fun to be with. They had started walking out together, but the more she tried to get close to Alan, the less Joy realized she knew about him. He would give her the occasional kiss, but always held back. One night, when she teased him, he had pushed her so hard she had hit her head against a wall. It had been frightening and had hurt her feelings terribly. Even worse, Alan had joined up and gone off to the Army without a word of warning.

But since then she had come to understand what was bothering him. She had gone – without Alan knowing – to see his family, who lived in a cramped terraced house in one of the old inner wards of Birmingham. It had come as a huge shock to her. Alan's father was in prison, his mother a wreck of a woman, seeming at least half out of her mind. The one person who reassured her was Irene Bishop,

Alan's elder sister, who had encouraged him to get away and work at Cadbury's. Irene had helped him in every way she could.

Joy understood now how ashamed Alan was of his background, how hard he had tried to make a different life and not to be anything like his father. And so far as anyone else could see, he had succeeded. But he was still afraid of himself and what he might do.

'Maybe going off – the Army and that – will make a better man of me,' he'd said the last time Joy had seen him, one rainy afternoon when they stood together in the grounds of Cadbury's. 'I want to come back better – for you.'

They had poured out so many things to each other then; her admission of bewilderment, his of shame and, most importantly, what they felt for each other. Joy was moved by what he told her. She came away knowing for sure that she had not been wrong, despite all her doubts. Alan was her love.

She had one thing that was now her greatest treasure: the letter that Alan had written to her a couple of days after she had seen him, before the Army took him away to wherever he had gone:

I know that once we get to wherever we're going I shan't be able to write a letter without some Army bloke reading it, and I don't fancy that. I know I've not been much of a letter-writer. I just didn't know what to say and I'm sorry for that, Joy. So now I want to say a few things, because I might not want to say them later, knowing someone might read it.

The way things were the other day – us talking the way we did – well, I feel different now. Knowing you've seen the state of our mother, that you know everything about my family and you're still prepared to give me a go: that means everything. I know I've always loved you. You're the best – you're beautiful. But I never really dared think we could be in it for the long term. I never thought I was good enough for you. Your family are strong, solid. They are good, honest people – but mine! My father's a brute, if I'm to be honest, as well as a thief. It's a terrible thing to feel ashamed of your father, but the way he treated our mom and . . . Well, you know the rest. But I thought you would never have me if you knew about me. You saying you'll give me a go is like winning every prize there is in the world. It's like the World Cup and every other prize rolled up together!

I know we're in a war and something might happen to me. It's not nice to think of, but it easily could. So if it does, don't be sad; just say it wasn't to be and live a good life. You're such a girl, Joy – your name is so right for you. But you did say you'd wait for me, so . . . Well, I'll do my level best to come back in one piece for you. It means everything knowing you're there.

In the meantime I'll try and write as best I can. But I wanted to send this – private – to say I love you and I'm honoured that you say you'll be mine.

Until we meet again, my love,
Alan

Joy knew the letter almost off by heart and could never read it or think of it without welling up. Even now, she had to wipe her eyes on the sleeves of her overalls. How she had felt before – so unsure of Alan, so angry, and going off with Lawrence Dayton like that – those feelings were all gone. She loved Alan, and only Alan, and she was going to wait for him. In the meantime she would throw herself into everything going on here at Cadbury's for the war

43

effort: knitting for the WVS, helping with dancing classes. Anything to make her feel useful and help the time pass until she and Alan could be together again.

Norma was working behind her and couldn't see her tears, but the chatty girl next to her could.

'You all right, Joy?' she called over.

Joy turned, forcing a dazzling smile on to her face. Because she was all right – she just missed Alan like mad. 'Yes,' she said. 'Just thinking, you know.'

The girl laughed. 'Oh, you don't want to do too much of that.'

Seven

Len came in after work, grunted a greeting through the kitchen door and went straight to the stairs. Ann hurried out of the kitchen.

'You on tonight?'

'Only if there's a raid.'

He didn't even turn round. She looked at him, the solid body of the man she knew so well, grey trousers, his jacket creased at the back, the thick neck, slight curl at the ends of his hair. He looked exhausted, bowed down. Ann listened as he disappeared from sight. Len did not go into their bedroom, but straight up to Marianne in the attic. Ann rolled her eyes as she waited, listening at the foot of the stairs. She thought she heard a faint cry from the top of the house, but nothing more after that.

We can't go on like this, she thought. But nothing else came to her in the way of a solution.

She and Len were still sharing their bed – for sleep at least. There had been no real intimacy for a long time. They slept at the far sides of the bed, turned away from each other.

On Easter night, after he had brought Marianne home, they had argued in hissed whispers.

'She can't stay here!' Ann erupted – quietly. 'What the hell d'you think you're playing at, Len? Bringing her to your mom's like that: are you mad?'

He sat in his vest, hunched on the edge of the bed, his back to her.

'*Len?*'

He turned, as if propelled by anger.

'Where the hell else could I take them? You should've seen the state of that place. A lav between God knows how many . . . Hardly any food – and the place stank. I couldn't just leave them there, could I? She's got no one else.'

She realized he was close to tears. Her tone softened a fraction.

'What happened to her family?'

'She was orphaned, young. The grandmother brought her up, and she's an old witch by all accounts.'

Ann nodded. She sank down on the side of the bed. 'There must be somewhere she can go . . . What about Miss Prince?'

Miss Prince was an elderly lady who lived along the street, who had often shared Margaret and Cyril's air-raid shelter, for company.

'There's a lodger in with her. Some wench down from the North to do munitions work . . .' He turned to face her, humble now. 'D'you want everyone knowing our business?'

They stared at each other. There was so much to say that Ann could not begin and ended up saying nothing.

She thought Len would come straight down again, but he stayed and stayed upstairs, even when she called, 'Tea's ready!'

Martin came down from doing homework and sat at the table in the back room. Ann fetched the food in from the kitchen.

'Where's Dad?'

'He'll be down in a minute.' She could feel rage rising

in her. Joy was out, but Martin was still here, having to see this. The lad was troubled by all of it, she could see. Of course he was. But she could not think of anything useful to say. She just caressed his shoulder as she walked past.

She had made some turnovers, stuffed with carrot and potato softened in dripping. Enough for all of them: they had turned out big and very unglamorous, but they were not going to go hungry, with some thin vegetable gravy and mashed potato added on. But even once she had brought everything to the table, still there was no sign of anyone coming down.

This was happening every night now. At least, previously, Len and Marianne had come down for the meal. But Len spent every night up there with her. Ann quietly boiled over.

'I'll go and get him.'

She almost flew up the stairs, propelled by fury. Yes, *she* was a sinner. Yes, *she* was a betrayer – but she had done her very darnedest all those years not to give in to her feelings, not to let any of that get in the way of Len, of her marriage. But now she was not only having to live with her husband's mistress, but do all the flaming work as well. The least they could do was come down and blasted well eat the meal she had cooked!

Stopping at the attic door, she heard sobs from inside. The girl, Marianne, was crying. Ann stopped, the wind taken out of her sails. Did she love Len – really love him? How must it feel to be here in this strange house, with the man you loved, while he slept every night in the bed downstairs with his wife, the woman who had brought up their children over so many years? Because whatever you felt for anyone, having children with them was a bond that never died . . . What hope did Marianne have of any future of her own?

She knocked, gently, and called through the door, 'Tea's on the table. Come down, will you?'

'Coming.' As Ann moved away, she heard Len get up and say, 'Come on, love. You can't stay up here all the time. Little 'un's all right. Come and have summat to eat.'

Ann went downstairs as fast as she could. 'They're coming!' she said brightly, to Martin.

Len appeared a few moments later with a tear-stained Marianne, who sat down at the table, looked at Ann, then at Martin, and mumbled, 'Sorry.'

Martin looked at Ann. He obviously felt sorry for Marianne. What he felt towards Len, she could hardly begin to guess.

'It's all right,' Ann said. 'Look . . .' She had been about to serve out the pasty-type experiment, but her better nature got the better of her, and the fact that her son was watching her. There was something about Marianne as well – something helpless. And there really was nowhere else for her to go, it seemed. 'We're all going to have to make the best of this, aren't we? So let's try and get along.'

Len shot her a grateful look and Marianne sniffed and nodded. She managed to look across at Ann.

'Thank you,' she said again.

Ann lay in bed that night, with Len – not asleep, she could tell – on the other side of the bed. It was very quiet. She felt nowhere near being able to sleep, her body charged with energy. She found herself almost wishing there would be a raid, so that she could put all this pounding of her blood into action. She listened, straining her ears.

'Len?'

He stirred beside her.

'If you could, would you move out and live with her?'

There was a long silence – so long that she was suddenly

choked with emotion again. She knew he was awake. She wanted to lean across and prod him, hard. Just *say* something.

'I dunno,' he said eventually.

There was a sound from upstairs suddenly, a baby's cry. For a moment Ann thought it was Elaine and was jarred all over again, on realizing it was George waking in the attic. She heard Marianne moving about and all went quiet.

'Do you love her?'

'Ann,' he pleaded. 'Don't.'

She wanted to be saintly and heroic. And she wanted to hurt him.

'I gave mine up. For you.'

Another silence, as if her words had to sink deep, travelling through mud. 'I know,' he said eventually. 'Maybe you shouldn't have.' There was another long silence until she thought he had fallen asleep. Then she heard, quietly, 'I love all of you as well.'

She lay for a long time, quietly, tears sliding into her hair.

Eight

'Sheila – over here!'

As Sheila walked out of the little railway station at Goring-on-Thames that raw afternoon, the place felt familiar, almost like home now, especially seeing Audrey waving at her enthusiastically beside the motor car. It hit her quite how much everything had changed. A year ago the idea of her living in a place like this, let alone being friends with someone like Audrey, would never have entered her head.

Audrey hurried over, all smiles.

'Let me take the case – your arms must be dropping off. Hello, Lainy darling – how lovely to see you both again!'

Audrey was very much the English countrywoman. She was neatly dressed, as ever, in a dark-red coat. Her brown hair, longer than it had been the last time Audrey saw her, was swept back under a jaunty hat, which matched both her coat and the lipstick that she had to dab off Elaine's cheek after leaning in to kiss her. She stepped back and her clear grey-blue eyes took in Sheila. Audrey looked very well. Sheila could not help thinking that widowhood was suiting her. Having known her husband, Maurice Vellacott – a bully of a man, who had died in a night of bombing in London – she could completely understand why.

'You do look tired, Sheila.'

'Yes,' Sheila replied. 'Well.' Where did she even begin? She was certainly not going to pour out to Audrey all the shameful goings-on in her family, but there was another reason . . . Blushing, she said, 'The thing is, Audrey, I'm expecting again.'

'Oh, how lovely!' Audrey's hands went to her face. 'Oh, my dear, that's marvellous news! How are you feeling?'

'I'm mostly over the sicky bit now,' Audrey said. 'It's all been very much like it was with Elaine.'

'I'm so glad. But you shouldn't be lugging all these heavy things around!' Audrey scolded as they walked to the car. 'It's so wise of you to come back: the air must be fresher, and you'll get much more sleep. The boys are *so* looking forward to seeing you when they get home.'

'Are they?' Sheila felt warmed by this. Audrey's lads, Edward and little Charlie, had not found it easy when she and Elaine were first evacuated to Goring. But then they had also been affected by their father and his dark moods. Things had gradually improved during the time Sheila lived there, and now she found herself actually looking forward to seeing them as well.

Audrey drove through the pretty village, with Sheila and Elaine in the passenger seat. Sheila found herself smiling, seeing the church, the sandbagged post office, the beautiful old houses with their anti-blast tape criss-crossing the windows. She knew Birmingham would always be home, but she had gradually grown very fond of this quaint little place.

'How is your husband?' Audrey asked. 'He must be so pleased to hear your news! Is he still on the east coast?'

'Grimsby, yes. He's all right.' Kenneth, Sheila's North Star: solid, loving, never changing. At least there was one person she could really rely on, she thought bitterly. A wave of grief passed through her – she was expecting another of his children, when he had hardly seen the first – grief for all the family life they were missing.

'And your sister, Joy?' Audrey was saying. 'What about her chap – is he in Greece, d'you think, or North Africa?'

'We don't know for sure yet,' Sheila said. Joy was so happy these days, but the thought of the great world out there, full of war and danger, chilled her. Alan could be anywhere, and anything could happen. Thank the Lord they were keeping Kenneth in England. She needed to stop feeling sorry for herself.

'Right, here we are . . .' Audrey swept up the steep drive and braked abruptly outside the beautiful house. Rosebuds were just beginning to appear on the old plant, which the summer saw sprawling across the warm red brick. 'Come on in – let's get the kettle on. We've time for a cup of tea before I go and fetch the boys.'

It was surprisingly nice to be back, and soon Sheila felt as if she had never been away. She had been there when Audrey received the news about her husband Maurice's death – and when a woman suddenly turned up, claiming that the little twin girls who were with her were Maurice's children. Sheila had seen the brutal, loveless marriage in which Audrey had been trapped.

All of this came back to her as they sat drinking tea that afternoon. Elaine was starting to pull herself up, holding on to pieces of furniture, and they laughed as she headed towards a round stool with a chintz-upholstered seat and dragged herself to her feet.

'The boys used to do that,' Audrey said, smiling. 'It's a good walker, that stool!'

Sheila looked round the cosy sitting room. A few things had changed: a dark-brown leather chair that had previously been there was gone, and a picture of a hunting scene, which had taken up half of one wall.

'Maurice's chair was such a gloomy old thing,' Audrey

said, seeing Sheila take in the changes. 'I was glad to get rid of it. And that picture went to his brother.' She looked steadily at Sheila. 'I've done my best in the village to play the role of wife in mourning weeds, but I'm not going to pretend with you, Sheila.'

'No point in that, really, is there?' Sheila said, hearing a dryness in her voice. Even though she knew what Maurice Vellacott had been like, had seen him be truly vile, she felt raw in herself. For a moment her mind flickered towards her parents, then shied away, horrified. Was *anyone* faithful and true? At least Audrey had stuck it out, she thought, as she sipped her tea. She had been faithful and done her best.

But Audrey had heard her tone. 'D'you think me dreadful, Sheila?'

'No.' Sheila leaned forward and touched her hand. '*No!* Of course I don't.'

Edward and Charlie came in, in their school uniforms with caps and satchels, all of which made them look like formal little men. The sight of them made Sheila feel tense, remembering some of the behaviour she had seen in them when she first arrived. Edward had slapped Elaine that first day when they arrived, and she was prepared for them to resent her just as much now.

But the boys actually seemed pleased to see her. Sheila was surprised by Edward especially. He was eight now, and so much calmer than the angry, vicious little boy she had met last year. He came across to her, gave her a shy smile and said, 'Hello, Mrs Carson.'

'It's all right – you know you can call me Sheila, remember?' Touched, she stroked his hair and the boy blushed and turned away, shyly.

Charlie who was nearly six, ran in, said hello to Sheila

and knelt down in front of Elaine, who laughed at the sight of him and said, 'Tarw-ie!' He giggled, delighted.

'Hello, Lainy! Shall I get the toys?'

Sheila and Audrey exchanged looks and a sad, sweet smile spread across Audrey's face. *My boys*, her smile said – *see how lovely my boys are*. How awful that the only way they could be sweet and gentle and free was once their father was no longer in their lives, Sheila thought, but that was how it seemed to be.

They all ate tea together and Sheila was surprised by how much the atmosphere had changed. She realized she was in a happy, relaxed household. The boys chatted about school and laughed at Elaine. She played up a bit for them, flicking some mashed potato across the table.

'Oh no, you don't, missy,' Sheila warned. 'Don't encourage her,' she said kindly to the boys. 'She's becoming a bit of a madam.'

'Mummy said that you work in a chocolate factory,' Edward said suddenly.

Sheila was startled. It was the first time either of them had ever asked her anything, as if previously they had not seen her as a person who had any existence outside their own house. But now they seemed curious. She laughed.

'Well, I did, before I had Elaine. And a lot of my family work there – it's the factory where they make Cadbury's chocolate, and cocoa and all those things. It's in a city called Birmingham.' They stared at her. Sheila glanced at Audrey, both of them amused.

'A factory?' Edward said doubtfully. 'Does that mean we're better than you?' There was nothing rude in his tone, but Audrey was horrified.

'Edward, don't be so rude! *Of course* it doesn't.'

Sheila was stung, but she could see the boy was only repeating something he had heard from the grown-ups around him. She knew what snobs people could be. It was not the boy's fault.

'Have you ever seen a factory?' she asked.

Edward and Charlie looked at each other and shook their heads.

'Well, it's a very big place with a lot of buildings, and inside there are machines where they make things. If we didn't have factories, we wouldn't have the things we use every day: no chocolate, or anything! The big room where my father works is where they mix the chocolate. There are great big – really big – vats where they mix the cocoa crumb and milk and sugar, and stir it all round . . . And then it goes on to somewhere called the Moulding Department, where they make it into bars, or Easter eggs and things . . . Not so many things, now the war's on. It's hard to get the milk, you see. They all go down big conveyor belts to be wrapped up in the wrappers. And then they get put into lorries, and that's why you can see them when you go to the sweet shop.'

They listened, spellbound. 'A chocolate factory,' Charlie said, as if this was a concept almost too hard to imagine.

'It wasn't always a big factory,' Sheila said, raking around in her memory for the history of the place. 'It started off in the middle of Birmingham in somewhere called Bull Street . . .'

'Did they sell bulls?' Edward giggled.

'No,' Sheila laughed. 'I don't think so. But the Cadbury brothers, one had a draper's shop and another one set up a shop selling tea and coffee, and then they began selling cocoa as well. And later, when they started making chocolate in bars and things, they didn't have enough room, so they moved out of town to Bournville, where I come from. It was all countryside then. So they built a big factory with all green round it, gardens and playing fields . . .'

'We'll have to go and see one day, boys,' Audrey said.

Sheila smiled, but she didn't think Audrey really meant it.

Once they had got the children to bed it was exactly like old times, the two of them by the sitting-room fire, as the nights were still chilly, drinking cocoa before they went to bed.

'I'm glad to have you back – at least for my sake,' Audrey said. She leaned close to the fire, wrapped in her dressing gown. 'How is your poor mother getting along?'

'Oh, much better, thanks. Her ankle still gives her trouble, but she's very well – it's a miracle really.'

'Thank goodness,' Audrey said. 'What an awful thing. Has it been bad up there lately?'

'Off and on,' Sheila said. 'There was a terrible raid just before Easter. I didn't want to chance it, after that.'

She wasn't going to tell Audrey the main reason she had left home. A flush of pain and anger went through her, thinking about it, and she hoped Audrey would think it was just the heat from the fire.

There was a silence for a moment, then Audrey said, 'I'm glad to say I'm not having any trouble from *her*.'

Sheila knew who she meant immediately. Monica Gordon – the woman who had been Maurice Vellacott's mistress. She had arrived before Maurice's funeral with her little girls – three-year-old twins.

'I make sure she has what she needs, for the time being, while the girls are so young,' Audrey said. She did not even sound angry.

'She seemed . . . all right,' Sheila said.

Monica had come to the funeral, without the children that time. She stood discreetly near the back of the little village church, then melted away afterwards to avoid any questions.

'Oh, she's a decent enough sort, I think,' Audrey replied.

As you are, Sheila thought. You could both have done with a much more decent man. Once again, she was almost tearfully grateful for Kenneth.

'Anyway,' Audrey said, her voice changing suddenly. She sat up. 'I've been thinking . . . Up until now I've done absolutely nothing for the war effort, and now you're here might be an opportunity. You wouldn't mind taking the boys to and from school, would you? It's only a case of walking down to the main road . . .'

With the petrol shortages, some of the local school children, like Edward and Charlie, were being transported the few miles to school by horse and trap.

'You see . . .' Audrey's face lit up suddenly with excitement. 'I've never got out and *done* anything. I've always just been the little wifey. But one thing I can at least do is drive, so I've decided to go and drive buses – in Reading!'

Sheila was startled. She had been expecting Audrey to say that she was going to start knitting or doing local WVS work.

'No, of course I wouldn't mind,' she said.

Nine

June

Ann sank on to a chair by the kitchen table. There was a bundle of whites on the floor, waiting for the wash, and the water in the copper must be hot enough by now. But she could not seem to find the energy to make herself walk into the scullery and get started.

Everyone was at work or school: Len, Joy, who was back on days, and Martin at the grammar school. It would be nice to think she had the house to herself, but no. *She* was still creeping about upstairs.

The struggle to keep everything appearing normal was telling on them. On her and Len, at least: he looked worn to a wafer. For herself, she see-sawed between a sense of detachment – where she could tell herself just to put one foot in front of the other, and to keep things calm in front of Joy and Martin – and rages that rose up in her hot and fast, making her whole body feel she was going to explode.

She rested her elbows on the table and put her head in her hands, hearing the hiss of the kettle heating.

'Oh God,' she whispered. 'Help me . . .' She had got into the habit of always carrying her latest letter from Tom somewhere on her – today tucked into the pocket of her frock. Feeling the crackle of it, the mere touch of the paper, always made her feel stronger, feel loved. It kept her going in the madness that seemed to have taken over her life.

So far as everyone else was concerned, Marianne was a 'cousin' of Len's who had been bombed out. A lot of people these days had lodgers squeezed into newly found corners of their houses: strangers from northern towns and from Ireland, who had come to work in Birmingham, or stray relatives turning up for one reason or another.

It was only Hilda who said, 'Cousin? Where on earth did *she* spring from then?'

Ann, her face hot with blushes, mumbled something about her being a relative on Cyril's side of the family, while realizing she really needed to get her story straight, and feeling terrible telling Hilda, of all people, such fibs.

'Well, how long's she staying for?' Hilda asked, 'and why didn't she stay with Len's mom and dad?'

All Ann could do was shrug: Margaret didn't think she could cope with such a young child in the house, with her not getting any younger . . . She babbled excuses.

Sheila was the only person who had come out and said it. 'You're as bad as each other! How could you? *Both of you?*'

And Ann asked herself the same question. Sometimes she felt she was living in a dream – or a nightmare, depending on the day.

But it was Joy and Martin she was most worried about. Joy acted as if none of it was happening – or as if Marianne really was a cousin of Len's, nearly a decade older than herself. She was bright and breezy, played with George if he was about and kept out of the way as much as she could, as if to say, *Well, I don't know what you've all been up to, but I'm just going to live my own life*. Which, when you came down to it, was fair enough, Ann thought.

But Martin . . . he'd be fifteen in three months and they were working him hard. Next year would be School Certificate exams, and he had already said he wanted to stay on and do the Higher Certificate. Ann glowed with pride. He was clever – a lovely lad. But here he was, now almost a grown man. And even before Marianne had turned up, Martin had become more withdrawn, seemed to have taken against Len as if they were strangers suddenly, who had nothing in common. And it was true: they didn't have much. Martin was going beyond what either she or Len had ever had in the way of schooling, and he was not especially keen on football – Len's main passion.

And now this pretty, blonde young woman was living in their house. Marianne was closer to her daughters' ages than to Martin's, of course, but even so . . . Ann looked for signs that he was disturbed by Marianne, but she couldn't find any. Martin was polite to her, never unpleasant, but distant – as if it was all the same to him whether she was there or not.

A couple of days ago, when Joy and Martin were home before Len, Ann had reached a point where she felt she would burst if she didn't say something to them.

'Come in here a tick, both of you.' She beckoned them into the kitchen, already having to swallow hard to fight back her tears. Len might be back any minute and she needed to keep a clear head.

Closing the door behind her, she faced her two youngest children. Joy stood with her arms folded, her back to the cupboard. Martin stayed by the door, arms hanging down, awkward-looking. They didn't look hostile, she realized, just helpless.

'I . . .' She thought she knew what she wanted to say, but now it seemed impossible. All she could think of was to blurt, 'None of this should be happening. I'm sorry for . . . all of it. I don't know what else to do.'

She didn't cry, didn't want to blackmail them with tears. She saw Joy glance at her brother, then look very directly at her. *You've got to tell him about his father*, her eyes seemed to say.

'Why doesn't Dad leave – take her away, somewhere else?' Martin said. His voice thickened. Ann realized her boy was close to tears and she felt as if her own heart would burst. 'It can't be nice for her living here and . . .' He didn't have to finish. *It's not nice for any of us, either.* He never had other lads round now, his school pals – he always went to their houses.

Ann struggled to know where to begin. There are no homes to be had, and it would be double rent and . . .

'He doesn't want to leave you – us,' she said. 'We're his family. And Marianne's only here because of being bombed out, twice, otherwise this would never have happened.'

'Oh, so this is Herr Hitler's fault,' Joy said sarcastically. Suddenly she burst out, 'I understand, Mom – in a way . . .' Her eyes said, *We can't talk about all of it, can we? How this is not just one-sided.* 'It's all a mistake and a mess, but it's horrible. We can't be normal or have anyone round. What do I tell Norma?'

'Marianne's a cousin – remember? Of course you can ask people round. Norma can come any time.'

They both stood there looking at her, so sad and embarrassed. These were the sort of adult, shameful things they didn't want to know about, never, ever thought could happen in their family.

'Look, we've got to get through this until she can move on.'

'What, with our stepbrother . . . half-brother – whatever he is,' Joy pointed out. 'She's never going to disappear now, is she?'

'This goes on more than you'd think,' Ann said, pleadingly. Though she had no real idea if this was true.

Joy stared at her. 'Doesn't it just?' she replied.

The memory of this conversation pierced Ann as she sat at the table. She was about to drag herself to her feet – there was washing to put in to soak while she dashed out to queue at the shops; she must get on! But she heard feet on the stairs. There was a pause as Marianne put her coat on in the hall, then walked into the kitchen with George in her arms, coat on and a dark-green wide-brimmed hat that Ann had never seen before.

'Oh, are you going somewhere?' Ann said. 'I thought you might go and do some of the shopping.' She bit back the words *for once*.

Marianne looked back at her, a brazen glint in her eye. She was hard to fathom. When the rest of the family were around, she was a sweet, apologetic little shadow, always trying to keep out of the way. But gradually, over these two months of dodging round each other in the same house, Ann had noticed that on the rare occasions they were alone together, Marianne had become a lot less apologetic and definitely less sweet. There was a defiance now, a look in her eye that said, *Your husband loves me, and you know it – and I know all about you as well, so don't you go thinking you're above me.* It gave Ann a powerful desire to slap her.

'I'm taking him up the clinic to be weighed,' she said haughtily. 'And then I'm going to check on my nan. I'll bring the pram back after the clinic – I can't take that on the tram.'

Ann's mind was racing. Marianne would likely need the eleven bus and a tram. Did she have the fares? She wasn't going to ask – no doubt Len was handing over what she needed. And here was she, worrying because Martin was growing out of another pair of shoes.

'No chance of them rehousing her, I suppose?' Ann asked hopefully. She doubted whether Marianne's grandmother, lodging in one room in some cramped little house, had even tried to find a new place to live.

'Not as I know of.'

'Well, when you get back, there's your bucket of nappies to see to.'

Their eyes locked together. Marianne was getting better and better at forgetting to do things she found unpleasant. When she first arrived, she had kept up with things, always trying to come to the kitchen when Ann had finished whatever she was doing. But now she was letting things slide. It felt to Ann as if she was doing it on purpose. A couple of times she had left the nappies soaking for so long that a rank smell began seeping through the house. Finally Ann, muttering with fury, had felt bound to wash them out herself. But she damn well wasn't doing it again.

'Aren't you doing washing this morning?' Marianne said.

'Yes. *Our* washing.'

'Only I thought . . . I mean, it doesn't take long.'

'No – so you can do it when you get back, can't you?' Ann said. 'Best get going on with it or you'll run out of nappies.' She gave a little smile, tight and insincere.

Marianne turned away, fussing over George. Had she even given the child any breakfast? Ann wondered. She hadn't seen her downstairs. She gritted her teeth, hearing Marianne putting George into the family pram, which they had oh-so-kindly said she could use. George was a strapping boy and Marianne could hardly carry him everywhere . . . He was also placid, thank the Lord. The noises of wheels squeaking on the linoleum, and of the door opening and shutting, finally ceased.

Just as Ann bent down to pick up the washing, there was a knock at the front door.

'For heaven's sake!'

She thought it was Marianne having forgotten something, but after dumping the sheets again and yanking the front door open with her pinner on, she found Margaret on the doorstep.

'Oh!' Ann gasped. She had hardly seen her mother-in-law since Easter and Marianne's arrival. 'Hello. Is everything all right?'

'You tell me,' Margaret said. 'Got a minute?'

Ann stepped back to let her in. The shopping would have to wait.

'I was just about to soak the sheets,' she said. 'Give me a tick.' She pushed the back door open, letting in the early summer air, and dumped the pail of George's nappies outside, before pushing an armful of whites into the steaming water in the copper and poking them with her wooden tongs. The soap moved in the water in white swirls.

She came back in from the scullery to find Margaret looking round the kitchen as if she was perhaps in a foreign country where customs were different – even though nothing had changed.

'Sit down, won't you?' Ann said carefully. 'The kettle's boiled.'

As Ann made tea, she could feel Margaret's gaze drilling into her back. Joy and Martin often went down the street to see Margaret and Cyril, but Ann did not feel she could. Beneath all the tension and difficulty of this awful situation lay the grief at losing their trust, and she felt tears rise in her eyes again.

'Len looks worn out,' Margaret remarked.

'Yes.' Ann turned and put cups on the table. She didn't care if nothing got done – shopping or washing. This was much more important. She knew Margaret was right about Len; she heard him tossing and turning beside her at night. But what could she do about it? Even though there had been few air raids to speak of since April, the war was exhausting everyone. He had all this going on, with Marianne on top of it. But then, she thought, sinking on to a chair, so do I!

'I saw her go out,' Margaret said. She gave Ann a very direct look. 'Looks respectable enough. Is she pulling her weight?'

Ann found she could hardly speak. Margaret was being sympathetic to her, and her throat seemed to close up. It felt that if she managed to say anything about Marianne, she would begin raging and shouting like a madwoman. She managed to give a small shake of her head.

'She's handed over her ration books?'

Ann swallowed hard, gripping her teacup. 'Oh – yes. Course.'

'The boy's bonny, I'll say that. But as for her: going with a married man like that.' Margaret seemed to have transferred most of her wrath towards Marianne – and Tom, for that matter. 'Whatever you've done in the past, Annie, this isn't right.'

Ann could not hold back then. She burst into tears, laying the cup down for fear of tipping it over, and sobbing so hard she could hardly breathe.

'I'm worried about the young 'uns,' Margaret said. Ann was nodding, tears streaming down her cheeks. 'They come round – I mean, they seem all right. Cheerful, both of them, bless them. But it's not right, them having to live like this, knowing who she is as well . . .'

Ann was nodding. *I know, I know. I feel as if I'm going mad.*

'That man, Martin's father . . . Is he doing what he said he would?'

'He's . . .' Ann blew her nose, pulled herself together. 'He's set up a savings account for Martin, and he's been as generous as he can be. I mean, he couldn't do the work he was trained to do, after the war, because of his arm – and his sight.'

Margaret nodded, respectful in the face of Tom's war injuries.

'Len didn't want him paying *us* anything – not a regular thing. It would have just rubbed his nose in it. But Tom's set up this account for Martin – for later.' A glimmer of happiness lit within her at being able to say Tom's name in an honest way. Tom – Martin's father.

'I don't know what to say, Annie.' Margaret's hard disapproval was gradually melting into her natural kindness. 'All my married years I've never thought of anyone but Cyril – nor he of me. We've been talking, of course. The other night he said to me, "You know, really, we've been lucky, you and me, Maggie. I suppose it's not everyone picks right first time, and most of them that don't are stuck with it."' She looked at Ann. 'Len's my son. My only surviving son now, and I hate to see him hurt, though that doesn't mean I think the sun shines out of his backside, Annie. But I do believe you stick with the person you made your vows to in church.'

Ann nodded. Her eyes filled up again and she could not speak.

'When did you meet Tom? At the hospital?'

She nodded. '1916.'

'You and Len were engaged?'

Again, a nod. Ann looked down. 'I'd promised Len. Maybe I should have done something then . . .' She found courage to look up. 'But you and Cyril were so good to me. I loved *you* both as well. And I thought, with Tom and him coming from somewhere else – I thought it would pass. I was never going to see him again, so . . . for both of us. And I did love Len. I just . . .' She didn't finish. *I didn't know how much more there could be.*

Their eyes met, then Margaret looked away.

'Well,' she resorted to saying, eventually, 'I never, ever thought I'd see the like of this in my family.' She let out a long sigh. 'Until Ida turned up.'

Ann heard the prickle of discomfort in her voice. Ida, the sister Margaret had been told was dead, had been 'put away' as a young woman, carrying the child of a man who had no thought of marrying her. Margaret had come across Ida – now calling herself Lizzie – one morning after a bombing raid, when she was working with the WVS serving tea to bombed-out survivors in a church in Balsall Heath. Lizzie, or Ida, had been returned to the Agatha Stacey home where she had spent so many years of her life.

As if speaking to her lap, Margaret said, 'I went to see her – a couple of days ago.'

'How is she?' Ann ventured to ask.

'She's . . . she's all right, I suppose.' Ann could hear her mother-in-law's voice thicken with emotion. 'More . . . with it, somehow, once she was back in her . . . the place she's used to. She kept saying to everyone, "This is my sister!" She sounded so . . . proud.'

Margaret's composure crumbled and she could not speak any more. Ann reached out and placed her hand over Margaret's, which were clenched in her lap. Her own throat ached with tears.

'I feel so ashamed,' Margaret wept. 'Not of her – of *us*. Of my family. How could they do that? All these years.'

'It wasn't your fault,' Ann said. 'You didn't even know, did you? All you can do is visit her now – she likes to see you.'

Margaret nodded, trying to wrestle her emotions under control. Her lips tightened and she got up.

'All I'll say is: you've both made your beds, you and Len . . . And somehow we've got to keep this family on the right road, for the children, if nothing else.' She buttoned her cardigan, then looked up at Ann, her eyes filling again. 'Drop in and see us occasionally, will you, bab? Cyril's missing you.'

Ann's chest heaved and more tears came.

Margaret turned at the door. 'Sheila all right?'

Ann could still only nod, recovering from all this. When Margaret had gone, she sank down at the table and wept. All the tasks she had not yet begun seemed like a mountain to climb. She felt like a candle, burned right down to the stub. As she calmed, a thought came to her, like a lightning bolt. She got up from the table, took off her pinner and put on her raincoat, even though the day was fine. And, trying to ignore the pain niggling in her ankle, she set off up Linden Road.

Ten

Marianne stepped off the tram near the middle of Birmingham and turned into Gooch Street. Looking warily around her, she pulled her hat down low and her collar up, even though the day was warm, cuddling George close to her face.

'Won't take long, Georgie,' she murmured to him. 'Let's just get this over with.'

George's round, amiable face stared into hers, glad of her undivided attention.

'What a lovely little lad!' the nurse had said.

Marianne had turned up at the clinic wearing her mother's brass wedding ring and calling herself Mrs Gilby. Thank God it was years since Len's blasted wife had had a child – no one was going to ask any questions.

'He's your first then, dear?' the nurse had said.

'Yes.' She looked as wide-eyed and new to all this as she could manage.

'Well, you've got a lovely bouncing boy! A good weight – he's coming on a treat.'

Marianne hurried along the busy shopping street now, past queues of women standing with baskets and ration books, chatting and having a moan to each other. Heart pounding, she turned at the corner where the Sir Charles Napier pub marked the entrance to Bissell Street and scuttled along, head down.

Mother of God, how she loathed this place – the sooty frontages of the buildings, the blue-brick pavements –

exactly like the yards in Aston she thought she had finally escaped. Every person she passed caused her heart to thud in alarm, in case they recognized her. It was a relief to turn along the narrow, stinking entry into a back-court – a yard of four houses backing on to others on the street.

But one of the greatest dangers could still lie ahead of her. Marianne tiptoed to the end of the entry and peered into the yard. A woman she did not know was turning the mangle next to a maiding tub, which was leaking a trail of water across the yard. Wet clothes hung limply on the line, strung between one of the gaunt brick back-houses and the wall on the other side. The woman doing her washing was young and thin and looked caught up in her own thoughts. There was no sign of Mrs Sullivan, that tittle-tattling hypocrite.

Marianne hurried to number two and tapped on the open door.

'Is that you now, Marianne?' Mrs O'Riordan said, appearing at the door. 'I'd hardly know you, under that hat. Oh – and look at the little one!' She tickled George under the chin with her stubby fingers. 'What a lovely boy you are now, aren't you?'

Clare O'Riordan was a fleshy, down-to-earth woman with four married daughters and another still at home. She had made herself a friend to Marianne's grandmother – a friend indeed, when she had nowhere to go.

'Will I put the kettle on?' Mrs O'Riordan asked. 'You'd fancy a drop?'

'Thank you,' Marianne nodded absently, getting inside the poky little house as fast as she could. 'Is she in?'

'Well, where else would she be now?'

'Is that you, Marianne?' Her grandmother's voice rang down the stairs, making the hairs stand up on Marianne's neck. 'I'll not come down – my feet are troubling me today.'

'No need to shout, Grandmother,' she said. 'I'll come up.'

'Will I bring you up a cup, the two of you?' Mrs O'Riordan asked.

'Ah no – just call, and I'll come and fetch it.' Marianne forced a smile as she went to the bare wooden stairs. 'You're very kind.' She had a lot for which to be grateful to Clare O'Riordan, so thank heaven and all the angels for her, even though the woman irritated her half to death.

The attic room was painted a faded pale green, the walls showing wounds where lumps of the plaster had chipped off, and half the ceiling was mould-stained and bulging with damp. It contained only a black iron bedstead, and a china po' with a cloth over the top – which, by the smell, had not yet been emptied – tucked beneath. A bodged mat, small and grey with age, was the single covering on the dusty floorboards, and the only other furniture was a small chest of drawers and a wooden chair with a frayed string seat, plus the wooden-armed, semi-comfortable chair in which her grandmother was sitting.

The chair was half-turned towards the narrow gable window, which – if you were to stand on something to see out – looked over the yard. It was the only illumination coming into the room, and a murky beam of light picked out the bitter features of her grandmother's face. As ever, the old lady wore her black widow's dress, some relic from the time of Queen Victoria, smelling of ancient sweat and mothballs.

The sight of her turned Marianne's innards. That dress – the dutiful Catholic wife, making a display of mourning for that marvellous figure of a man who had been her husband. It made her want to vomit into her grandmother's lap.

Teresa Walsh was seventy-six years old and had begun her life on a Wexford farm, coming to Birmingham in 1883 to marry Patrick Walsh, a distant cousin with whom she had only a scant acquaintance and for whom she developed an even scanter liking, once she had endured more of him. She had borne him thirteen children, eight of them surviving. Two of those were lads lost in the First World War – one of them Marianne's father, and not one of the surviving six children came anywhere near her. At least her elder two daughters sent her money now and then, so that she could subsist and cover the rent.

Teresa Walsh's pale eyes swivelled in her sharp face, the thin hair scragged back into a bun.

'I see you're still painted up like the whore of Babylon.' Her gaze scorched over Marianne's hair. 'And you've brought *that* with you.' Her eyes fixed with disgusted loathing on George.

Marianne caught her breath. Her grandmother's viciousness could still feel like a burn, even now. How had she managed to spend those weeks after she had been bombed out in Selly Oak, living back under the same roof as this vile, embittered old harridan? Every day of living with Len's family was like a punishment, but at least he was there to protect and look after her. And his family were a mild ordeal, compared to living with Teresa Walsh and her poisonous tongue.

'George,' she said, her voice heavy with irony. 'This is your great-grandmother Teresa. Do you remember her?'

Teresa turned away, her face twisting with contempt. 'No good talking to the creature as if he understands you. He's probably feeble-minded, coming into being through the sins of the flesh . . .'

She withdrew a little square of white cotton from her sleeve and wiped the corners of her mouth. Marianne watched, her grandmother's every tiny movement utterly familiar and sending ripples through her of memory, as well as powerful, hateful feelings.

Why did she still have anything to do with this spiteful old lady, she asked herself? This bitter harridan who had never protected her from her grandfather's evil molestation, who could do nothing but condemn her and bring down the wrath of God and the Church upon her? Loathing burned in her as if she had swallowed acid.

But Teresa had not always been as bad. When Marianne was four and her mother died, her grandmother took her in. It was only later that she came to hate her – as much for what she did not do as for her actions . . . And Marianne had no one else: her grandmother was the only living blood relation she ever saw. Marianne also knew that it was thanks to her getting into trouble with John and James Brady in the way she had, and because of all the threats from the Brady brothers, that she and the old lady had had to escape across town, to live far from the Aston neighbourhood they had always known. And now, because of the bombing, Teresa had been forced to move once again. After that, Marianne felt she owed her – at least to see that she had a roof over her head.

'Has anyone been?' Marianne asked, swallowing all the hurt and rage that Teresa's nastiness brought out in her.

Tight-lipped, her grandmother shook her head.

'Why would they now? Those Bradys'll not be looking for you here.'

Marianne hesitated.

'It's just . . . her.' She jerked her head towards the yard. 'That Mrs Sullivan. I don't like the way she looks at me. She goes to Mass, I suppose?'

73

'Sure, she goes to St Anne's, same as I do. And all you have to do is make your confession and you can come back to the church yourself – instead of living out there with those Protestant pretenders . . . Quakers or whatever it is they call themselves! Godless heathen,' she added with burning contempt.

Marianne ignored this; she had heard it so many times before. But that job, Cadbury's and working at Rowheath, had been her salvation. Or so she thought – before she met and fell for Len.

'D'you think she knows someone – from over there, in Aston? Only, people talk . . . No one's said anything? Not to you?'

They heard footsteps on the stairs then.

'Your tea'll be after stewing – will I bring it up?'

Mrs O'Riordan was already panting her way up, without waiting for an answer to this question, and her pink face appeared round the staircase.

'There you are – I've put you a little bit of sugar in, so.'

As had happened many times before, Marianne was startled by the sudden change in her grandmother, who became somebody halfway civil.

'That's good of you, Clare,' she said. 'You'll have this before you go, Marianne?'

Marianne, who was frantically searching her mind, wondering if Mrs O'Riordan could have heard any of what she said, managed to say thank you, and the woman's sturdy frame disappeared downstairs again.

Her grandmother's eyes met hers over the rim of her cup, which she lowered after taking a slurping sip. 'You've not heard anything from those Bradys – still?' she said.

'No.' Marianne shook her head, shifting George on to her other hip.

'You're a fool, you know. You don't look so different as

your own husband wouldn't know you. It'll catch up with you one day.'

'Not if I can help it.'

On the way back Marianne stopped in Selly Oak and went into the chemist's. Once she had got back to the house and up to the attic, she slipped the little bottle of hydrogen peroxide out of her bag and pushed it right to the back of her top drawer. She bent to look in the mirror, anxiously examining the parting in her hair. As soon as she had a moment when no one was in the house, she would sort her hair out again – before the roots started to show through.

She sank down on the edge of the bed, taking George in her arms again and cuddling him.

'What're we going to do, Georgie boy?' she murmured over the top of his head.

The little boy turned to look at her, his big, innocent eyes filling with puzzlement as he saw the tears that started to roll down his mother's face.

Eleven

Later that afternoon, knowing that Marianne was back and the two of them were alone in the house, Ann went to the foot of the attic stairs.

'Marianne? Come down a minute, will you? I want a word.'

She heard furious shushing directed at her from the top of the stairs and Marianne came hurrying down.

'I've only just got George to sleep!' she hissed.

'Oh,' Ann said blandly. 'Sorry. We'd best go down then.'

Marianne followed her. Ann gathered herself, feeling the young woman watching her from behind. She knew she was still quite trim for a woman of forty-seven, her figure gently curving, with only a few threads of grey in her brown hair. Joy looked very like her, with her dark eyes. But now she could only feel like a worn-out matron compared to Marianne – *twenty-five*, blonde and fresh-faced – and it was not a nice feeling.

'*Dear Tom,*' she had written when she got back at dinner time, '*I know I can't go on like this, in this situation. So I've decided to make some changes . . .*'

On the kitchen table she had placed the ration books: all of the family's and Marianne's, in a neat pile.

'Right.' She didn't ask Marianne to sit down. 'From now on, things are going to be different around here. Now that my children are so grown-up, I've got no excuse not to do some kind of war work. So next week I'm going back to work at Cadbury's on munitions, and you'll have to take on more of the work. I don't expect you to do my family's washing, but I do expect you to do your own. You will share the cooking with me – and with Joy, when she can. And I'd like you to do the shopping.' She nodded pointedly at the ration books.

'Me?' Marianne looked flabbergasted. 'But I can't keep going to the shops!'

'Why on earth not?'

'Well . . . I've got Georgie to look after!'

'You have,' Ann agreed. 'Which gets you nicely out of bringing any money into this household. But I s'pose you managed to get to the shops when you were on your own? There are plenty of young mothers who feel up to standing in the meat queue with a pram – because if they don't, no one gets any tea, do they? And the pram's useful for carrying things. This isn't a hotel, bab.' She folded her arms, feeling as if she had suddenly turned into an old matron, reading the riot act like this. 'You're going to have to pull your weight, like the rest of us: you can start with a practice run today.'

'What?' Marianne was outraged. 'You're just going to go out and leave me to do everything? You only want me here as your skivvy!'

'Marianne.' Ann leaned in close, hands on hips. 'Me, want you here? At all – for anything? Are you joking? If you can see anything from anyone else's position, then for a sec, try looking at mine!'

Marianne's eyes burned back at her. 'He loves me. He does! He always said you were a cold fish and never gave him what he—' She stopped, quelled by the expression on Ann's face.

Ann had to grip her hands tightly together so as not to slap the uppity wench. She was not going to start discussing her life, or her husband, with *her*.

'Two months you've been here – in *my* house. And you've hardly lifted a finger. Well, madam, that's going to change. By the way . . .' She turned away. 'Len likes his tea on the table in good time and so, come Monday, you'd best get weaving, hadn't you?'

'Does Martin know Len's not his father?' Marianne's voice was low and cruel. 'You're not so lily-white yourself, *Mrs* Gilby! Be terrible if someone let that slip, wouldn't it?'

Ann turned, slowly. She was starting to tremble with rage, wanted to lash out and claw the girl's face. But she was determined to hide it. Somehow, with this spiteful little bit standing in front of her, she felt strong. She gave Marianne a pitying look.

'He will know one day. At the right time, when I'm ready to tell him. I don't know why you'd think he'd believe anything *you'd* say.'

Ann went into the kitchen, looking round, defeated. She'd got nothing done – not the shopping or the washing. She racked her brains. The milkman had been, luckily; there were a few potatoes . . . She'd have to cobble some-thing together later.

She put her hands over her face, shoulders shaking as she heard Marianne's footsteps recede up the stairs. Sink-ing down at the table again, she felt more alone than ever before in her life, locked into this nightmare, with no apparent way out of it. But she pushed her emotion down. Enough of that!

There was something she was going to do about it – and why shouldn't she? She could not struggle on any longer alone under the weight of all these secrets. She desperately needed a friend, someone in her life she could turn to; and she already had one, didn't she?

*

By Sunday afternoon Ann finally had Hilda to herself, to pour out her woes to. The thought that Hilda might never speak to her again was more than her mind could cope with. Sitting at the table in the back room in Sycamore Road, she blurted out all of it: Tom. Martin. Len. Marianne. The whole thing. Her need was so great by the time she got there, after several days of Marianne sulking and looking daggers at her, that out it all tumbled, holding nothing back. Her mess and shame of a life.

Even though she was frightened to death of what her friend was going to think, Ann had to stop herself smiling at the sight of her face. Hilda was staring ahead of her as if someone had unplugged her.

'I've never known you this quiet, Hilda.' She waited. 'I'm sorry,' she said eventually. 'For coming and letting all this out.' Tears ran down her cheeks. 'I just can't go on like this.'

'I knew there was summat.' Hilda looked closely at her suddenly. 'I've said to Roy, more than once: there's summat not right with those two. And that cousin – so-called . . . But fancy Len, and you, all this time . . . And not telling me about Martin. You're a dark horse, you are.'

She sounded completely stunned. Ann waited, her heart pounding. Was Hilda about to order her out, telling her never to darken her door again?

'I've known you get yourself into some scrapes, Annie.'

Inside herself, Ann was begging, *Please say you're still my friend! You're my oldest, best friend!*

'But this . . .' She looked into Ann's tearful face. 'I'd never've thought any of this of you. It's . . . well, it's a right mess, isn't it? It's going to take me a while to get used to it.'

She seized hold of Ann's hand, her own eyes filling with tears.

'You could be dead. We all thought you might die after that bomb. But you're here – and what's the use in doling out judgements and being all nasty about it? That never helps anything, does it? You're my friend, and you always will be, even if you are a prize—' She couldn't seem to think of a word adequate for this. 'Dear *God,* Annie!' Hilda shook her head. 'I think I'd best put the kettle on again. We can string out those dregs a bit more.'

As she got up, Ann looked adoringly at her, buoyed by her friend's kindness. There was someone she could turn to, at last.

'Thanks, Hil. You're a real pal.'

Holding the kettle, Hilda turned. 'What about Norma? Joy's got all this on her plate as well.'

Their daughters had always been close friends. Ann hesitated, then nodded. 'All right then. You tell her, if you like.'

Hilda stirred the grouts around in more hot water and poured the weak brew.

'Talk about maid's water – it can hardly clamber out of the pot. So, where're they putting you?'

'In the new sheds, I think. Munitions of some sort.' Though married women had not been able to work at Cadbury's before the war, everything was changing now. All hands were needed to service the great war-machine that Birmingham had become.

'Well, it'll be nice to have you back, kid.' They raised their cups and chinked them together. Ann smiled, feeling happier than she had in months. 'Even if you are a complete flaming mess.'

Twelve

July

'Where're we going again?' Norma panted, trying to keep up with Joy. They had got down from the tram in town and off Joy went up the hill, like a firecracker.

'The Town Hall. I can't wait!'

'Slow down,' Norma grumbled. 'It'll still be there when we get there.'

'Don't tempt fate,' Joy laughed, curbing her enthusiasm a little and slowing down. 'We've managed three dances with no raids – let's try and get through this one as well.'

The Town Hall, like a Greek temple with all its columns, loomed ahead of them in the mellow evening light.

'Joy,' Norma said suddenly. 'D'you feel sort of . . . guilty, going out dancing and that – with Alan away fighting?'

'Guilty?' Joy was fishing in her bag for something. 'Oh, phew. Thought I'd left my lipstick behind. Not guilty exactly. I just . . .' She had slowed down, her face serious now, and turned her liquid brown eyes to look at Norma. Alan's latest letter was at home under her pillow. She knew where he was now: somewhere in the North African desert, a place she could barely imagine. She carried his loving words around with her in her heart. 'I really love him, Norm, I do. And I just want to keep busy – do everything I can to fill the time while he's not here and I can't dance with *him*.'

'I don't know what I'd do if Danny had to go,' Norma said. 'Dunno how you stand it.'

'I'm doing everything I can think of at the factory: knitting and packing parcels for the lads.' Joy had volunteered as a 'Cadbury Angel', as they had first called the girls in the last war, who made up parcels for the lads serving overseas. 'And I do a bit of country dancing . . . But now and then it's so nice to do this!' Her face lit up again. Joy was never miserable for long. 'It's what life's about! And anyway' – her smile faded then – 'the more I keep out of the way at home . . .'

Their eyes met. Norma had told Joy that she knew what was going on in the family: about Marianne and all that. They had talked a bit, but it was all so shocking and embarrassing and difficult, and there was nothing much Joy or Martin could do about any of it. Joy was determined to forget about it as much as she could, the moment she closed the door behind her. She had her own life to live, never mind their mess.

'Come on!' She grabbed Norma's arm and they ran the rest of the way, tripping and laughing.

There was a band at one end of the grand interior of the Town Hall. Warm, fuggy air gusted into their faces when they reached the door, laced with the smells of hot bodies, scent and smoke and the sound of music. The windows were shrouded with blackout curtains and the place was alive with couples weaving their way through the dances. Some women were dancing together, but there was a good sprinkling of men, both in and out of uniform.

Joy sashayed round with her latest partner, Bob, a man in his thirties who was in a reserved job at Newman Tonks.

He was quiet, mousey-haired and not an especially good dancer, but nice enough. But the words of the 'Anniversary Waltz', to which they were dancing, brought a lump to her throat. It was a dance you were supposed to enjoy with the person you loved most. For a moment she imagined she was held in the arms of Alan, not Bob, and that his good-looking, amiable face was smiling down at her . . .

'You all right?' Bob said.

Joy nodded, swallowing hard. 'Yeah. Course.' She must pull herself together and she tried to raise a smile at him. She caught site of Norma, her autumn-leaf hair glowing under the lights as she glided past, and they grinned at each other.

'Fancy another dance?' Bob ventured as the music came to an end. A few people clapped and there was laughter and chatter. Cheeks glowed in the warm summer evening.

'Oh yes, maybe,' Joy said vaguely. She had promised herself that she would not get stranded with one dancer all evening. Most men who danced with her wanted to keep her to themselves, but that was not what she wanted. 'Just one more . . .' she began to say, when among the lively crowd and the interchange of partners, the sight of a familiar face burned its way into her attention. She didn't think or hesitate. 'Sorry – thanks. 'Scuse me . . .'

She hurried across, not giving a thought to the person she had left behind, and later felt badly about this when she thought back on it. But that face: the dark, lively eyes, the slender build, the dark-brown hair and moustache of one of the best dancers she had ever known – other than Alan. He was chatting to a woman beside him. Joy went up and gently touched his arm and he turned immediately.

'Joy!'

She felt the full impact of Lawrence Dayton's energy as he turned to her – something almost electrically alive, which had attracted her immediately the first time she met him and they had talked in that air-raid shelter, then danced together in the smoke-filled moonlight.

'How lovely to see you!'

Lawrence turned to his dance partner. For a split second Joy wondered if she was his wife. But why would she be here in Birmingham, when they lived in Southampton and had a small child?

'This is . . . Bella? Joy.' He introduced them, courteously.

Bella, a pleasant, round-faced woman, said, 'Well, you two obviously know each other. I'm just going to . . .' She indicated the way to the ladies and left, looking disappointed.

'Sorry for interrupting,' Joy said. They were having to talk loudly amid the hubbub, and a foxtrot was starting up.

'"The Wise Old Owl" – that's ever so good!' she said.

'Al Donahue!'

Lawrence beamed, holding his arms out. 'Slow, slow, quick, quick . . .'

And they were off, Joy laughing, overjoyed to see him. They were both such expert dancers that they scarcely had to think of their feet at all as they swept around the floor, avoiding other couples by instinct and smiling into each other's faces.

'I thought I might run into you again, sooner or later,' Lawrence said.

'It's lovely to see you,' Joy replied. 'I've . . .' She was about to say 'missed you', which would have been true, but suddenly she was all blushes, remembering the last afternoon she had seen Lawrence, last winter. He had taken a room in a hotel in town. He was always gentlemanly, and she knew by then that he was married. But with the war on, and the threat of death falling from the sky each night, the feeling that every day might be your last, only the present seemed to matter. She had almost – almost – climbed into bed with him and let him make love to her. She had thought she was in love with him, wanted him, but at the last moment she froze. Lawrence was married. What future could they ever have?

Now, remembering how foolish she had felt, backing off like that and leaving with fumbling apologies, she felt horribly embarrassed.

'I'm sorry,' she mumbled, mortified. 'About – you know – last time.'

'Nothing to apologize for,' Lawrence said, looking at her in that intent way of his that made her want him all over again. He smiled. 'Well, except for the best dancing partner I'm ever likely to find disappearing into thin air!'

Joy laughed. 'I could say the same of you,' she said. 'Although there is someone else.'

'Oh yes?'

'My . . . fiancé. Alan.'

Lawrence nodded, unperturbed. 'And where is Alan now?'

'Army. In the desert.'

He nodded gravely. 'Poor fellow. Keeping safe, I hope?' He shrugged as if knowing this was a stupid thing to say. 'It must be a worry.'

'It is,' she said. 'How's your wife? And family?'

'Oh, they're doing well, thank you.'

There was a gentleness between them. Joy was grateful to Lawrence and very fond of him. For all his desire for her, he had never been pushy or unpleasant and she liked him a lot.

'Can you dance the Lindy Hop?' he asked.

Joy winked. 'Of course.'

'Not likely to happen in here – all rather staid,' he said. 'We'll have to give it a try somewhere.'

Neither of them could resist dancing almost every number together. Joy introduced Lawrence to Norma during one break.

'I've seen you before, haven't I?' Norma said.

'Yes, we've danced together before, haven't we?' Joy said. 'He's ever so good.'

Norma smiled. 'I can see. We'd best be off soon, Joy,' she warned.

The quickstep was called and the music started up.

'Oh, we've got to dance this, Lawrence!' Joy's eyes lit up. 'One last one, Norma.'

The two of them swirled away across the dance floor. Quite a number of couples were having difficulty keeping up, and before long many had stood aside so that Joy and Lawrence, and a few others, had an audience watching in awe – two swans gliding beautifully round the room, their feet paddling expertly below. When the dance ended, everyone clapped. Joy curtsied, holding her shimmery skirt, and Lawrence bowed. Their eyes were locked together, their lips turned up in delighted smiles.

'Oh, thank you,' Joy cried. 'That was the best night I've had in ages.'

'Me too – very definitely. I've hardly been dancing lately.'

Norma was coming towards them and Joy said hurriedly, 'Can we do it again?'

Thirteen

September

Sheila stood waiting beside the quiet main road with Elaine in her pushchair. Elaine was excited – she loved meeting the boys from school. Within a few moments they heard the clip-clop of hooves.

'Can you hear the horsey?' Sheila bent down over her, feeling the almost full-term weight of the child inside her as she bent over.

Elaine squealed with excitement, squirming in her pushchair. 'Tarley! Ebward!' At nineteen months she was learning new words every day. Her favourite one these days was 'Duck!', called with great vigour every time they saw a mallard on the river. Her hair had grown and was soft and fair, curling a little at the ends. Her cheeks were pink from the country air and she had a jolly, gurgling chuckle, which never failed to set the boys off laughing too.

Sheila straightened up, smiling. When she had first arrived back in Goring and Audrey announced that she wanted to go and work on the buses, Sheila had thought she was mad. Reading? That was miles away! Audrey argued that she would not drive there, because it would take most of her petrol ration – but she could go by train and it was only just over a mile's walk to the station. 'It'll do me good,' Audrey said. 'I don't get enough exercise.'

At first Sheila had been a bit fed up. She had been look-ing forward to Audrey's company, looking after Elaine and the boys, with no Maurice coming home, corrupting the atmosphere like acid eating metal. But she was Audrey's guest and she could see her point of view: Audrey was excited by the thought of a new challenge. They all had to put personal niggles aside, for the war effort.

'I hope it won't feel too much for you, now you're expecting, Sheila,' Audrey said. 'Mrs B will be here to help some of the time. But I suppose you'll want to go home to have the baby?'

'Oh yes,' Sheila said. This had seemed so far off when she first arrived that it didn't seem worth worrying about. So she took on more work in the house, collecting the boys, feeding them and putting them to bed if Audrey was working in the evening. Audrey worked five shifts a week, at irregular hours, but she was still home two days a week.

At first Audrey was a storm of nerves and excitement. She spent her initial weeks training. 'A bus feels so *big* compared with a car,' she giggled when she came home after the first time. 'It's terrifying. And that's with no one on board! But I know I can do it – I *want* to do it.'

She was lit up, loving the challenge and meeting a lot of different people, all mucking in together.

'People are so nice – well, except for one of the men training me, who's one of those who behaves as if all women are complete airheads and we don't know what we're doing there. But I do like it; it's fun!'

Over the past months the novelty had definitely worn off. Audrey was doing the job all right, but she found it exhausting, on top of having to get to Reading and back every day – sometimes coming home quite late. Even when she was at home, she often fell asleep so early that she was no company then, either.

'Oh well,' she had said last night, through enormous yawns. 'I suppose one just has to keep on keeping on. But my goodness, I do feel exhausted.'

Sheila's thoughts were interrupted by the clip-clopping growing louder, and the little trap came into view with the four children in it, pulled by a skewbald pony.

'Horsey!' Elaine said, delighted. Sometimes the old man driving the trap let her stroke the horse's nose. This time, though, he seemed to be in a hurry. Edward and Charlie jumped down from the back with their satchels, and the man tipped his hat and clicked for the horse to move on.

'Hello, Lainy!' Charlie called, and Edward smiled at her as well.

'All right, boys?' Sheila said.

'What time's Mummy coming back tonight?' Edward asked.

'She's on a late, I'm afraid,' Sheila said. 'So you're stuck with me.'

But they both grinned at her.

'Come on – I've made you some sandwiches.'

With Edward and Charlie walking each side of the pushchair, they strolled back to the house. Sheila suddenly felt a wave of happiness. This was all right. They were all getting along. Life could be a lot worse.

Later that evening Sheila came downstairs, feeling muzzy and ready for sleep herself, after sitting in the dark singing 'Golden Slumbers' and 'Baa, Baa, Black Sheep' to settle Elaine to sleep.

Peeping into the sitting room, she found the boys sitting together. The curtains were closed, the room was cosy and Edward was reading Charlie a story. She walked in and smiled at them.

'You've been real good lads. D'you want one more story before you go up?'

'I can read it myself – and Charlie can,' Edward said.

'I know, I just thought you might like—'

'*Treasure Island*,' Charlie said. 'Read us some more!'

As she sat down, Sheila felt a twinge at her side and took in a sharp intake of breath.

'Is it the baby?' Charlie asked, wide-eyed.

'Yes,' Sheila laughed. 'Don't look so worried. You get all sort of little aches and pains when you're having a baby.'

She put her arm round Charlie, though not Edward, who she knew thought he was far too old for that sort of thing, and read to them for a while, seeing their eyes begin to droop.

'Come on – up you go!'

By the time she had the two of them settled in bed and had tidied up the tea things in the kitchen, she felt grateful to sink into a chair. For a moment she sat, looking around Audrey's gracious sitting room with its chintz-covered chairs and curtains. When she had come here the first time she had been homesick, to begin with, and always felt awkward and in the way, especially when Maurice Vella-cott was at home. Now, she realized, she felt quite relaxed and at home. Audrey had been a friend to her and Sheila knew she would always be grateful for that.

Her mind drifted to Kenneth, wondering where he was, praying he was safe, and her eyes closed . . .

The next thing she knew there were odd noises, startling her awake. Her heart set off thumping like a piston. The front door closed with a thump and she could hear gasping, sobbing sounds. Jolted awake, Sheila could not make sense of anything for a second. Audrey – was that Audrey?

She hauled herself off the settee and hurried to the hall.

Audrey was trying to hang up her coat, the distressed sounds still coming from her. She was not behaving normally at all – she could not seem to get the coat to go on the hook and she was shaking all over.

'Audrey?'

She turned then and Sheila's hand went to her mouth. For a second she could hardly recognize her friend's face. It was swollen, one eye closed, blood oozing from one side of her mouth and from other cuts on her face. Audrey had her uniform on, but she looked filthy and crumpled. She was shaking and whimpering as if she had turned into someone completely different.

'Oh my God, Audrey, what's happened?'

Audrey allowed herself to be led into the sitting room and seated on the settee. Sheila closed the door carefully and sat beside her, as she broke into choking sobs. She was in such a state that for a while she could not speak at all.

Sheila hardly dared even touch her at first, but after a few moments she put her hand gently on Audrey's back, feeling her wince as she did so.

'What's happened?' she asked, softly.

'I was . . .' Audrey raised her head, gulping out the words. 'I'd finished my shift and I was going to the station. And I didn't see him . . . A man . . . He just jumped on me in the dark and . . . he pulled me – somewhere. Some alley, I don't really know where, but . . . I was struggling and he hit me across the face, again and again and . . .'

Very gingerly she touched one of her teeth.

'I thought he was going to knock them all out. And he pushed me on the ground and made me . . .' She mewled then, like a little child. 'It was . . . He stank – disgustingly – of drink, and he couldn't seem to hear anything I said . . . I couldn't . . . do anything.'

Sheila listened, rigid with horror.

'He went away after he'd . . . finished. And I just got up and came home,' she said, seeming astonished that she was here. More calmly, she turned her battered face to Sheila. 'I thought I was going to die.'

'Did you tell anyone – the police?'

'I don't even know where the police station is.' She took out a hanky and spat bloody saliva into it. 'There was hardly anyone on the train. All I could think of was getting home.'

Sheila was in shock. What were you supposed to do when something like this happened? Surely they should tell the police? At least Audrey had a telephone.

'Let me phone them,' she said. 'Someone's got to lock that man up – he'll only keep doing it again.'

Audrey didn't argue. She had gone limp. Sheila made her a cup of sweet tea, wrapped a blanket round her and went to the telephone. After phoning Directory Enquiries for the number, she dialled it nervously.

'Reading Police,' a voice said. He sounded half-asleep and fed up. Sheila's mouth went dry.

'I'm phoning to report a . . . an attack. An assault – on my . . . landlady.'

'I see. Where and when did this happen?'

'Tonight. About . . . well, maybe two hours ago. In the middle of Reading.'

Feeling more and more nervous at the man's uncon-cerned tone, not to mention suddenly conscious of her Birmingham accent, Sheila described what had happened.

'So,' he said eventually, 'she never saw the man's face, in the dark? She was out on her own – and she's no idea who he was?'

'No,' Sheila admitted. 'It wasn't anyone she knew.'

'And she didn't see anything at all?'

By the time she put the phone down she felt helpless

and foolish, as if she had been making up a story and he didn't believe her: a silly woman telephoning about another silly woman, who had gone out in the dark by herself and seen nothing and no one, and how did they expect the police to do anything about *that*?

She went back to Audrey, who looked really pale and sickly now.

'Well, I've told them.' Sheila wanted to say the police were doing everything they could, that they would go and look for him, but of course that was not true. She squatted down at her friend's side, talking to her almost as if she were a child. 'I'm going to run you a nice bath and make you some cocoa, all right? And then we'll get you to bed.'

Audrey was still shaking, her teeth chattering. 'Can I . . . d'you mind coming to sleep in with me tonight? I feel so frightened.'

'Course I will,' Sheila said. She helped her friend painfully to her feet.

'I can't do it any more . . .' Audrey started sobbing. 'I can't go on driving buses after this. I never want to go anywhere ever again!'

Fourteen

'I'm sorry,' Audrey sobbed. 'I'm being so selfish. You should be going home to your mother.'

The baby was due any day now and Sheila had planned to go back to Birmingham in good time for the birth, taking Elaine. Even if she had to stay with Kenneth's mom and dad, at least she would be near home. But Audrey was in such a state since she was attacked – five days ago now – that Sheila kept putting it off.

Audrey managed to pull herself together when the boys were around, but as soon as Sheila had taken them out to set off for school, she would come back and find Audrey sitting on a chair or the sofa, all curled in on herself as if freezing cold and seemingly unable to get started on anything.

'Would you like your sister to come and be with you?' Sheila asked.

Audrey shook her head emphatically. She did not seem to want any of her family anywhere near her.

Sheila didn't feel she was doing an especially good job of helping. Audrey insisted on them sharing a bed, because at night she was racked by nightmares when asleep, and her mind could not stop going over it all when she was awake.

'What if he's got me with child?' she sobbed over and over again as they lay side by side. 'Whatever could I do?'

It was almost too terrible to think about.

'I feel so . . . soiled,' she had said the night before. 'I feel horrible and disgusting. What was worse was that I had my . . . you know, the Curse.' She shuddered. 'That didn't stop him.' She was silent for a moment, then more calmly she said into the darkness, 'Does that mean . . .'

'What?' Sheila asked.

'Well, you can't fall for a child when you have your monthly, can you?' She sounded stronger suddenly.

'I'm not sure.' Sheila felt lost in ignorance and very alone in all this. 'Shouldn't you go and see the doctor?'

'Dr Harper?' Audrey's tone was full of disgust. 'Oh, heavens no – I'm not having him poking me about, on top of everything else.'

Sheila did everything she could to help, even though she was so heavy and exhausted herself. One evening after tea, when she was sitting with the boys, Audrey came down from upstairs. She managed a smile.

'Come on, my little chaps. Time for bed. You stay there, Sheila – you must be all in.'

After she had settled the boys, Audrey came down again, seeming calmer.

'They'd like you to say good night as well,' she said. As Sheila was getting up, Audrey said softly, 'You're a very kind person, aren't you, Sheila?'

'Oh, I don't know . . .' Sheila blushed.

She moved across to the door to go upstairs and felt suddenly wet. A bursting, soaking down below, and pinkish fluid was running down her legs and on to the cream carpet.

'My waters!' She pulled her cardigan off and trod it under her feet, trying to mop up the wet that was staining the floor.

'Oh, my dear . . .' Audrey seemed to come back to herself immediately. She took Sheila's arm. 'Right, just leave that, do. We must make you comfortable upstairs and I'll telephone the doctor.'

*

It was not a doctor who arrived, but a reassuring middle-aged midwife. She was quite tall, with a mannish haircut under her veil, vivid blue eyes and a kindly manner that immediately gained their trust.

'Yes, to tea and hot water,' Sheila heard her deep, refined voice saying to Audrey as she swept into the room. And as Audrey hurried downstairs again, she came over to Sheila. 'Hello, dear, my name is Nurse Jenkins and I am here to help you. I gather this is not your first?'

Sheila smiled. For the moment she was in respite from the pain. She liked the look of Nurse Jenkins – not least because she was not Dr Harper, whom she did not like the sound of one bit.

'I've got a little girl; she's nineteen months . . .'

'Ah, so you know what you're doing.' Nurse Jenkins was taking things out of her bag and talking, while attending briskly to several things at once. 'You don't sound as if you're from round these parts?'

'No. Birmingham.'

'Ah, I see. Husband away?'

'Yes, Air-Sea Rescue with the RAF,' Sheila said, feeling a flush of pride.

'Well, this'll be a lovely surprise for him, won't it? Now, knees up and apart, and feet together for me, will you, dear?'

Sheila disappeared into the rhythm of pain, waves crashing over her as she drifted in and out of awareness of what was going on around her. Nurse Jenkins and Audrey were both there, it seemed, all the time. Both spoke to her, making reassuring noises as she laboured on, turning this way and that as her belly hardened into a drum, pushing and pressing at the child within, then relaxed again. Audrey gave her sips of water and stroked her hair from her face.

'You're doing ever so well, Sheila,' she said. 'Won't be long – just keep going.'

Sheila was aware, in glimpses, that Audrey seemed much better than she had for days. She heard Nurse Jenkins say to her, 'What have you done to your face, dear?'

To Sheila's surprise, she heard Audrey tell this kindly woman, straight out, what had happened. Nurse Jenkins was shocked.

'My dear, that's appalling! Did you inform the police?'

'Sheila did. My husband is not away, you see; he was killed in London, in the bombing, and Sheila has been living with me – she's such a support . . . I don't know what I'd do without her. But of course I never even saw his face, so there's not much hope of catching him.'

'Men like that want a good seeing-to,' Nurse Jenkins said darkly, without specifying what she meant. 'Now, if you need me to take a look at you . . .'

Sheila heard Audrey confiding her worries that she might have fallen for a child, but that she had had her monthly, and Nurse Jenkins was reassuring about that too.

'Unlikely, dear, thank goodness. Let's hope and pray.'

In many ways it felt as if Nurse Jenkins had been a gift from heaven.

Just before seven the next morning Sheila, worn out but managing the final force needed to bring life into the world, pushed her second child into the waiting hands of Nurse Jenkins.

'Here we are, little love,' Nurse Jenkins exclaimed. 'Safe and sound – oh, and we're a little boy!'

Sheila held her arms out and the little one, who reminded her immediately of Kenneth, was placed in her arms.

'How lovely!' Audrey cried, tears running down her cheeks. 'My goodness, isn't he beautiful?'

'Now, we need the afterbirth and then we're all ship-shape,' Nurse Jenkins said.

Within half an hour Sheila was sitting up in bed, the baby nestled on one arm, with a cup of tea and toast on the go. Audrey bustled about, making more tea and toast for the whole household, getting the boys ready for school and bringing Elaine in to see her new brother.

Sheila saw her little girl come round the door, holding Audrey's hand, her face pink and fresh from sleep and serious with anticipation at what she was about to find.

'Hello, sweetie.' Nurse Jenkins held out her hand. 'Don't be shy.'

Elaine came over to the bed and Nurse Jenkins lifted her up to sit on it and snuggle up on the other side of Sheila.

'So, do we have any names?' she asked as Elaine stared and stared, drinking in this extraordinary new person who had just appeared.

'Well, we like the name Robert,' Sheila said. 'We're going to call him Robert Richard – after Kenneth's dad. Kenneth and I have been making our minds up for months!'

Audrey brought the boys in for a few moments before school and they were suitably awed.

'A boy,' Edward said approvingly, looking down at him.

Sheila watched Audrey leading them out, taking Elaine as well. She seemed so much better suddenly.

'Nice household you've got here,' Nurse Jenkins said, draining the last of her tea and packing her things away again.

'Yes,' Sheila said. She thought with a pang of home, of everyone being able to see Robert. Whenever was that going to happen? But the reality was that there was not enough room for her at home – not with that woman stuck up there in the attic. Sad as it was, it was better that she stayed here. 'It is,' she said. 'I've been very lucky.'

'Well, I'll pop in to see you tomorrow.' Nurse Jenkins went to the door. 'Any problems in the meantime, you've got the number. I can see you know the drill though.'

'Thank you,' Sheila said. 'You've been marvellous to us all.'

Nurse Jenkins's tired face broke into a smile. 'That was a lovely birth: one of the nicest I've been to lately. Well done. And your friend – that was a very nasty shock. Never underestimate what that sort of experience does to a woman. But she's got you here. I think she'll be all right.'

Sheila listened to her tread on the stairs, the sound of her motor car starting up outside. She cuddled up in the comfortable bed, feeling worn out and warm and spoilt and happy. She had given Kenneth a son! Little Robert was cuddled in her arms in a white blanket, his mauve eyelids and his bud of a mouth twitching as he slept.

'Hello, little one,' she said joyfully. 'Aren't you just adorable?'

Fifteen

'Ann! Fancy seeing you here! I never knew you were coming back.'

Jeanette Fisher threw her arms around Ann the first day she started back at Cadbury's. Ann and Jeanette had known each other for years before Ann married Len. Jeanette had never married, and they had lost touch while Ann was in the throes of bringing up a family. But Ann had always liked Jeanette, with her long pale face, brown hair neatly combed back and tucked under her work cap and her gently spoken ways.

'Well, you know, they take any old riff-raff these days,' Ann joked as the group assigned to munitions in the new waterside part of Cadbury's filed into their Nissen hut to start work.

Jeanette laughed. 'Some of us riff-raff are still here! It's nice to see you, Annie. I've seen Len around once or twice, but not to speak to. How's the family?'

Ann's heart started to race. Now that she was out of the house, it hit her hard, how having the most normal conversation about things at home was going to be impossible.

'They're all right,' she said. 'Growing up fast!' She gave a quick outline of the children: Sheila about to have another baby, and so on. This was what she would have to do – light, bright conversations, everyone all right, doing their best, and all that – none of the truth about the tangled mess that was really going on.

But it was good to see Jeanette again; and Hilda, who

she often saw in the dining block for a chat during breaks, even though she was working elsewhere; and quite a few other familiar faces.

Rows of Nissen huts had gone up close to the Cadbury wharf, and Ann was assigned to one where they were filling anti-aircraft rockets with cordite. 'A different sort of assortment box!' some of them joked. The straight white tubes with a black band around the end were arranged in circular racks, splaying out like the spokes of a wheel, reminding Ann of a big, upside-down lampshade. Their job, hands carefully protected in gloves, was to push the explosive into the rocket tube.

A lot of the workers were women – quite a few of them married. Ann's first shifts back on the job meant getting used to everything again: to the work and the hours, which seemed so long at first; to the other women working on her rack, who included Jeanette; and to all the changes at Cadbury's.

But she soon found she was loving it. She had missed being with other people. Now that Joy was working days, they could walk up to Cadbury's together and it was so nice to be back. Ann could leave the house, where she spent so much time feeling like a volcano about to blow up, and walk into another world of work and chatter, of singing along with the others. Even working long hours made her feel younger and more lively – and even if this was a way to get out of the situation at home, she could equally argue that it was for the war effort.

'Joy and Martin don't really need me much any more,' she told Hilda. 'Joy's always off out somewhere, and Martin spends most of his time with his pal Ian – and we hardly ever see him.'

'Well, you can hardly blame them for keeping out of the way, Annie,' Hilda said.

'I know.' Guilt knifed through her. 'They're good kids, both of them; and at least they're both getting on with their own lives.'

Hilda's situation was so different. She and Roy had done everything right. They were steady, loyal and loving, and it looked as if Norma and Danny would be the same. Ann felt such a failure in comparison. But at least Hilda was still prepared to be friends with her; there were others who might not be, if only they knew. And her own daughters would do better – she could see that. Sheila and Kenneth were as steady as a rock and she knew that Joy had given her heart to Alan, and would wait for him, whatever happened.

'What does Len think about you coming back?'

'Well, he's not happy about it,' Ann said.

Which was a bit of an understatement.

'What, you're just going off and leaving Marianne with it all?' Len had erupted when Ann told him she had been taken on at Cadbury's again.

They were in their bedroom, late enough for everyone else to be in theirs. Ann was conscious that if they talked too loudly, Marianne might well be able to hear upstairs, not to mention Joy and Martin. They had to carry out their ding-dongs in hissed whispers. The fact that Len went off every day and always had done, leaving *her* with it all, did not seem to cross his mind.

'Look,' she attempted, patiently. 'Marianne's a grown woman – and I'm not leaving her everything. I'll do our washing and some of the cleaning. But I've told her she's got to go to the shops and do some of the cooking. I don't see why I should do it all; and I won't be able to anyway, will I?'

She knew that Marianne was furious. And that Len had

spent the earlier part of the evening being told quite *how* furious, up in the attic.

'You know she doesn't like going to the shops,' he said weakly. 'Not with George and everything . . .' He knew it was a stupid thing to say, before it was out of his mouth, and had the grace to look sheepish.

'Well, she's happy enough to eat the food that's put in front of her,' Ann snapped. She was trying to hold on to herself, but by God it was hard sometimes. She could have screamed.

Len sank down on the side of the bed, his shoulders sagging. Ann watched, actually feeling sorry for him. He was not a man who was made for all this sort of carry-on. He was the sort who wanted an ordinary, regular life: go out to work, come home to find your tea on the table, day after day. No upsets. No complications.

'Look,' she said. It was no good them fighting. Where would it get them? 'I'm doing my best, but how do you think it feels for me, having Marianne under our roof like this?'

Suddenly she was in tears. It was unexpected. Mostly she kept her feelings detached. But the heartbreak of it all was there, just waiting to break out. She did not make a performance out of it, but Len heard the break in her voice and turned to look at her. On seeing her tears, his face grew even more wretched.

'I'm sorry,' he said. 'I am. I wish none of this had ever happened. I wish we could go right back . . .'

She was touched by his words. He was a good man. But the terrible thing was that, sorry as she felt for him, she could not simply say, 'So do I.' Because it was not true. She wiped her eyes and climbed into bed.

'Look, we've got to make this work somehow. Until Marianne can move out, or you can both . . .' But this was getting too close to the edge of a cliff. Len, leave? Break up the family? How could that ever be?

Ann could feel him watching her, looking to her, as if desperate for her to solve it all. The fact that he had the top button of his shirt undone, that she could see the skin at his throat – softer now, ageing – filled her with gentler feelings.

'It's not unreasonable asking her to do more,' she said. 'She's living here rent-free – and I suppose you're giving her money?'

'A bit,' he admitted. 'For the little 'un, you know.'

'So she can pull her weight. I know there're all the queues, but I used to have to do the shopping with Sheila and Joy, when they were little. Marianne's got the pram. It's not the end of the world, is it?'

Len looked worried, but as if he couldn't say why. He turned away. 'No, I s'pose. She's just a bit funny about . . .' He trailed off. 'But I think you should have asked me first.'

The next day when Ann got in from work, alone, as Joy was off gadding somewhere, she found a telegram on the kitchen table. Marianne was nowhere to be seen. The sight of it filled Ann with foreboding. Telegrams never brought good news.

She opened it with trembling fingers, then let out a cry of joy that brought Martin down from upstairs.

'You all right?' he asked, worried. And then, seeing her smiling, he laughed. 'What's going on?'

She handed it to him. 'It's from Audrey – Sheila's landlady. *"Robert Richard Carson arrived safe this morning, seven pounds twelve ounces. Sheila doing well sends love."* Oh, how nice of her!' Ann cried. 'She seems such a kind person. I must go down and see Sheila!'

II

1942

Sixteen

February

'This flaming weather may be stopping the Germans getting to Moscow, but it's not doing the rest of us much good, either,' Ann grumbled through her blocked-up nose, shivering in the depths of her bedclothes.

Her mother-in-law stood over her, still bundled up in her brown coat, a thick woolly hat pulled down over her ears and a black knitted scarf covering the lower half of her face. Ann had heard Margaret stamping ice and slush off her boots before she came up. Her coat seemed to give off icy-cold breaths.

'Never you mind, bab,' Margaret said, her words sounding, quite literally, woolly. 'You want to just rest up there 'til you're all right. No good overdoing it.' She peered at the gas fire. 'D'you want that put on? It's cold in here.'

'All right, for a bit.' They never lit the thing in the normal run of things, because they were up and out of the room so quickly it was never worth it. When Ann had first put it on, it had filled the room with the stink of burnt dust. 'I've put it on and off that many times . . .'

Margaret bent over, lit a match and sent a whoosh of flame through the honeycombed asbestos. It settled to a comforting hiss.

'I'll make you a cup of tea. Is *that one* in . . .?' She rolled her eyes towards the ceiling.

'No. She's gone out to the shops.' It hurt Ann's burning throat to talk.

'Big of her.'

Margaret, to her surprise, had been an ally in Ann's plan to go back to work. She still had no time for Marianne, and was convinced – George or no George – that she was just a chancer. She went off downstairs, leaving Ann to her feverish bed and the icy white glare from outside the window. It was nice to have someone do something for her.

Ann sat up and sipped gratefully at the cup of tea Margaret brought up for her, as well as one for herself. She settled on the chair. The room was getting warmer and she unwound her scarf.

'What a winter!' Margaret peered outside. 'It's difficult even to scratch a meal together.' The number of U-boats in the North Atlantic was taking a savage toll on merchant shipping, and the shortages of food grew worse by the week. 'Least they're giving us a break from old Wailing Willie.' After another sip of tea, she went on, 'She pulling her weight?'

Ann swallowed, screwing up her face.

'Yes. On the whole.' This was partly true. Marianne had been furious at first, being expected to do the shopping, but when Len backed Ann up and said Marianne really needed to help out more, she'd had no choice but to knuckle down. She even helped with more of the cooking and cleaning now and, Ann thought, seemed happier for it, instead of mouldering away in her room all the time.

She'd bring George down and sit him on the floor with some toys while she dusted or washed up. Marianne was quite organized, and even seemed to realize that sulking was not going to get her anywhere, so these days she simply got on with it. Things had eased, to an extent. Ann sometimes found Joy and Marianne having a cup of tea and a chat together, playing with George; and even Martin had got used to her, now that she had been 'lodging' with them all these months.

'I'll pop in again – let me know if you want anything, Annie.'

'You'd better turn the fire off now,' Ann said. 'I'm baking.'

Margaret looked at her pityingly. 'You do look a bit pink round the gills.' She cleared the cups and headed for the door. 'Have a sleep – do you good.'

Ann lay back, trying to relax. She'd had to take some days off work, but she did not like lying here. It was better to be busy. This room brought back so many memories, happy and sad: all the years she and Len had slept here together bringing up their family; the old familiar furniture, which had not changed in more than two decades; the chair with the curved back; the wardrobe over on Len's side of the bed and the chest of drawers on her side, with its mirror. The top drawer where she had always hidden her letters from Tom . . .

That night, months ago now but never to be forgotten, when Len had suddenly demanded love-making, with nothing loving about it. That night when he had fastened his hands around her neck. She had never worked out exactly why, but she knew it must have had something to do with Marianne, with the pressure he had been feeling. And it had not got any better – these days he looked frantic, worn to a frazzle.

She adjusted her position in the bed. Suddenly everything was uncomfortable, the sheet rucked up underneath her as if she was lying on hard strings. All she really wanted to do was get up. Lying here allowed her mind to fill with all sorts of difficult memories. And if it was not that, then it was the war. More than two years now and everything was getting worse. The Americans had been drawn in now, after the Japanese had bombed their fleet at Pearl Harbor in December. War was spreading across the north of Africa, Europe was under siege, ships sunk, battles lost and no sign of a reprieve. And, on top of that, another freezing, hard winter.

The only bright spark had been seeing Sheila and the grandchildren. Ann had gone down to see them after little Robbie was born. She spent a lovely couple of days with Sheila and Audrey – such a nice lady, with her boys – and with Elaine and Robbie. Even Kenneth had had a couple of days' leave to see his newborn son. She had missed them all being there at Christmas, but where would they have slept? And she loved knowing that Sheila was safe and happy and no longer seemed to be quite so angry with her.

Cold again, she pulled the eiderdown right up to her nose and closed her eyes. She was just beginning to still her racing mind and sink into a doze when she heard a sound. She raised her head. Was that the front door?

It came again. A peremptory knock. Ann sank back on to the pillow. Oh no! Who on earth could that be? She really didn't feel like getting out of bed. She listened. Maybe Marianne would go. But there was no sound of anyone moving and the knock came a third time. Whoever it was, they were not giving up.

Cursing both Marianne and whoever was banging on her door, Ann climbed out of bed and pulled on the longest cardigan she could find, shoved her slippers on and went giddily to the stairs, holding on tight to the banister as she went down.

Icy air gusted up beneath her nightdress as she clung to the door latch, trying not to open the door any wider than necessary. Outside stood a heavyset man dressed all in black: a long coat and scarf and a trilby hat. Even his eye-brows were a thick beetling line.

'Good morning.' He made a vague attempt to raise the hat, though with an air of irritation at having to bother with such a thing. Ann realized he was an Irishman. 'I'm looking for a Mrs Brady.'

Ann stared blankly at him. The cold was making her whole body shiver and she had to clench her teeth.

'I was given to believe she might be living here. I'm Father Doyle – from the parish in Selly Oak.'

'No,' Ann said. 'Sorry – I've never heard of her.'

The priest looked impatient. 'Are you sure now? A Mrs Mary Brady. I'm after having a message from St Anne's parish in town to come and find her here.' Clearly this was all a great annoyance to him. He spoke in a way that indi-cated he was someone used to people doing as he said.

Ann bristled. 'Well, I don't know about that,' she said as politely as she could, through her chattering teeth. 'I think if I had a Mrs Brady living in my house I'd know about it. Look, I'm not well and I need to close the door . . .'

The priest looked very put out. Perhaps he had been expecting a warm welcome and cups of tea? Well, he wasn't getting that, she thought. She felt ill and she didn't like his manner, or the look of him in general. Catholics were a strange lot, in her book.

'Very well.' He turned away, flinging words back over his shoulder. 'If you hear of her, contact me at the presby-tery in Selly Oak.'

It was an order, not a request. Closing the door, Ann felt that even if she did know a Mrs Brady, she wouldn't be telling this man about her. What was he doing, follow-ing some woman about the city like that?

She crawled back up the stairs, feeling wobbly, using

her hands on the steps as well as her feet. Marianne was hovering on the upstairs landing, holding a toddling George by the hand.

'Sorry.' She was unusually apologetic. 'I should have answered that, as you're poorly. Who was it?'

'Some man – a Catholic priest. Asking for a Mrs Brady. Mary Brady, whoever the hell she is. You're not Mrs Brady by any chance, are you?'

To her surprise, Marianne gave a little laugh. 'No! I wonder what poor Mrs Brady has done, having the priest following in her footsteps.'

Ann was already sinking back into bed. 'He liked to give the orders, I could see that. Bossy, I thought.'

Marianne put her head round the door. 'What did you say to him?'

'I just said I'd never heard of her.'

Marianne smiled again. 'I don't suppose he's very happy. D'you want another cup of tea?'

As the young woman's footsteps receded downstairs, as she went to put the kettle on, Ann lay back, thinking that occasionally Marianne could be quite pleasant.

Seventeen

February

'He can come!'

Joy danced up and down the narrow hall that evening, with Lawrence's note in her hands. Ann emerged from the back room and stared at her.

'Lawrence: to the Valentine's Day dance! Ooh, I can wear my new skirt!' She had made a new, swirling skirt from a remnant of silky deep-plum material.

'Lawrence?' Ann said vaguely. Her mind was on other things. 'Who *is* this Lawrence?'

'Oh, just a friend,' Joy said cheerily, running upstairs. She wanted to get her whole dancing outfit ready – even if it was days in advance. Turning halfway up, she saw her mother watching, smiling up at her, and her heart lifted. Things had been so odd at home, but at least this felt normal, for once. 'Can I borrow your necklace? The one with the little green beads?'

'I s'pose so,' Ann said, pretend-grudgingly. She turned away, shaking her head. 'You're a one, aren't you?' But she looked happy that Joy was going out to enjoy herself.

Lawrence was waiting for her at the corner of Bournville Lane. Even in the dark she would have known him anywhere. He gave off a kind of energy that had always excited her.

'Hello!' She hurried up to him.

'Joy, how lovely to see you! Not that I can, very well,' he laughed, giving her a peck on the cheek.

'It's freezing – let's get inside,' she said.

It seemed natural to walk arm-in-arm in the darkness. There was a shred of moon in the sky and, as they walked into the Cadbury site, Joy pointed out the shadowy movements of spotters up on the rooftops.

'My dad might be up there,' she said.

'Not so much need now, is there?' Lawrence said. The raids had all but died out, now that Germany had turned its attention to Russia.

'No, but you never know, do you?'

He stopped her for a moment. 'It was nice of you to ask me. I hope we can, you know, be friends: no hard feelings?'

They were face-to-face in the shadows. Even now, Joy felt, it would be so easy just to step into his arms as she had so many times before, as she had in that hotel room where she came so close to giving herself to him. But no. Lawrence was married, with a wife and child in Southampton – and she was going to marry Alan.

'We can't even say we might die any moment now, can we?' she said wryly. 'Of course we can be friends. And anyway . . .' She paused.

'What?' Lawrence sounded amused by her, as he so often did.

'You're still my number-one available dancing partner.'

'And you, mine. And you are my Valentine for tonight!'

Laughing, they linked arms again and headed inside.

The Valentine's Day dance, in the factory's East Dining Room, was a popular event, and Joy was soon tripping around amid the tightly packed crowd, held in Lawrence's arms, beaming up at him, in heaven. She saw a few familiar faces – a lad she had worked with years ago, on leave from the Navy; a few of the girls, including Norma, who had dragged Danny along with her this time. It *was* Valentine's Day, she had insisted. Norma made comical faces at Joy as she and Danny jived past them; Danny was not the world's greatest dancer by any means.

Joy introduced Lawrence to them – what was the harm now? He was a friend, there were no secrets to hide and she felt proud to be seen with him, tall and slender, his dark eyes and his expressive face full of life and charm. They all talked amiably while resting from the dancing and having a drink.

'No alcohol here then?' Lawrence said wryly.

'No, virtuous beverages only,' Joy said, grinning. 'Want some ginger beer?'

But mostly they danced and danced. Joy's new skirt felt lovely, twirling about her legs. Her whole body felt in tune, each dance step almost perfect, her cheeks pink, her smile wide. She saw Lawrence gazing at her face during one dance.

'What's the matter?' she asked.

'Just you: you're so damn lovely. If you keep beaming at me like that, I shan't be able to help myself.'

'Well, you're going to have to,' she said, putting on a strict, schoolma'am voice. 'I'm engaged to Alan – and that's just how it is!'

'I know, it's all right,' Lawrence said sheepishly. 'And your Alan, he's a good dancer, you say?'

'The best. Although,' she conceded, 'with you, it might be a tie.'

'Where is he, d'you know?'

'In the desert. He was evacuated from Crete and then they went to . . . well, I don't know where he is exactly, but he tells me things like how he's learning all about stars. It's the only way they can find their way around, some of the time, so he knows about the Plough and Cassiopeia and . . . I can't remember the others. And it's freezing cold at night. You wouldn't think so, in a desert, would you?'

'Not much cloud, I suppose.' Lawrence sounded interested. 'It must be very strange. Nothing much but rocks and sand.'

'He had his picture in the works magazine,' Joy said proudly. 'He met someone there that he knows from moulding . . .'

'Moulding?'

'The Moulding Department: where they make the bars and suchlike. Their photographs were side by side. "*Alan Bishop (Packaging)* . . ." She laughed. 'So at least I've got a tiny picture of him.' She looked up into Lawrence's face. 'How's your wife – and the little one?' It felt nice, being able to talk openly, honestly – to a friend. Or so she told herself.

'They're well. I got down to Southampton last weekend. In fact it's possible I'll be able to go back – in a few months.'

Joy felt a pang. The thought of never seeing Lawrence again hurt more than she expected. But who was she, to make any claims?

'Come on . . .' A foxtrot was starting up. 'Let's enjoy it while you're here, then.'

When the dance ended, they all streamed out into the darkness. Joy could hear couples talking, peals of laughter and voices calling, 'See you soon!' ringing out as everyone dispersed across the works and headed for home.

'It's going to take you an age to get back,' Joy said. Lawrence's lodgings were across town in Erdington.

'Oh no, it'll be all right. And anyway,' he chuckled, 'what does it matter?' He sounded carefree, like a young lover.

They were both aware of couples who were holding back for a kiss in the deeper shadow of the buildings and, as they walked, Joy knew the atmosphere between them was electric.

Don't be stupid! She ticked herself off inside. *He's someone else's – and so are you!* But desire streamed through her. Lawrence was holding her arm tucked through his, as they climbed the steps up to Bournville Lane. It was quiet, apart from the sound of a few people receding in the distance.

Lawrence pulled her aside for a moment. 'Joy?'

She could feel him looking down at her, though she could only just make out the faint glint of his eyes. A few seconds passed as they gazed at each other's almost-invisible faces in the darkness, before they moved into an embrace and their lips hungrily searched for each other's.

The next morning, Sunday, Joy lay in bed until so late that there were already smells of dinner in preparation. She heard the family moving about, footsteps on the stairs, Martin's voice, 'What's cooking, Ma?' and, a moment later, 'We'll all *look* like carrots soon.'

Joy smiled. She felt warm and comfortable, bathed in memories of the dance, of Lawrence . . . Guilt clutched at her, cold and reproving. Lawrence's kisses, the way the two of them had stood pressed passionately together last night for . . . well, it must have been nearly an hour, judging by the time she came creeping into the house. Mom had given her a key, thank goodness.

The memories filled her with desire, the way Lawrence always had. But guilt followed on hard. Alan: she did love

Alan, she knew she did. Knew him inside out, now that they had talked properly – about his real life at home, his family. She drew on all the memories she could think of: standing outside at Cadbury's chatting with their friends and workmates; the time they went to the fair together and came home biting ravenously into toffee apples; dancing, so much dancing, and Alan, good-looking and light on his feet, learning any dance as quick as a flash. They were perfect partners as well.

But God, it was so long since she had seen him. More than a year. She loved his letters, even if they were short. She wrote affectionate ones back, telling him all about life at the factory and how she loved him. But it felt like half a lifetime since she had seen his face or been held in his arms.

'Forgive me,' she whispered. 'It's only for now, me dancing with Lawrence – because of the way things are. Just having a bit of life. But I love *you*, Al. I do.'

'Oh, look who came in with the milk!' Martin joked as Joy finally appeared downstairs, in time to help lay the table.

Mom was bustling about in the kitchen, shouting, 'Mart, come and take this in, will you?'

To Joy's surprise, Marianne was already downstairs with George, feeding him on her lap.

'All right?' Joy said. She felt sorry for Marianne, in a way. Imagine if Lawrence had got her pregnant and she had had to move in with him and his wife! Her father was another matter: what the hell had he been playing at? But she tried not to dwell on things too much. Why let it spoil her own life? And it was nice, in a way, having George in the house, the little pudding. She was his sister – sort of. She missed having Sheila at home with Elaine, who could always lighten things.

'If you like, I'll come out with you this afternoon, take George along to the park? Would you like that, Georgie?'

Marianne nodded and gave a shy smile. 'Yes, ta. That'd be nice.'

Eighteen

March

Sheila sat feeding Robbie while Elaine played on the sitting-room floor. She caressed her son's fair head as he sucked vigorously. He was nearly six months old now and she was completely besotted with him. Robbie was a beautiful child by any standards: fair, with big blue eyes, and he had a sweet, amiable nature. Elaine also adored him. Sheila's world had mainly, for the moment, shrunk to that of the house and her children – and her letters.

Every letter from Kenneth set her heart pounding with love and relief. He was alive and safe! She would sit, drinking in his words, seeing his loving face in her mind. Her mother's letters were full of local snippets: *'They've opened the Market Hall again – fancy that. Eighty stalls already, it says in the paper.'* And the fact that, to Sheila's astonishment, Mom had gone back to work at Cadbury's, on munitions.

News that reached her on the wireless – the fall of Singapore, the Japanese now taking over great swathes of Asia – all felt so distant, in this safe, green place, that it barely registered, except to create a general sense of gloom. When would this war ever be over, so that she and Kenneth could be together again with their little ones? Sometimes Sheila sat, aching to see him and weeping when she thought about how much of Elaine's life, and now Robbie's, Kenneth had missed.

Soon after Robbie was born, though, both Mom and Joy had managed to get down for visits to see her. They didn't discuss how things were at home: nothing about that Marianne woman or Dad, or any of their troubles. They just came and cuddled Elaine and met Robbie – as well as Audrey and the boys – and it was all lovely. The day glowed in Sheila's memory.

To cap it off, Kenneth had been given leave to visit and see his new son.

'How marvellous!' Audrey cried when she heard he would be able to come. 'He's very welcome. It'll be so nice to meet him – and have someone else around.'

Kenneth had stayed three nights before having to go back to the east coast. Audrey had been so tactful when all the visitors came, leaving them plenty of time to be alone as a family and, by the end of it, Sheila felt very loved and closer to them all.

She smiled now, looking down at Robbie's round cheek, sucking away. Things had been so nice since Audrey stopped her work on the buses. It had taken time for her to stop feeling nervous when she went out anywhere – and she still would not venture out after dark. But in the main Audrey was back to her normal self and the two of them had an easy, friendly routine with all the children.

'We're so lucky, little Robbie.' Sheila cuddled him close. 'All we need now is for this wretched war to end and your daddy to come home.'

Audrey went to church most Sundays. Sheila had gone along a few times before Robbie was born, but now – what with Elaine being so restless and herself with a new little one, as well as the boredom she felt, in truth, sitting through it – she felt she had good excuses to stay home. The part afterwards, all the chit-chat outside, had always felt awkward as well. She felt there were some people who were looking down their noses at her: 'Oh, that's the evacuee. From *Birmingham*, you know! *So* kind of Audrey Vellacott to keep it going this long. I hear they're not even being bombed any more.'

Sometimes Edward and Charlie rebelled and demanded not to have to go to church, so Audrey would let them stay at home with Sheila. So that Sunday, Sheila had spent an hour with Robbie on her lap, while Edward and Charlie set up a complicated Hornby railway set on the floor. Elaine was being very good and watched, fascinated, without interfering.

Sheila took charge of the cooking that day as well, so she left the boys playing and took Elaine into the kitchen, setting her to play with some wooden spoons and pastry cutters at the table. Robbie was in a basket safely on the floor, out of the way.

'These potatoes are going to be delicious!' she said to Elaine, basting the dish of nicely browning spuds.

There was a sudden rumpus at the front door and Elaine's face lit up. 'Audwey!'

The boys came clattering in as well, like rampaging lions.

'Now, now – go and have a run around outside if you've been in all morning,' Audrey said. 'You'll only get under Sheila's feet.'

'You're late back,' Sheila said, as the boys went hurtling out again. 'Were you having a nice chat?'

To her surprise, she saw Audrey blush. 'I was, rather,' she replied, leaning over the table in her Sunday frock, which was brown, printed with swirls of coffee colour, very elegant on her, along with her usual string of pearls. 'That chap, Mr Richardson, rather buttonholed me.'

Sheila frowned.

'You know: big man, rather jolly. About . . . I'm not sure how old. Fifty-odd, I should think?'

'I can't picture him, I'm afraid,' Sheila said, getting the knives and forks ready.

'Let me do that.' Audrey took them off her. 'No, I suppose he hasn't been there that often.'

'Just got to do the gravy,' Sheila said.

'He's very keen on gardening,' Audrey went on. 'Said he'd happily come and have a look at ours. It's so hard to keep up, now Maurice isn't . . . here.'

Maurice Vellacott had used to spend a lot of time out in the garden when he was home at weekends – at least when he was not on the golf course.

'I must say,' Audrey went on, drifting out of the kitchen, 'it would be jolly useful to have a chap about the place some of the time.'

'I'm surprised you want a man anywhere near you,' Sheila remarked.

'Well,' Audrey put her head on one side, 'this is a very different sort of man, I suppose.'

Sheila watched her. Audrey seemed altered suddenly: off in the clouds. She tried again to think who this Mr Richardson was, but nothing came to mind.

'Boys!' She yelled out of the back door. 'Dinner's ready!'

Sheila was soon to find out who Mr Richardson was, because the next evening he appeared at the house.

'Oh, I asked Terence over for a drink this evening,' Audrey announced in a light voice that morning, as if she had forgotten this. 'You must come and join us and meet him.'

'All right,' Sheila said. 'As soon as I've got the kids down.'

She was not mad keen to meet this Terence Richardson. She was tired and, in any case, mostly she felt like a fish out of water when any of the neighbours were about.

By the time she had Elaine and Robbie settled in her room and had remembered to tidy her hair and put on some lipstick – hoping for the best in the light from the landing, so as not to wake the kids – the bloke must have been there for quite a while already. What Sheila really wanted to do was curl up on the bed and go to sleep, but she had promised Audrey.

Opening the sitting-room door, she saw a large, forceful-looking person seated in the biggest armchair. Seeing this sandy-haired, pink-faced man, she did recall having met him once before. He was laughing merrily and loudly. Audrey was opposite, perched on the edge of the sofa, an empty sherry glass held between both hands. Her cheeks and nose were pink and she was also laughing and animated.

Terence Richardson leapt eagerly to his feet. He reminded Sheila of a large dog.

'Ah!' he cried, coming towards her, 'the evacuee. So glad to meet you at last!'

He took Sheila's hand and pumped it, like someone trying to draw water. His hand was big and hot, and she murmured 'How do you do?', not liking to point out that they had met at least once before in church, before Robbie was born.

'This is Sheila Carson – Terence Richardson . . .'

'Oh, Terry, please!'

'Here you go.' Audrey handed Sheila a glass of sherry. 'We're on to our second – at least I am.' She giggled. 'Another Scotch?' She lifted the decanter over Terence's glass and he winked at her.

'Why not? I don't often find myself in the company of two lovely ladies.'

Sheila settled into the other, smaller armchair and sipped her sherry. To her surprise, Terence Richardson sat forward, leaning his arms on his thighs, and started to ask her questions.

'Bournville, eh? How fascinating. The Cadbury place – one hears such good things about it, as a firm.'

'Yes,' she said. 'It's a very good place to work.'

'And they've gone over to war work, you say?'

'To some extent, yes.'

'Most of Sheila's family work at Cadbury's, don't they?' Audrey said.

'Jolly good,' Terence said. 'Good chaps, those Quaker businessmen. Quite odd of course, in their way, but they make a good stab at business . . . I was saying to Audrey here: lot of respect for anyone who can run a good firm. Fine city, Birmingham.' He sat back in the chair at last and crossed one large, tweedily clad thigh over the other.

'Yes,' Sheila agreed. There did not seem to be much she could add. Should she be asking him something? But before she could get a word in, he was off again.

'Told Audrey here I'd come and give a hand with the garden. Spring coming – everything'll be running away before long. Hard to cope.'

'I'd be so grateful,' Audrey said. 'If you can spare the time?'

'Oh, plenty of time.' He beamed. 'No good mooning about at home, is it? I've a son in the Air Force, daughter's married . . .' He looked at Sheila, who was wondering about his wife. 'Jean passed away: two years now.' His face folded into a mask of woe for a moment, before recovering. 'Terrible business.' He shook his head. 'No good moping.'

'No,' Audrey agreed, her head on one side, the picture of sympathy and fellow feeling. 'Losing one's other half is so . . .'

'Quite,' he said, nodding vigorously. 'Yes. Just so. No good dwelling.'

Watching Audrey, Sheila thought about Maurice Vellacott. But what was Audrey supposed to do, other than play the grieving widow?

Audrey got up. 'I've a few little crackers – to go with the drinks . . .'

As soon as she left the room, Terence Richardson turned to Sheila, smiling, but his eyes were intent.

'So, still bombing heavily up there, are they? I rather thought things had settled down?'

'Birmingham, you mean?' She could feel a pressure in his question. 'Yes, things are not as bad as they were. Not since—'

He cut her off. 'So I suppose you've no real need to be hanging about down here now, then?' Again there was the jovial tone, but there was something in his eyes that she didn't like. 'Will you be back off home soon?'

Sheila was spared answering when Audrey came back in with a few water biscuits on a plate, saying, 'Here we are!'

Terence kept looking at Sheila for a few seconds, during which the message was unmistakeable. He wants me out of the way, she thought. She found herself mentally digging in her heels. She wasn't going home to live with her father's mistress in the house. Not that she was ever going to mention that to Terence Richardson. But she wasn't being damn well pushed about by him, either. She pulled her face into a fake but defiant smile.

'Damn glad to have your company, ladies,' Terence said, raising his glass. 'Here's to a lot more of it. Cheers.'

Nineteen

July

Ann lay in bed, hearing the low murmur of voices from the attic. It was a muggy night and they had the windows open, but it was hard to get a flow of air through the blackout and she pushed back the bedclothes. It was one of those moments she tried to avoid, if she possibly could, of thinking: I am still sharing a bed with my husband, but he is upstairs with another woman.

She and Len never had physical relations now. Did he sneak up to *her* whenever he could for . . .? And if so, when on earth? What with work and the Home Guard, he scarcely ever had the time. She wanted not to mind – *didn't* mind, most of the time. Any desire she had ever had for Len was long gone. But all the same, the idea of him with Marianne . . .

Her thoughts whirled, as they always did if she ever allowed them to stray to this subject. Who was she to complain and criticize, when her love had been directed for so long towards another man? And on it went.

A moment later she heard Len coming back down the stairs and she turned away from him as he came into the room and softly closed the door.

'Ann?'

'Um?'

'Can I talk to you a minute?'

She rolled over and the soft gold eiderdown slid off the bottom of the bed as she sat up. Len stood there looking nervous, wretched almost.

'What's up?' she asked in a neutral voice.

'It's just . . . remember that camp, last summer? When you and Martin came out for tea?'

When the Home Guard had one of their training camps last summer, wives and families had been invited to join them for a Sunday tea, with long tables set out in the field where the men were camping. She nodded.

'It's this weekend. Out near Bell Heath.'

She stared at him. 'That's all right. You'll have to go.' The penny dropped suddenly. Len was watching her, looking terrible.

'Oh, what: you want me to come? Play at Happy Families?' She couldn't help it, the bitterness in her voice.

'Ann . . .' He sounded so wretched. 'That's not what I was going to say.'

Another penny came clanking down.

'Oh, I see. Course, yes – take Marianne. Your "cousin". And baby.'

'I thought it'd be a change for her, that's all.'

'Well, it would, yes.' Ann was only a little bit sarcastic now, because she realized that, deep down, she didn't mind. Getting both of them out of the way for a bit would be so peaceful. And already the seed of something else – something joyful – was forming in her mind. 'Good idea. Yes, go on, let her go. It'll do her and George both good.'

Len nodded, surprised. 'All right then. I'll tell her, tomorrow like.' He climbed into bed and turned to look at Ann as she lay down again. 'Thanks,' he said humbly. 'Can't be much fun for her: all of this.'

It's not much fun for any of us, she thought, but said nothing. She was long past all the argy-bargy and recriminations. She tried to stay floating over it all, detached. Who knew what was going to happen, but while the war was on they were all somehow going to have to keep going and get through it.

After Len had turned the light out and shuffled about until he was comfortable, Ann lay with her eyes wide open in the dark. A daring, wonderful plan was forming and she was already composing a letter in her head:

Dearest Tom,
Please, please say you're free, next Sunday 12th – I might be able to come away and meet you!

Her heart pounded so loudly she thought Len must be able to hear it. Tom – actually to be with Tom again! It wasn't something she had expected, not really. The last time she saw him was in December 1940, after she was injured in the bomb blast near St Thomas's Church, close to the centre of Birmingham. Such sweet, tender moments they had shared – until they were interrupted. Len and Margaret had arrived. Her last image of Tom was of him walking out along the ward, shamed by Len, not even daring to turn and wave.

Please, she prayed, *let this happen. Let us see each other – just for a day.*

Ann arrived first, feeling she was in a dream as she got down from the train, still hardly daring to believe that she was here, that she had found the courage to take off like this.

'Don't come all the way down here,' Tom had written. *'Oxford's halfway – and lovely!'*

But she would not believe it until he was here. All the time she expected everything to be jinxed: that even this one snatched day of happiness between them could not be possible. Last month there had been a big raid on Southampton and she had hardly slept until she heard from Tom. Jeanette and the other girls at work kept asking if she was all right.

It was still early – only just gone ten. They had decided to take the earliest trains possible. When Ann left, Joy had still been asleep and Martin was staying with his friend Ian. She wrote a note for Joy and left the house feeling dizzy with freedom.

She crossed platforms and stood in the cool shade of the Oxford station platform, waiting nervously for his train. So many times she had asked herself whether all she was doing was living a fantasy. All those years during which she had not seen him, had been married to Len, trying to bury any thought of Tom and what they had meant to each other in those fleeting weeks when he was a patient at Fircroft, recovering from his wounds. She told herself that those had not been normal times. Everyone's emotions had been running high. Once the war was over, everyday peacetime life would calm things down and they would forget.

But then she had seen him again. That dreamlike afternoon in a hotel room in the middle of Birmingham, which had given her Martin, their lovely son. And then again, when Tom came to see her in hospital. And each time she had known. When she saw him, nothing had changed. Even so, the same doubts came crowding in again while she waited, her bag over the shoulder of her pale summer mac, feeling as if she had a neon sign with the words 'Scarlet Woman' shining out above her head.

The loco thudded in, obscuring the platform in steam and smoke. As it cleared, suddenly there he was, walking towards her among the other passengers. Tom, unmistakeable. She saw, with a shock, that he now wore spectacles, one lens misted, which helped to hide the patch he wore over his missing eye. There was the brown coat, the pinned sleeve, his broad shoulders, his face lifting into a joyous smile as he saw her. Him. Her Tom. And every doubt vanished as home and rightness and love walked towards her. Again and again, each time she saw him, she knew . . .

They stood to one side, out of the scramble of passengers, holding each other without a word. Ann breathed him in, the slight smoky smell of his coat against her cheek, his strong back, remembering him with her fingertips, the warmth of him. Tom. Her man and her beloved. At last they drew back and looked into each other's faces.

'Ann,' he said. 'My dear Ann.' His face was full of emotion and, melted by it, she reached up and stroked his cheek.

'We have a day,' she said. 'A whole day.'

Ann felt almost drunk as she walked all morning in the summer warmth, arm-in-arm with Tom, her mac now slung over her other arm. On every side were the old, elegant, smutty-faced buildings of this small city. Wisteria and ivy trailed up its mellow walls. There were streets of houses with sleepy front gardens, the ancient stones seeming to bask in the summer sunshine. There were cobbled back-alleys, whiffs of old books through shadowy doorways.

But these days, of course, like everywhere else, sand-bags shored up the faces of the buildings, signs multiplied across the walls with warnings about careless talk and instructions to reach ARP posts and shelters. There was white paint on kerbs and poles and tree trunks, just like in every other city. Men in uniform bustled about here too. But it was still extraordinary.

'It's so beautiful,' she said.

'It is. I'm glad to be able to show it to you.' Tom had

been in Oxford a few times on visits. 'Let's hope to God it stays that way. I can't imagine they haven't got it in their sights – not after what's happened to Canterbury, and Exeter.'

It was the beginning of what were being called the 'Baedeker raids' – the bombing of beautiful old cities that appeared in the Baedeker guidebooks. People were horrified, grief-stricken by the destruction.

'But there's nothing here to bomb, is there?' she asked.

'There's quite a bit of industry – Morris and the Cowley works, for a start.'

'Oh,' she said, her head back to stare up at a church spire, its pointed pinnacle so high it made her feel dizzy. 'Yes. Course.'

Tom tugged gently on her arm. 'Come on, let's go and find some lunch, shall we?'

The time passed so quickly. They talked and talked, ate gristly sausages and mash in a pub and afterwards walked the streets again, mixing with military personnel and students, and women from the government departments now transferred to Oxford colleges.

'Let's go in here – it'll be peaceful.'

Tom steered her through the gate into a wide park, the path edged with mature trees, with a cricket pavilion in the middle and green laid out all around. Soon, as they strolled, they found themselves in sight of a narrow stretch of river with a little bridge arched over it and, without needing to consult each other, they sank down together on a bench.

'It's so lovely and warm.' Ann stretched for a moment, catlike, then sank back as Tom put his arm round her. 'Isn't it nice to be somewhere where no one has any idea who we are?'

'Bliss,' he said. 'Can we just stay for ever?'

132

They both laughed, slightly grimly. Through lunch, she had told Tom all about Martin, about how well he was doing at school, how clever he was and that he was planning to stay at the grammar school and take his Higher Certificate. She told him what a good lad he was. Kind. Funny. *Yours*, she kept wanting to say – *he's your son!*

But it was only now that they were not looking straight at each other, across a table, that Tom said softly, 'Are you going to tell him – ever, I mean?'

Ann's head whipped round for a second. 'Yes! Of course: I've got to, haven't I? I just . . .' She sagged, the reality of home seeping through her; it had been so good to escape for the day. 'But I don't know when. My children have got a lot on their plate. Len – and Marianne. It's horrible for them: a strain.'

'And so have you,' he pointed out.

'Well, yes. But I've got you.' She turned to smile at him, but she could see that Tom looked troubled. 'Sheila's the one who had the most to say about it, but of course she's not there now. Joy seems to be dealing with things well. She gets along all right with Marianne most of the time. It's surprising, but I s'pose she's more easygoing. Sheila's very black-and-white, but then that's most people for you, isn't it?'

'And Martin?' Tom asked gently.

'He's never said much – not had a go at me. As I say, he's kind-natured. But I can't really say what he thinks. He's working hard and he's out a lot: with friends, they go to the pictures, do whatever lads do at that age . . . He's not very keen on sport, not like Len.' She shook her head. 'Marianne's Len's "cousin", as far as everyone else is concerned.' She shrugged. 'I will tell Martin. Course I will. When the right moment comes.'

Tom stroked her back. 'I don't have a right to demand

anything. I'd like to know him – I really would. Be able to do more for him. But it's up to you, and to him.'

There was a pause.

'Thanks,' she said awkwardly. 'For the money you're putting away for him.'

Tom waved her away, embarrassed. 'It's the very least . . . Don't thank me.'

Up until now they had kept things light and joyous, as far as possible. It was their rare, golden day together, so why spoil it with sadness? But they couldn't hide their feelings for ever. Into the silence that fell suddenly, Ann said quietly, 'I'd come to you, you know. If it weren't for the kids. I feel pulled in half. As though I'm being unfair on you – on everyone.'

'No!' Tom said, distraught. He pulled her even closer to him. 'My God, I love you, Ann. And there's nothing I want more than to be with you. But I've caused enough damage already. If anyone needs to move themselves, it's me. But I don't see how, not with . . . You've got your family; and there's the business, my father . . .' He looked down tenderly at her. 'You don't change, d'you know that?'

She smiled, tearful now. 'I feel about a hundred years old.'

Tom shook his head. 'You're lovely. And, you know, every day I am glad simply to be alive. Knowing you are there is just another . . . blessing. And maybe one day—'

Ann put her hand gently over his lips. 'One day. But don't tempt fate. Wait and see.'

They both ran out of words, faced by the difficulties of it all. Tom's lips met hers and their kisses poured all of their longing into each other. Wrapped together, loving, desperate, they stared across at the green beyond the river.

'You see that bit of land over there?' Tom said as he held

her close. 'The river splits here, so there's land in between. You know what they call it? Mesopotamia. The land between the two rivers.'

Ann gazed across at it. 'That's where I live,' she said sadly. 'Between. In Mesopotamia.'

Twenty

'That's where I used to go to school.' Joy pointed to the Cadbury Continuation School. 'I mean, once I'd started working here. We had classes every week – swimming and everything – that's the pool, over there.'

Lawrence laughed, holding her by the arm.

'You really do have the lot here, don't you?'

'It's not bad, is it? Now your guided tour is nearly over . . .' She had walked him round the camouflage-draped factory and they headed around the edge of Bournville Green, which was fenced off for sheep to graze. 'It doesn't normally look like this,' Joy laughed. 'And Rowheath, where we're going, is more like a farm now!'

It was so nice to see Lawrence. They hadn't met up for ages. And Rowheath Lido and its grounds were now open for the summer, for what Cadbury's was calling 'Holidays at Home'. Now that the children had broken up, it was packed out a lot of the time. Best of all – so far as Joy was concerned – there were dances being held in the grounds. And this time Lawrence had said he could make it to one of them.

The year so far had not been easy for Joy. Alan's letters were not regular. She see-sawed between fretting when she did not hear from him, to the point of losing her appetite, and being flooded with happiness and relief when a letter finally arrived. When the news came in June that Tobruk had fallen to the enemy and Allied troops were being rounded up in their thousands, she had lived on her nerves for days. She didn't know exactly where Alan was anyway – he might have been miles away. But the silence and the not knowing were terrible.

She had been on the point of going over to Edgbaston to see if Alan's mother and sister had had any news, but she dreaded the thought. The one time she had been there, she had had a shock. She had been driven to go by a need to know who his people were, when Alan was being so evasive and mysterious with her.

Irene Bishop, Alan's sister, was a strong, capable young woman who, Joy realized, had coped with a lot in her young life. She was only a couple of years older than Joy herself, but she seemed older and much more grown-up. But Alan's father was in prison and when Joy saw his mother, it had been the greatest shock of all. Mrs Bishop was a wrecked wisp of a woman, who hardly looked in possession of her own mind.

'Mom used not to be like that,' Alan had told her, when she finally confronted him, needing him to be truthful with her. His mother, he admitted shamefacedly, had been in the asylum at Winson Green more than once. 'The old man drove her to it. So far as I'm concerned, they can keep him in prison 'til he rots.'

Joy was almost afraid to go back there again. But just as she was getting really desperate and on the point of going, a letter had arrived from Alan:

Dearest Joy,
I hope you haven't been too worried. We've been on the move a lot and there's been no time to write . . .

She took the letter to her room and burst into tears. He was all right! He ended the short letter:

You're the main thing keeping me going. There's not much here but sand, and sometimes I try and see your face in it – like a screen at the pictures. I can't wait 'til all this is over and I can be with you properly and for good.

Joy lay on the bed, hugging the letter against her. Every so often she stared at it again and kissed the thin sheet of paper.

'Oh, Al,' she wept. 'This blasted war – it's spoiling everything!' For a moment she thought of all the things they might have been doing, if there was no war like a dark pall over everything. Both of them were twenty years old and the best years of their lives, which should have been full of life and love, were being spoilt by all this stupid fighting that had nothing to do with them. She wept with frustration, feeling very sorry for herself.

But the effect of getting a letter – even though it made her heart leap with joy when it arrived – soon wore off and she had to start worrying all over again. Sometimes Alan felt like a distant memory. She had hardly seen him for two years now. It was so hard to hold on to her feelings.

I want him here now, not always on the other side of the world like some ghost, she thought. She sat up on the bed, wiping her eyes. She might never even see him again. What did it matter if she went dancing with Lawrence a few times? It didn't mean anything, did it?

The band had arranged itself outside the Rowheath pavilion. All across the wide lawns, couples danced in the mellow afternoon light. Joy was not wearing her usual evening dance skirt, but a cotton frock that she had had since before the war and which still just about fitted: cream, with bunches of red cherries on it and a full skirt. Clothes rationing had come in a few weeks ago – points for this and points for that. Any new purchase had to be thought about very carefully. Lawrence was in his grey flannels and a white shirt, looking slender and athletic, as ever. The sight of him, the way he moved and his lively brown eyes, filled Joy with feelings that she kept trying to forget about.

Some of her workmates were there and she introduced Lawrence as a friend – they all knew Alan. Norma and Danny were about somewhere; Danny was trying to avoid the dancing at all costs, and they had sat down to have a drink with some of his pals.

'Oh!' Joy cried as the next lot of music came on. 'My favourite!'

'Everyone's favourite,' Lawrence laughed as the band struck up 'In the Mood'. The two of them flung themselves into the dance, their feet and bodies moving completely in tune. As the dance got going, they bent their legs more, leaned out, holding each other by one hand, before Lawrence pulled Joy close and she twirled round and under his arm . . . And as had happened on some occasions previously, their dancing was so electric, so expert, that a space appeared around them and gradually other people stopped dancing to watch.

Joy and Lawrence beamed at each other. She was lit up – this was living. It was heaven! Her feet had a life of their own, the steps as familiar to her as breathing, and Lawrence moved in perfect time with her. As the music stopped, he bowed and they both finished, laughing as their audience clapped and cheered.

'Blimey, you two are something!' Norma said. 'I came over and there you were – doing a solo suddenly.'

'Our first dance was under the moon,' Joy laughed. 'After that night in the shelter, remember?'

Norma was giving her a bit of a funny look. She had met Lawrence – Joy introduced them – but until now she had not realized quite how much time Joy had apparently spent with him.

'You going to drag Danny out here?' Joy teased as the music struck up again.

Norma glanced back at him and made a face. 'Not a chance!' she laughed.

Joy and Lawrence whirled off into another dance.

'Please see if you can get time off again sometime, won't you?' she said as they left the Rowheath grounds amid the weary dancers, right at the night's end.

'I'm not sure if . . .' He was serious suddenly. 'Look, I know you only live up the road, but can we walk a bit? I need to talk to you.'

'Oh dear,' she joked. 'That sounds ominous.' They turned along Heath Road. 'We can go round the block. As many blocks as you want.'

Arm-in-arm, they walked in the sweet-smelling summer night. Roses in the gardens were giving off their perfume after the warmth of the day.

'The thing is . . . Just stop a moment, Joy.' Lawrence put his hands on her shoulders. 'They're moving me back to Southampton.'

'Oh no!' She was taken aback by the immediate tightness in her chest, the tears that threatened.

'I did tell you it was on the cards. I've done all I really can up here and they're putting me on some other development work down south. I have to go: orders. And the family . . .'

'I know. Of course I know.' But she burst into tears.

'Oh, Lawrence – I'm going to miss you so much.' She loved Lawrence, Joy knew. Not the way she loved Alan, but as a friend, a wonderful companion and dancer. She knew how much he felt for her as well.

'I know – and I'll miss you. But we understood, didn't we? That this would happen.'

She nodded, tears rolling down her cheeks. They could scarcely see each other's faces, but he could hear her choked voice.

'Oh, come here, little one.' He pulled Joy into his arms and they stood rocking from side to side, comforting each other.

'I'll never forget you,' she said. When Lawrence left Birmingham, she knew she would never see him again.

'And I, you. When I think of the war, there you'll always be – little Joy, the most wonderful dancer of my life.'

She smiled sadly, pressed against his chest. She knew not to suggest writing. It felt wrong. She pulled back and they reached for each other, kissing passionately in the darkness. It didn't mean anything – not about the future. It was a goodbye.

After they stood taking leave of each other fondly for a good long while, Lawrence walked her home. When they reached the end of Beaumont Street, she said, 'Let's say goodbye here. Don't come to the door. I don't think I could stand it.'

Again they were standing face-to-face in the dark.

'Goodbye, Joy,' he said, the last time she would ever hear his deep, tender voice.

'Bye, Lawrence – and thanks for everything.'

She backed away and walked home, seeing him in her mind's eye moving further and further from her along the street. And now, in the secrecy of darkness, she could let her tears fall.

As Joy came into the house, wiping her eyes, she realized that her mother was in the kitchen. It was gone eleven, but Ann had a look of only just having got in. Joy could hear faint voices from upstairs: Dad and Marianne, she guessed. Her sadness increased further. Home – and all this carry-on, still.

Her mother was at the stove while the kettle was heating, simply standing there. She looked nice, Joy saw, in her yellow summer frock. Ann looked round, hearing Joy come in.

'They're all back then?' Joy rolled her eyes to the ceiling. 'Where's Mart – in his room?'

'Yes, he's not long back, either. And where've you been?' She took in Joy's tearful face. 'What's up?'

'I'm all right.' Joy sank down at the table. 'It's just . . . Lawrence, my dance partner.' She told Ann that was it: he was leaving.

'Oh dear,' Ann said. 'He seemed a nice man – and you said he was a good dancer.'

'*Very* good. Oh well.' Life felt so flat and sad. She looked at Ann. 'Thanks for the note. Where've you been?'

Her mother stood there, seemingly unable to reply.

'You've been to see him, haven't you? Tom?'

Ann nodded slowly, unsure of Joy's reaction. Joy, who had sent the telegram to Tom while Ann was in hospital, asking him to come. But that was then . . .

'You do love him, don't you, Mom?'

She saw her mother's eyes fill with tears. Ann nodded.

'And he really loves you?'

'He does, yes.'

Joy got up, as if tired suddenly. 'Well, that's good. I

want to know that somewhere there are people who really love each other.'

'Joy . . .'

Walking to the stairs, she could feel her mother watching her. She sank down on the edge of her bed, staring wearily ahead of her, the sadness a physical weight in her body.

'Oh, Lawrence,' she whispered.

He would not write to her, she knew. And it would be wrong if he did. He had just walked out of her life, and she already ached with missing him. He had been one of the few bright lights during the dark wartime days and already she was left with a sick feeling of loss. She knew she loved Lawrence – and he, her – during these strange and fractured times. It did not mean they loved other people any the less, and they had had very little time to see each other. But now it felt as if a cheering light had been put out.

She put her hands over her face and let her sobs break out, falling sideways on the bed and having a good cry. Reaching down under the bed, she pulled out her little chocolate box containing Alan's letters and hugged it close to her.

'I love you, Al,' she whispered. 'You know that. I'll always love you.'

Twenty-One

August

'Of course you can come with us,' Ann said. She and Joy were clearing the table after a bit of dinner – bread and cheese and some lettuce from the garden. Ann looked at her daughter in surprise. 'I'm quite flattered you'd be seen out with me.'

'Mom! Don't be daft,' Joy said, gathering the plates up from the table. 'I walk to work with you nearly every day, for a start.' She rolled her eyes at the racket coming from the hall, where Marianne was struggling to get a tired, cross George upstairs for a nap.

Len had already escaped to the garden and was doing something busy-looking in the veggie patch. Ann's eyes met Joy's – let's get out of here! They both smiled. An understanding that Ann had never felt before seemed to be growing between her and her younger daughter.

'I've got nothing else to do, have I?' Joy went on, filling the sink to wash up. 'Norma's off somewhere with Danny, sorting out a wedding cake supposedly, though God knows what's going in that – chalk dust and tacks, I should think! Who else am I going to go out with these days? Anyway, Jeanette's nice.'

The sound of George's roaring receded upstairs. Marianne had been out somewhere or other and had come back rather late for George's dinner. He was not happy.

'I don't think I'll bother having children,' Joy remarked.

'Famous last words,' Ann said. 'Look, I'll wash up. Go and ask Martin if he fancies some fresh air as well, will you?'

'They're off cycling somewhere – him and Ian – he didn't say where,' Joy said when she had come back down. 'Those two are thick as thieves these days.'

'Yes . . .' Ann said vaguely, watching Len, bent over his spade. He was thinner, worn down, she could see that. Margaret kept commenting on what a state he seemed to be in, but there was nothing much either of them could think of to do about it.

'Ian's a nice lad,' she said. 'And they're at least doing something outside, after all those exams.' Martin had taken his School Certificate at the end of this year. Both he and Ian were planning to stay on, and Ian, a quiet, freckle-faced lad who was very good at maths, was talking about university.

Ann narrowed her eyes, her hands automatically swilling plates in the sink. Len had straightened up. He seemed to be muttering to himself.

The 'Holidays at Home' season was still in full swing. There was swimming, dances and bands, a putting green – even a dog show! Ann walked along the road in the sun with Joy, each with their swimming things in a bag, feeling as happy as it was possible to, in the circumstances.

Jeanette was waiting for them just outside the Row-heath grounds and waved merrily seeing them coming, her pale face lighting up.

'All right, Annie, Joy? It's getting really busy in there! Fancy a go on the putting green, if we can get on? Get warmed up for a swim?'

They walked in past the ornate white pavilion. Along

the front were seven arched entrances with glass doors, and a long balcony above them with a wrought-iron balustrade. The lawns sloped away from the long frontage, and today they were packed with people picnicking and lounging, chatting and basking in the sun.

Shrieks and splashes were coming from the pool, with divers climbing up to the high board and soaring down. Jeanette linked her arm through Ann's, and Ann smiled at her in surprise. The two of them each worked on the ack-ack rockets with a group of other girls, and there was plenty of chat and laughter. They were a nice bunch. But she seemed to see more of Jeanette than of Hilda these days. Ann and Jeanette spent all their breaks together and had become close.

Or as close as I can be to anyone, Ann thought regretfully. There were whole areas of her life that she couldn't open up about to anyone. Although she had confided in Hilda, she was still not sure what Hilda really felt about her now.

The three of them had a lovely afternoon, playing on the putting green, then getting into the crowded pool for a dip. Jeanette, though quiet and almost mouse-like when you first met her, knew how to enjoy life and they had a lot of fun and laughter. She was a kindly, gentle woman who had looked after her poorly mother until she died.

'Look at us,' she said as they wriggled into their costumes. 'I mean, your face and hands . . .'

'You are – you're yellow, both of you,' Joy said.

Ann looked down at her hands. 'No, we're not. You're having me on! It's TNT does that, isn't it?'

'D'you know,' Jeanette said, 'after the Great War some of the munitions girls – the Canaries – had yellow babies.'

'Did they?' Joy said, horrified.

Ann grimaced. 'Ah well – too late for me.'

'And me!' Jeanette laughed. 'Come on: race you in!'

They all ran over to the pool and managed to find a gap to jump into the water, shrieking. After their swim they bought some glasses of lemonade and sprawled on the grass.

'Well, that's brought some colour back into your face,' Ann said to Joy, who had a pink nose and roses in her cheeks again.

She looked so pretty, with her dark eyes and tousled dark hair and she felt a surge of pride.

'Your boy all right, is he?' Jeanette asked Joy. 'You heard from him?'

'Yes, he writes when he can,' she said. Sadness passed over her face like a cloud, but she managed to smile. 'He's very funny about the Italian soldiers – says they all stink of aftershave. And at least he's getting his chocolate,' Joy laughed. 'Which is more than we are.'

At the end of July chocolate and sweets had been rationed to two ounces a week per person, though there was talk of the ration increasing soon.

'I know,' Jeanette laughed. 'I used to eat more than that every shift when I first started at the works. It soon cured me though – I ate enough chocolate to last a lifetime. Give me a sherbet lemon any time: at least you can still get those!' She reached over and squeezed Joy's hand, her face serious again. 'It's terrible though, all you young people being separated like this. It's not right. Let's hope it'll all be over soon and you'll have him back with you, eh?'

But there did not seem much hope of that. All year there had been bad news from the Desert War. Two names had begun to dominate the news: Rommel, the German general over there, and now General Montgomery, who had arrived to lead the Allies. But there was no sign of any breakthrough and it felt as if the war would drag on and on . . .

'I'm keeping busy,' Joy said. 'You know the dances they have before the night shift? I've been asked to go along and do a bit of teaching – for people who don't know the steps. I didn't want to do it when I was working nights, but I don't mind now.'

'And you helped out with the party Mrs Elizabeth held last week, didn't you?' Ann said.

'At Manor Farm,' Joy said. This was the home of Mr George and Mrs Elizabeth Cadbury, a huge Georgian timbered mansion out in Northfield, with extensive grounds. 'It was so nice – she invited lots of children. There were pony rides and everything!'

'Ah, how lovely,' Jeanette said. 'They're such good people, they are. Mrs Elizabeth came to see our mom when she was ill and had to leave work. I've never forgotten how kind she was.'

As Joy and Jeanette talked, Ann lay back on the grass, her head resting on her rolled-up cardi. The sky was a deep-blue arc above her, patched with little flat-bottomed clouds. She felt floaty, almost as if it was she, and not the clouds, that was moving slowly. The sky looked so clean and fresh, like another world into which she could escape. If only she could stay here and float away from all her problems, and be taken up into that pure, clear blue . . .

'Mom? She's dozed off, I think,' Joy was saying.

'She's obviously finding us lively company,' she heard Jeanette say, and Ann opened her eyes. 'Oh, back with us now, are we?' Jeanette teased.

'Oh Lor'!' Ann sat up, in a panic. 'How long have I been asleep?'

'Half an hour or so,' Joy said. 'We didn't want to disturb you.'

The light had changed. As Ann sat up, muzzily, the

grass seemed a deeper green, the shadows longer and families were starting to pack up to go home.

'I'd best be off,' Jeanette said. 'I've got a few things to catch up on.' As they parted outside the gates, she said, 'That was a really enjoyable afternoon. I hope we can do it again sometime?' She looked at Joy. 'Your mom's such a good friend.'

Ann was warmed by this. 'Course we must! See you Monday.'

'She's so nice,' Joy commented as they wandered back along the road.

'I know. It's been good going back and getting in touch with people. I remember Jeanette when we were both fourteen.'

Joy walked quietly for a moment, her bag with her costume and towel slung over her shoulder.

'Mom? Can I ask you something?'

Ann felt her heart pick up speed a little. 'Yes. Course you can.'

'Do you think you'll ever . . .' Joy stumbled the words out. 'You and Tom. It's not as if Dad . . . We're all living a pack of fibs really, aren't we?'

Her words stabbed into Ann. All this muddle and mess that she and Len were inflicting on their children – on each other. It took a while before she could answer.

'The thing is, love, it's not only Dad, is it? You're all my family: you and Sheila and Martin – you're the world to me, the three of you, you know that? And there's Nanna Margaret and Cyril . . . I'm not going anywhere.'

'But I suppose we'll all grow up and leave, sometime.'

Ann was moved by her daughter's quiet thoughtfulness, a way of thinking that went beyond other people's judgements.

'I just think . . . If Dad wants to go and live with Marianne . . .'

'He's never said so.' Ann sighed. She suddenly felt weary to her bones. 'I'm not sure he knows what he wants. What I want is to keep my family together.'

Joy nodded. 'I know, Mom. But none of this is right – for any of us. You're sticking by Dad, and us, and . . . Marianne's got no one else.' She spoke as if trying to work things out. 'I wish we could all . . . People are such nasty gossips, aren't they?'

'I do love your dad.'

Even as she said it, Ann asked herself if it was really true any more. It was so hard to separate out her feelings from all the day-to-day things – looking after the house and the children they shared, all those ordinary habits of caring for everybody. That was all love of a sort, wasn't it? Of course it was. And yet . . . She knew, and could not help knowing, that with Tom there was something more.

'I know. And I do think' – Joy looked up into her face – 'that you can love more than one person at a time. You just can.'

Ann waited.

'My friend Lawrence. He's married. And I'm engaged to Alan. But . . .' She thrust her chin up. 'I love him, all the same.'

Ann put her arm round her daughter's shoulder for a moment, in wonder at this sudden openness between them.

'Well, lovey,' she said, 'it's probably just as well he's gone then, isn't it?'

Twenty-Two

October

'There's someone creeping about after me – I'm sure of it. Have you said anything to anyone?'

Marianne stood in her grandmother's grim attic room, George in her arms, wriggling because he wanted to get down.

'Stop it, George!' she snapped. She was warm, after hurrying along in all the clothes she had on – her winter coat with the big collar pulled up. Outside it was all damp and grey, the pavements soggy with leaves and chilly, but the air in this attic felt thick and fetid, the window not even open a crack.

Teresa Walsh stared back at her with an I-told-you-so face on her.

'Of course I haven't. But you can't go running for ever – John Brady's lot will catch up with you in the end.'

'That priest who came: who told him there was someone living at that address in Bournville?'

'Ah, now, that was months ago.'

'No, he came back – last week. Thank God *the wife* has no idea who Mary Brady is, but . . .'

'But how can they possibly know?'

'It's *her*,' Marianne snapped. 'That Sullivan bitch – I'm sure of it. You should see the looks she gives me. Too much of a coward to say anything to my face, but I'll bet she knows someone . . . John's family, or some old witch of a gossip in the parish over there.' Their parish, when Marianne was growing up in Aston, had been the Sacred Heart. 'They're like the flaming Mafia.' She jiggled George so furiously in her arms that he started snivelling.

'Put that child down, for the love of God – you're mollycoddling him.'

Marianne squatted thankfully and placed George on the floor. He looked about him, bewildered.

'I wouldn't put it past her to be following me about herself.'

'You'd not miss that one – the size of a house.'

'Or send someone else. She's had her evil eye on me from the moment I came here.'

For once, for a few moments they were united. Nora Sullivan was a self-righteous pillar of the parish who had waxed fat on gossip, chewing over the sins and misdeeds of others.

'Here.' Marianne reached into her bag and pulled out a ten-shilling note. 'Len gave me this. I'll send what I can, but I'm going to have to get away for a bit. They're getting too close.' Her face twisted in disgust. 'It's not as if John Brady really ever even wanted me as a wife, the bastard. Only to beat me black and blue.'

'It'll be the brothers – the male pride – you taking off like that. They'll be wanting to bring you to heel.' Teresa swelled visibly with rage. 'I'd have the lot of them castrated, if I had my way. All the male species is a plague on the earth. You took it into your head to marry that bastard, Mary . . . But you can be sure, if they unearth me here, I'll not be breathing a word to those filthy bog peasants.'

She stared ahead of her, her bitter old face unusually troubled. Suddenly words gushed from her lips. 'I should never have let *him* start on you. I know that. No wonder you're the way you are. It's a weight on my soul.'

Marianne's head jerked back in shock, never having expected to hear such words from this rigid, angry woman. She had harboured no hope of any contrition from Teresa, for having turned a blind eye to her grandfather's foul molestations. Marianne's eyes burned with sudden tears. It was the first time such a thing had happened – and it would be the last.

A moment later the old lady's face was hard again, eyes narrowing.

'And where, in God's name, d'you think you're going to go?'

Marianne slipped back into the house in Bournville at midday. She closed the front door and stopped to listen, running through the family in her head. Ann and Len would both definitely be at work. And Joy. And the lad, Martin – he must be at school? She shrugged. He was never going to come bothering her in any case. He wasn't a women's man, that one, it was obvious.

'Come on, Georgie. Let's get you something to eat, and then you need to go to sleep without playing me up. I've got things to do.'

On fire with impatience, she lay George in his cot and leaned over, patting him, trying to settle him. But the child seemed to sense how strung up she was and started to wail.

'Holy Mother of God!' Marianne straightened up, gripping the top bar, frantic with need to hurry. 'There's no time – just be quiet and go to sleep! Oh, sometimes I wish I didn't have you weighing down my life.' A moment later she was full of remorse. 'I didn't mean it; course I didn't, my little love.' She forced herself to be calm, then patted his chest until he quietened. 'That's it: you go to bye-byes.'

When at last George's eyes closed and he was lying quiet, Marianne tiptoed about the room. Her ration book, which she had retrieved from the shelf on the kitchen, lay on the counterpane. She slid her little suitcase out from under the bed and flung it open, hurriedly pulling things from her chest of drawers. Her attention was caught by something at the back of the top drawer. She lifted out a crumpled paper bag with small bottles clinking inside it. After looking inside to check the contents, she laid the little bag at the bottom of the case. At least now she had a plan. She could get away from here – and she had someone to get away with.

Twenty-Three

'Heaven knows what this is going to be like,' Ann said, delivering a dish to the tea table.

Joy and Martin were already sitting at the table. Martin leaned over.

'I can smell sulphur.' He wrinkled his nose. 'Positively volcanic. Do I detect powered egg?'

Ann gave him a look. 'I haven't had long since getting in. It's potatoes and runner beans – what we've got left from the garden. Cooked with a bit of milk and some powdered egg. And a tiny bit of cheese grated on.' She poked dubiously at the patchy crust on top.

Joy and Martin exchanged looks.

'It can't be worse than curried carrots,' Martin said. 'Although it's a fine line.'

'What won't fatten will fill,' Ann said in warning tones. 'Where's your father? And where's *she*? I don't know if she's already given George some tea.' Her brow furrowed.

'Dad's just come in,' Martin said. 'He's putting his bike away.'

'I'm here!' Len called from the kitchen. 'Just washing my hands.' He came bustling in, in his Home Guard uniform. Once again Ann was struck by the change in his face – he was hollow-eyed and thin. Startled, she thought: Is he ill? 'Got to get this down me and off again . . . Where's Marianne?'

'D'you think she's fallen asleep?' Joy asked. 'I heard her up with George last night – she must be tired.'

'*She's* tired?' Len muttered. He had sat down, but now got wearily to his feet. 'I'll go.'

Ann was dishing out plates of potato-egg gloop when they heard him coming back down. She could see by his face. They all looked at him.

'She's gone.'

'Where?' Joy said. 'What d'you mean, gone? I expect she'll be back in a minute.'

'No. Her things aren't there. Nothing.' Len looked awful, as if he'd been punched. 'Just the cot – empty.' He sank on to his chair. 'And George . . .' He pushed the chair back and leaned forward, stroking his chin in agitation, lost in his own panic. 'What do I do?' He straightened up, aghast. 'What do I do, Ann?'

Everyone else looked at each other. Ann felt the shock seep into her and the first sparks of anger.

'D'you mean she's really gone?'

She ran up to the attic, needing to see for herself. The bed was unmade, the cot empty. Even the cot bedding was gone – bedding on which her own children had slept. Drawers empty, nothing but a cup and saucer on the little table by the bed, containing cold tea grouts.

'Right,' she said to her assembled family downstairs. 'There's nothing more we can do, and I've cooked this meal, such as it is, so we're damn well going to eat it.' She looked at Len. 'You need to get cracking – you're on duty tonight.'

He seemed to come to his senses. He sat up and looked at the contents of the dish cooling on the table. 'What the hell's that?'

Now there were so few raids, Len was not up all night nearly as often as before. Ann lay in bed, waiting to hear him come in.

Of course she, Joy and Martin had been talking about it all evening. Ann's fury with Marianne had been building up. The ungrateful little madam, going off like that without a word, after turning her family upside down and living off them all these months. It was a good job, for her sake, that she wasn't here!

'Does this mean we can go back to normal now?' Martin asked wryly. They all looked at each other. Normal? What was that?

'We won't see George, I suppose,' Joy said. Ann was surprised to see tears in her eyes. 'The little monkey. Where d'you think she's gone, Mom?'

'I've no idea,' Ann said. It all felt like a dream. 'I can hardly take it in.'

Already she had begun to suspect that there were all sorts of things they had no idea of, about Marianne. That priest turning up, for a start. Who knew what that was about? Was Marianne even a Catholic? She had not shown any signs of taking herself off to church, or Mass, or whatever they called it. He'd asked after someone with another name – Mary-something. At the time Ann thought it was all a misunderstanding, but now . . .

Lying in the bed, with the light on, she heard the back door open and close and after a few moments Len's weary tread on the stairs. But his steps passed their bedroom and went on up to the attic. She heard him open the door, switch on the light and go in. Everything went so quiet that it felt as if the house itself was straining to hear. The silence went on and then, from upstairs, she heard a muffled sob. She could picture him, on the edge of the bed in his Home Guard uniform, head in his hands, weeping. For *her*.

Don't you dare make a noise, she thought, clenching her teeth, fists bunched with fury. Did Joy and Martin really need to hear this? Their father crying up there over that woman?

Ann lay rigid, fists clenched, listening, full of turmoil: rage at Marianne, at both of them, and – for Len – sorrow and pity. Did he love Marianne the way she loved Tom? Is that what he felt. Imagine if Tom had behaved the way Marianne had. But she knew in her heart that Tom had no secrets from her. She was his only secret. With Marianne, who knew what on earth had been going on?

Len came down eventually and crept into the bedroom. He sank down on the edge of the bed and sat, sniffing. She wondered if he was going to start crying again, but a moment later he dragged himself to his feet and started undressing for bed. All the while she pretended to be asleep.

Of course at home they could talk about little else over the next days, which turned into weeks. At first Ann could see that Len thought Marianne would simply walk back in one day, carrying George, and they would all go on as before. But she did not.

Ann went round to tell Margaret and Cyril a couple of evenings after Marianne disappeared. She felt really awkward coming with this news, but she also knew how awful it would be for Len to have to do it.

Cyril opened the door. 'Oh! Hello, bab, nice to see yer!' He had always been more forgiving than Margaret – or just let it all wash over him, or couldn't take in any of what was happening; it was hard to tell. But he had soon gone back to being as affectionate as ever. 'Come on in, it's cold out there.'

She came in from the chill, smoky darkness and followed Cyril, in his slippers, along the hall into the back room.

'Have a cup of tea with us. I was just brewing up. Look who's here, Maggie.'

Margaret, who was sitting stroking the cat on her lap, looked up, startled.

'Hello, Annie,' she said cautiously. 'You all right?' She pulled herself up straighter. 'What's the matter? Has summat happened?'

'Sort of, yes.' She was going to have to come out with it.

'What d'you mean, gone?' Cyril said, hovering. He had made Ann sit in his chair, opposite Margaret.

Ann knew they found it hard to talk about Marianne at all. They would rather have pretended none of this had happened and she did not exist. But they had to know. Margaret sat stony-faced. It was Cyril who asked the questions about wherever could she be, and what did they know? Ann could feel Margaret's anger swelling like a tidal wave waiting to break, across the room.

'Why don't you make that tea, love?' she said, tight-lipped.

As soon as Cyril had left the room, Margaret said, 'I never liked the look of that little madam, but my God, I never thought she'd do something like this. No note or anything?'

'Nothing.'

'Well, what about George? He's Len's son!' She too looked suddenly very upset. They had all grown fond of little George – despite everything, he was blood and none of this was his fault.

'I don't know,' Ann said helplessly.

'How's Len taken it?'

'He's . . . I don't really know.' She did know. She had never seen her husband closer to breaking down and she was worried about him, but she did not want to pass her fears on to her in-laws. 'He's been quiet.'

159

Margaret sat back, grim-faced. 'My God, if I could get hold of that little wrecker of a—'

'Now, now,' Cyril said, coming in with the teapot in its cosy and clinking cups. 'There'll be a reason. Maybe she's had to go and look after a sick relative.'

Margaret snorted. 'The only person that one ever looks after is herself, if you ask me.'

The first inkling of what had happened in fact reached Ann when she was at work. She and Jeanette and the others were in their usual positions in the waterside Nissen hut on the Cadbury's site. Now that the summer was over, a thick mist often hung over the murky water of the cut when they arrived in the morning and it was beginning to feel noticeably colder in there.

'It's going to be bad in brass-monkey weather,' someone observed as they all traipsed in to begin their shift. 'I hope they're going to get us some heating.'

'Oh, they will, I expect,' Jeanette said, pulling on her gloves to start filling the rows of rocket tubes. 'By the way,' she said quietly to Ann, 'there's some funny business going on – have you heard? It's Mr Harris. I used to work with him in the cocoa block. Nice man: a quiet sort. Apparently he's run off with some woman. No one can believe it. Just upped and left his wife.'

Ann, who had quite enough on her mind already, without adding gossip about someone she didn't know, nodded and dismissed this from her mind. But later, when they were in the canteen at dinner time, Hilda came up and sat with them.

'You all right, Annie? Long time, no see.'

'Yes, we're all going along,' Ann replied, looking down into her bowl of soup. She felt annoyed and upset. She didn't want to have to tell Hilda about these latest dramas in her household.

'Kids all right?'

'Yes, going along. What about Norma and Danny – getting ready for the big day?'

Hilda made a wry face. 'It's going to be a cardboard wedding cake, by the looks of it – I should've baked them a cake before the start of the war!'

Norma and Danny had decided they wanted a Christmas wedding; it might be cold, but at least there would be a bit of festive feeling, and Norma loved Christmas.

'Terrible about Ted Harris.' Hilda leaned closer, speaking quietly. 'Have you heard. No one knows where he is, but there's some woman involved. He's left his wife and vanished into thin air! There are three kids – all grown-up now, but even so . . .'

'D'you know him then?' Ann said. She had never heard of this person before.

'Not really, but Roy knows him. Len must know him, surely? I'm almost certain he's in the Home Guard.'

It was only then that the seeds of a sudden terrible suspicion began to unfurl shoots in Ann's mind, but she tried to act as casually as possible. Marianne had been to the Home Guard family tea. And now both she and Ted Harris were gone.

'Oh,' she said. 'P'raps he does. I'll ask him.'

Twenty-Four

November

'Oh my goodness, can you hear that?'

Audrey was already in her smart shoes for church and she hurried to open the front door so that they all could hear better. 'Boys, come and listen to this!'

From down in the village came the jubilant sound of church bells, rung as if for a wedding, peals of sound rising and falling. Sheila, with Elaine in her arms, and Audrey and the boys all stood outside the door, smiles spreading across the adults' faces.

'Isn't it *marvellous* to hear that!' Audrey said, in yearning tones. 'Ringing all over the country, I imagine. I wonder if this might really be the beginning of the end. Good old Monty! I never thought they'd be able to beat that Rommel fellow – even his name has a sound of doom.'

It was the first time church bells had been rung since the middle of 1940; they were only to be rung in case of an invasion. But now the glad sound rang out in celebration. A few days ago they had sat by the wireless and heard the first promising news in months: victory at El Alamein. The Allies, under General Montgomery, had cut off the German and Italian forces from reaching Egypt, the Suez Canal and the oil fields in the Middle East. It was a major turning point. At last some signs of the Allies' fortunes changing.

Sheila had a letter from her mother immediately afterwards. 'The first thing Joy came out with was, "Does that mean Alan will be coming home?" I don't know the answer to that – I wish I did.'

'I'd best be off,' Audrey said. 'Who's coming with me? Boys?'

Their faces fell.

'Oh, all right,' Audrey laughed. 'If Sheila doesn't mind.'

'No, you get along,' Sheila said as the boys scurried back indoors to their games. 'They'll be as good as gold, I'm sure.'

'You're a gem,' Audrey smiled. She was turning to go, but suddenly came back. 'Oh, Sheila . . .?' She looked apologetic. 'It's just that Terence is popping round for a little while this afternoon and . . . well, I wondered . . .'

'You want me to go out? What, take the boys as well?'

'If you really wouldn't mind?' Audrey gushed with relief. 'Only you're so good with them, and they'll be bored staying in . . .'

'I'll take them to the playing field – kick a ball about,' Sheila said.

Audrey put her hands together in thanks and hurried away.

Sheila watched her neat figure walking carefully down the frosty drive. 'I'm certainly happy to get out of *his* way,' she muttered, turning to go inside.

It was a bright, beautiful afternoon, the green of the park speckled with bronze and yellow. The leaves still left on the trees glowed in the slanting sunshine.

The boys dashed back and forth with their football. A few other parents were out, giving their young children an airing, and said hello to Sheila as she walked along slowly pushing Robbie in the pram, but at Elaine's pace. The little girl kept stopping every yard or two to pick up another leaf for her collection – the reds and yellows and browns a bouquet in her little gloved hands.

'Those are nice! D'you want this one?' Sheila held out a leaf, ablaze with gold.

Elaine looked seriously at it and nodded, trying to stuff yet another stalk into her clenched fist.

'I could carry some of them for you, if you like?' Sheila said. 'We could put them in the pram. Robbie can keep them for you.'

It was a long walk down into the village for Elaine, so although she was quite capable of walking, Sheila would sometimes sit her at the foot of the pram, though it made it a real slog pushing them back up to the house.

'Excuse me,' a voice said as she bent over the pram, stashing the leaves on top of Robbie's blanket.

Sheila stood up to find a middle-aged woman in a sludgy green wool coat and knitted brown hat, with a hairy dog on a lead.

'Sorry, dear – didn't mean to make you jump. What a *lovely* little girl!'

Elaine looked up at the lady with big, solemn eyes. Her blonde hair was tucked under a tartan tam-o'-shanter that Audrey had given her and she wore a little red coat. She really did look lovely.

'Thank you,' Sheila said quietly. She always felt rather shy of people in the village.

'Ah, do I see Audrey Vellacott's boys? You must be the evacuee?' The lady was quite kindly, but Audrey was getting a bit sick of being talked to like this, as if she was a zoo animal.

'My name's Mrs Carson,' she said. 'Sheila Carson.'

'Ah well, I'm Dottie Freeman and this is Archie.' She

pointed at the not especially prepossessing dog. 'Say hello, Archie!'

'Hello, Archie,' Sheila obeyed, before realizing that the woman was in fact talking to the dog.

'Oh, he can't hear you – deaf as a post!' The woman chortled.

Sheila nodded, not quite sure what to say. There was a silence, but one in which she sensed the lady wanted something from her – or was waiting to broach some subject. It didn't take long.

'You know . . .' Dottie Freeman turned to face into the sun, screwing up her eyes, 'I suppose you know dear Audrey pretty well by now?'

Sheila nodded, supposing she probably did.

'I don't know whether I should say this, but I'm going to anyway. I believe in being straightforward. Better out than in, sort of thing.' She gave a snorting laugh. 'I gather that Terence Richardson fellow has started sniffing around her?'

Sheila felt her ears almost physically prick up. She was torn between wanting to protect Audrey's privacy from the gossiping villagers and a strong need to find out what the woman was about to say. She had never taken to Terence and the more she saw of him, the more uneasy she felt, though there was nothing she could exactly pin down – except his blatant desire to get rid of her.

'I'd have thought you'd be best off getting back home now – not much danger of a raid,' was the sort of remark he kept making, ever since he had first come to Audrey's house. Whenever he arrived there, the look he gave Sheila always suggested the phrase, 'Oh, *you're* still here, are you?'

Terence was all charm, but she didn't like his eyes: there was something else behind them.

'He has been calling round quite a bit, yes,' Sheila said.

'Well,' Dottie Freeman leaned closer, even though no one else was anywhere near. 'You tell her to watch out. I knew Jean Richardson, his wife. They lived two doors away from me. She never said much, but that was not a happy woman. House was far too tidy, for a start – never a good sign!' She snorted again. 'She would never say anything – she was the reserved type, very loyal. And of course she had nowhere to go, if she'd tried to get out. Well, I mean she could have come to me, but she would never have owned up to the fact that Terence was a brute. I saw bruises on her more than once. Not the sort you get from just banging your elbow, if you catch my drift.'

Sheila did. Horribly clearly. Small things came into focus. The way Terence steered Audrey about, physically grasping hold of her. The way he had of getting what he wanted, turning on the charm. 'Oh, go on, Auds – don't be a spoilsport. You'll love it when you get there . . . Oh, don't be silly, Audrey: you're imagining it!'

'Make sense?' Dottie Freeman said, head on one side.

Sheila looked at her. She nodded. 'You are sure?'

'Oh yes. I know a bully when I see one. And as I say, I saw the results. If there's anything you can say to Audrey . . .'

Sheila nodded again, letting out a ragged breath. 'I'll try.'

The sun went down early these winter afternoons, the shadows and mist creeping across the fields from the river, wrapping them in a chill damp. Sheila soon had to take the children home.

She prayed that Terence would have left, but of course they had only been out for a couple of hours and they all walked in to find a cosy scene. The sitting-room fire was lit, and Audrey and Terence were sitting side by side on the settee. Audrey smiled when the boys ran in, followed by Elaine, but Sheila sensed tension in the air. *Please behave yourselves*, she could almost hear Audrey praying to herself.

'Haven't you boys got a playroom of your own?' Terence said in a chummy tone. 'Be better if you went and played in there, wouldn't it?'

Sheila, who had hardly got through the door with Elaine, looked him straight in the eyes.

'This is their home,' she said.

'Oh yes, of course!' Terence agreed. He gave a little laugh and looked at Audrey, waiting for her to agree with him. 'Not yours though, is it?'

Ignoring him, though her heart was pounding hard at having come out with such a thing, Sheila said, 'I'm going to put the kettle on. Would you like a cup of tea?' She looked at Audrey.

'I'll give you a hand.' Audrey jumped up.

Sheila was filling the kettle at the sink when Audrey came in, her face tight. 'Was it really necessary to speak to Terence like that?' Sheila could hear that she was furious. 'After all, he's right – this is not your house to say what goes, is it?'

'Sorry,' Sheila said, turning away.

Audrey obviously thought she was really upset, because she came straight over and touched Sheila's arm.

'Oh, don't worry. I know you were only standing up for them. And he can be a bit bossy at times – typical man, eh?'

Sheila forced a smile. 'Yes,' she said, wondering if Audrey had ever known any other sort of man. 'I'll take my tea upstairs.'

*

A week passed. Terence came and went. He turned up most days now, and Sheila was getting fed up with feeling that she had to take the boys out or hide away with them in the back room.

Then, one evening after Terence had left, Audrey came upstairs and knocked on Sheila's door. Sheila had just got Elaine off to sleep and she dashed over to open it before any more banging woke her again.

'Sorry,' Audrey said. 'Can I have a word?'

On the landing, with the only light coming from downstairs, she spoke quickly, as if wanting to get this over somewhere she didn't have to look into Sheila's eyes.

'I was wondering, Sheila, whether you are thinking of going home for Christmas – maybe staying on? After all, there are not really any raids now, are there?'

In fact Sheila was thinking of exactly that. Audrey did not know about the situation at home. Mom had written and told her that Marianne had left, so now, if Audrey didn't really want her company, there was no reason why she could not go back to her attic room in Bournville. In fact she realized she was longing to do so.

'Yes, all right,' she said.

'Of course we'll miss you.'

Yes, you will, Sheila thought. Audrey was certainly going to miss her taking the boys off her hands almost all the time. As Sheila did not reply, Audrey, out of nerves, startled babbling at her.

'I don't want you to feel you're being pushed out. Only Terence and I would like a little time alone, to get used to each other, and Christmas seems like a good moment for us all to try and be together – as a family.'

'Yes,' Sheila said. She kept her tone even, despite feeling hurt – and worried for Audrey. 'That's all right. I'll write home and tell them I'm coming. Straight away, if you like?'

'Oh, there's no rush!' Audrey was obviously feeling guilty. 'There's plenty of time until Christmas. And I don't want you to think—'

'You do know he's another Maurice, don't you?' Sheila interrupted. Her heart was pounding. The last thing she wanted was a row with Audrey. They had been such good friends until now. Until Terence.

Audrey seemed to flinch.

'What d'you mean?' she said, her voice hoarse and furious. 'How *dare* you say that about someone you barely even know? He's been kindness itself to me. I'd never have thought of you as spiteful, Sheila – but I want you to take that back.'

'Look,' Sheila said. She felt like crying. This was so horrible. 'I just don't want to see you back where you were before. That's all.'

But Audrey was walking away. 'I think you'd better pack and go home as soon as you can,' she said. 'I thought you were the sort of person who could be happy for me, but I was obviously wrong.'

Twenty-Five

19 December

'And now you may kiss the bride!'

A murmur of happy approval rippled around Bournville's Parish Church, St Francis of Assisi, as Danny and Norma exchanged a kiss and then turned to give everyone their radiant smiles. The church, already looking festive for Christmas, had been decked out even further with garlands of winter greenery and vivid red berries for a winter wedding.

Ann felt as if her heart was being squeezed, with all the mixed emotions she was experiencing.

'Oh, I remember that dress!' she had exclaimed the week before when Hilda got out her old wedding dress. The two of them had got married the same year. 'Oh, my word, Hilda, how lovely that you've still got it. You don't have to knock up a dress out of parachute silk!' She caressed the silky, faintly yellowed material. 'Doesn't it make you feel old, though? It does me!'

'I've hardly had to adjust it for her,' Hilda said, eyeing Norma's trim figure. She rolled her eyes. 'Those were the days, eh – look at me now!' She ran her hands over her substantial hips. 'I'm not slender like you, Annie.'

'You're all right,' Ann said, laughing. It was true that Hilda had a more matronly figure, but she still had her striking looks. 'And your Norma's going to be a picture in that.'

'And Joy. They should be in a magazine!'

Joy, as bridesmaid, dressed in her shimmery grey dance dress, was standing to one side in the church, now that the main part of the ceremony was over. She waited, hand-in-hand with the other little bridesmaid, Norma's five-year-old niece, her brother John's daughter. Norma beckoned to her and Joy went to stand beside her, with Danny's pal, who was his best man, next to him, as they all got ready for the final hymn.

Ann's eyes filled with tears. Joy and Norma always looked an attractive pair together, with Norma's flame hair and Joy's darker, vibrant looks complementing each other. But it seemed incredible that Norma was getting married now. Where was that little girl with the curly, carroty hair who used to come round and play, what seemed about five minutes ago?

And what had become of her, Ann, who had stood in this very church making her vows to Len not long after Hilda had made hers to Roy? How the years had rushed past. Len was sitting at the far end of the pew, looking white and strained. He was not well, she knew. The thought of herself and Len then, back in 1919, tore at her heart. He had come back from war; she had been nursing for part of it, as some of the other Cadbury girls had, and she had met Tom, who she had loved deep in her very soul, but had never expected to see again. And that day she and Len had both believed they were doing the right thing. They had been promised to one another all through the war . . . Ann felt like breaking down and weeping at what had become of them.

At the same time she was full of happiness. As Norma and Danny processed out arm-in-arm, beaming round at everyone, she wiped her eyes and smiled back. She blew

Norma a kiss as she passed – the girl was almost like one of her own.

As Hilda, in her mother-of-the-bride hat, passed her on Roy's arm, they both gave her big, happy smiles and a little wave, and Ann smiled back, so happy for her old friends. It was as if they were all family – and part of the Cadbury family too, because they had all grown up working there.

And now, for the first time in months, she had all her own family together – and no Marianne living in the attic. There were rumours, but no one was sure what had happened.

'I hear Ted was seen at Snow Hill station with some woman with black hair,' Hilda told her. Someone else reckoned they had seen them in Alcester. It was impossible to know for sure, but Ann knew in her heart what had happened. Marianne had bewitched her husband – and now she had managed not only to turn her charms on Ted Harris, heaven help him, but it seemed actually to lure him away with her from his family and all that he had known. God, the poor fool!

It did at least mean that Sheila was back home with the children. Sheila was now beside her with Kenneth, home on leave. Kenneth was holding Elaine. Martin, sitting next to them, had been helping to keep the little girl amused, making faces at her, and Elaine was giggling. Sheila, who was holding Robbie, looked round and smiled at Ann.

'Pass him to me?' Ann held out her arms. Sheila leaned over and placed the little boy in her arms. Robbie gazed, wide-eyed, up at his grandmother.

Everything's all right today, Ann thought. Tomorrow might be another matter, but now the whole family was home. Christmas was coming and they were all celebrating a really happy wedding. Whatever else might be on the horizon, that was all she needed to know for today.

III

1943

Twenty-Six

March

'It's all right, I'll get it!' Ann went into the hall as the post clattered through the letterbox. 'For goodness' sake – it's cold. Get back to bed!'

But Len was in the hall, in his pyjamas. He looked terrible, unshaven, thin and ill. He was already shivering as he bent over the mat and picked up the letters.

'I'd bring it up to you if there was anything,' she said, her voice less harsh this time. She was worried about him. He had been ill on and off ever since Christmas and this sort of carry-on was not going to help. 'You haven't even got anything on your feet!'

Len was feverishly looking through the post. Ann, ready to set off for work, watched nervously. She could see that one of the envelopes looked as if it might be from Tom, although she could not be sure. Len's face darkened and he pulled the envelope out and held it out to her, threateningly.

'That *him* again, is it? His Lordship?'

Ann almost laughed. A title less apt for Tom he could hardly have come up with.

But Len's face was hard, ugly. 'Writing to *my wife*?'

Ann felt as if her head might explode at any moment. Len had come downstairs, sick and feverish as he was, desperately looking for something from Marianne. Nothing else could have brought him down.

'Len,' she whispered, trying to take his arm. 'Look, let's get you back to bed. You've got a temperature.'

'No!' He flung her off violently, dropping the envelope on the floor, this thin, haunted man whom she hardly recognized. 'You don't want me to see! Why can't you just be my wife?' His face contorted and she thought he was going to start crying again; there had been a lot of that, however much she pleaded, 'I'm trying my very best – I *am* your wife, aren't I? I'm not going anywhere.' But right then Sheila came out of the back room.

'You get off, Mom,' she said. 'Come on, Dad – I'll make you a cup of tea. Let's get you back to bed.'

But Joy came hurrying down, ready for work, blocking the stairs. 'You ready, Mom?' She took in the scene of her distraught father, and her eyes filled with sadness and worry. Then she caught sight of the pale envelopes on the mat.

'Is there anything for me?'

'I'm afraid not, love,' Ann was saying as Joy pushed past them, frantic. Days and weeks were going by and she had heard nothing from Alan.

'Come on, Dad, up you come,' Sheila urged. 'Joy, just watch the kids a minute for me, will you?'

Ann watched as Sheila helped her father back up the stairs to bed. She could hear Joy cajoling Robbie to eat a spoonful of milky slop, and Elaine chuckling. Thank heaven for the kiddies. There were so many emotions swarming about the house – even Martin seemed far off, as if he had things on his mind that he never talked about. Sometimes she felt as if she was going mad, but the little ones kept them all pinned to the ground, having to be cheerful and positive and their best selves.

'I'm getting really worried,' Joy said as they walked up the road to Cadbury's. 'Alan did say they looked to be moving somewhere else soon. I know it's hard for him to write sometimes, but it's three weeks now.'

They turned into the Cadbury works. Now that the contract for filling anti-aircraft rockets was finished, Ann and Jeanette and their group had moved over to a new job, sticking rubber on to aeroplane petrol tanks. If the tanks were shot at, the rubber would swell to close over the holes. Joy had recently been moved to the same work in another waterside hut as well.

Ann felt the onset of real worry for her daughter. Alan, who always said he was not good with words, had in fact continued to write faithfully to Joy. Ann knew now how devoted Joy was to him and she was glad. Alan was a nice lad and she had always liked him.

'I wonder if they've heard at home,' Joy said miserably. 'I might go and see Irene.'

'Alan's sister?'

'At least that would be something I can *do*.'

Ann could see how upset Joy was, and how she was burning with restless energy. But as they turned in through the gate of the works, Joy shook herself out of her own worries.

'Is Dad going to be all right?' She sounded like a little girl again suddenly.

'He will be – he's just got run down,' Ann said. But in her heart of hearts, she wondered as well. Len looked so broken, almost deranged at times. Margaret was worried, she knew, and sometimes came round in the day to keep Len company. He already had Sheila there, but he was bad-tempered with everyone, and kept telling them to leave him alone.

'Nothing from *her* – still?' Joy asked. She sounded

disgusted. 'She's a piece of work, that one. She could at least let him know how George is.'

'Not a word,' Ann said.

It was four months since Marianne had disappeared. No one had heard anything definite about her. It was no good calling the police – she had gone of her own accord, and that was that.

For the first few weeks leading up to Christmas, Len had been in shock. He thought she would come back. But Marianne did not, and as 1943 broke upon them and the weeks passed, he started to fall to pieces. He kept being ill. He was overwrought and flared up at the least thing. One night after the New Year he had a go at Martin for being out so much.

'Use this house like a hotel, you do,' he snarled, so nasty suddenly that Ann could see Martin really caught on the raw.

'Any reason why I'd want to be here?' Martin asked sullenly. The easy relationship they had had when Martin was younger was fast going downhill.

'Don't you speak to me like that, you little . . .' Len advanced on him, his fist drawn back. And Martin stood, without flinching.

'Little what? What d'you think *you're* going to call *me*?'

Ann was so frightened that for a moment she forgot to breathe. Len's teeth were clenched, his fist drawn back. But it was what he might say that terrified her. She really thought that if he came out with the truth about Martin's father now, like this, she might . . . Well, she didn't know what she might do.

But Len backed off.

'That's enough, you two,' Sheila said, coming into the room. 'Go on, Mart – just keep out of his way.'

Martin, pink with anger, nodded and left the room.

Sheila's eyes met Ann's for a second, as if to say, *For heaven's sake, you people . . .*

'That's not going to bring her back, is it, Dad?' Sheila said, while Ann watched as Len sank back in his chair, amazed at the change in her elder daughter.

The other letter that had arrived that morning was addressed to Sheila. Once she had got her father back into bed, she came down, on her dignity as usual. Ann could see that Sheila's attitude was that she was a bit superior to all of them. A married woman with a loving husband fighting for his country, and two children she was bringing up without him – while her parents behaved like fools. Ann could hardly blame her: it was the truth.

But it was still so good to have them all home.

'Letter for you,' Ann said, as she and Joy went out of the door.

Sheila took it and raised her eyebrows. 'Audrey.'

Soon after Sheila came home in December, a Christmas card had arrived from Audrey, cheerful, affectionate, not saying anything except the usual season's greetings. Sheila had stuck it on the mantelpiece without saying anything.

That night, when Ann got in, Sheila was in the kitchen, bent over *Wartime Cookery*, which was open on the table – a now well-worn little green booklet that Ann had dipped into many times. Her finger rested on 'Tripe and Liver Hotpot'.

'There's tea – stewed, but . . .' Sheila said, eyes still on the recipe.

'Where're Elaine and Robbie?'

'With Dad.' Sheila stood up then.

Ann raised her eyebrows. Len must be feeling better. She tiptoed to look into the back room. Robbie was sitting up on the hearth rug and Elaine was with him, chattering and showing him a little wooden horse on wheels and her doll, with its wool hair. Len, in his pyjamas and a jumper, was sitting forward on the chair playing with them. Ann's heart contracted. She knew he was missing George, and the sight of him with Sheila's two little ones, a faint smile on his lips, made her see the old Len again. Her eyes filled with tears and she moved silently away.

'Everyone seems happy,' she said, back in the kitchen. She smiled, swallowing her emotion. 'Any news from Audrey?'

'Yes.' Sheila was tight-lipped, and only now did Ann see that she was absolutely furious. 'She wrote to say she's got married.'

Ann poured a cup of not very inviting-looking tea.

'To that . . . What's-his-name? And she didn't invite you?'

'Terence flaming Richardson. Yes – I suppose she knows what I think of him. He's a wife-beater!' Sheila erupted. 'She's going from one awful bully of a man to another: what the hell's the matter with her?' She went and started mashing vegetables in the saucepan with energetic fury. 'Now he's got a ring on her finger, he'll start. *Really* start,' she ranted. 'I can see it coming. That's what that lady told me – the neighbour who knew his first wife. He's a bully and a fake, and Audrey just can't see it!'

Once again Ann was taken aback by all that Sheila had seen and learned, in a place that had sounded as if it was roses all the way. She had become a much stronger person, steely and definite.

'There's not much you can do, is there?' Ann said. 'You warned her.'

'I know.' Sheila paused her violent mashing. She looked upset. 'That's the trouble. Why's she taken in by him? What is it with some women?'

Ann rolled her eyes, thinking, And some men.

Twenty-Seven

Joy stood in the waterside Nissen hut that April morning, sticking a neatly cut sheet of rubber on to the side of one of the petrol tanks. The rubber sheets came from the Dunlop works across the city and had to be cut into strips to fit.

Her mind was hardly on the job, which she could do automatically, fast and skilfully. All she could think of was Alan and her heart was as heavy as a rock. Tears dropped on to the black surface as she pressed the edges down with her fingers. Still no word – nothing. He's dead, I know he is, she thought. He would never not write to me . . . And more tears ran down her cheeks.

'Well, there's gonna be no danger of a fire with you about, is there?' A voice at her shoulder made Joy almost jump out of her skin. Mr Jarvis, the foreman, had appeared behind her, a short, jovial man with thin hair combed over his bald patch. They had all been told that the material they were working with was dangerous – almost as dangerous as Ann's job, filling rockets – because the static that built up in the layers sometimes spontaneously caught fire.

Joy straightened up quickly, wiping her eyes. Mr Jarvis's kindly eyes searched her face.

'What's up, bab? This isn't like you.'

His sympathy was too much and Joy burst into tears.

'It's my fiancé – I haven't heard from him for weeks. I don't even know where he is!'

Norma, seeing that there was a problem, stopped work

and came over as Mr Jarvis was saying, 'I'm sorry to hear that – I truly am. I hope you have better news soon.'

'Hey.' Norma put her arm around Joy for a moment. She knew how desperate she was feeling. 'It'll be the break soon – we'll go and have a sing-song, eh? Try and chase the blues away.'

Joy nodded glumly. Everyone was so kind; but there was Norma, married, with Danny working only just across the Cadbury's site, whenever she wanted him. The thought made her feel even more desperate.

Joy had heard that the nearby reservoir in Edgbaston had been drained some time ago, to half its size, so as to be less of a target for enemy bombs, a great many of which had fallen in that neighbourhood. And as she walked across to Alan's family, she passed the wrecked Docker's paint factory some streets away and a lot of bombed-out houses. The day was chilly, with a raw wind, and the force of it made her eyes water.

Stour Street, Ladywood, where Alan's family lived, with its corner shop and its drab brick house-fronts, looked much as she remembered it from her previous visit. By the time she got to the front door, her legs felt wobbly with nerves. Especially when it occurred to her to wonder whether Alan's father, Alfred Bishop, was still in prison? If not, was she about to meet him face-to-face? She had built him up in her mind as a giant, beetle-browed and terrifying. She realized in that moment how sheltered her life had been – she had never met anyone who had been in prison.

Close to the house she passed two little lads sitting out on the pavement playing with a handful of marbles and she managed to smile at them, thinking how cold the poor mites must be. And then she was there.

She knocked and stood back. A moment later a man appeared at the door, whom she immediately realized must be Alf Bishop. In that instant she saw where both Alan and Irene had got their good looks. Alan's father was a powerful, upstanding man somewhere in his forties, with the same strong, curling hair as Alan, though of a more muted brown, and the vivid blue eyes he had handed on to both his children. The only thing that indicated trouble was the scar snaking across the left side of his face, from the cheekbone down towards his top lip.

'Yeah?' he said, his expression blank. He seemed to have a lot on his mind. 'Who're you?'

'Hello, Mr Bishop?' she tried. 'I'm a friend of Alan's. I was wondering . . .' Here her throat started to close up, so desperate was she feeling that she only just managed to speak without bursting into tears again. 'Have you heard anything from him?'

Alf Bishop shouted over his left shoulder, ''Rene! Some wench 'ere asking after Alan!' He stepped back – 'Come in' – then walked off as if none of this was any of his business. Joy heard feet climbing the stairs and she was left alone in the dank, faintly mouldy atmosphere of the front room.

Footsteps approached from the back and Irene Bishop appeared. Joy was shocked by the sight of her. The forceful young woman she had met two and a half years ago, when she called round, was not as she remembered. Irene's strongly sculpted face had shrunk, giving her eyes a shrewish look they had not had before. Last time her hair had been pulled back into a jaunty bunch behind her head, but now it hung loose. But, like last time, she was friendly enough.

'Oh – Joy, isn't it?' she said. 'Come in, it's warmer back here.'

Nervously Joy followed her into the back room. A fire was struggling in the grate, but there was definitely less of a chill in the air. Sitting huddled beside it was Alan's mother, the woman she had only glimpsed before, looking half out of her mind.

'Mom,' Irene said. 'This is Joy – Al's girl. D'you remember her?'

Mrs Bishop uncoiled herself and sat up straighter, smiling. To Joy's relief, she seemed much more herself than the last time she had seen her. Though she was only in her mid-forties, her hair was already fully grey, but instead of hanging in a wispy mane around her face, it was shorter and tied neatly back.

'Hello, Joy,' she said. She looked really pleased to see her and there was a sweetness to her face, although Joy wondered if she really did remember her at all.

'Hello, Mrs Bishop,' Joy replied, relief coursing through her at how much better she looked.

'Cup of tea?' Irene said. 'You've come all this way.'

'Yes – if that's . . .'

Irene made a gesture with her hand that Joy should sit in her chair. There were two, one on each side of the fire, with shabby green upholstery and wooden arms.

'How are you?' Mrs Bishop asked politely. Her voice was soft, sweet, and she sat slightly hunched, her hands clasped in her lap. She wore a dark-green frock, which looked too thin for the weather, with a baggy jumper over the top, the colour of porridge. Her feet were pushed into old sheepskin slippers.

'I'm all right, thanks, Mrs Bishop,' Joy said, smiling back. She wanted desperately to ask about Alan, but wondered what his mother knew and how she was, and whether it would be bad for her to talk about it. But this was why she had come and she could not hold back. She turned to Irene, who was putting out a cup and saucer for her.

'Have you heard from him?' she burst out. 'Because . . . I haven't – not for ages and I'm so worried.' And the tears came. She couldn't help it.

Mrs Bishop suddenly leaned forward, and Joy jumped slightly as Alan's mother took hold of one of her hands and squeezed it, her eyes wide and sweet.

'We were hoping you might have done,' Irene said, bringing Joy a cup of tea. She pulled an upright chair over from the table for herself. 'I'd thought of coming over to see you, but I wasn't sure where you live exactly.'

'We're ever so worried,' Mrs Bishop said. 'He's a good lad, my Alan. It's not like him.'

'I know . . .' Joy's tears were flowing, but it felt so good to be able to share her worries with the other people who loved Alan. 'He wrote to me every week at least.'

Irene nodded. In the shadowy room her cheekbones seemed even more prominent, and Joy could see how much the worry was eating at both of them. It felt suddenly as if the three of them had been drawn close together by all this, even though they barely knew each other.

'There are so many things could've happened.' Irene began. 'I mean, he could be in hospital somewhere . . .' She trailed off.

Alan could be . . . anything. The worst possibility was one they did not want to name. In the silence they heard Alf Bishop's noisy tread hurry down the stairs again and the slam of the front door.

Irene rolled her eyes at her mother. 'Going to look for a job – or so he says. Anyone'd think it was hard to find one.'

'How long has he been . . .?' Joy began.

'Not long,' Irene said.

Mrs Bishop was listening intently to her words, as if learning what to say when faced by similar questions. She looked such a sweet person and Joy had warmed to her this time, as soon as she saw her.

'Look, here's my address,' she said, pulling the slip of paper she had prepared from her pocket. 'Please, if you hear anything . . .'

'Alan's always been a good boy.' Mrs Bishop's eyes filled with tears suddenly. She was so small, a wisp of a person, that she looked like a lost little girl. 'I know he's a good boy – wherever he is. Not like his father.'

'He is, Mom.' Irene agreed soothingly. Joy felt such admiration for this young woman, for all she had to deal with. 'And you'll let us know if . . .'

Joy looked down for a moment as she spoke. 'If anything . . . you know, bad happened, they'd let you know first – you're his family.'

Irene nodded. 'Don't worry. We won't make you wait. Drink your tea; it'll get cold.'

As she showed Joy out, Irene said softly, 'Come again, will you? It's nice to see you. After all, if things were different, we'd be sisters-in-law.'

Joy smiled. 'Yes, course, if that's all right. D'you want me to let you know first?'

'Sundays're all right – like today. Just come. We aren't going anywhere.' She glanced back into the house. 'It's a funny thing, but when there's summat real – you know, not just me dad messing with her mind – our mom deals with it better sometimes.'

'It was nice to see her looking better,' Joy said.

Irene gave a faint smile. 'Yeah. Well, she's up and down. See yer, Joy.' She gave a little wave as Joy walked off, and shut the door.

*

186

Back home, when she walked into the house, she heard voices and laughter from the front room. Mom's friend Jeanette from Cadbury's had come round for a cuppa. Joy's spirits lifted. It was so nice to hear laughter in the house. She liked Jeanette; she was a kind lady and having someone else in the house made things easier.

'Hello, love!' Jeanette said as she walked in. She and Mom were on the sofa and Sheila was sitting on the rug by the fire with Elaine, and with Robbie in her arms. To Joy's amazement, her father was also there, in his chair by the fire. He had recovered from his long bout of flu and was still thin, but even he looked quite cheerful.

'Bring yourself a cup, Joy,' Mom said, the remains of laughter in her voice. Then her face sobered, remembering where her daughter had been.

'Any news?' Sheila asked.

Joy shook her head.

'Oh dear, you poor girl,' Jeanette said.

'Don't!' Joy forced a smile. 'Or you'll set me off. Any more tea for anyone? And then I'm going to play with these little ones and try and forget about everything.'

Twenty-Eight

July

'There – that's enough now!'

Sheila poured a final jug of water into the little tin bath out in the garden, with a few soap bubbles mixed in. Elaine, now nearly three and a half, giggled delightedly as bubbles caught the sunlight in rainbow colours. Robbie, twenty-one months and a sweet, stolid little lad, watched wide-eyed and went to dip his hands in.

'Now, Lainy, you watch Robbie for me a minute,' Sheila said. 'I'll bring you a few things to play with and I'll do the spuds out here, all right?'

She hurried back into the house to the sound of Elaine bossing Robbie about. 'You need to *be careful*, Robbie . . .'

All the time she felt tense, under pressure. As well as looking after the children, a lot of the work in the house fell to her now. Not that she minded exactly – it was better to be busy, and better for Mom to be out at work, with all that had been going on. If she herself was going out and standing in queues and cooking, she had less room in her head to worry about Kenneth or to miss him.

A few minutes later she came out with a bowl with a few potatoes to peel, and various bits and pieces for the children to play with: wooden spoons, a ladle, a little tin teapot and a tin mug. She sat at the outside table, smiling as the two little ones lifted cups of water and sloshed them back into the bath, giggling.

'That's it – try not to spill it all or you won't have any water left.'

'If we spill it, isn't there any more?' Elaine asked, frowning.

'Oh, I 'spect we might be able to find you a drop more,' Sheila laughed. 'But try not to spill it all – I don't want to be running in and out all the time. And when you've had a play, we'll wash your hands and Robbie needs to have his nap. And I want you to have a little sleep today, all right?'

A great game began of splashing, then watering plants, and this led on to making mud pies. Sheila fetched more water. Just as the two of them were at their muddiest, she heard, dimly, someone knocking on the front door.

'Bother it,' she muttered, hurrying inside. In passing, she placed the pan of spuds on the unlit stove for later.

Irritably, she pulled the front door open and for a second could not believe her eyes. The solid body dressed in his RAF uniform and cap, the smile spreading across his face.

'*Kenneth!*' Sheila stood, stunned for a second, then threw herself, squealing with delight, into his arms. 'Oh my God – what're you doing here?' She drew back quickly, suddenly full of foreboding. 'What *are* you doing here? Is everything all right?'

'Shall we go in?' he said, laughing as he dumped his bag in the hall. 'I've come to see my wife and kids, if that's OK. Sorry I didn't warn yer – it was all a bit last-minute.'

'The kids are out the back.' Grinning, Sheila took his hand. 'Come on – shh.'

They crept to the back door. The garden was long and narrow, with the chickens and veggie patch and, at the far end, the air-raid shelter. Its layer of soil had long ago self-seeded with grass and wild flowers. And framed in the light, in front of Len's growing potatoes, cabbages and beans, the two children were bent over the bath, happy and filthy and playing together.

'Elaine?' Sheila called softly. 'Robbie.'

They looked up, both blank-faced at the sight of the big man beside their mother and suddenly solemn.

'Daddy's home: come and say hello. Oh, we'd better clean you up first!'

She hurried over and rinsed most of the mud from their little hands in the remaining murky water.

'Is that Daddy?' Elaine asked, quiet and unsure.

'Yes, he's come to see us. Come on, Robbie.' Inside Sheila felt like crying. The children had hardly an idea who their father was.

It took them a while to come round. They all sat in the back room. Kenneth did not push it too quickly with the two of them, but joined in with a game of building a tower with blocks on the floor. Soon they came to him and Elaine was on his lap and asking him endless questions, and Robbie stood by his knee, staring solemnly up at him. He was not talking a lot yet, but you could see he was taking everything in.

Sheila watched them: all her family together, just for once! She felt herself relax. If only things could be like this all the time.

'Now then, you two,' she said eventually. 'Nap time. Daddy'll be here later, but you need to go upstairs – come on.'

'No one else'll be in for a bit,' Sheila said when she came downstairs. 'But they sleep in my room . . .'

Kenneth, in the back room, held his hand out, and she could see all his desire for her in his eyes.

'I don't care where,' he said, pulling her down on to his lap, a hand closing over her breast. 'God, Sheila, I don't half miss you . . .' Their lips met and they began to make love immediately, both so hungry for each other that it was soon over. They readjusted their clothing and sat side by side.

'That's better.' He smiled, kissing her again.

'How long can you stay?' Sheila asked, already fearing the answer.

'Couple of nights.'

She cuddled up against him, arms wrapped around his solid body. Each time she saw Kenneth, he seemed bigger than she remembered.

'I'm going to tie you up and not let you go,' she murmured. Already she was dreading him leaving, and he had only just arrived. It felt so cruel that life had to be like this. 'We never noticed, before the war, how good normal life was, did we? Being able to see each other when we liked; no bombs, no going off and not knowing . . .' She stopped, scared she might break down. She didn't want to spend these precious hours crying.

'How're things?' Kenneth asked. 'Your mom and dad – and Audrey?'

After Robbie was born, Kenneth had come to stay at Audrey's house and had liked her. Sheila shrugged. She felt hurt by Audrey, by the way she had been booted out when Terence Richardson moved in on her.

'I know it's her house, and everything. Audrey can do what she likes. But we've gone through a lot together. And I'm worried for her. She's a bad picker.'

Kenneth laughed. 'I'll say.'

'To be honest, Kenneth . . .' Sheila pushed herself up straighter, serious now, relieved to be able to talk. He knew all about the goings-on in their family. 'Things here are . . . well, not easy. Dad's been in a right state since Marianne went off, and we've no idea where she is.' Even as she spoke, Sheila could hardly believe she was talking about all this as if it were normal. 'Mom and Dad are . . . well, you know. It's like living in a pressure cooker. And Joy's feller, Alan – there's been no word for weeks.'

'He was writing before?' Kenneth asked.

'Yes, all the time, whenever he could. And suddenly – nothing.'

Neither of them spoke for a moment.

'We don't know for sure where he is. Joy thinks Alan might have been moved out east somewhere.' She gave him a tense smile and leaned forward, arms resting on her knees. 'So things haven't been very easy.'

'I'll say.' Kenneth stroked her back.

'If it wasn't for Nanna and Grandad, I think I'd go mad sometimes, but I can take the kids round there. Cyril's always the same – offering to make us chips!'

'They're solid, those two.'

'Yeah, golden.' She turned then, rolling her eyes and giving a wry smile. 'My family! I'm surprised you'll still have anything to do with us.'

'I love you, Sheila,' Kenneth said seriously. 'And if that's what comes along in the package – well, so be it. I'm very fond of your family, even if . . .' He trailed off.

'They are a complete madhouse?'

Kenneth grinned. 'Well, I wasn't going to say it!'

Everyone was delighted to see Kenneth, and by the time the whole family had eaten tea together, Elaine and Robbie were quite settled with him and wanted his attention all the time.

They passed a nice evening, with everyone doing their best to be cheerful. And Sheila – looking round at her father, chatting with Kenneth as he, Joy and Martin played with the kids, and at Mom handing out cups of tea and the driest cake any of them could remember – could almost believe things were normal. Usually these days the happiest times in the house were when Mom's pals came round, Hilda and Jeanette, and they could all joke and laugh as if nothing else whatsoever was going on.

At last the children were settled, and Sheila and Kenneth were able to cuddle up together in bed, make love again in the darkness of the room and lie close and loving afterwards.

Kenneth told her a bit more about his life on the east coast these days: his pals and a rescue that he had been on, out at sea for the best part of thirty-six hours, rescuing two downed RAF men.

'If it hadn't been for their Mae Wests, they'd have been a goner,' he said. He could almost see her puzzlement. 'Life-jackets – they fill with air and keep the men up.' He was full of stories, of banter and of names of men she had never heard before. Kenneth's life, like his body, had grown bigger and more muscular without her, as if everything about him had expanded. She started to feel small and left behind.

'It's so nice they gave you leave again – I wish they'd give you longer,' she whispered. They lay holding each other, their faces very close together in the darkness. She felt she was trying to pull him back to her; back to being the husband she had always known.

Kenneth went quiet suddenly.

She lifted her head for a moment. 'What?'

'Nothing,' he said. But she could tell by his voice that it was not nothing. There was something he was not telling her.

'Kenneth?' She scrambled on to her stomach, looking down at him, even though it was pitch-dark. 'What?'

'Thing is, Sheila – there's summat I need to tell you. I wasn't going to, not until . . . I don't want you getting upset.'

'What?' Her heart hammered, her mind running wild with crazed thoughts. Had she got everything wrong, and things were not as they seemed? After all that had gone on in her family, anything seemed possible. You heard heart-breaking stories about service wives left behind. Had Kenneth found some other woman: was he trying to tell her? She burst into tears. 'You're not going to leave me, are you?'

'*What?*' He sounded completely appalled. 'What're you on about? Of *course* not – you're my missus and I love you, Sheila. I'd never leave you! I mean, not leave you, you know, like that . . .' He sounded distraught.

She waited, wiping her eyes, a far-off feeling of dread growing closer.

'Thing is . . . we're on embarkation leave.' He spoke haltingly, knowing how much his words would hurt and frighten her. 'We're being posted overseas.'

The news sank into her, like something stabbing deeper and deeper into her guts. Of course this might happen sooner or later, but she had never thought it would. The Air-Sea Rescue people were so busy around the British coast; she thought Kenneth would be here all through the war. But now . . . She had never allowed herself to face up to the idea that he might be posted away somewhere.

Throat aching, so that she could hardly get the words out, she whispered, 'When? Where?'

'Soon,' Kenneth said. 'When I get back. But we don't know where – they don't say. I could guess, but I really don't know for sure.'

She could hear then that he was close to tears himself and it brought her round. She drew on reserves that she barely knew she had. She was going to have to be strong: for him and for their children.

'Oh, Kenneth.' They wrapped their arms even more tightly around each other. 'This war – this terrible, evil war. Whatever happens, we've got each other, and I love you so much!'

Twenty-Nine

When Kenneth left, it was not only Sheila who was tearful. Ann and Joy felt it as well – another person going off, to who knew where or for how long.

'It's terrible,' Ann said to Hilda that day, during the break at Cadbury's. 'All these young lives. They've only just got started, and heaven knows when he'll be back or . . .' She swallowed the words 'or if he will'. Tears rolled down her cheeks. She felt so sad for her girls: Joy's agony at not knowing what had happened to Alan; and now Kenneth, the one they thought would at least stay in the same country, going off into the unknown as well.

'Hey, Annie – this isn't like you,' Hilda said, patting her arm as she lowered her head over the table to hide her tears.

Ann struggled to control herself. So many emotions had come rushing to the surface: for her girls and all their uncertainty, which she was powerless to do anything about. She hated seeing both of them so sad. But it also brought back all her feelings on saying goodbye to Tom in 1916, the man she had fallen so deeply in love with, and whom she believed she would never see again.

'Sorry,' she said, wiping her eyes and trying to smile at Hilda. 'I know you've got your John to worry about.' Norma's brother John was in the RAF as well, flying night fighters – it was a constant worry for Hilda and Roy. 'It's been a bit of a year.'

*

Two weeks later, Ann and Len were in their bedroom and the rest of the family had turned in as well. It was gone ten o'clock. Ann waited for Len to get into bed and was turning over to switch off the light when there was a lot of banging and commotion from downstairs.

'What the hell was that?' Len asked.

'It can't be our door?' Ann said. 'Not at this time.'

More furious banging broke out below.

'Oh Lor' – what now?'

She leapt out of bed, grabbing a dressing gown, as did Len. Martin was on the landing.

'What's going on?' he said as both his parents rushed past.

'We don't know!' Ann called back over her shoulder.

'Here, let me open it,' Len insisted.

They kept the hall light off, out of blackout habit, to open the front door. It was summer-dark outside and in the gloom stood two men. All Ann could make out, past Len's shoulder, was that they each had dark mops of hair and wore heavy workmen's boots. From what she could see of their faces, they did not look especially friendly.

'What's up, lads?' Len said. 'Bit late to be knocking people's doors, isn't it?'

He spoke with a forced cheerfulness, but Ann could hear a tremor in his voice. She made out the dark brows of the two men – they looked alike and she wondered if they were brothers.

One of them stepped forward.

'We've come for Mary,' he said. 'She's coming back with us.'

Ann could hear that he was Irish and the worse for drink.

'Mary?' she said. 'Look, we've had someone round before, asking about a Mary. She doesn't live here and we

197

don't know who she is.' Though by now Ann was beginning to have more than a shrewd idea.

'She's been seen coming in and out of this house,' the man said, squaring up to Len. 'So you get her down here – she's coming home with me.'

'There's no one here called Mary,' Len said, 'and never has been. Goodnight.'

He went to shut the door, but the man kicked it open again. The other one came to restrain him, trying to pull him back.

'Loose me, James – I'm going to find that whore of a wife of mine . . .' He pushed so hard that the other lad reeled backwards into the road.

'John!' he shouted. 'Stop this now – you come away with me.'

John, the bigger of the two, was still standing in the doorway. Ann and Len had to back away along the hall, and Ann only realized then that Martin was standing behind them.

'Look,' Len said, 'who is this Mary?'

'Mary Brady – that's who she is, the filthy whore! And she's my wife.'

'Well, she's not here,' Ann said helplessly. She was really frightened now. 'And my daughters are upstairs trying to sleep. You just get out of our house.'

'I'll go when I've seen every room in the house!' John Brady roared.

'Oh no, you don't, you thug!' Martin suddenly erupted past his parents and launched himself at John Brady, shoving him backwards and outside the door. But the man grabbed Martin as he went, pulled his fist back and slammed it into the side of Martin's face. Martin reeled back and tripped over the step, falling into the hall.

A voice came from a few doors along. 'You stop all that racket or we'll call the police!'

Ann was seeing to Martin, who was curled up, nursing his bleeding face. Len slammed the door shut and the three of them squatted in the hall, listening as crash after crash came on the wood as John Brady hammered his fists on it. They heard the other man's voice. 'Come on now, John. That's enough.' And finally it went quiet.

'Mom?' Joy's voice came from the top of the staircase. 'What's going on?'

They all sat in the back room. Ann prepared warm salt water and was bathing Martin's cut cheek. His face was already swelling, but he seemed remarkably cheerful about it, almost as if it was a badge of honour. And, it seemed to Ann, she and Len felt as if they were a united front against this sudden attack. It was a nice, reassuring feeling.

'Look at you,' Joy said. 'You look a proper gangster.'

Martin laughed, then groaned. 'Thanks, Mom. That's enough.' He looked at Len. 'It's Marianne they want, isn't it? Must be.'

Ann watched Len, her pulse racing faster. Len looked shocked. He shook his head, then glanced helplessly at them all and said, 'Heaven only knows.'

'What I don't understand,' Ann said, when she and Len were alone in their room again, 'is why they've waited so long. That priest came round ages ago, thinking she might be here. They could have come then. I suppose he must have said she wasn't here.'

Len seemed poleaxed, but when he spoke, she realized that anger was mounting in him, fit to explode. His voice came out harshly.

'D'you think that was Marianne then? This Mary Brady person?'

Even for Ann, it was hard to imagine the Marianne they had known having anything to do with the heavy-browed, violent men they had just seen. But what other explanation was there?

'I think,' she said carefully, 'that we hardly know the first thing about Marianne Walsh, or whatever it was she called herself. She must really be called Mary Brady – and that bloke was her husband.'

'It can't be,' Len said, appalled. 'Surely. Not *him*.'

'Well,' Ann said, starting to get annoyed. How was it that Marianne was able to make Len delude himself even now? 'What other explanation is there for all this, d'you think? They said she'd been seen at our house. That priest coming round . . . It must be her. The woman's a con artist, so far as I can see – and she certainly conned you, and all of us.'

She had gone too far. With a violent movement Len turned on his side to face her.

'None of this would've happened if you'd been a proper wife to me! You made this happen – carrying on with that fancy man of yours all this time. It's time we put a stop to it. You need to tell Somers, or whatever his name is . . . Cut him off and behave like a proper wife. It's time we had some normality around here – time you behaved yourself. I don't want to hear another thing about him. I want my wife back, how things used to be. Is that clear?'

The next afternoon Martin sat on the bed in his room, with Ian at his side. By now he had a proper shiner spreading across the left side of his face, and a plaster over the cut. Everyone at school wanted to know all about it. Martin had acted very mysterious. *Wouldn't you like to know?* Making a joke out of it all.

'Go on,' Ian said. 'What did happen, then?'

Martin looked into Ian's freckled, kindly face and away again. He really couldn't go into it all – not what had been happening in his family for the last few months, even though he wanted to pour everything out to Ian. He felt closer to him than to anyone else in the world. But Ian's family were so solid and traditional – or at least, so they thought. He suppressed a slight smile.

'What?' Ian said.

'Nothing. Just a naughty thought. Anyway, it was just some bloke came round last night, had a disagreement with my dad. He cut up rough and I didn't like it, so I shoved him out of the door – and then he punched me. He was drunk.'

'Your dad?' Ian said. 'He wouldn't say boo to a goose! What on earth was all that about?'

Martin shrugged. 'Search me. He seemed a bit off his head, to tell you the truth. I'm not even sure he got the right house, but I wasn't having it.'

Ian leaned in close and examined the bruise around the plaster. 'Quite something, that!' Playfully he gave the storm-coloured bruise a little lick.

Martin flinched. 'Ow!' Then he laughed.

'Sorry!' Ian moved close again and, very gently, planted a kiss on Martin's cheek. They each reached an arm round the other's back and sat lovingly close together, with Ian's head resting on Martin's shoulder.

After a few moments he lifted his head and gradually, fearfully at first, their eyes met and, seeing the answer to their feelings in each other, their lips passionately found each other's.

Thirty

September

'If they said he was "Missing in Action", at least we'd know *something*,' Joy said to Norma as they sat in Hilda and Roy's kitchen, Norma with her little girl Lizzie in her arms. Norma's already creamy complexion looked even more so at the moment and motherhood had filled out her cheeks. It did not take a genius to work out that Norma must have been pregnant at the wedding, and she blushingly confessed that it must have been so.

'I didn't know though,' she told Joy. 'I mean, I felt a bit funny, but I didn't realize that was what it was.'

None of these things seemed to matter as much as they once would have done. Norma and Danny were still living with Hilda and Roy, as there was nowhere else available to set up on their own.

As soon as she started talking about Alan, Joy could hardly ever hold back her tears. 'I can't stand not knowing anything. Sometimes I have crazy thoughts, like . . .'

'What?' Norma reached over and gently stroked her arm.

Joy wiped her eyes, trying to get herself under control and not sob out all her grief and worry yet again. 'Well, what if Alan's run away and set up home with some other woman? What if he's not even in the Army any more?'

'I don't think—' Norma began.

'I know it's stupid, but . . .' Joy shrugged helplessly. 'I just go mad sometimes, with it all going round in my head.'

It was nearly six months now since Alan's last letter, and all of them were trying not to give in to the inevitable thoughts about what might have happened. Joy found it a comfort visiting Sycamore Road, being with her old friends and cuddling little Lizzie: a new life, innocent of all that was going on in the world. However, she could not help sometimes comparing her life with Norma's – here with her husband and child, safe and sound, when Joy herself did not even know if Alan was still alive.

Why had they not been told anything? That was the question that went round and round in her mind. She had been to see Irene and Ivy Bishop, Alan's sister and mom, twice more and they had not heard a word from the Army or anyone else.

That morning – and every morning – if the post arrived before work, Joy rushed to the doormat, her heart pounding with expectation, only to be disappointed again. Dad had picked up the one letter that had arrived. She saw his jaw clench and he went into the kitchen, from where a delicious smell of frying bacon was drifting.

'It's from him, isn't it?' she heard him say. His voice sounded forced out between clenched teeth. 'I told you to end it. Didn't I?'

Joy had stood listening, her own daily punctured hope of a letter forgotten for a moment. She heard no reply from her mother, only the sizzle of the frying pan, and then, 'Here's your breakfast.'

'What you need,' Norma said now, 'is a good dance. It'll take your mind off it and make you feel so much better. Only don't look at me – I'm tied to this little lady for the time being.' And she smiled down adoringly at

Lizzie. 'Tell you what, ask Thelma – that girl with the dark hair, worked in fillings with us? She likes a good dance. Go on, get your glad rags on and go out and enjoy yourself!'

Joy did not know Thelma very well. She was a shy girl, a little younger than Joy and seemingly slightly in awe of her.

'But you're such a good dancer!' she said. 'I'm not sure you'd want to be seen with me.' But Thelma seemed pleased to be asked, and a few days later they stepped off the tram in the centre of Birmingham. Joy did not mention any of her own problems and instead listened to Thelma's worries about her brother, who was in the Army, as they walked up to the Town Hall.

'Anyway,' Thelma said sweetly, 'that's enough of that.' She was a small, curvaceous young woman and had on an emerald-green dance skirt that Joy could not help admiring. 'Let's just try and have a nice evening, eh? It was good of you to ask me, Joy. I haven't been out in ages.'

Joy gave a wan smile. 'No, nor me.'

She was, as commanded by Norma, dressed up to the nines. It was the first time in months she had gone dancing anywhere, except at Rowheath during the summer 'Holiday at Home' season. She felt guilty even doing that, getting dolled up and enjoying herself, when she had no idea whether Alan was lying sick somewhere or whether he was . . . Her mind would stop when it went down that track, never wanting to reach the end.

But being out and, as they reached the Town Hall, the sound of music from inside began to lift her spirits. The dance was a fundraiser for the Lord Mayor's War Relief Fund – a banner outside the huge Grecian-style building was advertising the fund. When they walked into the grand space, with the huge gold pipes of the organ reaching to the roof at the far end, it was already packed with swirling couples.

'"A Zoot Suit . . ."' Thelma grinned.

'"For my Sunday Gal!"' Joy laughed. 'Come on, we'll have to dance together for now.'

They whirled off around the floor. Thelma was not a bad dancer in fact, and she entered into it all with great zest. Joy wondered why they had never got to know one another before. It was fun to find another friend. Norma was her closest pal, but her life with Danny was a bit Darby-and-Joan these days – inevitably, now that they had a baby.

'Look,' Thelma said, scanning the room. She was more lively and less mousey than Joy had realized. 'The Yanks are here!'

Joy had hardly ever seen any of the American service-men who had arrived in the country, and she looked round curiously. She could see one or two in USAF uniforms, looking very smart and dapper.

'Tall, aren't they?' she giggled. 'They must feed them well over there!'

'They've got black lads over here as well,' Thelma said. She craned her neck. 'Can't see any here though.'

Soon after the dance ended Joy was startled to find two of the young men – both of them tall, but one especially so, and very smart, in khaki – standing beside them. The taller one was a very solid man with cropped, light-brown hair just showing under his army cap.

'I think I spotted the best lady dancers in the room,' he said in a warm, drawling accent. He removed his forage cap and gave a little bow. 'May I have the pleasure?'

He was looking at Joy, and for a moment she looked in confusion at Thelma, who smiled and gave a little nod.

'And may I?' The other lad had darker hair and – as Thelma said afterwards – 'bedroom eyes', chocolate-brown and soulful. How could she resist!

The taller man had a twinkle in his eye, which Joy liked immediately. She took his arm, which he held out to draw her on to the dance floor, then gave a formal bow.

'Hank,' he said. 'Hank Eklund – from Philly. And who do I have the pleasure?'

'Joy. Gilby.' She smiled.

'Well, Joy, I'm sure looking forward to dancing with you – you've got style.'

The band struck up with a swing number and Joy gasped. 'Oh, they don't always do this one . . .'

'You like to swing?' Hank asked.

'Oh yes!' she replied.

After the first few moments of getting the measure of each other, fitting each other's pace and steps, Joy realized that she was with a wonderful dancer – at least as good as Alan and Lawrence. Her heart soared as they whirled round. Hank, with a relaxed, lanky style that fitted the dance perfectly, whirled her up in the air and down into the splits on the floor.

'Whoa, what a beauty,' Hank cried, admiringly. 'I've picked the champ here!'

People at the edges were clapping, and other couples turned their heads to watch. Joy felt her body come alive, responding to the music without her having to think. Another lad came to join in and, between them, he and Hank spun her over in a somersault, causing everyone around to applaud and cheer.

'Oh my, you're really something!' Hank laughed as the dance finally came to an end. 'And you're beautiful as well.'

Joy laughed. She could feel her face glowing, as if she

was coming alive again. What fun this was – it was exactly what she needed! She felt a bit drunk, even though she had had nothing at all to drink.

'Want to take a rest?' Hank asked.

'No!' she cried.

'So far as I'm concerned, you're mine for the evening, little lady,' he said, laughing at her enthusiasm. 'I'm not letting anyone else get their hands on the best dancer in the room.'

They both danced until they were fit to drop. Thelma seemed to be having a good time with the other lad and Joy felt able to forget about her.

'I'm so hot!' she said, her lips close to Hank's ear to be heard. 'Let's get a drink – and a bit of fresh air, shall we?'

They stood outside in the dim light, gulping down glasses of ginger beer and leaning against the cool stones of the building.

Up until that moment they had said very little to each other, except to exchange names. They had danced and danced and beamed at each other, their bodies completely in tune.

'Well, I've had a fine time tonight,' Hank said. 'In fact I can say this is the best night I've had since I've been over here in old England. So, Joy Gilby, you tell me something about yourself.' He offered a packet of Lucky Strike.

Joy laughed, taking a cigarette. As he held out a lighter, the flame gave her a clearer view of his features for a second. She hardly ever smoked; just socially now and again. But it felt like a nice, relaxing thing to do. 'What d'you want to know? I have a sister and a brother – I'm in the middle – and a mom and dad, of course.'

'Not everyone is so lucky,' Hank said. 'My father died when I was seven years old.'

'Oh,' she said, feeling foolish. 'Sorry, I didn't mean it like that.'

'I know,' he said, easily. 'Go on . . .'

'Well.' She stopped and almost laughed. My family: where do I start? she thought. *So far as I can see, each of my parents seems to be in love with someone else, but somehow we all keep going along as we are . . .* 'All right – well, most of my family work at Cadbury's.'

'The chocolate factory?'

'I was packing chocolates when the war started; now I'm working on munitions instead.'

'I'll have to see if I can get some Hershey's for you,' Hank said. 'See what you think.'

'That'd be nice,' Joy said. 'Hershey' sounded so American and exciting. 'Where are you based, then?'

'Place called Pheasey: you know it?' He took a drag on the cigarette and blew out into the night. 'Used to be a farm, I think.'

'Near Walsall?'

'Yep, thereabouts. They took us on a tour of one of the leather factories there – that was swell.' He turned to face her. 'I'd sure like to meet your folks, Miss Joy Gilby?'

'All right . . .' She hesitated. 'Are you married, Hank?'

'No, ma'am, I am not.' He said it jokingly with a click of his heels and a mock salute. 'Are you?'

'No. But I'm engaged. Supposed to be . . .' She told him about Alan, haltingly, determined not to cry and spoil the evening.

'Six months?' Hank said. 'Oh my.'

Put like that, it sounded bad. A stab of utter desolation went through her.

'I know,' she said. 'But I'm going to wait. He's . . .' She wanted to say, *He's my love*, but then she really would cry. 'Just so's you know, that's all.'

'That's OK,' Hank said warmly. 'You poor girl. But you dance like a dream – and I'd still like to meet your folks. People have been real kind to us around the camp, inviting us in for afternoon tea, and so on. But I've never met any gal who can dance like you. Come out with me again?'

Joy hesitated. Was it wrong, walking out with another man when . . .? But Hank knew how things were.

'All right,' she said. 'I'd love to go dancing again.'

Thirty-One

Christmas

Ann hurried along the street, carrying the bag of vegetables. All the time she had been waiting in the shops, where everything seemed to take an eternity, her heart had been banging like a crazed drum and she was breaking out in a sweat, even though it was a freezing day.

It was five to eleven. She walked as fast as she could, trying not to draw attention to herself, praying there would not be a queue outside the phone box. She was so relieved to see a man coming out as she approached, and no one else waiting, that she almost burst into tears.

Just as she pulled the door open, the phone started ringing. She dropped the bag and snatched up the receiver, dreading that the call would be for someone else.

'Ann?'

'Oh, Tom!' She was so relieved that, once again, the tears nearly came. The door was slowly shutting. She had a few blessed private moments here, with him.

'Are you all right, dear?'

'Yes. Oh yes! I just hurried from the shops, that's all.' There was a pause. 'Are you all right?' Partly she wanted to scream. It was so difficult, this distance, and the knowledge that in every silent second his money was dwindling away.

'Yes. I'm very well. How are things at home?'

'All right. Well, I mean . . .' She had told him most of it: Marianne going; how Len had been very up and down, one minute depressed, the next trying almost to bully her into loving him; trying to forbid Tom's letters. And she wasn't having it. Not now, after all that had happened. 'Len's not too bad at the moment really. It's the girls I'm worried about.'

'Poor things,' Tom said gently. 'We remember, don't we?' The warmth of his voice brought back their old intimacy – as least so far as was possible. 'And how's Martin?'

'He's doing very well,' Ann said. 'He's been quieter lately, goes out with his friends a lot, though you can hardly blame him, with all that's been going on in the house. But he's getting good marks – he's talking about university.'

'Goodness,' Tom said. She could hear the pride in his voice. 'That's very impressive.'

'Well, he doesn't get it from me, I can tell you that!' she laughed. There was a pause. 'You know, love, before he leaves school, we shall have to tell him, don't you think?'

Tom hesitated. 'Whatever you think best, Ann. I just don't feel I have a say – after all, it's Len who's been there in the heat and burden of the day. But . . . I would love to get to know Martin, if and when it were ever possible.'

'Tom . . .' She hesitated. She was so sick of feeling sinful and divided. Feeling wrong for loving. 'Let's try and meet again – soon.'

'If it's ever possible. Yes, my love. You know I'd always . . . whenever you think.'

'It's so nice to talk to you,' she said longingly. But she tried to keep the sorrow out of her voice. 'All I want sometimes is to lie somewhere, right up close, and talk and talk.'

'That would be bliss.' His voice quickened suddenly, as

if someone was coming. 'I'm needed – I'll have to go, Ann. I'm so sorry. I do hope Christmas is all right.'

'Oh, it will be. There'll be plenty of people about – the whole family – and we've even got a Yank coming, a friend of Joy's!'

'Goodbye, my darling.'

'Tom? I love you.'

'I know. And I, you – always, you know that.'

When the phone call cut off, she felt desolate. Wiping her eyes quickly, she pushed on the door of the phone box and walked home in a daze with her heavy bag, wondering, How long is it going to be like this?

Sheila was in the attic, changing Robbie's napkin. She had left Elaine downstairs, playing with her Uncle Martin, who Elaine adored and looked up to like a god. Martin, tall and lanky now at seventeen, was funny and gentle and a good tease. Elaine followed him about like a puppy whenever he was in the house.

'There you are, you little lump,' Sheila said, neatly pinning Robbie's nappy. 'We need to get you potty-trained, that we do.'

She heard the faint bang of the front door closing – Mom coming back from shopping. A moment later music from the wireless came floating up the stairs.

Robbie, a placid soul, chortled at her as she pulled his romper suit over the nappy. She tidied him up and pulled him to her, cuddling him. Just then the sound of Bing Crosby's latest hit drifted up the stairs: *I'll be home for Christmas . . .*

She already knew most of the tear-jerking words, of lovers aching to be together. Her feelings all welled up at once, so that she was sobbing helplessly. 'Oh, Kenneth – I want you here. Why can't you be here?'

She clung to Robbie, tears falling on to his curls. Here she was with their two children, looking forward to Christmas, but with their daddy somewhere across the world. They'd be grown-up before he ever saw them again, at this rate!

Robbie made a little sound and she loosened her grip on him. His big eyes looked up into her tearful face, full of worry.

'Oh, I'm sorry, little sweetheart – it's just that I miss your daddy so much, sometimes. It's like being a child, stuck here with Mom and Dad all the time.'

Robbie reached out and touched the tears on her cheeks and Sheila heard feet on the stairs. Her mother appeared.

'Oh dear,' Ann said. 'Poor love.'

She came and sat down beside Sheila and put her arm around her. Sheila felt even more like a little girl again, accepting her mother's comfort and, with Robbie on her lap, the three of them sat together, rocking back and forth for a few moments.

'I don't know when I'll see him again.'

'I know.' Ann's fingers wrapped themselves around hers, stroking them. 'It's rotten.'

After a moment Sheila straightened up and wiped her eyes. 'Get the shopping all right?'

'Yes.' Ann smiled brightly at her. It was only then that Sheila noticed her eyes – was she imagining that Mom looked as if she had been crying as well? 'Nanna said she'd bring her puddings. She made them ages ago.'

'What's she found to put in them?' Sheila forced a laugh. 'Sawdust?'

Ann smiled, getting to her feet. 'Quite a bit of apple, I think.' From the doorway she said, 'Was that card from Audrey?'

Sheila rolled her eyes. 'Yes. All bright and breezy.

Marvellous life, with that Richardson bloke.' She sighed. 'She's a funny one, Audrey. I don't really feel I know her any more.'

'Oh my, this is a nice warm house!' Hank said, beaming and rubbing his hands as Joy showed him into the hall.

'Hello!' Ann came out of the kitchen, hastily untying her apron. There were handshakes and introductions. Joy smiled, grateful for the warm welcome her mother was giving this stranger, here in her house for Christmas dinner. 'Are they not keeping you warm over in Pheasey then?'

'We call it "Little Russia" over there, ma'am!' Hank laughed. 'And they're not far wrong. Anyways, I gotta tell you, all us GIs have been getting fifty invitations or more to come to an English house for Christmas – but, for me, there was no contest. I had to come and meet the Gilby family!'

'Well, we're glad you're here,' Ann said, charmed. Hank seemed to give off a happy sort of energy. 'Come on in and sit by the fire. Len!'

Len came out of the front room and shook Hank's hand. 'Nice to meet you, pal,' he said, looking Hank's uniform up and down. 'Army then, are you?'

'Yes, sir. Army dentist in fact.'

Len nodded, impressed. 'Well, you can take a look for us, if you like!' he joked, baring his teeth. 'Save me a bob or two, that would! Course I was in the last lot . . .' Len said. 'In the Home Guard here now, though.'

Joy and Ann exchanged smiles as the two men disappeared into the front room, exchanging talk about armies and wars. Joy thought she had not seen her father light up like that in a very long time.

✳

Joy followed her mother to the table, each triumphantly bearing a Christmas pudding. Everyone was squeezed round, with an extra little folding card table added on at one end. The room was very warm, the windows running with condensation. As well as Margaret and Cyril, Ann had invited Jeanette, who had no family to speak of. And now Hank was here too, to sample a British Christmas, with everyone pooling whatever rations or goodies they had. There were cheers as they carried the puddings in.

'Well, they don't look too bad,' Margaret said, peering doubtfully at them.

'Are we going to set light to them?' Martin asked.

'That'd make anything taste all right,' Len joked.

Joy looked at him, startled. Her father was sitting at one end of the table, with Hank on one side and Jeanette on the other. She had not seen him looking so cheerful in a long time.

'Those look mighty fine,' Hank said. 'Ma'am, it looks to me as if you have worked a miracle.'

Joy saw Margaret and Cyril, her grandparents, give each other approving looks. Hank was so amiable and easygoing. He had quickly settled in and got along well with everyone. Before dinner, he and Martin had been arm-wrestling and teasing each other.

'You'd be the age of my kid brother,' Hank said, ruffling Martin's hair. 'And he beats me every time these days!'

And the big bag of rations Hank had brought to contribute to the feast had provoked squeals of excitement.

'Oh, look – bacon!' Joy heard from Mom. She had gone into the kitchen to find Ann and Sheila exclaiming over everything: 'Real coffee!', 'Ooh, look: orange juice!', 'There's lard!', 'Sugar! – oh, and what's this? Rice!', 'Ooh, soap!' And so it went on. 'Mom, look,' Joy dipped her hand into the package, 'there's even Coca-Cola!'

'Well, he can come again!' Sheila said. She had been a bit sniffy at first at the idea of Joy bringing Hank the Yank home. She thought it disloyal, when Joy was still waiting for Alan. But Hank definitely added to the fun, with his old-fashioned manners and his sunny temperament – not to mention all the goodies.

'Right.' Len stood up, once the puddings were installed. 'This is my job, I believe.'

Joy took her place next to Hank as her father set light to the spoonful of cheap brandy, sending a mauve flame licking across the pudding.

'Say, I've never seen that before,' Hank said. 'You going to set light to the holly as well?'

'It usually goes out too quickly for that,' Jeanette said, as Len struck a match to set about the second pudding.

'Are there sixpences?' Martin asked. 'Don't go swallowing the sixpence!' he said, wide-eyed, to Elaine.

Mom managed to serve the pudding somehow so that Elaine found the sixpence in the first pudding, and everyone laughed at the expression on her face.

'You're set up for life now, bab,' Cyril joked, tweaking her nose. 'So, my lad. Hank. How're you finding our country? Did you come by ship?'

'It's very fine, sir. Yes, we sailed from New York to Scotland and then came down here on the railroad. I reckon your Birmingham is a little bit like our Detroit.'

'Well, they make cars there, don't they?' Jeanette said. Her cheeks were pink for once and she was smiling and animated.

'Yes, they do. In fact, one of our lads comes from Detroit. When we arrived here, it was dark as could be and we all marched up to the camp singing, *"The Yanks are coming . . ."*'

'*"Over there, over there . . ."*' Jeanette started singing, smiling. She had a good singing voice. For a moment they all joined in with the song.

'And we're very glad you're here,' Ann said, sitting down after serving out the puddings. 'Custard, anyone?'

Joy, sensing her own cheeks glowing, and feeling warm and nicely full of dinner, looked round the table at her family. It was a long time since she could remember such a happy day. Mom and Dad cheerful and relaxed – especially now all the cooking was done; her sister and the little ones; Robbie full of excitement at the first Christmas he could actually understand. And Nanna and Grandad, always there, as they had been throughout her life. Mom's friend Jeanette, who was gentle and nice, and somehow always created a good atmosphere around her.

And, of course, Hank – arriving with all his presents of nylons and lipstick and 'candy' and soaps, as well as the food supplies – brought a feeling of plenty into the house, which had not been there for a long time. And he was winning everyone's heart. A terrible pang passed through her. Oh, Alan, she thought, where are you? She knew she was beginning to resign herself to the terrible idea that she was never going to hear from him again. Not after all this time. She had to swallow down her tears as the family were raising a toast to 'absent friends' and to 'the end of this terrible war'.

'Come on now.' Mom got up and they started stacking the plates. 'Let's clear away and we can listen to the King and then have some games.'

Joy felt Hank's hand slip over hers and squeeze it tightly, and she could only smile back into his sunny face.

'Your folks are just the best, Joy. I picked the number-one spot!'

His eyes met hers and they were full of feeling. He's falling in love with me, she thought. Even in her muzzy, post-dinner state, she was suddenly filled with panic. Because she knew, after the nights they had shared of dancing and laughter, and by the way Hank fitted in so well with her own family, that she was enjoying being with him much more than she ought to. She smiled and gave his hand an answering squeeze, but then quickly pulled her hand away and got up to help her mother.

Late that night, when Hank was leaving to get his transport back to the camp, he thanked 'the Gilbys' fulsomely.

'I reckon I've had one of the best Christmases of my life.' He took Ann's hand and kissed it, in gentlemanly style. 'One I won't forget, that's for sure!'

'Well,' she said, laughing, 'do come again, Hank.'

Joy was going to say goodbye on the step, but Hank murmured, 'Come out with me, baby? Just a minute? You can stand inside this jacket of mine.'

As soon as the door closed, he wrapped both his arms and the jacket around her, enclosing Joy in his warmth. He was tall, her brow only level with his chin, and she felt his warm breath on her forehead as they stood close together.

'Reckon this has been a lovely day,' he said. 'And you, Joy – well, you're the best. I know what you said, about your fiancé and all. But . . .'

She rested her head against his chest. It just could not be true. Not Alan disappearing for ever. When was she ever going to know for certain? Desolation rose in her and her eyes filled with tears.

'I just wonder . . .' Hank said gently. 'How long is it now?' he asked.

'Nine months.'

A silence hung between them, which spoke for itself. She felt Hank's big fingers, gentle under her chin, tilting her face.

'It sounds as if something's happened to that poor feller of yours, baby – or he'd never be neglecting a girl like you, would he?'

She looked up into his eyes, his words sinking into her. A moment later his warm lips were pressed to hers.

Ann piled the washing-up beside the sink. She felt slightly unsteady – unused to drinking, she had downed a good helping of sherry that night. The washing-up could wait.

For a moment she stood in the kitchen, holding the edge of the sink. Tom's voice yesterday . . . *And I, you – always.* She clung to the sound of his loving tones, desperately trying to hear him in her head before the memory faded, as she knew it would.

Voices reached her from the room next door: Margaret and Cyril here, with them, and things feeling almost normal; Sheila laughing at something Martin said; Len's voice as he chatted quietly with Jeanette. Ann closed her eyes for a second, letting the sound of calm wash over her.

IV

1944

Thirty-Two

March

The sound of the wireless came from the front room: Martin, glued to the Sunday broadcast of *The Brains Trust*. Ann listened proudly in the kitchen, mashing a pan of swede. *The Brains Trust* went right over her head – all those clever bods with their posh voices – but her intelligent boy liked it, even if the rest of the family teased him for it.

She added pepper and some parsley to the swede and, lost in her own thoughts, started making little rissoles, covering them in breadcrumbs. Things had felt easier since Christmas. Len was more relaxed – it felt a long time now since Marianne had left and he was better in himself, resigned to the situation. She could hear Sheila with the children in the front room. Joy was upstairs somewhere. All her family around her.

Her own worries recently had revolved around Tom. His letters had stopped arriving for almost three weeks. Ann was starting to feel beside herself with worry, but there was no one she could tell or ask about it. Yesterday the post had at last brought a letter saying that he had had a bad bout of flu, and his father had also been sick and was still gravely ill, though Tom himself had recovered. That was all she needed to know, and all day today she had gone about with a light heart.

Her attention was caught by a movement in the garden:

Len coming back. He had been with the Home Guard this afternoon. She saw his back as he stowed his bike in the shed. When he turned to come to the house he kept his head down, staring at the ground. There was something in the way he was walking that sparked alarm in her. That tight, shut-in look, which he had managed to lose over the past few weeks, seemed to be back.

She smiled as he came in the back door. 'All right? Rain held off then?'

Len sank down at the table.

'You all right?' She turned at the sink. 'Not feeling poorly, are you? There's flu about.' Seeing that he seemed somehow stunned, she wiped her hands and went and poured him a cup of tea.

'Ann. Shut the door.'

Cautious now, she obeyed and sat down opposite him, perched tensely on the edge of the chair.

'What's going on?'

All the tension was back in his shoulders, his face.

'It's . . . This afternoon, he's back – Ted Harris.'

Ann stared at him, struggling to think who Ted Harris was. Then the penny dropped. Ted Harris, the married man with three children who had disappeared at the same time as Marianne. *With* Marianne. The poor dupe. She felt suddenly as if her body was full of stones. What did this mean? That Marianne would be back too?

'They say he's been back in Brum a while. Before Christmas. He only came back to the Home Guard today. I s'pose he couldn't face anyone – had things to sort out with his missus. And had to try and get his job back. I don't s'pose they'd have allowed him back in peacetime, but he's a valuable worker.'

'Nice of them to have him back.' Her heart was thudding in a heavy, horrible way. 'So, did you speak to him?'

'Ted spoke to me.' Len looked down. He was in pain. 'Course he thinks Marianne's my cousin and she evidently didn't let on, either. God knows what she told him, but he still thinks . . . Anyroad he came to say . . . He was a state – I thought he was going to start blarting. Said he'd made the worst mistake of his life and—'

'Did he say where Marianne is?' Ann interrupted.

'I never asked.'

'Why not?'

'I thought he'd think it was a bit odd.'

'But she's your "cousin"!' Ann said, exasperated. 'Wouldn't he have thought it even odder if you *didn't* ask? Didn't Ted tell you anything?' She leaned towards him. 'Don't you want to know?'

Len shrugged, looking down at the table.

When he came home from Home Guard duty at Cadbury's a few days later, Ann could see again, even as Len walked through the door, that something had happened.

'What's up now?' she asked wearily, as he walked into the back room. She clicked off the wireless; they had had a concert on in the background. Sheila had got the little ones to bed and was sitting knitting, and Joy and Martin were there too.

Len sank into a chair. He hesitated, then obviously realized there was no point in hiding anything from the children.

'I had a word. With Ted Harris. After we'd finished.' He stopped, shaking his head. 'The bloke's a mess. Damn nearly broke down again when he was talking to me. He said he fell for her – Marianne – hook, line and sinker. Said it was as if she'd put a spell on him. I mean, he's a middle-aged man . . .'

Ann and Sheila exchanged glances, but none of them said anything.

'He said they went down to Worcester. Managed to find a room and he got some piffling little job in a valve factory, I think he said. It was a case of better than nothing. They lasted three months, nearly; course he was at work all day, never knew what she was getting up to. Then one night he came home and she'd gone.'

'Perfidious woman,' Martin muttered flippantly.

'Oh, shut up,' Joy said. 'Where'd she go then?'

'He's no idea. That was November time. He hung on for a week or two, then packed up and came home. Betty, his wife, has taken him back, but of course things are . . . Well, they're not going to be the same, are they?'

'Well, they wouldn't be, would they?' Sheila said bitterly.

Ann was so stunned she could think of nothing to say.

'She's a right piece of work, that one,' Sheila said. 'Marianne's been using all of us – the whole way along.'

Len nodded. He looked so humbled and defeated.

'But why does she keep running away?' Joy asked.

'When she was here,' Ann said, 'and those blokes were after her, one of them said he was her husband. By the look of him, I can see why she'd have wanted to run away.'

'But why go off again?' Sheila said. 'And where the hell do you go when you've got a four-year-old child to look after?'

At the mention of George, Ann saw a stab of pain register on her husband's face.

Marianne stood washing up in the old stone sink in the scullery, waves of her thick ginger hair – with just tips of black remaining at the ends – falling over her shoulders. If she stood on tiptoe she could just see out of the little window, which looked out over a strip of untended garden in which hens pecked at the ground. Beyond it lay a damp, scrubby meadow into which a young deer had wandered, this chill, misty morning. It stood cropping the grass, raising its head every few seconds to look around nervously, its tail waggling.

She had boiled a kettle to wash the dishes and although the water was cooling fast, it was still a comfort to have her hands in the sink, when the farmhouse was so cold and draughty. Thank the Lord spring was coming. Things had to get better.

She stood listening for a second. Things were quiet upstairs, no stick thumping on the floor to demand that she come upstairs and answer his needs: tea, a shave, to do his business. At least the sick man did not need her to answer any other sort of needs – he was too far gone for that. The only sound was George, scraping at the last of his porridge from the bowl.

The back door opened into the kitchen and a pink-cheeked woman came in, wearing an ancient tweed coat, a wool hat pulled down over her ears and with a basin in her hand. She pushed her boots off at the door.

'I'm back!' she announced unnecessarily. 'Ooh, it's still right brass-monkey weather out there – but I do believe there's a touch of spring in the air. The hens are laying well.'

Marianne emerged from the scullery, smiling. She liked Jen Checkett – it would be hard not to like this cheerful, harried, overworked woman, left to run the farm almost single-handedly by the war and her husband's increasing infirmity. When she had first met her, in Worcester, Jen was weeping in the street. This was before things had gone down the pan with Ted Harris and she had decided to cut and run. Marianne was out shopping, with George, and

Jen had brought trays of eggs into town to sell at the market. But she had tripped and dropped a whole lot of them as she moved across to put them on her little stall. She was picking herself up, breaking into sobs of desperation, while the eggs lay smashed and slimy all around her. It seemed to be the last straw.

Marianne helped Jen pick up and rescue whatever eggs she could, as Jen poured out her troubles to this stranger: trying to run the farm almost single-handed, her invalid husband, the shortage of labour . . .

The day she decided she couldn't stand Ted with his endless guilt and his slack lips any longer, Marianne waited for market day and, taking George and her few belongings with her, went to find Jen Checkett again.

'I can help,' she offered. 'If you can give me somewhere to live.'

Jen Checkett leapt at the offer and that evening Marianne and George travelled back to the farm on the cart with her. As they moved deeper and deeper into rural Worcestershire, where the further they went there seemed to be fewer obvious signs of the war, she could see John Brady in her mind's eye, shrinking smaller and smaller to a little black dot. He was never going to find them here.

Now Jen pulled her hat off, revealing faded brown hair, all in a frizz. She hung her sagging coat on the hook by the door, beside an old brown gaberdine of her husband's, long unworn by him, and slipped on her ancient sheepskin slippers.

'Everything all right?' She looked at Marianne across the homely kitchen, then rolled her eyes ceiling-wards. Harry Checkett was not the easiest of patients. Even the doctor joked wryly that 'patient' had never been the right word for him.

'So far,' Marianne said. 'He ate nearly all his porridge.'

'Ah,' Jen said absent-mindedly. 'Well, that's good.'

Marianne could see that she no longer thought of Harry as her husband exactly. More as just another of the long list of daily duties she had to perform. And this on top of trying to get any workers to stay for more than a week or two on the farm, see-sawing prices and the list of war regulations that the government kept handing out to farmers. It had all been an eye-opener to Marianne. This was a place of unrelenting hard work, but it had also been a safe haven for her. She was happy enough to take on whatever needed doing in the house. She'd had worse – far worse. And Jen was out dealing with the farm work a lot of the time.

'Well there, Georgie,' Jen said, leaning over the table with the basin. 'Our girls're laying well today, so you can have eggies for your tea!'

She looked across at Marianne.

'They're sending me a couple more hands this week – let's hope to goodness they last,' she said. 'If they could just take on the milking, I'd be glad. It's a heavy job . . .' She smiled, never downhearted for long. 'You know, I praise the Lord every day, for you and this little 'un being here with us!'

Thirty-Three

As spring arrived and the weather warmed, Joy found herself living a double life. One life at Cadbury's, working in munitions, packing forces parcels as a Cadbury Angel, with a little bit of dance teaching.

Every so often she went over to Edgbaston to see Irene and Ivy Bishop. Joy liked Irene and they all shared the same terrible, grinding worry about Alan. It was a worry that had gone on for so long, though, that they were all secretly – and then not so secretly – becoming resigned to the worst.

'I don't think he's coming back,' Irene said to her when she last visited. 'I've never wanted to say it before.' She looked at Joy, her face pinched and tears in her eyes. 'Not to you, specially. But we've got to face it. Alan's not the sort to go off and not get in touch, unless there's summat really wrong. So . . .'

She couldn't finish the sentence. Joy nodded, with a huge lump in her throat that stopped her saying anything. Ivy Bishop sat silently, looking so sad and wisplike that the sight of her made Joy buckle inside even more. Even though it was so painful, she knew she would keep visiting them. To give up would feel like giving up on Alan and, during these helpless days, it was the only thing she could do.

But then there was her other life. Whenever Hank had time off and they could coincide, he came down from Pheasey like a shot. A couple of times Joy had met him in

Birmingham with his friend, Joe Litsky, the dark-eyed young man who was with him when they first met. Joe was very different from Hank: shorter, dark-eyed and a fast-talking New Yorker, who worked as a barber in Civvy Street. Thelma seemed to have found him a bit much, after dancing with him, so that relationship wasn't going anywhere. And Joe always had a different girl on his arm. He was lively and entertaining, and Joy enjoyed seeing him. But it was Hank, with his fairer looks, gentle, relaxed ways and wide smile, who really attracted her.

Most times when Hank came, he was alone. And he obviously had designs on getting Joy on her own as well. At first she resisted. 'Look, just come and see my family,' she had insisted, back in the winter.

Hank had been a real hit at Christmas and everyone was keen to see him again. And it was not only because he came bringing more goodies and rations with him, though that was an attraction. The GIs were like a prize to have visiting your family. Hank even brought stockings, which sent Sheila into seventh heaven. But mainly it was because they all liked him. He was like a big, friendly breath of fresh air, striding in good-naturedly and bringing a wider world to them. He was a huge hit with everyone – even Len, who, Joy realized, enjoyed having another man in the house who he could chat to.

One afternoon when spring could be said to have arrived, Joy walked with Hank around the park in Bournville. She loved walking beside him, with Hank's long, relaxed stride, his arm stealing around her shoulders. She enjoyed the looks other people gave them – this handsome couple, he a tall Yank in khaki and Joy pretty and slender in a burnt-orange frock.

'I like your family, Joy,' he said easily. 'They're all swell.

But, you know, it's you I really come to see. I can't stop thinking about you. You're in my dreams, every night.'

His amiable face smiled down into hers.

'I know I'm from a place so far away you can't imagine . . . But Philly isn't the boondocks. It's a big city, with lots of history. That's where we have Independence Hall – it's real old. It's like here in some ways, and you'd feel right at home.'

Joy's head jerked up to look at him, utterly startled. Was he saying what she thought he was saying?

'Hank, hey, just hold on,' she protested. 'You know I'm – promised to someone . . .' But all her doubts welled up. There was her whole past with Alan, all the future they had hoped for, and yet now the present reality with him was an echoing void into which she was shouting, desperately, again and again, but was never getting an answer – and would perhaps never do so again. And now, here was this attractive, loving man looking down at her, loving her . . .

'You're so beautiful, Joy. Those dancing eyes.' He stopped and gently stroked her cheek with his warm palm. 'I've never met a girl who makes me feel the way you do. You'd fit right in where I come from. We have great dance halls – and my folks would love you!'

Joy opened her mouth and closed it again, so full of panic that she could not find any words.

Hank leaned forward and solemnly kissed her forehead. When he drew back there was a cloud over his expression. For a moment he talked, looking out over the top of her head, as if to the trees beyond.

'The thing is, no one really knows what's going on. All "hush-hush", as you Limeys over here say. But we're here for a reason, that's for sure, and something's brewing.' He looked down into her eyes. 'What I'm saying is: I don't know how much longer I'm gonna be here, baby. Or what's waiting for us, wherever we're going.'

Suddenly Joy found herself looking down at him as he knelt gallantly before her on one knee, on the grass.

'You'd make me the happiest man there ever was if you would promise to be my wife, Joy, my darling? Whenever all this is over – if I survive it?'

Joy felt as if all the air had been snatched from her lungs. Her mind was a storm of panic. She liked Hank so much, didn't she? Loved him even. He was a very loveable man. If it had not been for Alan . . . And must she wait for ever for someone whose silence had gone on for almost a year now? Should she be facing the reality that Alan was never coming home? That day when they had stood together in the rain at the end of Birdcage Walk and promised themselves to each other felt an eternity away now. Wasn't that promise something that had been overtaken by circumstances? By this terrible war? But how could she let go, just like that, of all she and Alan had been – of the hope she was clinging to that he would be home with her again?

And Hank's words, asking her to marry him, to go to America with him, an ocean away from her family: how could she even begin to take that in?

'Oh!' she gasped. 'Hank. I . . . I like you so much! But I don't know what to say.'

'Say yes, baby?' He stood up, taking her hands in his. 'I didn't come here with a ring or anything like that. I didn't want to presume. But I want you to know how much I love you. We could have a good life together, you and I. I have a good job. We could start a family – how about six kids?' He pulled her close again, holding her gently. 'Oh, you'll make a fine mother. I love you, baby, like no girl I've ever met; and I think you feel something for me too?'

'I do. Oh, Hank – I do!' In a storm of confusing

feelings, Joy threw herself into his arms and reached up to kiss his cheek. 'But it's such a big thing you're asking me – I can't answer you straight away. Not yet; just give me some time, will you?'

Hank looked down into her eyes.

'Take all the time you want, Joy, baby – only try and give me an answer before I disappear, will you? Knowing you were going to be my wife would be my magic charm!'

Thirty-Four

'But she sent a telegram.' Sheila held it out to her mother, who had just come in from work. 'It came this morning. Frightened the life out of me – I thought it was about Kenneth . . .'

Ann, still standing in the hall, read it, frowning.

'That was a bit thoughtless of Audrey, I must say; she should have known what a shock it'd give you. Why not write you a letter?'

'I don't know what to make of it,' Sheila said, frowning. 'It doesn't really say anything. And it's the first I've heard from her in months.' The whole tone of the telegram was strange: *'Do come down and stay. Very soon. We should so like you to. All love, Audrey.'*

Ann gave a tired sigh, heading for the kitchen. 'It's quiet – where are the kids?'

'Upstairs with Martin,' Sheila said. 'I was about to bath them and then get the tea on. What d'you think I should do?'

Ann took the telegram again and stared at it, as if it was a puzzle.

'Reading between the lines, I'd say you'd better pay Audrey a visit.'

It was a cool April Saturday when Sheila stepped off the train at Goring. She had dropped Audrey a note to say that she would bring Robbie down for the weekend. Elaine was excited about spending a special weekend with Great-Nanna Margaret and Great-Granddad Cyril.

Sheila looked fondly round the little station, remembering the first bewildering time she had arrived there with Elaine as a baby, to be met by Maurice Vellacott, Audrey's husband. The thought made her heart sink. Now she was going to have to face this new husband. Had they even had the wedding yet? Surely if he was living in the house, they were not living 'in sin'. But although Audrey had mentioned that they were getting married, if they had had a wedding Audrey had not told her a thing about it.

Terence Richardson. He did not like her and Sheila definitely felt the same about him. It was not an inviting thought.

Audrey would have met her with the car had she wanted her to, Sheila knew, but it was so sunny that she had decided to walk, pushing Robbie in the pushchair. He was two and a half now and getting a bit old to be pushed around – but it was a long walk, too far for his little legs. Sheila lugged the thing up and out of the station, holding Robbie's hand on the steps, then strapped him in and set off.

The house was as lovely as she remembered, the pink roses that grew right across the front of the old brick already in bud, with the sound of birdsong from the hedges all around the wide garden. What a lovely place it was, Sheila thought with a pang. She could never imagine living here in the long term, but she did miss the beauty of it, after staying here all those months.

'We're going to see Auntie Audrey,' she told Robbie, whose eyebrows puckered, puzzled.

Sheila pulled on the rope bell beside the door and heard the soft tinkling inside.

The door flew open a moment later and Audrey, her face alight – rather too alight, Sheila realized later – exclaimed loudly, 'Oh my goodness: how *marvellous*! What a lovely surprise. Terence, do see who's come to visit! Hello, Robbie darling.'

Sheila was immediately confused. Had Audrey not received her letter saying they were coming? After all, Audrey had *asked* her to visit. She heard footsteps approaching and Terence Richardson appeared. He was wearing gardening clothes: a short-sleeved checked shirt and trousers smeared with mud.

'Ah, hello.' He managed a tone of social welcome, his fleshy pink face moving into a smile. 'Back again, are we, eh? How nice to see you.'

'Yes, you too,' Sheila muttered awkwardly. This style of talking where no one said quite what they meant – in fact often quite the opposite – was something she had never got used to.

'Bit of a surprise, eh?' he said, with more acid in his tone now. 'Perhaps give us a bit of warning in future.'

Sheila's bewilderment increased.

'Come in, come in!' Audrey was saying, in the strange fizzy tone she seemed to have taken on. 'I see you only have a little bag – aren't you staying?'

'Well, only until tomorrow,' Sheila replied as they released Robbie from the pushchair and went into the house.

'If you'll excuse me, I'll just finish off what I was doing in the garden,' Terence said, waving a pair of secateurs at her. Sheila nodded – of course. He leaned over and kissed Audrey's cheek.

'Why don't you make some coffee, darling? I won't be long.'

Was there something pointed about the way he said it?

Sheila wondered. Like a warning. But then she told herself she was imagining it.

'Let me get you a drink . . . And you, Robbie: what would you like?'

Audrey bustled them both into the kitchen. As she walked ahead, Sheila saw how much thinner she was, almost bony. Audrey closed the kitchen door behind them, then stood for a second, seeming to listen. The door to the outside closed behind Terence. Sheila realized the house felt almost eerily quiet.

'Where are the boys?' She had been rather looking forward to seeing them, and usually they came running to find out who was visiting, if the doorbell rang. They had not appeared to greet her and she felt a bit disappointed.

'Oh, have I not told you?' Audrey said, filling the kettle. 'They're both away at school now.'

'What, you mean . . .'

'Boarding? Oh yes. Maurice always wanted them to go; and Terence and I thought the sooner, the better. He said I'd left it rather late – I suppose I'd always held off rather. Selfish of me.' She turned with a wistful smile. 'I didn't want to let go, I suppose. And after Maurice . . . died. Anyway, they've gone rather late, compared to some boys.'

Sheila realized Edward was now eleven and little Charlie nine. It seemed terrible to her, sending them away; boarding school was another thing she had never got used to.

'You must miss them.'

Audrey looked across at her, face very sober suddenly, and her eyes filled with tears.

'Oh, I do – *terribly*.' Blowing her nose, she added briskly, 'But it must be done. We mothers just have to buck up. Good for them to stand on their own two feet.

Now, tea for you? Pot of coffee . . . Robbie darling, would you like a biscuit?'

She handed Robbie an arrowroot biscuit and a cup of milk with such sweetness that it tore at Sheila's heart, seeing all the love and care Audrey could not now give her own sons. It was *him*, wasn't it? she wanted to say. He *made* you do it.

But she did not have to say anything, because at that moment Audrey seemed to switch into another gear. Her face tight, her whole manner hurried and urgent, she came over to Sheila.

'Let's take our tea into the morning room. He's round the other side . . . I need to talk to you, Sheila. Come on, Robbie, I'll find you some toys.' But she kept talking as they went. 'Quickly, before he comes back. You have to help me . . . I just don't know what to do. I'm beside myself.'

They sat at the table in the pretty, sunny room, with the hollyhock-embroidered cloth on the table and Robbie on the floor with a treasure-trove box of the Vellacott boys' toys. Sheila felt a sick sensation arise in her. What on earth was going on? She felt for Audrey, but she really did not want to be dragged into this. She made herself say, 'You're looking a bit peaky, Audrey. Is everything all right?'

'I . . .' Audrey stammered into speech. Sheila felt really worried for her. 'I'm sorry, Sheila, you are the only person I could think of who I could call upon. I feel so foolish, but I don't know what to do.' Words tumbled out of her mouth. 'Terence wants me to sell the house – my home, the *boys'* home – and go and live in his house. Says it's silly having two houses, and how much money it would free up. And of course he's worried about appearances: him living here instead of me going there, now everyone thinks . . .'

There was a thud as the back door closed again and Audrey stopped talking as if a switch had been turned off.

'Audrey, is that coffee ready?' Terence's voice rang through the house.

'Yes, darling – in here!'

'Don't say anything,' she hissed at Sheila. 'We'll find time to talk—'

She cut herself off abruptly as Terence opened the door.

Soon afterwards Audrey provided some leek and potato soup – 'all from the garden!' – with a little cheese. Just as when Maurice Vellacott had been in the house when Elaine was very small, Sheila found herself relieved to have a child there, for her to pay attention to.

Audrey asked after Kenneth and Elaine and the rest of the family, then chattered away about village gossip.

'I thought after lunch we'd pop in and see Marjorie Sykes,' she said brightly. 'You were always such good pals with her, and her two little girls are absolute poppets – they'll be lovely with Robbie.'

She fixed Sheila with an intense gaze and smile. Sheila could vaguely remember the name of the woman she was talking about. She had come across Marjorie at some mothers' group in the village hall, but they had barely spoken to each other.

'Oh.' Terence looked up from his bread and cheese. 'Going for a stroll? I thought I might come along with you.'

'I think, darling,' Audrey said coyly, 'you might get a bit fed up with all our girlish chatter. Marjorie invited me over for a kiddie cuppa and a chat, if you know what I mean.'

Terence made a face. 'Yes, well, she certainly can talk. I think I'll bow out of that one.'

*

As soon as they had reached the bottom of the drive with Robbie in the pushchair, Audrey took a nervous glance behind her, then started talking.

'I'm so sorry about all this subterfuge, Sheila. This is what Terence has reduced me to. He'll hardly let me out of his sight. The only way I can get out is to pretend I've got all sorts of involvements with other women – and, of course, I do have a few friends to escape to. Even now, we'd better go towards Marjorie's house. I wouldn't put it past Terence to follow us. I know you probably have no idea who she is.'

'Audrey.' Sheila put a hand on her friend's arm, feeling its skinniness even through her coat. 'What the hell is going on?'

'I'm . . .' Audrey stopped for a moment, putting a hand over her face. 'No.' She recovered quickly, walking on again. 'Mustn't do that. He might be behind us.'

Sheila turned to look.

'There's no one there. Look, what's got you in this state?'

'It's him. Everyone thinks we're married, you see, and I don't know what to do. Terence made me send the boys away and he wants to take over everything: make me move into his house and . . . He found out about the money I was sending to Monica every month, for her and those little girls.'

Sheila had met Monica Gordon, the woman who had had an affair with Audrey's husband, Maurice Vellacott, and had fallen pregnant with twins.

'Monica has been very dignified; she's never come with a begging bowl, and of course Barbara and Ella are seven now and at school. She's working again. But I have always felt guilty about her – responsible somehow. I send her five guineas a month.'

'Five *guineas*?'

'It's not so much really – not in London, in the grand scheme of things. And Maurice left us comfortable. He was canny with money and he earned a lot. But Terence said I should no longer be sending her money, not after all this time. And that I had been remiss in not getting the boys to prep school as boarders much earlier.'

Sheila bit her lip, trying not to say something rude.

'But, Audrey, are you married or not?'

They had reached the bridges that spanned the two branches of the river in the village and they stopped to look over at the brown surging water. Robbie was asleep, a blanket wrapped snugly around him. Audrey glanced at Sheila.

'Terence said, one day, that he was taking me out. Shopping and a meal – in Reading. So off we went. I'd dolled up a bit, of course. I hardly ever go anywhere, and Reading doesn't hold very nice memories for me. But I thought he was trying to give me a treat.' She swallowed. 'You know, after what happened, with that man, I think I was . . . I don't know. Not myself. Fearful.'

'I'm surprised you even looked at another man.'

'Yes, but that was . . . He was an oik, an *animal*. Terence was different. He was a gentleman. I never felt safe afterwards, and I thought Terence was going to make me feel safe.'

Sheila managed not to make any comment.

'We drove to Reading and all of a sudden he was marching me into the Registry Office. This was quite early on as well, and his plan was that we'd get married – just like that! – with a couple of witnesses we didn't even know. Then go out for a celebration lunch, and that would be that. I panicked. I mean, if he'd asked me properly . . . But he'd ambushed me. That's certainly not my idea of how you get married, in that hole-in-the-corner way. I ran off, refused to go through with it. Terence was *furious*.'

'My God!' Sheila said.

'But then he must've gone round telling people in the village, because they all started congratulating me, saying what a dark horse I was. Terence made me write and tell you we were marrying as well. And then talking about how I was going to sell my house. I could hardly go round saying we aren't married, after all that – with him living here. I've hardly been able to face anyone since. I don't know what to do. Terence says I'm being silly. I suppose I *am* being quite silly, when he looks after me so well.'

'And he's been living in your house – all the time?'

'Yes! Before that, he was back and forth, keeping up appearances, but he's moved in on me . . .'

'But,' Sheila could hardly believe what she was hearing, 'why the hell have you gone along with all this?'

'Well, because . . . he's so sweet to me, you see. And he does do a very good job on the garden – and the house. He takes good care of me. I've a lot to be grateful for.'

'Audrey.' Sheila grasped her by the shoulders. She wanted to shout, but she kept her voice down. 'Does he hurt you? Like Maurice did?'

Audrey's eyes widened for a moment. 'Oh – no. No, he's not like that. Well, hardly ever. He just . . . confuses me. Whatever I say, he's got an answer, and I always seem to end up feeling I'm the one in the wrong. Terence was so upset with me for not marrying him, he actually cried.'

'You didn't run away from that Registry Office for nothing, did you?' Sheila insisted, repressing the desire to shake Audrey. 'You're not married – so he has no legal hold over you. And you're quite capable of organizing your life without a man around; you did that most of the time, even when Maurice was alive. So if you don't want this bloke in your house, tell him to get out!'

Audrey lowered her head. 'I can't.' She spoke barely above a whisper.

'Why not? D'you want him there? Do you want to marry him?'

Audrey looked up, cringeing, her thin face crumpling as she shook her head. 'But I can't. Everyone thinks . . . And I've just let it go on – I'm so ashamed. I haven't told anyone else, Sheila. I'm at my wits' end. I've even thought of calling the police. I really don't know what to do. You're so much more sensible than me: you have to help me, please!'

Thirty-Five

'Look, the dancing's about to start!' Jeanette took Ann's arm and propelled her to where everyone was gathering on the lawn. They were in the grounds of the big black-and-white-beamed Manor House belonging to the Cadbury family.

Amid the crowd sitting around on chairs, as the group of children assembled in the middle of the space, was their host Mrs Elizabeth Cadbury, for many years now a widow, tall, still straight-backed though she was in her eighties, with tightly curled steel grey hair. She had opened her home once again, for a tea party for wounded Polish servicemen and local children, and Ann and Jeanette had offered to help. They had spent the morning arranging trestle tables and making sandwiches, with Mrs Elizabeth supervising kindly – always there, taking part in the work. There had been games and the usual thrilling rides on donkeys for the children. Now that the hard work was over, for the moment, Ann and Jeanette had some time to relax and enjoy the entertainment.

The Polish Army and Air Force men – mostly young, though not all – were given pride of place for the entertainment. Ann could see several in plaster casts, or with bandaged heads, sticks and crutches. Many of them spoke some English and all were calm and polite to a fault. A couple of them had even been talked into playing instruments.

The group of young people lined up to dance were in

national costume – or what they had been able to piece together. The boys wore dark trousers, white shirts and little rust-coloured jackets; the girls, bright flowery skirts and garlands atop their heads. They set off dancing, in pairs, to the jaunty music, all smiling brightly.

'Ah, how lovely!' Jeanette said. 'Bless Mrs Elizabeth – what a nice day everyone's having. And those poor lads, they're so far from home. I can't really imagine it, all they must have suffered. This must make them feel a bit more at home.'

Ann watched, smiling. The dance stopped and everyone clapped like mad before they launched into another.

'You all right, Annie?' Jeanette leaned round and looked into her face.

Ann almost laughed, thinking, Where do I start in answering *that*?

'Well,' she admitted, 'it's been a bit of an odd week.'

The two of them linked arms and strolled around the back of the crowd as the lively music kept playing, and people cheered and clapped. Over these months working together, the two of them had developed an easy, kindly friendship. Ann saw more of Jeanette these days than she did of Hilda.

'Sheila came home from her weekend with Audrey – you know, her evacuation host down there. Nice lady, I've met her. But from what Sheila said, Audrey called her down because she's got herself into such a fix with some man who's pushing her around, trying to force her to marry him.'

Jeanette gasped. 'Oh dear – there are some right chancers about, aren't there? You'd think, a woman like that . . .'

'According to Sheila, Audrey's not nearly as on top of everything as she seems,' Ann said, blushing again at the thought that the same could very easily be said of herself.

'Her first husband was a bully and, by the sound of it, she's landed herself with another.'

Jeanette tutted. 'I don't understand some women. Can't be without a man. But what's the use of them, if all they're going to do is push you around?'

Ann looked at her friend, startled. Jeanette always seemed such a sweet, placid person, but her voice now contained steel.

'Goodness, Jeanette! Has there never been anyone for you?'

'Not that was worth having, no,' Jeanette said drily. 'You should have met my father – he showed me the worst that men could be, and it's been hard to trust any of them after that.'

Ann was really startled at this revelation. Jeanette had never mentioned her father before, only her gentle, beloved mother, who she had lived with and cared for, for years. She had put Jeanette down as a bit of a mouse, sheltered from the world, but now she was seeing her with new eyes.

'It's not that I wouldn't have liked to meet someone and get married – course I would. But I'd rather fend for myself than get stuck with some bully or idle sod, who I had to run around kowtowing to.' Jeanette smiled, now her usual sweet self again. 'So, there it is. Anyway, so Sheila's got herself involved in all this lady's problems, has she?'

'She came back last Sunday. Audrey was begging her to stay, but Sheila had her ticket and, anyway, she thought the bloke would smell a rat if she was there any longer. But she's ever so worried. She said to me, "Mom, I don't think Audrey's got it in her to give him the push, and the only other person who knows about this is me." Audrey was begging Sheila to go back down and . . . well, I don't know what really. Just not leave her alone with him. To be honest, in the past I'd never've thought Sheila had it in her to say anything to him – but now I'm not so sure.'

They turned back to watch the end of the dancing: all the bright costumes moving in orderly lines in front of the house. Everyone was going to have tea after the dancing.

'Thanks for listening,' Ann said. 'Oh and, Nette, you will come for Sunday dinner again tomorrow, won't you?'

'You sure?' Jeanette said. She blushed with pleasure. 'I don't want to impose – or eat you out of house and home. But it is lovely being part of a family.'

'It's nice having you there as well,' Ann said. This was far truer than she could say. Jeanette's gentle, humorous presence helped to soften a lot of the prickles of her family situation. And being able to invite anyone round to the house, now that Marianne had taken herself off, felt like the beginning of a new life.

'And you always bring something,' she laughed. 'You're giving us more than your fair ration, I'm sure!'

Thirty-Six

'I can't do it without you there.' Audrey's voice down the line from her home sounded small and tinny. Sheila was in a telephone box. 'The one night he's out is a Tuesday – he goes to the Catherine Wheel to meet a few chaps that he drinks with.'

Sheila held the receiver to her ear, looking out into the spring twilight with a feeling of unreality. She was not used to telephones, let alone what Audrey was suggesting at the other end of the line.

'If you could just come again, *please*: I'll pay your fare, Sheila, I don't want you to be out of pocket on my account. I could say it, if you were there to back me up. You've seen what I'm like; I can't do it on my own. I'm frightened of Terence: of what he might do. You said he used to hit his first wife and he hasn't done that to me – well, except once . . . I try to keep him happy, you see.'

Sheila stood, her head whirling.

'If you were to come this time next week – be here for when he gets back . . . Sheila, are you still there? Please say you're still there. You're my only true friend. I can't think of anyone else I could begin to talk to.'

'I'm here,' Sheila said slowly. 'And I think you might have more friends than you think.'

'Leave the kids with me,' Nanna Margaret said. 'This is a dreadful business and you need to be able to give your whole mind to it.'

They sat drinking tea in the back room of Sheila's grandparents' house, a room that always stayed reassuringly unchanging – the table and chairs always positioned in exactly the same way, ever since she could remember; the same painting of children in a cornfield over the mantelpiece.

Cyril was shaking his head. 'Man wants locking up. Poor woman.'

'She sounds like a bad picker, that's for sure,' Margaret said.

'You sure you can cope for a couple of days, Nanna?'

'Your mother and Joy can come and get the children after work and put them to bed,' Margaret said. 'And Cyril can get me on a stretcher and carry me up to bed.' She winked at Sheila. 'We'll be all right. But it makes me realize why you're supposed to have children when you're young!'

'Oh, thanks, Nanna – you're golden,' Sheila beamed at them. 'And you, Grandad.'

'Don't you fret about us, bab,' Cyril said. 'You just go and help your friend; she's given you a roof over your head when you needed it, and now she needs you.' His blue eyes became more intense for a moment. 'And you speak up to that rotten feller – don't you leave him in any doubt that he needs to skedaddle.' He made an emphatic gesture with his thumb.

Sheila sat up straighter, churned up inside with nerves. 'I'll try, Grandad.'

She arrived in Goring in the late afternoon in a steady drizzle. It seemed strange to see rain, as there had been none for weeks, and Sheila felt naked and peculiar being out with no children and no pushchair to hold on to in front of her. But Margaret and Cyril's house was home from home for Elaine and Robbie, and she had no worries about leaving them for a night or two.

Walking up through the village under an umbrella, she did not head straight to Audrey's house, but turned along the side road where she knew she would find Terence Richardson's own house. Audrey had shown it to her more than once: a big, imposing brick place with gables and a wisteria growing up the front.

The houses on each side were rather less hefty, though still built of warm brick. Sheila walked back and forth between them uncertainly until she heard a sound from one of the back gardens – the low woofing of a small dog. Aha, she thought, Archie.

The door had a window in its top half, four bevelled panes in a black iron frame. Steeling herself, Sheila lifted the knocker. There was no sound from the hard-of-hearing dog, but a moment later she saw a movement behind the glass and heard the sound of unlocking.

Dottie Freeman seemed smaller and wirier than she remembered, her strong, cropped hair grey turning to white.

'Ah,' she said. 'The evacuee.'

'Sheila.' She smiled nervously. She could not help liking Dottie. At least she tended to say what she meant.

'Trouble at mill?' Dottie enquired.

'You could say that, yes,' Sheila said.

Dottie stepped back. 'Want to come in?'

'It's not usually my style to get mixed up in other people's mess,' Dottie said, over teacups and strangely shaped but delicious pieces of flapjack. 'But I can see the woman's put you in a proper bind. Quite wrong in my opinion – if you want it.'

Actually, Dottie's opinion came as a bit of a relief.

'Is he allowed any?' Sheila asked. Archie was snuffling hairily at her knees as they ate.

'Good Lord, no – he's a dog!' she said, as if this was a feature of the animal that Sheila might not have noticed. 'No good spoiling them. Down, Archie!' she bellowed. 'Leave our visitor alone – have some manners!'

Archie lay down close by, showing the whites of his eyes pitifully.

'Look,' Dottie said. 'As I say, I usually keep out of things. But I know this fellow of old, and I think he's an absolute bounder. Don't relish the thought of getting stuck in with him, but maybe someone should have done it years ago. P'raps I should – except one doesn't reckon to go wading in on other people's marriages. Feel a bit of a coward when I think back, but then Jean was so private, so determined to keep up appearances . . .'

'Audrey said he'd be out between about seven and nine,' Sheila said. 'And I'd best turn up then.'

'Well . . .' Dottie eyed a loudly ticking little ormolu clock on the mantelpiece. 'We've got a couple of hours nearly. You stay here. And then I'll come with you.' She made a comical face. 'For better or worse.'

By the time they had walked up to the Vellacotts' house under a shared umbrella, Sheila was sweating, even in the chill evening, her hands clammy and her legs weak with nerves.

'I feel horrible,' she said to Dottie. 'I think if you weren't here, I'd have turned tail.'

'Quite,' Dottie said. Her face looked small and sharp under the hood of an old bombazine rain-cape. 'Not exactly looking forward to this myself.'

Audrey's motor car was in the drive, shiny with rain, and another car – Terence's – was parked beside it. Sheila hesitated, but assumed Terence would have walked down to the pub.

'Here goes,' she said, pulling on the doorbell.

A few seconds later Audrey opened the door. She had obviously been waiting, primed to rush and open it. She looked utterly taken aback.

'Oh! Is that Miss Freeman?'

'It is,' Dottie said. 'Sheila called in to see me, and I thought the best thing . . .'

'Who is it, Audrey?' Terence's voice rang tetchily from somewhere in the house. Sheila felt herself freeze in horror.

'Oh God.' Audrey was in pieces. 'He didn't go, because of the rain. Oh God . . .' She was dithering from one foot to another. 'What do I do?'

'Well,' Sheila said. 'You might as well let us in, so we can get it over with.'

'You do the talking,' Dottie had said to Sheila. 'It was you she asked to come. I'll just be back-up. Try and look forbidding, that sort of thing.'

As Audrey showed them into the hall and took their wet coats, Terence Richardson came out of the front sitting room. The light in the hall was not on and he was straining to see who was there.

'Ah, ladies! Miss Freeman – this is unexpected! And . . . is that Sheila?' His voice hardened. It was odd enough for Dottie to turn up like this on a wet night, never mind someone who was supposed to be miles away in Birmingham.

Neither of them said anything. They all went into the sitting room, and Sheila knew she had to speak – quickly and decisively. If they started making polite conversation, she might get stuck in it for ever and never say what she had to say. She took up a position in the middle of the room, with Dottie standing firmly beside her. Thank *God* for Dottie, she thought. How awful if she had had to walk into this situation on her own . . .

'Do sit down, everyone!' Terence gestured towards the sofas. 'Don't have to stand on ceremony. What are we drinking, Audrey?'

Sheila suddenly realized, from his tone, that he was actually nervous.

'I don't want to sit down,' she said, keeping her voice calm and neutral. She could see Audrey standing within her vision on her right, her hands clasped by her chest. 'We've just come to say to you . . .'

She stumbled for a moment. Terence sank into his arm-chair with a mocking expression, as if waiting for some female storm-in-a-teacup to erupt over him, which he could then dismiss.

'You need to leave,' Sheila said. 'You need to get out of this house. You must leave Audrey alone. She doesn't want you. She doesn't want to live with you, and she doesn't want to marry you.'

Terence sat back, flabbergasted. A smile spread over his face.

'And from what privileged source have you gleaned this information, pray?' he said, grinning at Audrey.

There was a silence. Audrey was pale and glassy-eyed. She did not contradict anything Sheila had said. The silence became very tense and heavy. Then Dottie stepped forward.

'I knew Jean, don't forget.' She stepped closer to Terence. 'I know what you are. I should have said something years ago. I saw the bruises on her. Saw her waste away, living with you.'

'My former wife died of cancer,' Terence said.

'She died wasting away in the poisonous shadow of *you*,' Dottie replied ferociously. 'You are as the Upas tree – everything dies within your shade. She was a good woman, Jean was. And she should never, ever have married you.'

'And I am not your wife,' Audrey said, in a thin voice. 'I don't want to be your wife, Terence. At first I thought we might get along well. I thought you were a nice man. But you're not. You're a bully and a con man. And now . . . I don't want to live with you. I don't want to marry you. I don't want you telling me what to do about my own sons, what to do with my money, my house, my clothes . . .' Her voice rose almost to a scream. 'I want you to get out and leave me alone! Leave my house and don't ever come near me again, d'you hear?'

There was no mistaking that she meant what she said. Sheila felt a weight fall from her. All she had had to do was open up the way, and Audrey had made tracks along it.

Terence Richardson looked at the three of them, lined up against him. His lips were clenched shut like a trapdoor. He had started to swell with rage, but he could not seem to think of anything to say.

'You'd better collect your things and go back to your own house,' Dottie said. 'And make no mistake. Everyone in the village will be told what you've been up to: the way you have duped Audrey – and them. We shall be watching you.'

'And if you come back here, I'll call the police,' Audrey said.

Terence Richardson stood up and left the room, tight-lipped. They heard him climbing the stairs.

'Don't worry, dear,' Dottie said. 'We'll stay until he's gone.'

'I'm staying the night anyway,' Sheila said.

'And we must give you a lift home, Miss Freeman.' Audrey was shaking and, at last, her face crumpled. She came to Sheila, holding her arms out. 'Oh, Sheila, I feel such a complete ninny. Thank you – both – so much!'

Thirty-Seven

'Joy!' She heard Martin's voice come to her up the stairs that Sunday afternoon, sounding happy and amused.

'Is it Hank?' She slipped her feet hurriedly into her shoes, which were creamy-white with a slim heel, snatched a look in the mirror – her hair, longer now, pinned back and hanging in waves, her favourite yellow frock that she knew Hank liked as well, her eyes dancing as she smiled at herself – then pulled her cream cardigan around her and tripped lightly down the stairs.

'Come and see this!' Martin was at the front door and stood back to let her past.

'Hey, baby!'

Hank, one foot resting on the kerb, looking solid and muscular in his Army uniform, was grinning at her from the seat of a Norton motorcycle, his teeth glinting in the sun.

'Fancy coming for a spin, little lady?'

Joy gasped, bursting out laughing. 'Where did you get that? And petrol as well!'

'Oh, belongs to a neighbour of ours in Pheasey. Feller says he hardly uses it since the war – only to get to work sometimes. A little bartering got me the use of it for the day, and a ration of gas! Coming?'

'I'll go, if you don't want to!' Martin said.

'Go on then.' Joy gave him a push. 'I've just done my hair. Give Mart a spin first, while I work up the courage.'

Martin, not needing to be asked twice, hopped on,

gathering up his long legs to ride pillion and smiling from ear to ear as he hung on to Hank, who sailed off, waving, along the street.

'What was all that about?' Ann came out of the kitchen, wiping her hands on a tea towel.

'Hank, he's taken Mart for a ride on his motorbike – well, someone's motorbike, anyway. It's swell!'

Ann gave her a look, then peered along the street, but the pair of them had already disappeared.

'He's quite a feller, that Hank, isn't he?'

They were not gone long. While Joy was waiting at the door, she saw Jeanette coming up the street.

'Hello, Joy,' she started to say, as the bike came roaring back towards them and braked outside the house so sharply that Martin almost tumbled off.

'Hey, easy there!' Hank said. 'Sorry, it's taking me a while to get used to this here machine.'

'It's OK – that was super!' Martin was laughing. Joy hardly ever remembered seeing him so lit up. 'I'm going to save up and get my own one day.'

'Oh no, you're not, they're dangerous,' Ann said, coming outside. But she was smiling.

Joy saw her father following on. He always enjoyed Hank's visits. Ann went inside with Jeanette, and Joy stood leaning in the doorway as the three men talked about motorcycles and engines and fuel use. She was half-amused – it was nice to see Dad and Martin getting on, and that they liked Hank – and half-irritated. Hank had come to see her, hadn't he?

'Go on, lad, take it round the back while we have our dinner,' Len said eventually. 'It'd be terrible if someone made off with it – specially as it's not yours.'

Once the motorbike had been safely stowed, Hank came back and took Joy in his arms.

'Hi there, sugar.' He kissed her, then smiled down at her. 'I'll take you out on it for a spin later, my beautiful baby!'

'The hungry gap'll be over soon and we'll have our own spuds, I hope,' Ann said, sharing out the roast potatoes on to everyone's plates. 'But I managed to get just enough – they're a bit old and ropey now though.'

'They look marvellous, Ann; don't go apologizing,' Len said, with such warmth that she looked at him, startled. 'You always do a good Sunday roast, rationing or no rationing.'

Everyone made noises of agreement around the table. Jeanette and Martin jokingly clinked their water glasses together, and Hank offered his to Joy to do the same.

'No Sheila?' Hank said. 'And the little ones?'

'Ah well, now there's a story.' Ann looked round to check that everyone had all they needed and sat down. 'Sheila's with her friend down south, and Elaine and Robbie are along the road with their grandparents. There's been a bit of a to-do. I went out and phoned Sheila last night, down at Audrey's – everything seems to be all right.'

She explained about Audrey and Terence Richardson.

'Oh my!' Hank said, seeming astonished by this carry-on.

'You don't think he'll come back, do you – start making a nuisance of himself all over again?' Jeanette asked.

'Our Sheila's sorted him out, by the sound of things,' Len said, chewing hungrily on a mouthful of tough beef.

'With some help from a neighbour,' Ann went on. 'From what Sheila said, Audrey's telling everyone now that they're not married and that Terence tried to force her into it. He can't really come back after that, can he?'

'Well,' Jeanette said doubtfully, 'I hope she's safe. You never know, with men like that.'

Ann looked at her, startled again by the close knowledge of life that Jeanette had, which she had never suspected before.

'Sheila's going to stay down there a few days, I think,' Joy said. 'To make sure things settle down.'

Len looked along the table at Ann. 'You'd never've thought it of our Sheila, would you?' He smiled at Jeanette. 'She always used to be a timid sort.'

'How things have changed,' Ann said.

As they talked, Joy felt Hank reach for her hand under the table. He turned and looked so directly into her eyes that her skin began to tingle. She felt full of a terrible tension – between the past and what she had now – and then a sudden feeling of falling, of surrender. If Alan was alive and still loved her, wanted her, he would have let her know somehow. And here was Hank, so loving and fun, so much liked by her family that he already felt a part of it. What else could she do but accept that he was her future, however much she grieved for Alan? Perhaps this was what was really meant to be. She looked deep into Hank's eyes and smiled back at him.

'Come on now, sugar – I didn't get hold of this motorcycle for nothing,' Hank said, once the dinner was cleared away.

Joy put her head round the door of the front room. The adults were sinking into a snoozy Sunday-afternoon restfulness, sprawling, looking satisfied and sleepy in their chairs.

'We're going out for a spin,' she said.

'Have a lovely time!' Jeanette looked up at Joy, startling her by giving her a little wink.

'You go careful, my lad,' Ann said to Hank, pretending to be fierce.

Hank popped his head in to the room, above Joy's. 'I'll take good care of her, Mrs Gilby – don't you worry.'

'Help, I'm going to fall off!' Joy squealed, perched on the back of the Norton, clinging to Hank for dear life with one arm, and trying to keep her skirt from blowing up and showing her knickers to the world with the other.

'No you're not – just hold on there.' Hank's words came in snatches in the wind as they careered down Linden Road, heading south.

At first, sheltering behind Hank's back, Joy tried not to look out at everything whizzing by at terrifying speed. But gradually they settled to a fast, but not too alarming rate of travel, or maybe she had simply got used to it. The houses thinned out. No one much was around now, so she didn't have to worry about anyone seeing her underwear. She put both arms round Hank, started to peer around him and let the wind take her hair – and enjoy it. It felt wonderful!

Where are we going? she wanted to shout, but it was so hard being heard in the wind and she realized she did not care very much where they were heading. It was exhilarating: the warm sunlight on her face and the wind rushing past her cheeks. The solid figure of Hank in her arms, and her feeling of trusting him completely, warmed her heart. If this was what life was offering, this loving man, could she accept it?

Thinking of Alan made her feel guilty all the time. But as Nanna Margaret had said to her the other day, 'It's hard for you, bab, but it's no use pining for a life beyond the grave.' The words had shocked her, sinking down in her like a stone. If only she could be absolutely sure Alan was never coming back – that was the worst of it. But now, after all this time, she knew that her grandmother was right and she was grateful to her.

Hank parked the bike by an ivy-covered wall on a narrow village street and they set off to wander the lanes. Joy had hardly been out of Birmingham – only to the seaside in North Devon a couple of times. Hank was absolutely fascinated by the curving little main street and the old houses of the pretty village.

'Look at that!' He stood in awe, gazing at a cottage at the edge of the village, its thatched roof mossy and neglected-looking. 'I've never seen a house like that before. You know oftentimes, when our boys see any place in England, we compare it to the States. "Oh, Birmingham, it's like Detroit" or "It's like Pittsburgh." But I can't think of any place that I can say is like this.'

'It's so old, I suppose. Do you think you could live here?'

The words popped out of her mouth and Joy found a blush seeping through her cheeks. This day – when she could feel herself sinking into acceptance of things with this kindly, handsome man, who was head over heels in love with her – her own mind seemed to be running ahead of her. If she was to commit herself to Hank, to marry him, did that mean her having to leave home, leave her country and travel to that huge unknown, the US of A? Following your husband to wherever he needed to go was the normal thing. It seemed unthinkable. But might it be that Hank would love England so much that he would stay over here?

Hank seemed to sense the meaning behind her question. He put his arm around her and pulled her close. Joy wrapped her arms around him as he looked down at her, his expression so solemn that something in her shifted, like a pang or a melting feeling. *He's so nice . . . I love him. I do.*

'I'm an American, Joy. That's my home and that's where I belong. I can't imagine living anyplace else – that's the truth. And it's a fine place: you'd love it there.'

She looked up at him, scared and excited. Might she love it, that great land across the sea, which was full, it seemed to her, of music and the pictures and dancing? And she could feel herself letting go, little by little and falling towards him.

Hank leaned down and gently kissed her on the lips.

'Let's look around a little more, shall we?'

They explored lanes full of spring promise and birdsong, crossed a brook and walked along a rise at the edge of a wood, the land sloping away gently to their right. Hank was telling her more about his family: his mother, two sisters and kid brother. His father, who he had lost so young, had also been a dentist.

'I sorta went into the family firm,' he said. 'It's not a bad life – there's always someone who needs you, that's for sure. My uncle runs our family's practice, Eklund Brothers – I guess I'll take it over one day, if I get out of all this alive.'

He spoke lightly, but Joy felt a stab of ice in her heart, the realities of the war crashing into this warm, peaceful afternoon.

'It sure is lovely,' Hank said, before she could think of a reply. They stopped to look out. There was a farm in the far distance, the fresh green lines of new crops across the fields.

'It doesn't feel as if there's a war on at all, does it?' Joy said. They could see no signs of the war from here – no barrage balloons, no blackout, nothing except the gently rolling landscape dotted with farms, as it must always have been.

'Let's take a look at that.' Hank pointed at a building down in the dip at the bottom of the slope. It was a brick barn with a mossy-green tiled roof.

Joy glanced at him and Hank gave her a mischievous little smile. They joined hands and started to walk down through the long tufty grass.

There were a few greying end-of-the-winter bales left in the barn. With the doors closed, the only light slanted in from a high, square window at the far end, illuminating a small area of the floor, scattered with dusty old straw.

'Come on, baby!' Hank tugged at Joy's hand and they ran over to the bales, started playing like children, jumping from bale to bale and arranging the dozen or so that were left into a little nest, or a fortress, by the shadowy back wall of the barn.

'Ugh! D'you think there are lots of spiders?' Joy said, shuddering.

'Oh, I'm sure there are a whole lot of great, big' – he made teasing movements with his hands – 'hairy ones!' He tickled her neck and Joy screamed, then clapped her hand over her mouth, laughing hysterically.

'What if someone comes?'

Hank took off his jacket, laid it on the fusty straw, then threw himself down on it, holding out his hand to her.

'Can't be worse than a bomb, or some German feller with a gun, can it? We'll just have to tuck up behind here . . . C'm'ere, Joy – I want to kiss you real bad.'

She stood smiling down at him. Memories flashed in her mind for a few seconds: her last, tender kiss with Alan in the rain outside Cadbury's; Lawrence, in that hotel room, lifting her dress over her head . . . And, looking down at Hank, her body was alive with desire.

Keeping her eyes – eyes that said, *Yes, we are alive, this is now* – fixed on his, she lay down beside him, sweeping all memories from her mind.

'Oh, my baby,' he murmured, his lips moving towards hers. 'My beautiful baby – my own queen . . .'

Thirty-Eight

Sheila lay in bed in the familiar room in Audrey's house. And for once she could sink into sleep, sure of not being woken sometime in the night. On the other hand, she ached from missing Elaine and Robbie, the feel of their little bodies, their voices . . . But when she had spoken to her mother on the telephone last evening, Ann had reassured Sheila that the two of them were having a lovely time with Nanna Margaret and that all was well.

And tomorrow she would be back on the train to Birmingham and would be able to see them by the early afternoon. She pulled the bedclothes up closer around her and luxuriated in Audrey's comfortable mattress, a muzziness overcoming her, and her eyes closed . . .

'Sheila!'

She jarred awake, gasping in fright. Someone was patting her arm.

'Sorry.' Audrey was whispering close to her ear. 'I'd put the light on, but I think someone's in the house. I can hear noises downstairs.'

'Oh my God.' Sheila was wide awake now, her entire body pulsing. She felt a bit sick after waking so suddenly.

Audrey sat on the edge of the bed. Sheila could see, from the faintest change in the light, that the bedroom door was ajar. As they both sat so still, Sheila was sure she could hear the sound of her own rushing blood.

'Did he give his keys back?' She thought Terence Richardson had done, but suppose he had spares?

'Yes.' Audrey laid her hand over Sheila's. 'Thank heaven you're here – again.'

Sheila wanted to say, *I thought this might happen*, but it was better not to speak. A little sound came from downstairs, she thought. Was she imagining it? Perhaps a door being opened, stealthily.

'What the hell does he want?' Sheila whispered. 'If it *is* him. It might be a burglar!'

'Can you hear it?' Audrey's nails dug into her hand.

'Think so.' Sheila stood up. 'We need to go down, not sit here like ducks waiting for him. I wish we had something – you know, like a stick or . . .'

'Here.' Audrey got up and went closer to the door. A moment later she came back and took Sheila's hand, guiding it on to something, some kind of handle with a metallic thing around it.

'What the hell is that?'

'It's a sword. From the Boer War. Maurice had it in his study. He didn't think to take it, so I've had it in my bedroom. You know, in case of intruders.'

'Oh my!' Sheila almost got the giggles, imagining the two of them prancing about with this heavy great thing.

'You carry it,' Audrey instructed. 'You're much braver than me, where he's concerned.'

With no option but to take charge, Sheila pulled the bedroom door open. Her eyes were completely used to the darkness now and there was a faint light from the high window over the stairs, which Audrey had never blacked out – they just left the hall lights off instead. As she reached the landing, Sheila heard footsteps moving stealthily along the hall. She jumped back inside as if she had been shocked, her heart pounding crazily.

'He's down there.' Her mouth was right by Audrey's ear.

As they stood, frozen to the spot, the footsteps started to advance up the staircase. Sheila's mind was in a turmoil of panic. I'll wait to see what he does, she thought. If he tries to come in here . . .

The footsteps reached the top of the stairs, but they kept moving past, along the landing leading to Audrey's bedroom at the end. Sheila squeezed Audrey's arm to indicate that she was moving and slipped out through the door, opening it wide to make sure she did not clank the sword against it. Holding the weight of it with two hands, the long blade pointing upwards, she crept along the landing.

He went, as she expected, to the door of Audrey's bedroom. It was darkest at that end of the landing and she could only sense and hear, rather than see, him at the door, the tiny scratch of sound as the handle turned and he started to push the door open.

'What the hell d'you think you're *doing*?'

The screech came out of her mouth with such force that she hardly knew herself. She lunged forward and felt the tip of the sword come up against something that gave slightly. As a male voice let out a tremendous yell – 'Stop! What's that?' – Audrey leapt forward and opened the door of the next room, switching on the light, which flooded on to the landing.

The three of them were arranged in a triangle: Audrey, beside Sheila, who was clinging for dear life to the sword handle, its tip having nicked the substantial tweed of Terence Richardson's suit. By the look on his face, it had gone far in enough to cause him discomfort. He had his hands in the air as if Sheila was holding a gun.

As soon as he realized who was there, he lowered his arms and a contemptuous expression came over his face. He went to grab at the sword, but Sheila leaned on it and shoved it in a bit further until he gasped.

'What're you doing here?' she roared at him. 'You lying, scheming . . .' She searched for a bad enough word.

'Bastard!' Audrey finished for her. She stepped forward. 'What were you going to do? Come into my room and hit me, like you did your wife? Rape me, like you men do? Taking what you want, with no care for anyone's else's wishes, you foul, dirty beast!' She was the one shrieking now. 'Did you come to terrify me? Is that what makes you feel like a proper man? Is it?'

Even Sheila was startled. Audrey was beside herself. She went right up close to Terence.

'You're *disgusting*. You're a two-faced, deceitful bully and I'm going to telephone the police and have you removed from my house. And preferably from this village!'

'Oh, Aud, do cut out the hysterics,' Terence said contemptuously, though Sheila could hear panic in his voice. 'Look, get this thing off me. There's no need for this.'

'Oh, I think there is,' Sheila disagreed, still leaning some of her weight on the metal, so that he could not escape the point drilling into his upper belly. She sent up a prayer of thanks that she seemed to have shoved it in just far enough so that Terence did not dare move while she was bearing down on him.

'Look, enough of all this drama.' He tried to put on an appeasing voice. 'I only came to fetch the last few of my things, that's all.'

But Audrey was on her way to the telephone.

'She's unbalanced, you know,' Terence was saying. 'She says the most ridiculous things that simply aren't true. And that Freeman woman – very eccentric. Utterly unreliable.'

'Oh, shut up,' Sheila said. She could hear Audrey's voice downstairs, insisting urgently that someone come:

now. This was a new Audrey, and Sheila marvelled, even as she waited nervously with a squirming Terence pinned to the wall.

'Right, they're on their way,' Audrey said, coming up the stairs. 'Can he get away?' she said to Sheila.

Sheila shook her head grimly and leaned a little harder.

'No – stop, please,' Terence said in a constricted voice. 'I'm bleeding. I'll have you for assault. You could do serious organ damage.'

'It's a surface wound, you fool,' Sheila said, hoping to goodness that was true. A dark stain had appeared on his shirt.

'They said they'd be twenty minutes,' Audrey said. 'Shall I make a cup of tea?'

Sheila looked incredulously at her. 'What? No! Stay here and help me hold this flipping sword – it's heavy!'

An hour later the two of them sat in Sheila's bedroom with cups of cocoa instead of tea.

'I've never seen you like that before,' Sheila said.

'Nor me.' Audrey was still looking shocked. 'It just came pouring out somehow. I hate him. Hate *all* of them.'

'Not all men?' Sheila said, a bit shocked.

'All the ones I've had anything much to do with,' Audrey replied bitterly. She was sitting with her knees drawn up, sideways-on against the pillows, facing Audrey. 'Mind you, that policeman was rather nice.' She smiled suddenly, as if in wonder at the night's events. She started giggling. 'Seeing Terence in handcuffs!'

The constable who had arrived, after being told of Terence's intrusion as well as his attempts at forced marriage and deception, had ushered him into his car.

'And you with that sword – like, I don't know, Boadicea or someone!'

They both laughed, letting out a lot of the tension.

'D'you think it'll be in the papers?' Sheila asked.

Audrey reached round and put her cup down. 'The local paper anyway,' she said, with a wicked expression coming over her face. 'I think I'd better make sure it is, don't you?'

Sheila looked at the sword, lying on the floor at the side of the room.

'And that ought to go in pride of place over the fireplace!'

Thirty-Nine

Late May

Joy sat snuggled up to Hank in the back of the US Army truck, along with some other Army lads, including Hank's friend Joe Litsky, whom Joy always found fun to have around, and the girls who had come along to the dance. At the moment, though, Joe was enthusiastically kissing his dance partner, a girl with strong black hair and an interesting face called Ella.

'Um, that was *such* a good night,' Joy murmured to Hank, her arms around him, her head against his chest. Her cheeks were hot from all the exertion – they had all been to the dance in town – and she felt tired in a lovely, satisfying way. 'You know,' she looked up at him in the gloom, 'in the summer they're having the "Holidays at Home" at Rowheath again. There're lots of dances – it'll be fun!'

Hank was quiet, which was unlike him, as he was usually enthusiastic about everything.

Joy drew back, squinting, trying to see the expression on his face. 'Anything wrong: was it something I said?'

Hank stroked her back. He seemed to be looking at her with sudden seriousness. When he spoke, it was in a very quiet voice, so that she had to strain to hear it over the noise of the truck.

'Baby, thing is . . . it's all confidential. We don't know much and, what we do, we're not supposed to say. But something's coming – and it's coming soon, I reckon, the way things look.'

'But . . .' She realized she had not given any of this enough thought. 'You're a dentist! You won't be going anywhere, will you? I thought you were in a sort of . . . replacement camp, and you just send people out when they need more men.'

'We do. But, honey, they need dentists near the Front as well. No guy's gonna fight well with toothache.'

She sat, shocked. This again: loving someone and them disappearing, perhaps for ever. Tears forced up inside her and she swallowed them away. No, don't spoil this time now, she told herself. There'll be plenty of time to cry afterwards.

Hank squeezed her shoulders. 'It's rough, I know. But I love you – and I'll be back for you.'

Her eyes filled then. 'You promise?'

'Oh, baby, none of that.' He got out a handkerchief and gently wiped her eyes.

'I love you, Hank.'

'And I love you too. And I'm gonna come back.' He kept his lips close to her ear, speaking in a sweet, soothing way. He seemed so much older than her suddenly. 'I'm gonna come back and sweep you away with me to Philly and make you my wife. And we'll have a lovely house with a big yard, and kids and . . . You're gonna love it.'

'This the place?' The driver shouted back over his shoulder. 'Beaumont Road?'

'Yes!' Joy called, jarred. Now this meant they would have to say goodbye and she might never see Hank again. They jumped down from the back and Hank went round to the driver.

'Give me a few minutes to say goodbye to the little lady, will you, pal?'

The driver nodded solemnly, as he too understood that this might be a real parting, and not just a goodbye until the next dance. 'Everyone happy in the back?' he called over his shoulder.

There were contented sounds from the entwined couples inside.

'OK, we're gonna take a raincheck.' He crunched the gears, ready to move the truck closer to the kerb. 'Ten minutes, pal, and then I'm leaving.'

For a moment Joy and Hank stood at a loss, by the front door.

'Is there anywhere more private we could go?' Hank asked.

'Come on.' Joy tugged on his hand. 'I know where we can go!' In the dusky light she led him through the garden gate and along the path.

'Hey,' Hank laughed. 'Where're we going?'

'In here . . .' She had to shove hard to get the door of the air-raid shelter open. 'We haven't spent a night in here for a while now. I expect it'll be all damp, but . . .'

'Oh my!' Hank had to fold almost in half to get inside. He was astonished. 'You all slept in here?'

'We tried to. There are still a couple of old cushions,' she started to say.

'Baby, come here.'

He was already taking her in his arms. Both of them knew why they were here, each of them full of a frank, urgent desire that would not be thwarted, however uncomfortable the place. They had only been able to make love once before, in the warm straw-bed shadows of the barn. Now they were soon to be torn away from each other. Hank was kissing her hungrily, his hands inching her skirt higher and higher.

'Oh, baby, let me . . . just let me. I love you so . . .'

Swiftly Joy removed her underwear and a moment later they were on the narrow, hard little bench, and Hank was moving inside her, fast and urgent, both of their desires peaking fast and intensely. It all happened so quickly that afterwards she could hardly believe it had not been a dream, and they were replacing their clothes, hot and dazed, and Hank kept saying, 'Oh, Joy – oh, my baby.'

They had a tender moment to hold each other, close and still.

'I'm coming back for you,' he said. 'You're my gal.'

'I'll wait for you.' She pulled him in tight. 'I love you. Love you. Love you.' In that moment she meant it with all her heart.

'I have to go . . .'

Holding hands, they crossed the garden again.

'I haven't said goodbye to your folks,' Hank said.

It felt as if they had been away in another world, for a long time, but no one seemed impatient when they reappeared. Hank knocked on the front door, and everyone came out to wave him off. Sheila was home again, and Mom and Dad and Martin all called goodbyes and good lucks, as Hank kissed Joy again, waved and climbed back into the truck.

'What a nice boy,' Mom said.

'Yeah, good lad,' Dad agreed.

Joy, her body still tingling from their love-making, feeling sad and joyful and strange, stood with her family and waved. As the truck lumbered away along the street and turned the corner, she felt her mother's arm steal around her shoulders and give her a squeeze. They looked at each other for a moment and Joy smiled at her, suddenly full of gratitude. What a mother I have, she thought. All her mistakes, all the mess and muddle of this family – but because of all that, I know she understands.

*

Sheila, though, was less sympathetic.

'I don't understand you,' she said that night, even while Joy was still feeling raw and, once again, as if a piece of her had been torn away. The two little ones were asleep and the women of the house were all together downstairs. 'You just move from one man to another as if they're pieces of clothing.'

'Sheila!' Ann said. 'What a terrible thing to say! I know you're worried because you haven't heard from Kenneth, but there's no need to take it out on Joy.'

Sheila sat perched on the edge of the chair, holding an empty cocoa cup. Since she had come back from Audrey's – and everyone had been very impressed by the part she had played in that carry-on – she had been tense and bad-tempered.

'I only meant, I thought you were going to wait for Alan? That he was the love of your life. And then suddenly . . .'

Joy was so stunned and hurt by this attack that she could not speak – for the true guilt she felt, and because she was so close to tears.

'Sheila, Joy hasn't heard from Alan for well over a year. What does that tell you? The ones who've been taken as prisoners of war, they can write home. So what explanation can there be?' Ann glanced nervously at Joy, because it felt unkind to spell it out. 'Other than . . .'

'Either he's dead or he hates me,' Joy burst out. 'If he was alive, Alan would have written to me by now, somehow – I know he would!'

Sheila looked a bit ashamed of herself. 'Sorry, Sis. That wasn't nice of me.' She seemed close to tears herself now. 'I'm so worried about Kenneth. He writes every week usually, and I haven't heard a thing. It's just . . . if it was me, I'd wait, that's all.'

'Yes, well, it's not you, is it?' Joy snapped. 'Do I have to spend my whole life waiting for someone who's not coming back? Hank loves me and he's promised we'll get married. And I . . .' She started crying. 'I want some life, while I'm young.'

'Oh dear, oh dear,' Ann said, as both her daughters sat sobbing. 'Come here – both of you.' She pulled them over to the sofa and put her arms round them so that they were all in a big huddle, stroking their backs as Sheila and Joy let out their pent-up emotions. 'You poor girls. We thought the last war would be the end of all this.'

She comforted them until they stopped crying and could wipe their faces. Sheila and Joy looked at each other, both of them apparently having the same thought.

'Mom,' Joy asked guardedly. 'How's Mr . . . How's Tom?' She thought she saw her mother flinch.

'You speak to him, don't you?' Sheila asked.

Ann hesitated.

'We're not angry, Mom,' Joy said. She thought for a moment. 'Least, I don't think I am – mostly.'

'I do, sometimes,' Ann said carefully. 'He's a good friend.'

Joy and Sheila exchanged looks, but did not say any more. They all held hands and sat in a loving silence.

Forty

August

Ann and Jeanette were working away side by side in the waterside hut, cutting sheets of rubber to cover the petrol tanks. The door was open, letting in the warm air. Ann glanced across at Jeanette, who had started humming to herself. The more she got to know her, the more she liked Jeanette and found herself surprised by her. Jeanette had seemed a bit of a mouse – especially when they were young girls. But she realized now that Jeanette had a rod of steel for a backbone and was more worldly than her pale, quiet looks ever gave away.

'People will say we're in love . . .' The song Jeanette was humming threaded its way to her through the other noise and chatter. One or two of the other women started to join in, singing snatches of the words. Jeanette's face was pink, happy-looking and Ann thought suddenly, She's changed – there's something going on here that she's not telling me. I wonder who he is!

With a powerful ache, she was taken back to that hospital ward at Fircroft, the house the Cadburys gave over as a military convalescent hospital during the last war. Those tremulous days when she first met Tom, when she sat with him as he began to mourn what had been left of his body and spirit at Gallipoli. Those days when, quite unexpectedly, they had begun to love each other, having no idea how long and through what troubles it would last – even until now. Only two days ago she had heard his dear voice on the telephone. She was a shameful woman and wife, but life was too short and fragile not to spend some of it hearing Tom speak – and not just in letters. Especially considering all that had happened with Marianne.

She felt badly that Jeanette knew none of this. She must see us Gilbys as a happy bunch – a model family, Ann thought. But at least it now seemed as if Jeanette was finding something for herself. Who could it be, and how did she find the time?

'You ever seen *Oklahoma*?' she asked, partly to distract herself.

Jeanette looked round at her, smiling. 'No – my mom had a record though. She liked show tunes. We used to sing along. *The Band Wagon* and all those shows. "Dancing in the Dark" was her favourite song. Funny, really.' Her face sobered and hardened suddenly. 'Knowing what my dad was like, I don't s'pose she ever danced like that with anyone – in the dark or in the light.'

Ann was trying to think of something to say to this when a shout came from the doorway, their foreman running, lit up with excitement and talking before he had even got inside the hut.

'Heard the news, ladies? They've liberated Paris! The German garrison's surrendered!'

There were whoops and cheers all round. Ann and Jeanette linked hands and jumped up and down like children. Some good news at last!

'Anyroad, it's time for a break, you lucky lot – go and get yerselves a cuppa. Quick sharp lively!'

As they streamed over to the main building, chattering excitedly, Ann saw Joy heading over for her break as well.

'Heard the news, love?' she asked her.

Joy seemed to surface from a dream, as if she was miles away. Unlike everyone else, she looked pale and miserable.

'Oh, yeah,' she said absent-mindedly.

Ann felt for her. The poor kid had been put through such a lot – first, Alan, and now not knowing where Hank was. The list of casualties from the invasions on D-Day grew and grew. No wonder the poor girl was looking down-in-the-mouth. She put her arm around Joy's shoulder for a moment.

'It'll be all right, sweetheart – you'll see. We're winning, at last. And he'll come home to you.'

Joy looked at her, gave a wan smile and a nod, then looked away again.

Hank had been right. After he and Joy had had their impulsive, passionate parting, all leave was cancelled and soon afterwards everyone destined for the Normandy invasion was moved to the south coast.

As soon as news came of the invasions – the daily activities measured from 6 June as 'D plus one', or two or six – Joy had been filled with a heavy sense of doom. She had begun to give her heart to Hank and now, she felt sure, she would never see him again. It was not meant to be. Once again she was stripped bare, left with all her emotions spilling out like some disembowelled creature.

'He won't make it, I know he won't,' she had sobbed at home, back in June when the numbers grew and grew, of men lost in the terrible struggles on to the beaches from their landing craft, then inland, fired upon by the Germans.

'He's a dentist,' Sheila pointed out, trying to comfort her. 'He's not in the infantry.'

'But he'll still have had to get off that boat somehow,' Joy sobbed. She reacted angrily to anyone who tried to comfort her, because she felt so helpless. She had very little idea of how any of it worked, regarding who came off which ships and when. 'They're not going to *not* shoot him just because he's a dentist!'

After a month she finally had a card from Hank, saying he was safe. She lay on her bed and sobbed her heart out. These days it was as if she could not get any control of her emotions – she kept dissolving into tears and felt irritable and scratchy over the slightest thing.

'She's fretting about him.' She heard her mother and father discussing her changes of mood in the kitchen one morning when she came down. Joy hovered outside the door. 'She's had enough worry with Alan – and now Hank going off as well, the poor lamb.'

'Ah, I s'pose she has,' Dad said. There was a silence and then he added quietly, 'It's been quite a time, hasn't it?'

There was a silence and Joy could imagine her mother looking across at him and rolling her eyes, as if to say, *You can say that again.* But even loaded with her own sadness, she could sense a new gentleness between her parents.

She pushed the door open and they both looked round.

'All right, babby?' her father said, in such tender tones that she almost burst into tears there and then.

'Yeah,' she said croakily. 'Any tea on the go?'

Ann reached for the teapot, but she was still staring at her. '*Are* you all right, love?'

'*Yes.* I've just said so, haven't I?'

She sat down at the table with the cup of tea, feeling them exchanging glances over her head.

It was only a couple of weeks later, as the summer passed into August, with the grass browning and the light changing, that it began to dawn on Joy that for two months now she had not bled, and that all the mysterious feelings she had been having were not simply worry and loss, but something else altogether that was going on in her body.

By halfway through September she was sure. Three monthlies missed, a funny taste in her mouth, sometimes feeling dizzy when she stood at work, and queasiness – something she had put down to strain. The day that she faced up to it, she got out of bed with stomach ache and had to rush to the lavatory. It felt as if everything in her body was being disrupted. She sat feeling hot and strange. Was she just poorly in some other way? Weren't you supposed to be sick every morning, regular as clockwork, when you were in the family way?

But she knew, really. It was all beginning to add up.

Those fast, passionate few moments with Hank – even now her body flushed with desire at the thought – and now she had a piece of him for ever. Standing at the basin after washing her hands, she burst into tears again, lost in a collision of love and panic.

Wiping her eyes, she leaned closer to the mirror. Her dark eyes looked tragically back at her, her lashes pearled with tears, her hair rumpled over her shoulders. 'What in heaven's name are we going to do?' she asked her reflection.

'Joy? Can I come in?'

Sheila stood at her bedroom door a few evenings later. She had come up from the kitchen, still wearing an apron, as if driven suddenly by the need to speak. Today a letter had come from Kenneth, flooding her with relief, and she had more space and kindness to take in her sister's misery.

Joy, lying exhausted on her bed after a day at work, was struck by the way Sheila spoke to her. She had become rather bossy lately, but now she was talking in a humble, careful tone.

'Yes. What's the matter?' Joy half-sat up, then sank back as her sister came to sit on the bed.

Sheila thought for a moment, frowning. 'You know that day when we heard about Mom – when she was in hospital?' She spoke gently.

'After the bomb, yeah?' Joy said, bewildered.

'And we went through her things and found . . . you know: "Tom" and everything?'

Even though they knew about Tom, they both still spoke of him as if he was someone in a story that was not quite real.

Joy nodded.

'It was . . . I mean, we found out things' – Sheila was stumbling to find the words, hands clasped in her lap on the flowery apron – 'that we didn't expect. Didn't want to know, really. It was like that with Audrey; she couldn't admit what was really happening with her husband, Maurice, not for a long time anyway.'

She looked round at Joy, as if seizing her courage.

'It's no good, is it? Things have to come out in the end. We're all frightened of what people will say. And there's plenty will judge and tittle-tattle – but not the ones that really know you or care about you. And, from what I can see, their nasty words won't kill you.'

'Sticks and stones . . .'

'Yes, exactly.'

Their eyes met. A pulse of time passed. Joy felt her throat swell, emotion waiting to escape.

'How far gone are you?' Sheila leaned over and touched her hand. 'I know the signs.'

Joy sat up, slowly, glad it was Sheila she was having this conversation with, not Mom, even though she already sensed that her mother would not turn against her. How could she?

'We only did it twice,' she whispered. 'And the first time he used one of those . . . you know. But then' – she looked down, embarrassed – 'that night he came to say goodbye, we . . . well, we'd just been in the Anderson, quick like.'

Sheila's eyes widened. 'You brazen hussy!' she exclaimed, but fondly. Both of them exploded into desperate giggles. 'And that time you didn't . . .'

Joy looked up at her and shook her head.

'Oh, Joy, you stupid flaming idiot.' Sheila took her sister's hand between both of hers, half-tender, half-fierce. 'You're not going to be able to hide it much longer. We're going to have to tell Mom – and soon.'

Forty-One

'God Almighty,' was Mom's first reaction, sharp and worried. 'Are you sure?'

Sheila and Joy had cornered her in the front room when the men were both out of the way. It was one of those 'Sit down, Mom' moments. Sheila and Joy had sat side by side on the settee, and Ann had sunk down on the chair opposite them. Their faces had immediately told of something serious. Ann had braced herself. Now what?

'Oh, you stupid girl!' she burst out first of all, then counted urgently on her fingers. 'You must be due about . . . February?'

Joy, staring down at her feet, nodded numbly. 'I s'pose so.'

Ann didn't feel angry, she realized as she looked back into her daughters' strained faces. Not with Joy. Was she supposed to rage and cast her from the house – that was what many a mother would do? But she was only angry with fate. She felt worried to death for Joy. And tired. Very tired.

'You blithering idiot,' she repeated.

'That's what I said,' Sheila agreed.

'Oh, Joy.' Ann sat back and sighed out a long breath. She was reeling. 'Flaming Ada. Just give me a minute to take this in!'

Her eyes rested on Joy's sad, frightened face. Dear God, those weeks when she had first known she was expecting Martin – another man's child! At least she had had a marriage to hide behind, and could pretend it was Len's. But where did pretending anything get you, in the end? She got up and knelt in front of her daughter and put her arms around her.

'Come 'ere, you daft 'apeth. It'll be all right.'

'Will it?' Joy looked around at her, her tears starting to flow. 'How can you say that, Mom? I'm having a baby, by a man who's probably never coming back, and we're not married!'

'You don't know he's not coming back,' Sheila managed. Ann was struck by how much less rigid she was becoming in her views.

But Joy was too busy sobbing to listen to hope or reason.

Ann stroked her back, thinking that, before the war, all this would have seemed like a mountain blocking all paths – impossible. All the gossip and judgement that went on, over babies born out of wedlock.

'Aren't you cross?' Joy asked, looking like a little girl.

'Oh, bab, I'm long past being cross about anything. And I'm hardly in a position to be, really, am I?'

Ann looked around at her assembled family in the front room, after Sunday dinner: Robbie napping, Elaine playing by the unlit fire, and Margaret and Cyril there too. They had had to bring in a couple of extra chairs. Ann sat herself between Sheila and Joy on the settee.

'Right, I've got something to say to you all.'

'Oh dear,' Martin said with a nervous laugh. 'That doesn't bode well.'

'Let's get it over with,' Cyril said, trying to sound jovial.

Ann felt suddenly even more protective of Joy, as if what she was going to say was necessarily a tragedy. But

even Len did not know yet, and she was nervous of everyone's reactions.

'It's not necessarily a bad thing,' she said.

'Come on – out with it,' Margaret said.

Ann looked at Joy, whose dark eyes were communicat-
ing fearfully with her. Ann saw that Sheila was holding her
hand and she reached for her other one and held it.

'Well, our Joy is expecting a baby. Hank's baby.'

There was a silence, during which Ann could almost
sense everyone in the room rearranging the furniture in
their head to take this in.

'I wondered if it was going to be something like that,'
Margaret said eventually, stiff and disapproving.

'Well,' Cyril said, 'let's hope he can come back and
marry you, bab. Then everything'll be all right, won't it?'

Joy burst into tears at this.

'Grandad,' Sheila said, urgently, 'she can't know if
Hank will or he won't, can she?'

'I just mean it'll be hard for her – if he doesn't,' Cyril
said, looking wretched.

'I *like* Hank,' Martin said, as if trying to redirect things
on to a more positive path.

Joy was crying quietly as everyone talked above her
head.

'Look, love,' Margaret said. 'I don't hold with . . . that
sort of behaviour. You know I don't. And there'll be
those—' She stopped, as if deciding not to pursue that train
of thought. 'But times are changing. The war . . . And you
know we're your family and we'll look after you, whatever
happens.'

Cyril made noises of agreement. Margaret sat back. Her
hair was white now and Ann saw an old lady sitting there,
trying to adapt, her tired face settling into determined
lines. She had had so many things to adjust to and was

doing it without bitterness. Moved, Ann honoured the struggle.

'Things aren't as I thought they were meant to be once,' Margaret said, as if reading Ann's thoughts. 'Everything used to have its place. Having a baby out of wedlock was . . . Well, look at what happened to our Lizzie. Ida, as they call her. She doesn't even have her own name any more. And I lost my son to the trenches. I thought we'd had quite enough drama in this family. But I've not turned on your father and mother, for all their . . .' She eyed Ann and Len. 'Well, let's just say "mistakes". Though God knows, that's putting it mildly. And I'm not going to turn on you, either, bab.'

She reached across and patted Joy's arm and handed her a handkerchief.

'I'll pray for you that your young American comes back – he's a good lad. And you deserve some happiness, love. You can count on your grandad and me.'

Cyril was nodding in agreement and Ann saw he had tears in his eyes, which immediately brought them into hers as well.

'Thanks, Nanna,' Joy said, blowing her nose. She looked at her father and saw him nodding at her, unsure what to say. Ann could see from his face that he was on her side – and she would certainly have had things to say to him, if he hadn't been.

'I don't know what you're going to tell them at the works though,' Margaret said. 'You'll not be able to keep that under wraps for too much longer.'

Joy looked at Ann in panic. 'What am I going to do?'

Ann felt a moment of real anguish. Her Cadbury employers set such high standards of behaviour and were so good to people. And now one of this family, who had worked at the firm for several generations, was in a situation that would certainly not be approved of.

'Well,' she said slowly, 'I don't want any of us telling lies – not to Mrs Elizabeth or Miss Dorothy or any of them. You should be able to work for a bit longer. But with that Hank lad as the father, I can't see this baby being a small one! After that, you'll just have to give your notice. I'll leave it up to you to decide what you tell them.'

'Hank did ask me to marry him,' Joy said.

'Here, I'll borrow you this.' Margaret set about twisting her engagement ring off her finger, but her knuckles were swollen and neither of her rings would come off. She stared ruefully at her gnarled hands. 'I'm not sure even a bit of soap's going to shift that.'

Ann smiled. 'Take mine.' She twisted the ring, which Len had once given her, one tiny diamond in its silver setting, and handed it to Joy. A pang went through her, even as she rescued her daughter from more tittle-tattle than necessary. It felt as if she was removing something else, and she did not look at Len as she did it.

Joy carried on at work and seemed to feel a bit better in herself. Ann kept a close eye on her. As a fit, slender young woman, she carried her baby well and for the moment there was nothing too much to see. But it was only a matter of time.

It felt like a small lull before the main storm arrived. This was one thing Ann did confide to both Hilda and Jeanette. Joy and Norma were such old friends. And she already felt that she hid enough from Jeanette.

She did dread telling her though. Even though she realized Jeanette was not such an innocent as she had thought, Ann was surprised by her reaction when she told her. It was the dinner break and they were outside, crossing the bridge over into the girls' grounds at Cadbury's, to enjoy the late-summer sun.

'So,' Ann finished as they entered the pretty green space and she finally looked round at Jeanette. 'That's what's happening. We're all doing our best to stand by Joy. It's no good keeping on, is it?'

She was surprised to see a blush spread across Jeanette's face. There was obviously some complicated emotion going on in her and she gave a peculiar smile, as if she was embarrassed and trying to cover it up. Perhaps she was, Ann realized. After all, men and intimate relations had not seemed to play a large part in Jeanette's life.

'You are a very close family, aren't you?' Jeanette said warmly as they settled on the grass. 'I do admire you.' She gave a sweet smile, then asked, 'What does Len think?'

Ann almost laughed. *What does Len think?* Jeanette had no idea how bleakly funny *that* question was!

'Oh, he's standing by her – course he is,' she said. 'Especially as his mom was so clear about what she thinks.'

'She's a lovely lady,' Jeanette said. She reached into her overall pocket, brought out a hanky and fiddled with it, dabbing her nose.

She was being peculiar, Ann thought. But later, when she told Hilda, she was truly shocked. 'Oh, for heaven's sake,' Hilda said. 'Not her as well?' As if to say, *like mother, like daughter*. But once she had calmed down, she assured Ann that she would not tell anyone and that these things happened. However, Jeanette's reaction now was harder to fathom.

'All I'd ask is that you don't say anything to anyone,' Ann said. 'Joy's still at work for the moment and she doesn't need any trouble, if you know what I mean.'

'Of course,' Jeanette said warmly. She seemed to have

recovered herself and was back to being a kind, easy friend. She touched Ann's hand. 'I wouldn't *dream* of it.'

'All this business,' Ann said, trying to speak lightly. 'What with Sheila worrying about Kenneth, and poor Joy with Alan disappearing like that. I'm only hoping to goodness this is the last thing.'

Even realizing that Jeanette did not know the half of it, this was a wish that turned out to be tempting fate.

It was early September and school had just started again when the letter arrived. Ann, ever alert for a letter from Tom – or, for that matter, from any of her daughters' men – raced to the mat when she heard the post arrive.

The brown, official-looking envelope was addressed to Mr Martin Gilby. An icy feeling gripped Ann. She took it into the kitchen and sat down, staring at this bland rectangle lying on the cloth like a bird of doom. Call-up papers. Must be. She had hoped and prayed that her clever boy, who had stayed on at school beyond fourteen, and who might even be destined to go into a good apprenticeship or – something unheard of in their family – to university, would be left alone, that the war would finish before he reached any call-up list.

When Martin came home she almost wanted to hide the letter and pretend it did not exist. But it was not hers, either to open or to dispose of.

'This came for you, love.' She tried to keep the dread out of her voice. Perhaps she was wrong and it was something else altogether.

Martin frowned. He took up a piece of bread and marg from the table and ate it ravenously, slitting open the envelope. There it was, the headed notepaper: that was all she could glimpse. He looked up at her, still chewing.

'I've got to go and register – go for a medical.'

Sheila came in just as he said it. 'Mart? What, have you been called up?' She leaned over, reading it solemnly. 'Oh my . . .' She rubbed Martin's shoulder with unusual tenderness. 'My little brother.' She sat down with them, tearful suddenly. 'Which one'll you go into, d'you think?'

Martin was looking a bit stunned, trying not to be emotional. Ann knew he was not one of those lads who was desperate to go and join the fight. But he was brave and dutiful.

'I suppose the RAF,' he said. 'Reckon I'd make a good navigator.'

He went into the recruitment offices in Birmingham for his medical and interview. Ann was on tenterhooks, finding herself praying that he failed, that none of this would have to come his way: her beloved boy, Tom's boy. But she knew that Martin, although good with book work, was also fit and healthy. He was not going to fail a medical.

In a state, she talked to Tom about it the next time they spoke.

'I've got some not very good news, dear,' she said.

When she told him about the call-up, there was a silence at the other end of the telephone.

'Oh no,' she heard him say, eventually. She could hear desperation in his tone and she immediately became the one trying to make him feel better. 'How is he – is Martin keen to go?'

'No, not really,' she said. 'He's putting on a brave face. Says he wants to join the RAF.' There was silence down the line. 'Look, the war has turned,' she said, trying to convince herself as much as Tom, while she felt scoured with emotion. What if Martin, their son, went and lost his life before Tom had even got to know him? Might that be their punishment? 'It can't go on much longer, and he's got to train first – the war might even be over before he's posted anywhere.'

'I hope so, for his sake,' Tom said. 'You know, some people say that nothing makes a man of you more than being in the Army – or any of the forces.' He stopped to cough for a moment and, when he spoke again, his tone was bitter. 'All I can say is: what kind of man?'

Ann could hear the pain in Tom's voice. She ached to hold him, comfort him – both for his own experiences in the last war and for the pain of never being able to see or spend time with his son. Tom's sisters were all married and busy: his only close relative now was his ageing father.

'Tom.' She made herself speak. 'If it turns out Martin's going away – and we don't know for how long – I think it's time to tell him, don't you?'

Again a silence.

'I think that has to be your decision,' she heard eventually. 'But, Ann . . . only if you think Martin won't go away feeling distressed or angry. What would be the point of that: for him or for you?'

Forty-Two

'Joy – one for you!'

Martin heard the lift in his mother's voice as he got out of bed. Time to get some breakfast and head to his desk. He had started work on the final years of his Higher Certificate at his school in Kings Norton and there was a lot to keep up with.

From the landing came a squeal of excitement from Joy and he heard her hurrying down the stairs. He smiled slightly; he hoped it was something from Hank. He'd liked meeting him – especially that ride on his bike. It had felt marvellous clinging on behind Hank's burly figure and roaring along the streets. In this house with only sisters, it was a treat to have some male company. He had found himself wishing his dad was a bit more like Hank – more lively and energetic. The older Martin grew, the less he felt he had in common with his father.

Excited laughter was coming from downstairs and he pulled on his dressing gown and went down. Ann, Joy and Sheila were all in the hall, with Elaine and Robbie as well. Joy was smiling tearfully.

'Hank!' She waved the card at Martin, then pressed it to her heart, beaming.

She was looking a bit better now, Martin thought. Even though Sheila had already had two babies, this side of life was an utter mystery to him, something remote and female. But even he could see the pink in Joy's cheeks, after weeks of looking pale and queasy.

'He's all right then?' he said.

'Well, he was when he sent it,' Mom replied. Her face grew serious. 'But, love, there's one for you.' She held out another buff OHMS envelope.

Martin felt his heart begin to thud. His knees went weak and he had to grab hold of the banister, hoping no one would notice. He felt like taking the envelope and rushing up to his room to open it alone, but he didn't know if his legs would manage rushing anywhere. And in the end they would all have to know what it contained.

'Right,' he said, a catch in his voice. 'I'd better open it.'

Suddenly he was the absolute centre of attention. Mom and the girls followed him into the kitchen, quiet and awed. Mom handed him a knife.

'What if they're sending you to sea?' Sheila joked, as if to break the tension.

'Don't be silly,' Mom said. 'He asked to go in the RAF.'

The back door opened and Dad came in from the garden. 'What's going on?'

'Martin's got his letter,' Mom said.

She was behind Martin, leaning over his shoulder.

'I feel as if I'm in one of those pictures where the detective tells everyone who the murderer is,' Martin joked, trying to cover the fact that his hands were shaking.

Elaine and Robbie peered over the edge of the table, knowing something important was happening.

'Come on,' Joy said. 'Stop making us wait!'

He pulled the sheet of paper out and read it. He could make so little sense of it that he had to read it again. It was supposed to say that he would be required to arrive at some training centre for the RAF on such-and-such a date. But that was not what it said. The words blurred in front of his eyes.

'Let me see.' Mom almost snatched it from him. As she read, she sank down on to a chair, her face turning ashen.

'For heaven's sake, Mom – what is it?' Sheila said.

'He's not going into the forces at all,' Martin heard Mom say, while he was still reeling in confusion. 'They're sending him down a coal mine.'

When Martin was alone, after all the family exclaiming over it and asking what he felt, he sat in his room and tried to work out what he did feel, exactly.

'I don't really want to go anywhere,' he murmured to himself. Suddenly the ordinary days of his life felt glowingly precious: home, his books, even his exams.

He tried to think about the reality of coal mining and started to feel scared. Of course he had passed his medical. With all the weighing and measuring, tapping his knees and feeling his muscles, he knew there was nothing wrong with him. 'A good specimen,' as the doctor had told him, with a wink.

But coal mining! Did that not mean digging and bashing at a seam underground, for hours at a time? Dealing with underground railways and heavy lifting, and surely he just was not strong enough? How would it feel, being underground? It sounded terrifying and claustrophobic.

'On the other hand, if I've got to do my bit . . .'

He had been briefed to travel, in three days' time, to a pit near Doncaster. He imagined tramping to a coal pit in a file of other men. Manly men, all working together, going home together, to . . . where? Where on earth were they going to live? But, either way, all men: mostly young like him. He felt a tingle of excitement, of adventure. The idea of doing something physical and masculine with other men – proving himself, and not being a desk jockey all his life – suddenly felt like a thrill.

After getting dressed he went downstairs again. In the kitchen, his mother turned when he came in. Martin could see she was worried to death, and he wanted to reassure her. He also didn't want them fussing over him, coddling him. He pulled his shoulders back and breezed in, smiling.

'Well, it's not what I was expecting. But I don't have to kill anyone, do I? And I hope I won't get killed, either.'

'Put like that, I suppose we should be grateful,' Mom said, her eyes still full of anxiety.

'The country's crying out for coal, that's for sure,' Sheila said, having breakfast with the children at the table. 'And everything else, for that matter. I'd never thought of you being one of the Bevin Boys though, not in a million years.'

'No, nor me,' Martin laughed, sawing off a slice of the brown National Loaf – so wholesome! extra vitamins! – to make toast. 'But I suppose I'm going to have to make the best of it.'

'It's ridiculous though,' his mother said crossly. 'It seems as if they're just picking boys out of a hat, with no idea who they are or what they can do. What a waste of his qualifications, digging coal!' She carried a pan of porridge to the table. 'At least you can celebrate your birthday before you go.'

As she passed behind him and ruffled his hair, the way she had when he was a little boy, Martin tried not to bristle. He would be eighteen tomorrow. He was a grown man now: it was time to be treated like one.

'Happy Birthday to you!' they all sang, the next evening.

Mom had managed to make him a dry little cake with powdered egg. It had icing on the top, so thin as to be almost transparent, and the sponge contained a hint of vanilla.

'You'll be all right, Son,' Dad said, raising his cup of tea to him. 'Good, strong lad like you. 'Spect you're looking forward to it – see a bit of life!'

Martin was not sure whether this was encouraging or irritating. It was kindly meant, but he could not be sure that he would be all right. And when had Dad ever asked him what he *actually* felt about anything?

'You make sure you write, won't you?' Joy said.

'Yes, we want to make sure our little brother isn't getting into any trouble,' Sheila added.

They both spoke jokingly, but Martin was touched. He could hear that both his sisters were worried for him.

'It's not going to be the same round here, without your ugly mug,' Joy said.

Martin joke-punched her. 'Don't go pinching my room or taking a lodger, that's all. I'll be coming back!'

Later, when he had gone up to his room and was about to change for bed, there was a knock on the door. Mom's head came round it, smiling.

'Hello, birthday boy. This time eighteen years ago you were just a little dot, and I spent the evening smiling at you.'

'A *dot*?' Martin laughed to cover his tender feelings. He was soon to leave home, and apart from a couple of Cadbury holidays for young people, he had never been anywhere much without his family before.

'Can I come in? I want to talk to you.'

He gestured to the bed beside him and, as his mother carefully closed the door and crossed the room, he sensed that she was very nervous. She sat beside him, smoothed down her skirt on her lap and drew in a ragged breath.

'Is this your parting speech?' he asked, embarrassed and nervous. So far he had only taken off his shoes and socks and somehow, with his pale feet and ankles sticking out at the end of his trousers, he felt young and vulnerable.

'I hope not.' Mom's tone was so serious, it made his pulse thud faster. She swallowed and was obviously having to work up to it, which made him feel even more nervous. 'Martin, love. I need to tell you something.'

'Oh,' he said dully. 'Is it about Marianne?'

'Marianne?' She sounded astonished. 'No, why would it be about her?'

He shrugged.

'It's about . . . you. And me . . . And . . .' She was gasping for breath now, seemed in such a state that he was really frightened. 'I've put off having this conversation. For years. I'm . . . I'm so frightened of it. But you're all grown up now, and you're going away. I don't know when else I'll be able to speak to you.' She seemed so emotional that Martin squirmed and railed inwardly at having to witness this. *Don't tell me – whatever it is, please! Or do tell me, but just get this over with.*

'What, Mom?'

Ann seemed to pull all her courage together and looked into his eyes, tender and fearful.

'Look, I can't do anything but say it straight.' She took his hands and held them, gently. 'You are my boy. My beloved boy. And you were conceived and born in love . . .'

He almost pulled away. This was awful – really awful. But he could not do that to her. Ann looked ahead of her for a moment as she talked.

'You must remember that – always. I . . . I was going to say I made a mistake. That's how other people would say it, I suppose, but it's not how I feel. Because of you, because of love.'

Again she turned to him with that direct, naked look.

'Martin, Len, your father who has brought you up, is not your actual father.'

Despite the obvious seriousness of the conversation, this was not what he had expected. He almost laughed.

'What? What d'you mean?'

She drew a piece of paper out of her pocket and unfolded it, passing it to him. His birth certificate: 'Martin Thomas Gilby: birth, 26 September 1926; father, *Thomas John Somers, Marine engineer.*

She was talking fast, telling him how she met Thomas John Somers; that she loved him, that she knew that the father who had brought Martin up felt like his real father and maybe always would, but she wanted him to know the truth . . . Words entered Martin's head in chopped-up scraps: nursing, Fircroft, Southampton . . . Confusion, and things making sense: the way his father, Len, sometimes felt so alien, someone he had to try so hard with . . . And the way he had let them down, bringing Marianne into their lives. But also now it seemed that nothing was true, nothing was as he had been led to believe.

'Tom wants to know you,' Mom was saying. 'He loves you – he longs to spend time with you.'

Martin felt his legs propel him off the bed and he bent, fumbling on the floor to grab at his shoes and socks.

'Love, what're you doing? Come here! Oh, Martin, don't do this – please don't, my love.'

Her tears moved him not at all, not at this moment.

'You're all a bunch of liars!' he said, from the door. 'I thought Dad was bad enough, bringing that woman here, but at least he was honest enough to tell us! But you – you've kept this from me all this time. Is nothing in this family ever true or normal?' He made an enraged sound, then went crashing out. 'I'm going to Ian's for the night.'

He thumped down the stairs and Ann heard him open

the front door and slam it shut behind him, before he had even stopped to put on his shoes.

She lay back on his bed, reaching her arms out as if to embrace the mattress, the bed that smelt of him – her boy, who was going away. She lay weeping, feeling utterly broken.

Forty-Three

After that, all Ann could think of was to run to the phone box and speak to Tom.

'Mom?' Sheila called out from the back room as she scooped up some change from the hall table and dashed to the front door. 'What's up? Where's Martin gone?'

Ann could think of nothing but letting herself out, without even putting a coat on, and hurrying along to the phone box in the half-dark street. But as she lifted the receiver, longing to pour out all her distress to Tom, she realized what a terrible thing it would be to tell him Martin's first reaction.

She put the receiver down and went home again, feeling as if her body was weighed down with lead. Her boy had gone, so hurt and angry. She had never seen Martin like that before and it felt as if now she had lost him for ever.

She could not hide her upset from Len. She went straight upstairs when she came in. Later, as they both sat in bed Ann wept and wept beside him.

'Why did you tell him – then, just like that?' Len was indignant at first. Why had she not consulted him?

'I'm sorry. I'm so sorry,' Ann sobbed. 'You're right: I should have consulted you. I was in a panic, with Martin suddenly being called up like that, and I'm supposed to be at work tomorrow. I thought, If I don't tell him now, when am I going to? He was so angry – with all of us.'

Len shook his head. 'He's had a basinful, the lad.' He

sounded wretched, contrite. Ann was not the only one who had put the family through a lot.

'It was the last straw for him,' she said.

There was a silence, into which Len said quietly, 'How did we get like this, Annie?'

The words tore at her heart, sent her mind racing back to the early days when she first met Len at Cadbury's, hauling on one of the drums of liquid chocolate being transported between departments in the factory. A jolly, amiable lad, who loved football and his family – and her. It made her tears fall all over again.

Bit by bit, she wanted to say. *Drop by drop. Neither of us meant it to happen.* But she could not speak.

'Stay friends, whatever happens?' Len said. He looked at her suddenly, his eyes vulnerable, enquiring.

Ann was startled, but touched. Here she was, clumsily telling their son – who was not Len's son – the truth about his father; Len who had gone through all the days of bringing Martin up. And he was trying to keep things together, keep them as good as they could be. She touched his hand, so familiar, on the blanket beside her.

'You're a good man, Len.'

'No.' He shook his head. 'Don't say that, Annie. I don't feel it.' After another pause he went on, 'You can't blame Martin. But he's a good lad. Just give him a bit of time – he'll be back.'

There seemed no more to say. Their eyes met and each of them put their arm around the other's back. They sat for a while, warm and comforted, before lying down to try and sleep.

Ann heard Martin come in the next morning. Nothing would have induced her to go to work that day now, however much she was letting them down or might lose her job. She could no more have walked out of the house than flown off the roof.

Len and Joy were at work, and Sheila had taken the children to play with friends. Ann froze at the kitchen sink, hearing the front door close. She crept to the hall, almost as if fearing it was a burglar coming in and not her youngest child.

Martin turned from shutting the door and they stood for a long moment. He could not meet her gaze.

'I've got to pack – for tomorrow.' His voice was calm, but he seemed about to head up the stairs with no more to say.

'Martin.' Ann was surprised by how calmly she spoke when she felt so wretched, wanted to fall, begging, at his feet. But she managed to sound in control of herself, even commanding. 'You can't just go away as if nothing has happened. We need to talk about it.'

'*You* need to, you mean?'

He had half-turned a few steps up the stairs, but he swivelled round and sank down, his elbows on his knees, sinking his head into his hands. His shoulders began to shake.

'Oh, my love . . .' She hurried to sit beside him, taking him in her arms and rocking him. 'My dear, lovely boy.'

'I don't know who I am,' he choked out, once he could speak. 'And I don't know who any of *you* are, either. I thought it was bad enough with Dad, but now . . .' He pushed her away, but gently, and sat up. Sounding a little bit more like his usual self, he added, 'No one's who I thought they were – I mean, if we had a *dog* I'd be having to ask it some searching questions: *Are you in actual fact a dog, or a cat* pretending *to be a dog?*'

Ann smiled through her tears. She was holding herself

in, not wanting to sob and cry all over him – it was Martin who needed to be the emotional one.

'Look, love, I can tell you all about it. About your father. But your dad here, Len, he has brought you up and he loves you as his own. And Tom loves you too.'

'Tom.' Martin sounded faintly hostile again. 'Tom Somers. How can he love me? He's never even seen me.'

'Not in the flesh, no.'

His head shot round. 'You mean . . . Are you still in touch with him? You see him?'

Ann nodded, looking down, blood rushing to her cheeks. 'Well, not see him – hardly ever. I do keep in touch though. He wants to hear about you. Always. But, you see, Tom never wanted to disturb our family, or upset you. He's always said I should tell you if, and when, there was a right time. And now you're grown-up and going away . . .' Tears fell on to her clasped hands. 'He's putting money away for you – for your future. Because he knows he hasn't been able to do enough for you.' She laid a hand gently on Martin's thigh. 'You get your brains from him, I think. He was an engineer – before the last war. But he lost an eye, and his left arm.'

Martin was listening intently. She could see he was being drawn in.

'You love him, don't you?'

Fearfully she nodded. There was no point in hiding anything, not now.

'What about Dad – I mean, your husband?'

'We . . . yes. We . . . care for each other. Very much,' she said, stumbling over the words. She saw Martin take this in.

'Tell me.' He spoke barely above a whisper. 'Please tell me about Tom.'

*

Ann asked Jeanette to tell the works that she was absent because of family illness, and she went with Martin to New Street station the next day. She had told him to take his warmest coat – winter was coming on and he was heading north! – and he had an old brown suitcase.

'I thought the war might end and you wouldn't have to go,' she said as they travelled in on the train. 'If they had won at Arnhem . . .'

After the slog across Normandy there had been high hopes that victory was assured, but the Allies, in 'Operation Market Garden', had not managed to win through.

'I'd still have had to go, I suppose,' Martin said. 'There's always going to be coal needed.'

As they stood together on the station, Ann's heart was so full, she could barely find any words. Both Sheila and Joy had realized what must have happened. They had been sweet, loving with Martin – and with her. And Martin suddenly looked so very young, bundled up in his coat, with his grey flannel trousers up around his ankles – another growth spurt – and weighed down by his case. She felt she could not stand to let him out of her sight. He was not a weakling, but he was a slender, sensitive lad, and the idea of him having to do something like digging coal seemed inconceivable.

'I do hope you're going to be all right,' she said. 'I wish you were somewhere nearer home.'

'Digging for victory.' He gave a little laugh. 'Well, it's a training pit I'm going to. Six weeks or so and then, you never know.'

There was a tender, fragile sweetness between them. They had talked and talked yesterday, with Ann explaining about Tom, how they had met and what he was like. She knew Martin was still very raw, had so much to take in – but it felt as if they were friends again, she and her boy. As the train came in and slowed in front of them, she felt as if a piece of her was being torn away and she had to struggle to compose herself.

'Bye, Ma.' He leaned to kiss her and she could not help seizing hold of him for one last embrace. 'You be good – and if you can't, be careful.'

The absurdity of her son saying this to her made her truly laugh.

'You make sure you get enough to eat,' she said. 'And *you* be careful. Go on with you.' She propelled him towards the carriage door and he climbed aboard. 'Write, won't you?'

'Course I will.'

And the train doors were slamming and Martin was moving away waving, and then he was gone. The railway platform emptied and she stood there, still staring at the empty track, seeing him as a tiny boy running towards her, his little face all lit up: 'Mom! Mom!' She would not have missed a moment of his life for all the world, despite everything. Tears poured down her face, tears of loss and gratitude.

'Well, he's gone,' she told Tom that night, tearfully, from the telephone box. 'Bless him – I don't think he's got any idea what he's letting himself in for.'

'No.' Tom sounded worried, distracted even. 'It's not going to be easy; it's heavy work.'

'Love . . .' She blurted it out. 'I did tell him. Before he went.'

A pause. 'How did he take it?'

She was not going to tell him everything. 'He's curious. Wants to know all about you. I felt I had to say something before he left. It seems terrible that the girls have known all this time and yet Martin didn't. Actually I didn't tell him that – he didn't ask. Obviously he's got to get used to the idea, and he was a bit upset at first. But I'm sure, when the time is right, he'll want to meet you – get to know you.'

'Oh.' Tom sounded emotional, as if he could not manage to say anything else. 'Well, that must have been hard. Well done, my love. I just hope—'

A faint, agonized cry came along the wire from somewhere.

'What's that?' Ann asked. 'Was that from your end?'

'Yes, I'm afraid I'd better ring off. It's my father – he's not well at all.'

'You'd better go.' She felt a bit deflated; she had been looking forward to a long conversation. But then what more was there to say? And Tom's father had sounded very distressed.

'Bronchitis,' Tom said. 'I just hope it's not turning into anything worse. His chest sounds awful.'

There was another strange sound from behind him, half-cough, half-groan.

'My love, we'll speak again very soon.'

And he was gone. Ann stood, bereft for a moment in the little box in the dark street.

Forty-Four

December

'And she sometimes gives us tripe for breakfast!'

Martin had been regaling everyone with stories of his life in the coal mines through a lot of Christmas dinner and they were already on to the pudding – with things carefully arranged so that, once again, Elaine and Robbie found the sixpences.

'What's tripe?' Elaine asked, big-eyed, the shiny little coin lying next to her plate. She was sitting on one side of her beloved uncle, drinking in everything he said. Sheila watched her daughter's serious little face, so like Kenneth now, with her fair hair and blue eyes. Robbie was just as intent, trying to follow what Martin was saying.

'It's . . .' Martin lowered his voice, fairy-tale style, 'bits of a cow's stomach.'

'Eurrgh!' Elaine looked appalled. 'For *breakfast*!'

'It's all a bit hit-and-miss,' Martin said. The family was playing close attention, his mother and sisters, his father and grandparents all so delighted to have him home for a few days. 'Not like when the scheme started – apparently half of them had nowhere to live. By the time I got to Eastwood, they had built hostels for us.'

'If they're anything like our work huts, they must be freezing,' Ann said.

'They are,' Martin replied. 'But I suppose we might

move in there if Nancy gets sick of us. They put on quite a decent breakfast – starting with porridge.'

'You don't like porridge,' Sheila laughed.

'Oh, don't I? I'd eat anything now.'

'Well, that explains it,' Cyril said, leaning over Robbie's head to squeeze Martin's upper arm. 'You've certainly bulked out, lad. And you seem to have scrubbed the coal off you, for the moment anyroad.'

'He's filled out no end,' Ann said.

Sheila saw the glow in her mother's eyes as she looked across at Martin, who did look taller and was much broader in the shoulders than when he left. They had had his letters for the last three months: all cheerful and droll, but reading between the lines, the first weeks of PT and training must have been gruelling. Martin had never complained though.

From Hartshay Colliery, one of the training pits at Alfreton, Derbyshire, he had been moved to Eastwood, near Nottingham, where they had found what seemed to be happy, if not exactly luxurious, lodgings.

'We've survived our Nancy's cooking so far. As well as the cockroaches down in the back kitchen.' He grinned with relish at their horror. 'She's a good-natured person – her husband's in Italy. I get the impression . . .' He looked round the table with a mischievous glint, but could not say too much in front of the little ones. 'Let's just say she seems to be missing him.'

Margaret's mouth shaped into an O. Sheila saw her eyes meet Mom's for a moment. Martin had never been a great one for the girls and it was funny hearing him talk like this – he was growing up fast as a Bevin Boy!

'What's the other lad like who you're lodging with?' Dad asked. Sheila was struck by how happy Len looked – pink-cheeked and cheerful. So unlike the way he had been a few months ago.

'Jack? Oh, he's a good sort. Comes from London.'

'Goodness,' Jeanette said. 'What a long way to send him.'

'It's all pot luck in this,' Martin laughed. 'No rhyme or reason in who they send where, so far as I can see.'

Sheila's mind started to drift as Dad and Jeanette asked Martin all about the pits and how they worked, and what he was actually doing at Eastwood. She had had a card from Kenneth, just before Christmas. However short a message she received from him, she was always flooded with relief, feeling his love coming to her over the miles, even if he was not very good at putting it into words. At least she knew he was somewhere in the western Mediterranean. And things were looking better: they could feel that slowly, slowly, the war was being won. But what a long, weary time it felt since she had been with Kenneth. That last time when he came home and told her he was being posted seemed an eternity ago now.

Sometimes, guiltily, she had to work hard to bring his face to her mind, the sound of his voice . . . *I love you*, she spoke to him in her head, looking across the table at her children, who had also now lost interest in the conversation. Robbie wouldn't remember his father at all and that thought filled her with pain. All this time Kenneth had lost in his children's lives – time when they should be building their home and family together. Elaine sometimes asked about him, but less and less as time went by. Every night Sheila reminded them as she bent over to kiss them goodnight.

'There: one kiss from me, and another kiss from your daddy. One day soon Daddy will be home, and we'll all be able to live together again.'

Sheila blinked away her rising tears now, not wanting to wallow. Joy, across the table from her, had it far worse and she had been through such a lot. Her sister's dark, sad eyes were fixed on Robbie, a little smile playing round her lips. Sheila wondered what she was thinking. Was she wondering what her own little child would be like when he or she was three, the way Robbie was now?

Sheila pulled herself together. It was no good feeling sorry for herself. And she thought about Audrey, who had gone down to the school deep in the countryside to which Terence had insisted that she send her boys, to fetch them back. Audrey had written to her:

I have hardly ever felt so satisfied with myself. I just walked into that ghastly place, where they have them all marching about like little tin soldiers – I gave them no warning. Said I was taking my boys home, straight away. It felt absolutely marvellous. I have never felt so tall, as if I had grown ten feet! And you should have seen the children's faces, especially Charlie. The school was furious, of course, but I couldn't care less. They can keep the term's fees – that's what they'll be worrying about. Anything is worth it to have my boys back with me, and I have been able to get them tout de suite into one of the local schools.

And by the way, Terence has not been seen in the village for weeks, so far as I know, not after the hefty fine he had to pay for all his nonsense. And his house is up for sale.

Sheila could hear so much strength and satisfaction coming through Audrey's letter. It had made her laugh, reading it.

'Now,' Mom was saying, getting up as the last of the pudding disappeared. A lonely sprig of holly was all that remained on the plate. 'Let's make a cup of tea.'

'Oh, let me do it!' Jeanette said, trying to get up. But she was hemmed in between Len and the wall. 'We can't have you doing all the work, Ann.'

'You're all right,' Ann smiled. 'Sit tight – I'll pop the kettle on.'

Joy got up and followed her to the kitchen. It was a relief to be up from the table. She was seven months pregnant now and her back ached, and most food did not sit very happily in her stomach.

Quietly she got the cups and saucers out and laid them on a tray. She was fighting her emotions all the time these days. First, on leaving work, when she was almost five months gone. She had worn Mom's engagement ring ever since she had slipped it on to her finger. But an engagement ring was not a wedding ring. She was not a married woman and she knew she must leave, before her state became obvious to her employers. Wearing a wedding ring would be a lie – and she was not going to lie to the Cadburys.

But leaving, in October, had been so hard. Norma had left Cadbury's long ago, when she had little Lizzie, and she was now expecting another baby. And Norma knew what was going on, of course – Joy didn't keep anything from her these days. But it was hard saying goodbye to some of the other chocolate girls. What was she supposed to do now: just hang about the house? She could hardly go out dancing, especially now she was really starting to stick out at the front. All she could do was stay inside like a whale, getting bigger and bigger.

Mom turned and looked at her. Joy glanced at her and then away. This time last year they had had Hank here, full of fun and stories, and she knew both of them were thinking that. It had been hard enough when Jeanette brought it up over Christmas dinner.

'You must be missing him, love,' she said kindly. 'Such a nice lad.' Seeing Joy fill up, Jeanette quickly tried to lighten things. 'I didn't mean to upset you, dear. I suppose all the children up that way in Pheasey are missing the Yanks as well – all those sweets . . .'

'Candies,' Martin interjected.

'Yes – and the parties and everything. Such *nice* boys.'

'The lad could be on the Rhine, or in Belgium,' Len said. 'Any of those places.'

'I have heard from him,' Joy said, quickly wiping her eyes. 'He sent us a Christmas card – look.' She pointed to the mantelpiece. The card showed a snowy corner of France with a tank from the US Army crossing it. 'But I don't know where he is.'

She missed Hank so much – or at least she insisted to herself that she did. He had been lovely to her, and they had had such fun. But now he was gone, off into the mysterious field of war the way Alan had gone, with no guarantee that he would ever return. In her most honest moments she was not sure whether it was Hank she was grieving for or just her old, free life. But she had to miss him and love him now, didn't she? She was carrying his child. Suddenly she felt very old, as if her youth had been sucked away from her and was gone for ever.

'It'll soon be over, kid,' Mom said. She came over and stroked Joy's cheek tenderly. Joy wished she'd stop. She didn't want to be all teary on Christmas night.

'I know,' she said tragically. 'But it won't though, will it?'

The meal drifted on long into the afternoon. Once they had cleared the table, Ann was touched to see her three children all doing the things they always did as kids on Christmas Day. They sat around the table and set out dominoes and pick-up-sticks, and Elaine and Robbie were there too, joining in until their bedtime.

'We'll go and climb the wooden hill quite soon, I think,' Margaret said a little later as she and Cyril got up to leave. Wryly she added, 'We're not as young as we were, you know.'

'I ought to be on the move too, I suppose,' Jeanette said. She sounded warm and muzzy. 'It's such an effort to get up and go out in the cold.'

'Oh, you don't need to go yet,' Ann said. 'Stay as long as you like. Len can walk you home later, can't you?'

'Yes, course I can,' Len agreed.

Ann saw her in-laws to the door.

'Bye, bab. Thanks for a lovely day.' They took their leave, with Margaret and Cyril each kissing her goodbye. Ann stood on the step, arms folded in the chill, smiling fondly as the two of them set off along the street, both walking slowly these days bundled up in their winter coats – unmistakeable figures. Margaret turned and gave a little wave. 'Go inside, Annie, you'll catch cold.'

All things considered, life was good, Ann thought as they disappeared into the gloom. She and Len had an easier relationship these days, even if things would never go back to how they had once been. But it was friendlier at least, more contented. Her children were home; even her boy, who seemed to have been surviving his experiences. And despite everything, she loved Margaret and Cyril and they loved her. Things had healed, gradually, over the hurts and mistakes. The scars might be rough and imperfect, but it seemed they could forgive; they were loving people. She felt very grateful and blessed.

Closing the front door, she thought, I'll put the kettle on again. She popped her head into the front room.

A shock met her. They weren't sure she had seen them,

Ann realized. The children were all noisily absorbed in their game at the table. And as she looked into the room, Len and Jeanette had linked hands, where they were sitting in their chairs, and were gazing into each other's eyes. They released one another as if they had had an electric shock, but on their faces were the traces of something unmistakeable: warmth and a confiding love.

Ann yanked her face into a smile. 'Anyone like another cuppa – even if I have to reuse the grouts?'

V

1945

Forty-Five

February

'Nearly there now, babby – you can do it.'

'I can't!' Joy moaned. 'I just can't keep on any more.'

Ann squeezed her hand, remembering feeling the same hopeless exhaustion each time she was close to giving birth.

'Course you can,' the young midwife said briskly. 'Strong, healthy girl like you. Now, come along, best foot forward. A big push for me!'

Ann waited, full of emotion. It was hard watching her daughter suffer and she almost wished she could do it for Joy. Sheila was downstairs keeping the children out of the way, bringing up cups of tea every so often. Ann had been in the room with Joy through the night as she laboured, and all of them were getting very tired. Joy's hair was damp and tousled and she was definitely running out of steam.

'That's it,' the midwife said, her face intent. 'Yes, the little one's nearly here!'

Spurred on by this encouragement, Joy seemed to find more strength. There were intense, miraculous moments as first the head, then the long slither of a body appeared on the prepared towel on the bed. Ann held her breath, as if in sympathy with the child. Cry. *Please cry, little one. Please be all right.*

A second later she obliged: a loud indignant roar that left no doubt that she had arrived and looked in fine fettle. Tears ran down Ann's face. She felt like sobbing her heart out in relief. At last, at last!

'A little girl.' The midwife wrapped the baby in the soft towel Ann had provided. 'And she's a big bonny lass as well.'

'Her father's a big lad,' Joy said, straining her neck to see. She held her arms out and a moment later the small wrapped bundle was lying in her arms.

'Congratulations!' the midwife said. 'She's a beauty.'

Ann moved closer, overcome. 'Oh, Joy – she's lovely. And she's a really good size.' She gazed adoringly at the child. She did not look anything like Joy had done as a newborn. Ann realized the baby was probably going to favour Hank, with his strong face and solid build. She looked so healthy and strong.

'She's a whopper – eight pounds at least, I reckon,' the midwife said. 'And what is the little lady going to be called? Do we know?'

'Patty,' Joy said. 'Patricia. But Patty for short. Patricia Margaret – after Nanna.'

'Well,' Ann replied, mopping her eyes, which were disobeying her orders about *not* getting all emotional. 'That'll make her very happy.'

'Come along now,' the midwife said. 'We need to finish the job – afterbirth still to deliver.'

'And then everyone else can come and see,' Ann said. 'Elaine's going to be over the moon to see another girl.'

Joy had found these last months very hard. She was not a quiet, staying-at-home type and Ann had had to do a lot of jollying her along, but she knew it was hard waiting for a baby to come, even at the best of times. And she had given Joy as much sympathy and attention as she could manage, whenever she was home.

It had helped to distract her from the other things she had on her mind. She had only had short, snatched conversations with Tom. His father had been very ill, had rallied and then, only a fortnight ago, had died suddenly in his sleep. Ann felt terrible that she could do nothing to comfort Tom, though his sisters, who lived quite a way away, were able to come and help. But they could not help with the business, which Tom was also having to run. He assured her that he was managing perfectly well, but she heard the sadness and strain in his voice and longed to go and put her arms around him.

That moment she had seen, between Len and Jeanette, she had tried to put out of her mind. When Len set off to walk Jeanette home on Christmas night, she had said goodbye warmly to her friend – and this was not difficult, because she felt warmth towards her. But she did feel shocked and confused. Jeanette was such an honourable person. Was there something going on in front of her eyes, which she had managed to miss completely, or had she somehow got the wrong end of the stick?

Jeanette – and Len – both seemed happy and glowing. Len was so much easier to live with than during those awful weeks after Marianne disappeared. Was this the reason? But no one said anything, and so far as she was aware over the last two months nothing else had happened, and life went on as normal.

Jeanette was always grateful to be invited for a dinner or tea and went out of her way to help. 'You've got such a lovely family, Ann,' she would say affectionately. 'I admire you – I really do.'

And Ann believed her. What she had seen was perhaps just a friendly gesture; a relaxed moment after a happy

Christmas feast. But it was a piece of a puzzle that did not fit properly. Deep down, she knew what she had seen. Their eyes had held more than warmth. They had held love. Love was unmistakeable.

She did not feel jealous or angry. If things had been different, what she had seen would have been a major betrayal of her trust and hospitality. This woman, who came round as a friend and shared their home so often, behaving like that! And Len . . . But she was long past that, with him. Towards Len she felt friendly, mostly – but neutral.

Although she did feel confused. And she couldn't help feeling . . . interested. Unsettled. And resigned. God knew, life was not controllable most of the time. What was she to do, if this was the way things were going? All she could do was to wait and see.

Joy sat up in bed, eating a plate of toast as Sheila, with Elaine and Robbie, gazed in wonder at little Patty, who was fast asleep at Joy's side.

'Can she play with my dolly soon?' Elaine was asking as Ann slipped into the room, smiling at the sight of them all.

'Well, maybe not quite yet,' Sheila said. 'Don't touch her at the moment, love – she's tired after all the business of coming into the world. Just let her sleep.'

Joy looked up at Ann as she came in and smiled.

'All right now?' Ann asked gently.

'I feel as if I've done a few bouts in the ring – but yes. I'm all right. And she . . . well, isn't she the most beautiful thing you've ever seen?'

'Well, along with all of you, yes!' Ann said, perched on the other side of the bed from Sheila. Everything felt calm and loving, as if there was a glow in the room. 'Yes, of course she is. She's absolutely gorgeous.'

'She reminds me a bit of Elaine when she was born,' Sheila said.

'Now you say it . . .' Ann put her head on one side. 'Yes. I thought how like Hank she is.'

'Flipping typical,' Joy said. 'When he's not been here to do any of the work!'

They all laughed, but Sheila's face sobered and she touched her sister's hand. News kept coming that the German Army was retreating.

'He'll be here soon, I'm sure he will. Don't worry, Sis.'

Forty-Six

May

Someone was banging in a frenzy on the front door.

'All right, all right . . . !' Ann ran along the hall and found Margaret panting outside, her face lit up.

'You've heard, I suppose?'

'No – what? We've been – you know, all the kids . . .' They had not had the wireless on, perhaps the only household in the street that hadn't.

'It's finally happened. They've surrendered. And tomorrow's a national holiday.'

Ann felt as if her knees had turned to water and she almost had to sink down on the step. There had been talk for days of the Germans having to cave in, but now it had finally happened.

'What is it, Mom: is it over?' Sheila came running downstairs. Then Joy more slowly, with Patty in her arms.

'They've surrendered! Your boys will be coming home. Get your father – he's out the back.'

They all hurried out into the street, kissing and embracing. Cyril came steaming along after Margaret. Ann and Len threw their arms around each other, around their girls as well as Margaret and Cyril. Neighbours were coming out, laughing and talking excitedly.

'That little worm Hitler didn't even have the spine in

him to see it through,' Cyril said. Hitler had committed suicide in his bunker just a week ago.

The celebrations began that night – all the neighbours standing in clusters, bringing out beer and chairs and anything else they could find, wanting to laugh and chew over the events again and again, trying to take it in.

'Ooh, there'll be a party tomorrow all right,' Margaret said. 'You wait 'til we get organized.'

In the middle of all the chatter and laughter Ann saw Jeanette hurrying along the street, smiling from ear to ear.

'I had to come and see you all – isn't it wonderful news? Everyone's outside – everywhere. I can hardly believe it!'

She embraced Ann and they laughed, and then she flung her arms around the girls. Ann watched carefully as Jeanette and Len gave each other a hug. Was that an extra squeeze he gave her, as his arms settled around Jeanette's slender body? Was it an extra lingering look as they pulled apart? But it was slight – she had to look very hard. And again she told herself she was imagining things.

Standing with her girls, as Elaine and Robbie dashed about excitedly with other children in the street, she looked down at little Patty in Joy's arms.

'Fast asleep,' Joy rolled her eyes and smiled, full of happiness. 'She's not going to remember any of this.'

'No.' Ann put her arms around Joy's shoulders. 'But it does mean she should get to know her daddy.' She stroked her little granddaughter's cheek. Patty smacked her lips in her sleep, her eyelids fluttered slightly and she slept on, utterly content.

Victory in Europe Day, the following day, was the party that no one would ever forget, when almost every street in every city celebrated; when hearts were filled with hope and expectation, as well as with grief and loss. For that day euphoria was the main feeling, after all these years of darkness, of bombs and fear and worry. No more blackout: that had begun to be lifted the previous autumn. Now the lights of peace could blaze! No more worrying about boys overseas – they would be on their way home, and families reunited.

Except that it was not over, not everywhere. The war in the East was still continuing bloodily, though many of them did not know the worst of it. Not then.

For Sheila and Joy, at least, there was hope that their men would return. For that day, it was all they needed.

Tables were laid along streets, with all the food that could be gathered together to treat children and adults alike. Pianos and hurdy-gurdies were wheeled out; squeeze-boxes and penny tin whistles beat out all the tunes they knew. Fires were lit, with the dancing of shadowy figures going on for most of the next night. Who cared if there was work the next day? Who cared about anything – except peace? Hearts overflowed with relief and an opening out into the future. What might life bring now? There was to be no more war!

Ann and Len fell into bed earlier than many of their neighbours. The children needed their sleep, and all the family had finally turned in while the sounds of carousing and laughter and fireworks still came from outside.

Ann lay on her back, looking up into the gloom. Now that they no longer needed a blackout, the window was a grey, ghostly outline. She felt muzzy from drinking a beer – something she hardly ever did. And somehow careless, as if anything could happen.

'I can't believe it. What do we do now?'

Len gave a little laugh. 'Go back to work, I suppose,' he said, being literal-minded.

'Len?' She had no idea she was going to say it. It must

have been the effect of the beer, but she was full of a strange feeling, rushing her along like a waterfall. 'Are you and Jeanette . . . you know?'

There was a very long silence. In a low voice he finally said, 'What d'you mean?'

'You know what I mean.'

She realized she did not sound accusing; she didn't even feel it. But she had to know.

'She's a nice person,' he said carefully.

By the way Len did not leap to deny it, Ann was sure then. But she felt herself withdraw from the conversation. Tonight was not the time for this. What did any of it mean? The war had only just ended and she was not sober enough to think anything through.

'Yes,' was all she said muzzily. 'She is.'

It was as if a sudden quiet had fallen over everything. In some ways, nothing changed. There were still bulletins about the war in the East. Their street did not look any different. But summer was on its way and it was as if something in the very air had changed. The story of the war, going on in Europe, was no longer playing to them, giving their lives a wider context. Now things were quiet and they shrank back to a narrower perspective. The sun warmed the pavements, and vegetables were growing in the gardens.

Ann stood, pegging out laundry in the back garden one morning, a few weeks after the war had ended. She breathed in the scented air of early June, the warmth easing her muscles, and turned her face to the sun, eyes closed for a moment, until she heard Sheila and Joy bringing the children outside.

The girls spent a lot of time together these days and were closer than they had ever been as children. Elaine had just started school in Bournville and was settling in well. Robbie was holding Sheila's hand, and Joy spread a blanket on the grass for Patty to lie on. Ann smiled, watching them, feeling the preciousness of each day. If only Martin was home, everything would feel right. According to his letters, he seemed to be fine, although you could never be sure whether he was only telling her the brighter side of things.

'Ah, look at her.' Ann carried the empty wash basket over to where the girls were settling and looked down at little Patty, three and a half months old now and beginning to get over the newborn, milk-spots stage and filling out, to take on the look she would have as she grew older.

'Little madam,' Joy said fondly. 'She'd eat all day if I let her! I'm sure she's using me as a dummy as much as anything.'

'Well, she looks quite happy on it anyway,' Ann laughed. 'Don't you, darling? D'you both want a cuppa?'

'I'll come and do it,' Sheila said.

'No, you're all right. I'm going in anyway.'

She went inside and put the kettle on. With difficulty she managed to get the kitchen window open to let some air into the house. In fact she was so caught up in struggling with it that it took a while to dawn on her that someone was knocking at the front door.

Outside she found a woman with tousled ginger hair, dressed in very worn-looking clothes, holding the hand of a little boy with thick brown hair. She must have the wrong house, Ann thought, frowning.

'Yes? Who're you looking for?'

'Don't you recognize me?' The voice was low, almost as if she was afraid of being overheard, and apologetic. And her voice was familiar. She pushed the boy forward, though he seemed much keener to hide behind her legs. 'This is George.'

Ann's breath was taken away. Her eyes focused. She resisted a momentary impulse to slam the door in the woman's face. *What the hell are you doing here?*

'*Marianne?*' Of course she could see now. And George, the same age almost as Elaine, his hair darker now instead of blond, and thick, like Len's. Marianne was the very last person Ann wanted to see. She folded her arms tightly. 'What do you want?'

'I'm sorry, Ann.' She looked warily along the street. 'It's all right – I've not come to stop long . . . Can I come in?'

Ann stood back to let her pass. She did not want to hold this conversation on the front step, either.

In the kitchen, steam was pouring out of the kettle.

'The girls are in the garden,' Ann said. That was the strange thing, she realized. She didn't have to explain much to Marianne. She knew the family so well, was almost a part of it. As soon as she had come inside, things started to feel almost normal. 'Joy's waiting to marry her American – she's got a little girl, Patty. And Sheila's here . . .'

'What about Martin – and Len?' Marianne asked. Her voice was low, humble.

Ann told her about Martin.

'And Len's at work.' She hesitated, 'Look, you might as well come outside and have a cup of tea. We're long past having secrets in this house.' But as she turned to put tea in the pot she wondered, suddenly full of misgiving, if this was true.

Sheila and Joy stared in amazement as she led Marianne and George outside, carrying the tray with cups and Rich Tea biscuits.

'Hello,' Marianne said hesitantly.

'So, you're back, are you?' Sheila said sharply.

'Not to stay or anything,' Marianne replied hastily.

'Well, that's lucky – because there's no room,' Sheila said.

But both women smiled at the little boy. 'Hello, George. Here, you can come and play with Robbie. Look – he's a big boy now. Just mind you don't tread on the baby, all right?'

George had grown into a solid, rather sleepy-looking lad. The boys settled down with some wooden toys. Patty was still dozing away in the middle of them all.

'She's lovely, Joy,' Marianne said, sitting down right at the edge of the rug. 'And where's little Elaine?'

'At school,' Sheila said proudly. The familiarity of having Marianne there was softening them all.

'Oh. Yes.' Marianne looked at George, as if the idea of school had never crossed her mind. 'I suppose he should be . . .'

'So,' Ann said briskly, handing out tea. 'Where've you been and why're you back now?'

'Is that your natural hair colour?' Joy asked curiously.

'You can't get dye out on a farm,' Marianne said. 'That's where I've been – there's a woman called Jenny and her husband, out Worcester way. She needed help because most of her farmhands had joined up and the old man was poorly. He's passed away now, and she said to me she's selling up and I'd have to move on. I've nowhere to go, and my husband . . .' She looked round at them, her face tight and desperate now. There was no point in hiding anything.

'The Irishman?' Ann asked. 'Two of them came here one night – kicked up a proper stink.'

'John Brady. That would've been him and his brother, James,' Marianne said. Her face twisted with loathing. 'He's an animal, John is. If he sees me, he'll kill me – that's for sure.'

'He did seem very angry,' Ann said.

'I married him young.' Marianne's hand stroked the wool of the rug and kept her eyes down as she spoke. 'I had no one but my grandmother, and the old man, my grandfather, was . . . Well, never mind. He was not a good man. I married to get away; fell into the arms of the first man who'd have me, and John Brady seemed right enough. He was handsome and strong. But, you know, he'd not long come over on the boat and life was hard for him. He took a grudge over everything that happened to him. He was always a brute, but he got worse. Mad jealous, he was – of the air I breathed. And of our baby.' Her eyes filled and she looked away for a moment, wiping them hastily. 'When I was expecting the first time, he beat me so hard I lost it . . .'

Sheila and Joy both gasped. Ann felt pity for Marianne wrap around her heart. Whatever else she was, Marianne had had it hard and, by God, she was a tryer.

'I knew it'd be me next. John had no control over himself. So I got away and changed the way I looked – that's when I went blonde – got myself that job here in Bournville. God, that was a miracle to me.'

She glanced up for the first time and gave a brief, watery-eyed smile, before lowering her eyes again.

'I loved working there, at Rowheath. It was a good job; people were kind and I could start again where no one knew me. But it was lonely – and after a time I met . . . Len. We got along, had a bit of a laugh together and he was kind.'

She looked up again.

'That was all, for a good while. And I swear to God, he never told me he was married – not until we were in too deep. By then I was expecting George and he helped me pay the rent on that place in Selly Oak. Helped me as much as he could.' She shook her head. 'And then . . .' She shrugged.

The bomb that had caused so much damage in Katie Road that night, Ann knew. She had been there, the next morning.

'Ann . . .' Marianne reached out suddenly and grasped her arm, so hard that Ann winced. 'I've put you and your family through things I should never've done – I know that. I'm not a bad person, really I'm not. I'd never have done any of it if I wasn't desperate. But I was then, and I am now.'

She shook her head as if trying to loosen terrible thoughts.

'I can't be here in Birmingham. If I'm anywhere near, he'll find me. You saw what he was like. He never forgets a grudge, does John Brady. His pride won't let him . . . But how can I make a life now, with a child to bring up! I've got nothing and no one. Ann, will you take George? At least for now? Len's his father and you've got a home for him. You're his family.' She looked wildly between the three of them. 'You're all good with him. I know you all, and you know him. Will you let me leave George with you, just for a while, so I can get myself a life started somewhere else?'

The question was so flabbergasting that all three of them stared at each other in silence. Ann's head was spinning. Len. Jeanette. Tom. Marianne . . . *Are the tendrils of this family going to keep multiplying like some tropical plant, sending off stems in every direction? Stems that held secrets long buried, which must surely, eventually, come to light?*

Forty-Seven

Ann would never forget Len's face when he came in from work that afternoon. There was no way she could warn him, and when he came through the back door into the kitchen, the children were all at the table: Elaine, Robbie and George, all eating bread and tart rhubarb jam.

The kitchen was full of women – Ann, Sheila, Joy and Marianne – and it took him a moment to sort them all out. He stood there, with the door open, and Ann saw his face tighten with shock as he noticed Marianne.

But then his eyes fastened on George, and the most tender tumult of feelings seemed to pass through him. For a second Ann felt it like a stab in her own heart. Len's son – and the woman who had truly given him a son. Unlike her, his faithless wife, who had deceived him into bringing up another man's child.

None of the Gilbys seemed to be able to utter a word, except for Elaine, who said cheerfully, 'Hello, Grandad! George has come to stay again.'

It made everyone smile – even Len.

'So I see,' he said. He went over and ruffled George's hair. 'Hello, young feller.'

George hung his head, looking bewildered and a bit frightened.

'We've been on a farm,' Marianne explained timidly. Ann could see that at least she had the decency to look uncomfortable, scared of what Len's reaction might be.

'He's not seen any other children – or anyone much – for months.'

'Cup of tea?' Ann asked, her eyes meeting Len's. She knew that her eyes held a glint: *So now what do we do?*

'Yeah.' He took the cup absent-mindedly, appearing stunned, then looked round at everyone. 'What's going on?'

'You can both sleep in Martin's room for tonight,' Ann said as they all sat down in the front room. 'It'll give us time to think what to do.'

'Should they be in here?' Sheila mouthed at the others, as the three children settled on the floor in the middle of the adults. Elaine had taken charge of George, who, Ann realized, startled, was technically her uncle. They did resemble each other. Elaine's hair, at first blonde like her father's, was darkening to a gingery brown like George's. He followed her about like a lamb and she arranged toys for him and Robbie, bossing them both.

Marianne shrugged, knowing that she was not the one to decide anything.

'They'll be all right,' Joy said quietly. She sat holding Patty on her lap. 'If we just talk quietly, they won't take much notice.'

Ann saw that her husband was still looking shell-shocked. Len must have believed that Marianne really had disappeared into thin air, for ever. He did not seem capable of taking the lead in this at all. Wearily she thought, Well then, it'll have to be me.

'All right, Marianne.' She sat perched on the edge of the settee, between Joy and Sheila. 'You'd better tell Len where you've been and what the situation is.'

Marianne talked, explaining about the farm and Jen Checkett, who had taken her in.

334

'She wants us to take George in for a bit,' Ann said, ''til she can get set up somewhere.'

Len's look of astonishment only deepened.

'Len,' Marianne leaned towards him, her face tight with tension, pleading, 'I know what you must think of me. Taking off like that, without a word. But I knew the Bradys would get me, sooner or later. John'll kill me, if he ever sees me.'

Having seen the rage of the Brady brothers that night, Ann realized Marianne was not exaggerating. Her terror was obvious.

'Please, will you have George? For a while, 'til I can get on my feet? He can be here with all your family – you've been so good to me, considering . . .'

Her eyes filled then, something Ann had never seen in Marianne before. Ann had always thought her tough and self-contained. Seeing her now, she thought, She's had to be, I suppose.

Ann realized Len was looking at her. Now that the war was over, they were still fulfilling the last contracts for munitions, but surely that would not last long. And then would she stay on at work, when Cadbury's returned all its departments to making chocolate? Would they even let married women stay on, now it was all over? She was not sure what to feel.

'Look, you've got a flaming cheek coming here like this – as ever,' Sheila began sharply. 'The way you left was a disgrace; not even a thank you to my mother, after all you'd put her through.' She paused for a moment to let these words sink in.

Marianne was blushing, saying, 'I know . . . I know.'

'But I can see you're in a fix. Not everyone gets lucky with their husband, and yours sounds worse than most. I'm here 'til Kenneth comes back,' Sheila went on. She did not sound exactly delighted to have to take on another child, but it did make sense. 'I'm doing this anyway, and George and Elaine get along all right. I can take them down to Audrey's as well – she's asked us to stay, and she's got two lads. I don't suppose another little one'll make much difference, and they might be good for him – get George mixing a bit more.'

Joy looked at her sister in surprise.

'That's nice of you, Sheila.'

Ann and Joy exchanged looks. Neither of them could imagine the Sheila from before the war coping with any of this. Having children, and all that had happened, had made her a stronger, far more resourceful person.

'I can help out as well – while you're here,' Joy offered. 'Least until Hank . . .' She trailed off.

'And I don't know that I'll carry on at work,' Ann said.

They all looked at the three children playing together, Elaine wrapping something round and round George's head as she played at being a nurse. George sat passively, but he didn't seem to mind the attention. Marianne smiled as well.

'Where will you go?' Len asked. 'You need to be able to come and see him.'

Marianne looked uncertain. 'I don't know. Not far. Nottingham? Wolverhampton? But, Len . . . If I keep coming back, I'm worried John has his spies everywhere. Could you bring him to see me as well, sometimes?'

Len looked at Ann, as if fearing she would think this was asking too much. Ann had a strange floating feeling inside – a resignation. This was how things were: what else could she do about any of it? Once again they all had to rally round.

'Well, you won't be doing Civil Defence or the Home Guard and all that now, will you?' she said. 'So you'll have to find something to do with yourself. And, by the looks of it, it's not going to be football.'

Len was nodding rather helplessly in agreement when they heard someone knock on the front door. Marianne stiffened in fear. They all looked at each other.

'If that's my mom, tell her I'll come down and see them later,' Len said hastily as Ann got up to answer it.

It was not Margaret. It was Jeanette.

'Hello!' she said, smiling. 'Just thought I'd pop in for a cuppa, if you're not busy?'

Ann froze, trying to marry in her mind the reality of Jeanette, and her view of their family, with what was going on inside at this very moment. All she managed, to begin with, was a slightly hysterical laugh.

'Are you all right?' Jeanette asked.

'Yes. Yes, I'm all right.'

She stood for a moment longer, holding the door open. This family – the family in which Jeanette was more tangled up than she thought Ann was aware of – this was the reality. All their secrets building up over the years, the hiding things, the pretending . . . how could all of this go on? Ann stepped back and made a gesture of welcome.

'Come on in.'

'I *didn't*,' she said afterwards. 'I didn't do it out of spite. It wasn't that.'

Len was pacing around the bedroom, possessed by fury as Ann sat on the side of the bed. She watched him distantly. How she had tried to love this man as she had promised, when they made their vows. Tried – and failed, mightily. And tried again. But it was no good. All she could feel now was sorry, but detached.

But she felt strong and firm in herself. What she had said was true. Spite was not what she felt at all when she

337

led Jeanette into the front room. It was more like a sense of something exploding, finally, in her head. It was all too much. All that had happened: all those years of secrets, of things never being what they seemed; of living for her family in order to do the best for them, when her deepest heart was somewhere else – and perhaps, in truth, so was Len's. And it was tiredness. Deep exhaustion with half-truths and pretence, and a friend like Jeanette – who was perhaps also deceiving her, was she? – and not knowing the truth about anything. Love was not lies and deceit. Enough! Enough of it.

'Jeanette . . .' Ann had gone to stand in the middle of the room, close to the children. She did not once look at Len, did not want to see the expression on his face. 'Come on in. Have a seat there, on the settee.'

Sheila and Joy shifted slightly to let Jeanette sit down, both looking as astonished as might be expected.

'We've got some visitors, so let me introduce you,' Ann said. 'Marianne, this is our friend Jeanette. Jeanette and I work together. And, Jeanette, Marianne was living with us for a time during the war because she was bombed out and there was nowhere else for her to stay. Her little boy, George, is Len's son. Marianne is going to go away for a bit because she needs to escape from her husband, who is violent and who might harm her – and George is going to stop here for a bit with us.'

Jeanette's face had gone absolutely rigid. She looked at Len as if she had never seen him before, then at Ann.

'I know this must be a shock,' Ann said gently. 'But, Jeanette, we've been friends a good while now and I haven't been truthful with you, not really. You think we're some sort of ideal family – but we're not. Not in the way you think, anyway.'

Ann sank down on to one of the chairs by the table.

'I don't want you to think Len is the only one in the wrong.' She looked down at her lap for a moment, then at Sheila and Joy. 'It's no good, girls – this has gone on far too long. And now Martin knows all there is to know . . .'

Sheila got up, touching Ann's shoulder. 'Ears are flapping. I'll take the kids out . . . Come on, Elaine, George, Robbie: we'll go out into the garden for a bit.'

The three of them got to their feet, Elaine looking round, wide-eyed as if suddenly taking in the atmosphere in the room.

'Thanks, love,' Ann said. As the door closed, she looked directly at Jeanette.

'Martin is not Len's son. I was . . . unfaithful to him. His father is—'

'Ann.' Len's voice cut through, tight with warning. 'Jeanette doesn't need to know all this. Why're you doing this?'

'Because . . .' Her throat tightened and her eyes were blurred with sudden tears. 'She's our friend – you've been such a good friend, Jeanette. But you don't know what's gone on or who we really are. We've made so many mistakes and . . . I don't want you to go on thinking that we're . . .' She started to break down, her voice cracking. 'It's all a mess, and I know a lot of it's my fault. But I want to be able to tell the truth. I'm so sick of it all!'

'I think,' she heard Jeanette's voice dimly through her tears, 'I'd better go.'

Ann felt Joy's hand, warm on her arm. By the time she looked up, wiping her eyes, she heard Len's voice in the hall. 'Look, sorry, Jeanette – bad time.'

'It's all right, Len – just let me go.'

And then the door closing behind her.

'Ann, upstairs with me – *now*!' Len launched into the room, grabbing her by the arm.

339

As they got into the bedroom, she saw him come very close to hitting her, but he clenched his fists and backed away.

'It wasn't spite,' she insisted. The same feeling of resignation filled her, as if she was tipping over the waterfall and could not stop or do anything about it. 'Stop pacing about like that and look at me!'

Len turned and they glowered at each other.

'What did you think was going to happen – in the end?' she demanded. 'You've got a child by one woman, you're mixed up with another – oh, and there's me and your family! It's time someone, just for once, faced the truth around here.'

Len put his hand to his forehead. 'She must think we're . . .' He shook his head, despairingly. 'God Almighty, what a mess.'

'Well, maybe she does,' Ann said. 'But now she knows who the Gilby family actually are. Or you and me, anyway. What were you going to do: carry on living in some fantasy world where Marianne and I didn't exist, eh?' She got up to go downstairs. 'Jeanette knows now, doesn't she? And either we'll never see her again or she'll be back – to talk to us, like a friend. Because that's what a real friend does, isn't it? Takes you as you are, warts and all?'

She left Len stewing in the bedroom and went down to the others.

Forty-Eight

Joy pushed the pram along Bournville Lane in the evening dusk, stopping every so often to check whether Patty was any closer to dropping off. At four months, Patty was thriving: bonny, a good weight, smiling and full of beans, but her sleep was still unpredictable, even though Joy worked hard to try and organize things at regular times, as the health visitor had said she should.

She turned into the park to walk around the boating lake, which was deep enough only for toy boats. At the moment there were only a few people walking dogs and a few ducks circling on the surface.

Joy smiled, looking out across the lake. The place held so many memories. Nanna Margaret could even remember when the Cadbury family first opened the Rowheath playing fields in the 1920s. And Joy could remember Nanna and Mom bringing her and Sheila to the lake when it was first completed, when Joy was about ten. And Nanna telling her that Mr George Cadbury had taken on a group of men with no work and paid them and given them food, and helped them learn a new trade so they would have a job afterwards – and they dug out the lake. It took two years, and suddenly here was this lovely place for people to be out in the fresh air. And they had come here so many times as children for walks and picnics.

She had walked here with Alan, just a few times. Memories surfaced like a series of little blows in her mind as she pushed Patty around the curving edges of the water. She could remember one summer afternoon when she and Alan were about seventeen, there at the end of the lake; Alan pretending to push her in, then pulling her back at the last second, and Joy so helpless with laughter she could hardly catch her breath. She and Alan laughing and chatting; the two of them whirling around the dance floor; their kissing in the rain before he left the final time.

'Where are you?' she whispered across the sun-rippled water, full of an ache for the past: those innocent, fun-filled days together at Cadbury's and in dance halls all over town. 'What's happened, Al?'

But it was no good. Years of silence now. She touched her fingers caressingly to her lips and, with her heart aching, silently blew a kiss to him, to wherever in the wide world Alan's body lay. She had to accept it, to fold him – and the past – away.

'And now I've got you!' Little Patty, her little girl here in the place where she had spent her own childhood. Joy leaned over the pram, but a terrible pang of emotion seized her. For how much longer would she be here, in her familiar home? A pair of lively blue eyes stared back at her from inside the pram, as wide awake as ever.

'You!' She couldn't help laughing. 'You're a cheeky monkey, you are.' She leaned in and tickled Patty's cheek. The little one chuckled in reply. 'How many times am I going to have to walk round here before you doze off, Your Majesty? Now close those eyes and go to sleep!'

It was a warm June evening and Joy did not mind being out. Things were not easy at home, though she understood why Mom had said what she did, with Marianne suddenly turning up again and wanting to dump George on them. She felt defensive of her mother. Whatever Mom had done – having Martin, and all that – none of it had caused anything like the trouble and disruption that Marianne had. Joy didn't mind Marianne as a person; she even felt sorry for her. But everything had been so much better when she had stayed out of the way.

Anyway, now the war was over – on this side of the world, at least – she would soon be out of here, with Hank. Again her heart gave a lurch. He had written, full of how they were going to have a wedding in the United States, how much his family would adore her and she would love the country . . .

Sheila had heard from Kenneth as well, but even the boys in the European war would not be coming home immediately. How could they be sure that Hank would soon be on his way home, either? Might he not be sent out east, attached to a different part of the Army? Joy was startled by the rush of relief that thought gave her.

If she was honest, even though she longed to see Hank and for him to see Patty, with all that hope came a fear and dread that she could barely admit to. She and baby Patty, Hank's daughter, would have to travel halfway around the world and leave home, perhaps for ever. Would she ever even see Mom and Dad, and Sheila and Martin, again? And the little ones, Elaine and Robbie, who adored Patty? She was going to have to leave her whole family behind, and the thought filled her with such an ache that she almost burst into tears there in the park.

She felt a powerful tingle at the side of her breasts as more milk let down again. She told herself she was extra-emotional. All new mothers were emotional: it would pass and she would be herself again. But now she felt raw and at the mercy of everything.

As she strolled around the end of the lake, she saw someone coming towards her from the other end. The woman raised her arm and waved, and Joy saw, to her startled embarrassment, that it was Jeanette.

'I thought it was you, Joy,' she said, walking up and looking into the pram. 'Oh, she's such a little lovely, isn't she? Fast asleep!'

'At long last,' Joy said, trying to get her emotions under control.

'Are you all right?' Jeanette asked.

'Yes,' Joy said curtly, too afraid she might burst into tears to say any more. But Jeanette was still looking kindly at her. Joy swallowed. 'I'm surprised you're speaking to me, after what happened the other day.'

'Oh . . .' They walked on together, slowly. 'Well.' Jeanette heaved a big sigh. 'It was a shock, that I can tell you.' There was a long pause, before she added, 'But . . . no one's perfect, I suppose.'

Joy couldn't help laughing. 'Well, that's a bit of an understatement!'

'Did Hilda know about it? And Norma? I know you've all been friends a long time.'

'Some of it, yes,' Joy admitted.

Jeanette accepted this.

'It's nice that you and Norma both have children now.'

'Yes,' Joy said. 'I see a lot more of her these days.'

They took a walk round the lake, then turned automatically to head back along the road.

'Look,' Jeanette said eventually, 'I don't want to pry, but . . .'

'You're not prying,' Joy said. 'You had a whole lot of information dropped on you that you weren't expecting. I don't even know why Mom . . . Well, I do, I suppose. There have been so many secrets, and you're a friend. It seems wrong. But you must be wondering all sorts of things.'

'Well, yes, I am really. I mean . . . Martin's father?'

'Tom Somers? To be honest, Jeanette, Sheila and I found out about him without meaning to – after Mom had her accident: the bomb blast, I mean. I was getting her things for the hospital and I came across – well, our birth certificates, for one thing. Martin's. Tom's name was on it, not our dad's. It was such a shock for us, as you can imagine. Mom met Tom when she was nursing at Fircroft – she and Dad weren't married then, but they were engaged.'

It seemed only fair to her, now that Mom had opened the floodgates, to fill Jeanette in.

'But . . . Martin's younger than you and Sheila – much younger. So how–' She stopped, realizing she was really being nosey now.

'I'm not sure.' Joy's cheeks were burning. It was awful, having to talk like this. People didn't, did they: talk like this? But then other people were not the Gilby family, it seemed.

'But your Dad brought Martin up?'

'He didn't know – not 'til much later. And then I suppose none of us would ever have known about Marianne and George if it hadn't been for her being bombed out. Dad went and found her in some respite centre somewhere; he said it was grim. And he brought them back to our house.'

'Good heavens,' Jeanette said. 'And your mother had to take them in?'

'Yes. Well, she didn't *have* to – but she did. Sheila was away down south with Audrey, so they had her room. Marianne and George were there a few months. But there were people looking for her – her husband – although Mom and Dad didn't know she had been married . . . Sorry, this is all a bit complicated. Anyway, her husband is bad news, very violent. And one day she disappeared – took George and all her things and left. We had no idea where she was until a couple of weeks ago, when she turned up again.'

'And she wants your father to bring up George?'

'I don't know about bring him up – just stay with us for a bit is all, I think. Unless she does another disappearing act, and then I suppose Dad will have to bring him up.'

Jeanette looked at her intently. 'Don't you *mind*?'

'Yes, in some ways.' Joy examined her feelings as best she could in that moment. 'He is Dad's son though; he can't just ditch Marianne, can he? And the thing is, when we found out about Mom – and Tom – she was in hospital. She might have died. It made us think: what would be worse? We just wanted her back . . .'

Joy's voice was rough with emotion as she spoke. Her tears were so close to the surface, and she felt Jeanette lay a hand gently on her back for a moment.

'It was a terrible time, Jeanette. Finding out about Tom was only part of it, but losing our mom would have been much worse. And then Dad – well, yes, we were angry with him. But I think he was so hurt, after he found out about Martin. I don't know.' She shrugged. 'He's never said. He doesn't say much about anything. And I know they've both done bad things – or at least that's what people would say. But they don't *mean* to be bad. They've never run off and left us, or anything like that. I just think . . .' She hesitated.

'What?' Jeanette said gently.

'Well.' The thought of Lawrence brought blushes to her cheeks. And Hank. 'After all, this little one is born out of wedlock. I've not exactly been snowy white myself.'

Jeanette looked at her with a kind of wonder.

'You've got a wise head on you, young lady,' she said.

'I don't know about that.' Joy stared ahead of her. 'Having a family like mine has taught me a thing or two, I suppose.'

Forty-Nine

'You can stay here tomorrow,' Ann said. 'And then if you want to go and see your grandmother, I'll come with you.'

She and Len were with Marianne in the kitchen that Thursday evening while Joy was out at the boating lake.

'I should go,' Len said.

'No,' Marianne said, sounding panicky. 'Not to the yard. If anyone sees me with a man, I'm done for.'

'Well, I'll go with you to the station.' Len was bending over backwards to try and help, to make up for everything somehow.

'No,' Ann said, 'you won't. Who d'you think's going to look after George, if we're all in town?'

'Well, Sheila could . . .' he began.

'No,' Ann insisted again. 'There isn't always going to be some woman conveniently there to take him on. He's your son: you look after him for a few hours.'

Marianne looked a bit startled at this. 'I'm sorry,' she said wretchedly.

'It takes two.' Ann was looking at Len. 'If your son is going to live with us again, you can spend some time getting to know him – and do some of the work.'

She saw Len's eye wander.

'Oh no, you don't; you're not dumping him on your mother. She and Cyril are too old for all this. Anyway she's going to see Ida on Saturday – she told me.'

'All right, all right,' Len said. 'I get the message.'

*

347

Ann waited upstairs while Marianne said goodbye to George and Len, and then Len took George into the garden. Ann and Marianne set off, Marianne with a small suitcase containing everything she possessed. Len had given her the train fare and a few days' survival money.

'You going to be all right, d'you think?' Ann asked as they rode on the tram. She did not want Marianne back in her home, but she could not help feeling protective towards her. They were connected, whether they liked it or not.

Marianne was now blonde, having dyed her hair again last night.

'I'll be all right,' she said dully. 'I can get a job – if I had George with me, I wouldn't be able to do anything like that.'

Ann nodded. She didn't ask any more, because she knew there were no answers about the future that Marianne could give her.

Marianne took her along Bissell Street and turned into the entry. Ann felt herself tense. The house she had grown up in, in Selly Oak, had a front and back room and faced on to the street. She had only heard about the backyards in the middle of town; a sprawling Victorian ring of homes built to house workers near Birmingham's factories, along narrow entries hidden away from the street. These were in truth only half houses, sharing their roofs with another house, as basic as could be, with no running water inside, even these days.

She found herself in a shabby, blue brick yard where children were playing, a tap to one side, washing lines strung across and a shared brick wash house and lavs up at the end. A whiff of the lavs reached her. The bricks were rough and smut-encrusted, and pools of water lay in the uneven ground. There were a couple of children playing out, and a large woman stood at the far end turning the mangle.

'That's her – Nora Sullivan, the old bitch,' Marianne hissed, seeming to shrink down beside Ann as the woman's gaze turned on them like a searchlight. 'Come on, let's get inside.' She knocked briskly on a door with cracked paintwork and, to Ann's surprise, stepped straight inside.

'You're too late, you shameless Jezebel!' the large woman shouted in their direction. 'The old girl's after having passed on, months ago.'

Ann glanced at this horrifying-looking person and quickly stepped inside after Marianne. As they stood in the cramped room, with its cooking range and table and chairs, a woman came down the stairs. Ann saw a kindly-looking soul in her sixties.

'Holy Mother of God, Marianne! I never thought to be seeing you here again,' she exclaimed. 'And who's this with you?'

'A friend. Ann.' Marianne seemed very nervous and did not introduce the Irish lady to Ann.

'We couldn't get hold of you,' the woman told her, arms folded. 'Herself passed on last . . . August, I think it was. It was a quick death. But I'd no way of letting you know.'

'I know.' Marianne did not seem upset. 'I'm sorry. Did they . . .?'

'Those children of hers? They arranged her funeral, even though they'd no time for her in life. She wasn't an easy woman, but God, the bitterness of that family, even in the face of death! I'd have to suppose they have their reasons.'

Marianne nodded. 'I dare say they do. I came to thank you, Mrs O'Riordan. For taking her in. If I can't see her, at least I can do that.'

'Well, her bed and board was paid – I can at least say that of them.'

Marianne was turning to leave when Mrs O'Riordan said, 'The Bradys have been here, you'll know that? Herself out there told them your grandmother was here. I'd not be saying this to every runaway wife, but . . .' She put her hands on her hips. 'If it was me, I wouldn't be married to John Brady for all the tea in China.'

Marianne nodded, her jaw tight.

'I'm going now. I'll not trouble you again, Mrs O'Riordan.' As she and Ann went to the door, Marianne looked back. 'Thank you for all you've done – God bless you.'

'Good luck to you then,' Mrs O'Riordan said as they went out into the yard.

'Shameless whore, running off from your husband,' Nora Sullivan boomed from the other end of the yard. 'You needn't think painting yourself up and changing your hair means I don't know you!'

Marianne turned and gave her a look of pure loathing. She seized hold of Ann's arm. 'Quick, let's get out of here. I want to get on the first train out and never seen these people again.'

'What did Marianne say, when she left?' Sheila asked, later that night when the family were all in the back room, the children in bed.

As Ann parted with Marianne at the ticket barrier, Marianne had given a genuine smile.

'I've brought you a lot of trouble,' she said. 'Thanks for everything. God bless.'

Ann waved her off, marvelling, as Marianne disappeared towards the platform and the train to Nottingham, at her own feeling of neutrality. She was not jealous. She was hardly even angry. Who knew where this was going to end? It felt as if, every day, one day at a time was as far as she could get. And then came the added thought: If I'm allowed, I'll stay on at work for the moment.

'She was all right,' Ann said. 'Said thanks to everyone – that she'd be in touch.'

'Well, she'd flaming better be,' Sheila said. 'I wouldn't put it past her to vanish without trace now – leaving us all holding the baby. Look, Dad, I can mind George a bit. While you're at work. And I can take him down to Audrey's with me – one more makes no difference. But you've got to help. You can't just go off playing football and that, and leave all the work to the rest of us.'

'Yes, all right,' Len said. 'I know.'

Fifty

August

'I can't believe it – I still can't take it in,' Sheila said. Suddenly she was in tears. 'I can't believe it's all really over.'

'Oh, Sheila. I say, this isn't like you!' Audrey shuffled closer on the rug that they had spread on the lawn at the back of her house, the children playing around them on the grass. She put her arm around Sheila's shoulders. 'I'm usually the one who's a soggy mess that needs mopping up!'

'What's the matter, Mom?' Elaine said, planting herself in front of them. She was a sturdy child, her hair having darkened a few shades and thickened to be like Sheila's, though Sheila saw Kenneth more in her face all the time.

'Oh, I'm all right, Lainy.' Sheila smiled, wiping her face. 'I'm just happy because the war has ended, really ended, and your daddy will be home soon.' Before Elaine could start on her next line of questioning – if you're happy, why are you crying? – Sheila added quickly, 'Is George all right over there? He's very quiet.'

Elaine glanced over at George with all the haughtiness of a five-year-old girl.

'He's all right. He's looking at a worm or something.'

Sheila and Audrey exchanged looks. George was a strange little boy, something they put down to not having had anything to do with other children all these recent months. He was amiable enough, but he could sit staring, mesmerized at something, for minutes on end. Even Robbie, who was a quiet lad, happy to get on with things on his own, did not have George's powers of concentration.

'He's OK,' Audrey said. 'He needs drawing out of himself a bit, that's all.' As she spoke, Edward and Charlie went roaring past, chasing after the same ball, and she rolled her eyes. 'Not something I need to worry about, with these two!'

Sheila could see that Audrey was happy. The strained, tense woman who she had first met when Maurice Vellacott was still alive had later been replaced by a woman trying too hard to convince herself that things were all right when Terence Richardson moved in and started to take over her life. But now she was restored as the natural English rose that she was, the light back in her eyes, her boys at home with her. Terence had sold up and left the village.

'It's hard to take in, isn't it?' Sheila said, turning her face to the morning sun as Elaine went back to bathing her doll in a bucket. 'When, *if* Kenneth comes home . . .'

'Don't say that. He will.'

'I just don't want to chance it. But it means we can go on living our lives – like we did before, without even thinking about it. No war, living together in the same house, because we want to. Well, if we can find a house, that is. There's hardly a cellar to be had in Birmingham at the moment. But even in a cellar we can just be a family.'

'Yes,' Audrey said. 'It'll be lovely.'

Sheila looked round, hearing the wistfulness in her voice. 'Sorry, Aud, I didn't mean to—'

'No, don't be silly! You deserve to have your family, after all this. Even Maurice and I had some of that, before the war started. But I'd hate to lose touch – you've been such a friend to me.'

Sheila was touched. 'Me too.'

'I'd really like to come up and see you one day, when that's possible,' Audrey said hesitantly. 'And meet the rest of your family.'

'I'd like that,' Sheila said, still surprised – even though she knew she and Audrey really were friends – by the strange way things had turned out. Who would have thought it when she first turned up in Goring from the city, Birmingham, which seemed to everyone like a foreign land?

There was a pause as they watched the children – war babies all, but now children of the peace – playing in the summer sunshine.

'I hope we're all going to be OK,' Audrey said.

'You'll be all right.' Sheila turned and grinned at her. 'Just don't go speaking to any strange men.'

Joy tiptoed up to the pram, which she had placed to one side of the garden, shaded by the hedge, and looked down at Patty, who was fast asleep. She was such a bonny child, a happy little soul, almost six months old and growing up in the very heart of her family.

Satisfied, Joy crept back to the kitchen chair that she had brought outside and sat down, looking along the rows of Dad's potatoes towards the old, neglected air-raid shelter at the far end. It was a play place for Elaine and Robbie and George now – nothing more.

She raised her face to the sun and tried to stop her mind spiralling back: to the time when there was no shelter at the bottom of the garden, when she was young and things seemed so simple . . . Although, she reminded herself with a jolt, things had not always been simple with Alan, even then. But the last time she had seen him, his face full of tender hope, and had felt the way he kissed her, it had made her forgive him everything. But it was no good. *Don't think about it*, she urged herself. It only brought pain.

Every day now though, she felt more restless. Her body had recovered from the birth and she was back to her lithe self, barring a few stretch marks. The life before having a child now seemed like another place, where she used to live and dance and be free to do as she liked. It was hard to adapt, but now she had more of her energy back – and Patty was a good sleeper. It was hard to keep her mind from going round and round everything, and her hands twitched and moved restlessly on the skirt of her yellow summer frock. If only she could feel carefree again and just think about new outfits and dancing!

According to the news, the American servicemen had started their return home, shipload by shipload, on a points system: the sick and injured taking priority, and those who had done longest service. Hank would not be at the top of the list, but sooner or later he would be sent. She knew he was not injured – he was all right. He had written to her, telling her so.

In the meantime she knew that a whole crowd of young women such as herself – some already married to their GIs, others not, some of them already looking after a child – were waiting to be shipped to the USA. So far she had only met one: a girl called Cynthia who was married to a man from Illinois. Cynthia hardly knew where Illinois was. It was not clear how long they would have to wait.

Now Joy was in a hurry to start her new life. After all, she was going to marry Hank and go and live on the other side of the world. She had borne his child: what choice did she have? And she was getting to the stage where thinking about it made her more frightened all the time. She had done so much waiting – and grieving. Now she just needed to make the break and get it over.

On opening her eyes, for a second the colours of everything seemed so vivid. All the everyday surroundings – the vegetable patch and the washing line with its wooden prop, the scrubby bit of lawn where the children played, the hen coop – seemed lit with a glow of beauty. Home. England. *'There'll always be an England.'* Her family, her town. Cadbury's and Bournville Green. The wireless, all the voices reading the news, the chimes of Big Ben – would she ever see or hear those things again?

Thinking of these details of her every day, which she usually took so much for granted, she leaned over and burst into tears.

Fifty-One

'She's got a job then?' Ann said, folding clothes for ironing by the kitchen table.

Len put the note from Marianne down on the table, with the look of embarrassment he wore every time her name was mentioned.

Ann, though, had to admit that she was rather impressed with Marianne. She could be uppity and deceitful – she was a survivor, after all. But since moving to Nottingham she had found a job at Boots the Chemist, a lodging room with an Italian lady who seemed to be well disposed towards her, and now she was taking on extra work behind the bar in a pub, several evenings a week.

'She's going to be very tired,' Len said.

'She may be tired, but she wants to do her best for George. She doesn't want us bringing him up without her,' Ann said. 'I'd say she was doing her best.'

'Yes, I s'pose so,' Len admitted. He had been the one most deeply affected by Marianne's disappearances, finding out the truth that lay behind all her running and hiding: that when he met her she was a married woman, and he did not know. But then, Ann reminded him, he had been a married man, and Marianne had not been given that rather important piece of information, either.

She knew Len did not love Marianne. Any feelings he had for her had been smashed apart when she left with George, without a word. But he did feel responsible.

'I just wish . . .' He sat at the table with a half-finished cup of tea, looking really weary. 'I know it's bad of me, but I wish she'd stayed away. That I didn't know anything.'

'Look,' Ann stood holding a pair of trousers ready to fold, 'you and Marianne are going to have to look out for George all the time he's growing up.'

'What, like Tom Somers?' Len snapped at her.

Ann turned away sharply. It was in moments like this that she disliked Len – truly disliked him.

'He didn't know. Now he does. And you *do* know, so you can't pretend you don't.'

They didn't have many conversations like that. Mostly life just went on, with all these things humming somewhere beneath the busy surface of work; and Sheila and Joy with their turbulent emotions, both waiting for their men to return – and all the children in the house. If they kept things superficial, she and Len could get along amiably enough. They had gone on that way for years.

But if she let herself look deeper, Ann knew there was something else. Every time Jeanette came round to the house, Ann was on high alert for signs. Jeanette was a good person, she knew. A friend. Not deceitful or dishonourable. Ann was quite sure that Jeanette would be fighting her own feelings, trying to do the right thing.

She still came often for Sunday dinner and would sit with Ann and Hilda during breaks at work. The factory was beginning to adjust back to peacetime, but there were still shortages of everything, and still contracts to fulfil that did not concern the production of chocolate. For Ann, working at Cadbury's made at least something feel normal. It meant she saw her friends and it got her out of the house. It held her steady amid all the other carry-on.

Even though Jeanette was doing her very best, Ann sometimes caught a look between Len and Jeanette: warm, with a very obvious sense of comfort and affection. A look that Len had not directed at her for a very long time. You could say it was just a look of friendship. Friendship merging into love. Whatever it was, it was there. At times Ann even felt that she was in the way, in her own home.

Later that day as she stood over the ironing board, dipping her hand in a pan of water to sprinkle over the crisp-dry washing, these thoughts would not leave her alone. She had spoken to Tom a few days ago. Tom was at a crossroads: his father having died, he was now left with the business and could either continue to run it or sell it.

'I s'pose I always thought I'd end up in the business.' His voice came down the line to her, and she could hear his anxiety. 'But not necessarily. If things had been different – I mean, I wasn't working for Dad before the last war.'

She could hear the strain in his voice. Tom had loved being an engineer, but most of this was lost to him, with the injuries he had sustained. He never truly wanted to run his father's business; he loved designing and making things.

'Things'll work out, love,' she commented, feeling useless and silly. How exactly were they going to do that? She did not know what to say.

But now, with her arm moving across the sheet she was ironing, a thought broke over her like a wave. Somehow, in this family, it was always she who had to say something. To crack the shell of hesitation or fear or lies – whatever it was. She stopped ironing abruptly. This could not continue. It was ridiculous. Now the war was over, were they all going to just carry on like this?

Let's get Joy settled first of all, she thought. The government was apparently in no hurry to release Martin from his work – which, to her bewilderment, he seemed content enough to be doing. And Sheila was expecting

Kenneth home. Steady old Sheila; she would go on as always. But Joy, well, that was going to be a huge step. And then . . . what was Len thinking, in his heart of hearts? Dare she ask: could she find the courage? *Sometime*, her heart begged, *please let all this be over*.

'Damn and blast!' She jerked her hand up, the singeing smell filling her nostrils, and stared in dismay at the brown shape of the iron, right in the middle of the sheet.

Fifty-Two

November

Joy's hands were shaking as she bent down to scoop up a startled Patty from her blanket on the floor. Still holding the fateful sheet of paper, she tore out of the house and along the street, to hammer on her grandparents' front door.

'All right, all right.' Grandad Cyril opened up. 'No need to bang the door down . . . Oh, bab. What's up with you?'

It only took one look at her face.

'Margaret!' He shooed Joy into the house. 'It's Joy!'

A few moments later Joy was sitting in the back room, a place so familiar for all her life, with its comfy old chairs and cat ornaments on the mantel and crocheted blankets, that the sight of it made her burst into tears. Sitting with Patty on her lap, she held out the sheet of paper to her grandmother. Margaret's face turned stony.

'Oh my goodness. Look, Cyril.' While he was digesting the embarkation orders that were the start of Joy's transport to her new life, Margaret's eyes filled as well. 'So it's really happening? I was beginning to think it never would.'

'I know,' Joy sniffed. 'Me too.'

There had been protests down in London. Pictures in the papers of the American president's wife, Eleanor Roosevelt, on another brief visit to London, with women and children lined up outside her hotel, carrying placards reading, 'We Demand Ships' and 'Forgotten British Wives'.

Even Norma had started saying things like, 'D'you think you *are* going to go, really?'

But now there it was, in black and white.

'I've been waiting all this time,' Joy said, leaning forward tensely, hands clenched in her lap. 'And now it feels as if it's happening too soon!'

She could see the grief plain in her grandparents' faces. If she went, would she ever see them again? The thought made her buckle inside. But there was no one else at home and she had to tell someone.

'Well,' Margaret said, straightening her back as if to try and bear it. 'Things always feel worse when you're waiting. And you've done a lot of that.'

'You have, bab – it's been hard on yer,' Cyril agreed. His eyes looked watery too, which made more tears roll down Joy's cheeks.

'It says you've got to go to a camp to wait and be processed,' Margaret said. 'Tidworth. Where's that, Cyril?'

'I don't know.' He shook his head sadly.

Joy didn't know, either. They all looked at each other, shaken and bewildered.

'Well,' Margaret said, gathering herself, 'Hank's not your husband – yet. But he will be. And she's his child. You've got to go to him, haven't you?'

Slowly Joy nodded.

Joy's embarkation instructions knocked the family for six, even though it was news they had all been expecting. Joy could see everyone trying to cope. Everything was shifting, so that life as they knew it was not easy to recognize.

'I feel as if I'm losing my sister,' Sheila wept that night as they sat together on Joy's bed.

'You're not losing me,' Joy tried to insist, though she knew exactly what Sheila meant and she felt the same – as if she was losing everyone. 'You'll soon have Kenneth back, and you'll be so busy you won't have time to think about anything. You could come and see us – over in the States?'

'Oh. Yes, I s'pose I could,' Sheila said, but vaguely. Joy knew that, for Sheila, this was like talking about going to the moon.

As for Martin, it seemed she was not even going to be able to say goodbye to her little brother – not so little any more, but a man with wide, strong shoulders and a laugh that had become full and confident.

Mom and Dad were trying to be cheerful, doing their best to back her up in her decision. But she heard them talking a lot in low voices. And she came across her mother crying in the kitchen – more than once. The first time Mom wiped her eyes and pretended nothing was wrong, talking in a bright, cheerful voice about making tea. The second time they just looked at each other across the carrot peelings on the table and then walked into each other's arms.

'I don't want to go,' Joy sobbed.

It felt so reassuring, Mom cuddling her. When would she ever be able to receive this comfort if she was thousands of miles away? The bitter thought passed through her mind: those urgent, thrilling few moments in the airraid shelter before Hank went away, that was all it had taken to break open both her body and her future – and send her spinning across the world to a completely different life. If she had not had Patty, would she be going now?

'I mean, I do want to,' she added hastily. 'But I don't want to leave you – and everyone. I don't know what it's going to be like. I don't have any picture in my head of how it'll be.'

Ann held her tightly, rocking her slightly but saying nothing, and Joy realized that Mom was too full up to speak. After all, what could she say? After a time they stood back from each other, both choked with emotion. All Ann said was, 'Well, love, you're going to have to get a lot better at writing letters.'

Mom asked her if she wanted a party: a send-off before the date in November when she was due to leave.

'No,' Joy said immediately. 'I don't think I could stand it. I'd rather say goodbye to people one by one. Norma and the girls. And . . . I really think I should go over and say goodbye to Irene and Ivy: Alan's sister and mom. I haven't seen them for ages.'

She could feel her mother examining her face carefully, sorrowfully. 'It's not your fault, you know – any of this. What happened to Alan.'

'I know.' Joy turned away. Of course it wasn't; it was the fault of the warmongers who had overturned so many people's lives. But she still could not help feeling guilty. If she knew how Alan had died, where he was, then she might feel better. She would be able to mourn properly. And she still felt as if Irene and Ivy must despise her for not waiting for him – just in case there was any chance . . .

But that was not how it felt when she was with them. She finally went to see them, knocked on their door with her heart pounding, Patty in her arms. Nanna and her mother had suggested that she start wearing a brass wedding ring, and she had given her grandmother's engagement ring back. It saved looks from the sort of people who made judgements. But she was not going to lie to the Bishops.

'Joy!' Irene looked really pleased to see her. She managed to hide the moment of shock when she noticed Patty in Joy's arms. 'It's nice to see you – our mom'll be really pleased. Come in! And who's this?'

Joy sat in the back room, which smelt of the usual cocktail of coal, boiled cabbage and bleach. Both Ivy and Irene looked better than when she had last seen them, so strained and worried. They had had time to recover, to accept that Alan was gone; and Irene looked younger again, her thick hair brushed back from her handsome face.

Joy explained about Hank, and that she was soon leaving for the USA. They fussed over Patty, wanted to hold her. Patty, now eight months, sat like a lamb on each of their laps, looking up at them, big-eyed. Seeing Mrs Bishop holding her, her thin, lined face looking down so tenderly, Joy felt a stab of anguish. If things had been different, Ivy might be looking at her own granddaughter – Alan's child.

'She's a lovely baby,' Irene said warmly. 'Really bonny.'

'You do know, don't you,' Joy began haltingly, 'that if things had been different . . . I mean, I would have waited for Alan to come home.'

'It's all right, bab, we know,' Ivy said, still gazing at Patty. 'We don't blame you for anything. You've done your best.'

These kind, forgiving words settled in her heart and Joy smiled tearfully at each of them. 'You would have been my family. I would've liked that.'

'So would we.' Irene reached across and squeezed her hand. 'But I s'pose some things are not to be.'

Joy left with their blessing, walking away along Stour Street, thinking, I suppose I'll never come here again. Everything felt like that, at the moment. Last time doing this, last time doing that. Every small thing she did was suddenly overflowing with meaning, and bright like a gem. All she had to hold on to was Hank – his kind, friendly face, his loving arms – as she strained to remember him.

The man who was to be her husband and was Patty's father. Because everything else about the future felt like sailing out of her own life into an open sea, grey and featureless, the land on the other side, its people and places, a mystery.

Her mist-shrouded future was to begin in a few days now. Sometimes it felt the most exciting thing she had ever done – at other times she felt terribly alone and frightened.

Fifty-Three

'Joy says the other girls she's with are nice,' Ann commented.

She and Jeanette were walking back to work. Some women had returned to producing confectionery, but the shortages of everything meant that the factory was nothing like up to what it had been, before the war. Ann and Jeanette were both still working for Bournville Utilities, which was slowly winding down its manufacturing at Cadbury's. In the main it was the married women who had been kept on, to complete contracts with firms like Lucas's, General Electric and H. C. Webb and Co., but Jeanette was still working there as well. They were now on machines that were winding coils of wire for General Electric.

'It must feel better now she's with some of the other wives – and fiancées,' Jeanette added quickly. 'They're all in the same boat together.'

'Well, that's what they're hoping!' Ann said and they both laughed.

On the face of it, they were chatting together like the old friends they were. They had been through a lot together. Jeanette was a close family friend. But there was a feeling – Ann knew it was there, and she knew Jeanette must be able to feel it too. An awkwardness. A secret. It had been growing over the months, and Ann was pretty certain she knew the reason for it. But she believed that Jeanette did not know she knew.

Jeanette had not asked Ann anything – not after her

outburst in front of the family about Marianne and George, and Tom. Months had gone by and they had continued in the same way, as if nothing had happened. Jeanette came round for Sunday dinner every other week or so, bringing rations and sometimes something she had made as a contribution – a cake or blancmange. They worked together, took their breaks together.

Ann was puzzled, but knew she had not imagined what she had seen between Jeanette and Len. She knew love when she saw it. But she had been so taken up with all the goings-on with Marianne, and then with Joy, that the rest of her life had been simply a question of battling on as normal. Was this how it was going to be, endlessly?

It was only that day, as they walked back from the dining room, that Jeanette suddenly touched her arm, so that Ann stopped. They stepped aside, out of the way of the other hurrying Cadbury workers.

'I need to speak to you, Ann.' Jeanette's pale-blue eyes looked into hers, intense and fearful.

Ann did not look away. 'Yes,' she said, her heart suddenly pounding. She both wanted and desperately did not want to start this conversation. 'Go on then.'

'I don't mean here, now!' Jeanette looked horrified. 'I meant – maybe after work. Could you come to mine, for a cup of tea?'

A turmoil of emotions rushed through Ann. Resentment: did Jeanette think that after a day's work she had time to sit around drinking tea? She had to get back and help Sheila, who was looking after not only her own children, but her father's illegitimate child too. Did she think that she didn't have a hundred things to do: get the tea and think about shopping for tomorrow? What the hell did Jeanette really know about family life?

But inside Ann there was a calmer, broader feeling – the

368

result of all the mistakes and joys and sorrows that had made up her life. Things happened: people felt things that did not fit the rules, the way things were supposed to be. Love did not fall within lines dictated by the law, by what other people thought. As well as resentment, there was gratitude. She did not love Len, her husband. She loved him as a grateful old friend; she loved him for all they had shared, for the children they had brought into the world and cared for together, day after day. But she did not love him as a wife. Not any more, if she ever truly had. Len needed love – the love she was not able to give him – and he had tried to get it from Marianne. She remembered his shock, so bad it had made him ill, when he realized Marianne had betrayed him. But now perhaps there was someone who could give that love to him.

'Look,' Ann said quietly. 'It doesn't need to take long, does it, to say what you want to say?' She let out a small sigh, then fixed her eyes directly on Jeanette's and reached out to touch her hand. 'If what you want to say is that you love my husband and that he loves you – I do know, you know.'

Jeanette's pale face froze with shock. She looked around in a hunted way, as if someone might be listening.

'You . . . you know? *How* do you know?'

Jeanette looked so frightened, as if she was expecting Ann to erupt with rage. Ann's resentment faded. A warmth flowed through her, surprising her, as if some channel had opened up in her that allowed kindness and possibility. She wanted Len to be happy after all, to be loved. Moving closer to Jeanette, she pulled her arm through hers, indicating that they should keep walking.

'I've seen the way you both look at each other,' she said.

Jeanette looked down, flushing. 'Oh,' she replied, her voice trembling on the edge of tears. She was in quite a state. 'There was me, thinking I was doing such a good job of keeping things normal, hiding it. I . . . I didn't realize that was what I felt at first. Len and I got along well – you've both been such good friends to me. I suppose I kept kidding myself that's all it was. And then one day' – she paused, drawing in a tremulous breath – 'we just knew, both of us. But I've tried so hard *not* to feel it. I thought you'd be so angry, even though I know, from what Len's said . . .' She trailed off, obviously not wanting to say something that would sound like an accusation.

They were leaving the Cadbury works, going the long way round for both of them, along Bournville Lane. It would give them more time to talk.

'Len and I have been through all sorts together, good and bad,' Ann said as they passed the entrance lodge. 'We're family: we have children, and his mom and dad and everything. I'll always love them – they've been so good to me.'

She walked on in silence for a moment, measuring her words, and Jeanette waited.

'I've tried, Jeanette. Over the years I've tried so hard to be the wife Len needs. To love him. I've done everything I'm supposed to do, in terms of bringing up the family – you know what I mean. But I can't . . .' Her emotions rushed abruptly to the surface and now she was the one battling tears. 'You'd think you'd get over someone, wouldn't you? If it was that long ago?'

'Tom?' Jeanette asked timidly.

Ann nodded. Words poured out of her. Things she hardly knew she felt.

'There's something, with Tom, that's *right*, somewhere deep down, in a way things never have been with Len – not really. I've tried to make things right, Jeanette, I really have . . . When Len found out about Martin, both of us tried so hard and I'll always be grateful to him, but nothing was ever the same again. I don't blame him; that was just how it was. I'm not a sentimental person. If you asked me whether I think there's one person: you know, someone you're meant to be with, your hearts entwined . . .' She gave Jeanette a lopsided smile. 'You know, all that stuff in the pictures, then I'd say no. But with Tom and me, that seems to be how it is, for both of us. He got married, for a short time. It was a disaster. And I stayed on here because I had a family to bring up, and because of Margaret and Cyril – and Tom being in Southampton. It all felt too big a wrench: for everyone, not only me. And I'd promised Len. That's why I married him when he came back, because I'd promised and he was away fighting and . . .' She wiped tears from her cheeks. 'I seem to have done all the wrong things by trying to do the right thing.'

She felt Jeanette squeeze her arm, but she could tell her friend did not know what to say.

'You and Len, you're good for each other,' Ann said gently. 'I can see it. You're suited.'

'D'you think so?' Jeanette asked. She seemed stunned, as if she could not take in that this conversation was happening, that any of it was happening.

'Have you talked to Len about Marianne?'

Jeanette shook her head and looked down, and Ann could see she was in pain.

'I'm sorry our family is so complicated,' she said wearily.

'I wouldn't want you to think the family I come from was a bed of roses, either,' Jeanette said drily.

They paused at the end of Bournville Lane to cross Linden Road.

'Len did say Marianne . . . well, wasn't very truthful with him. That she sort of took advantage.'

'It takes two,' Ann said, with a flare of annoyance. She felt broad and generous about what was happening, but not broad enough to take in Len being portrayed as the helpless victim. 'He didn't tell her he was married, either. But, Jeanette . . . I think he was looking for love. And I feel to blame for that, because there was always part of me that was turned away. And even though I tried so hard, Len could feel it – I'm sure he could.'

Jeanette nodded. 'Yes, I think you're right.'

'And maybe you're the person who can give that love to him?'

They stopped at the end of Jeanette's road.

'Len's going to have to be . . . well, involved, with George, isn't he? Even if Marianne takes him back to live with her?'

'George – and his other children,' Ann said. 'Yes. That's how it is, Jeanette.'

Jeanette stood for a moment, and Ann could see her taking all this in.

'What do we do?' she asked eventually. 'I've no idea what to do.'

Ann looked away down Linden Road for a moment. It felt suddenly as if everything was spinning and strange. She drew in a deep breath and let it out slowly, then managed to turn and smile at Jeanette.

'I suppose we're all going to have to try and tell the truth, aren't we – all of us? But, Jeanette, I don't want to do anything until my girls are settled. They've suffered a lot, both of them, but especially Joy. Let's get them settled with their husbands first, all right?'

Jeanette's shocked face softened into a smile. 'You're an extraordinary person, Ann. Yes, of course we must.' With tears filling her eyes, she held out her arms and the two of them held each other for a moment, there in the street.

VI

1946

Fifty-Four

January

'Where does yours live then?'

A voice penetrated Joy's dazed state as she stood on the path between two snowy patches of scrubland, waiting to enter the reception office at Tidworth Camp in Wiltshire. It had previously been a US Army camp, but was now a transit camp for GI brides finally on the point of joining their husbands after this long wait.

Everyone in the queue of women was as smartly dressed as they could manage, in hats and coats; some, like herself, were carrying a small child on their spare arm and, in the other, little cases and handbags, with an assortment of rugs and shawls draped over their shoulders to protect against the freezing weather. The trunks that they had been instructed to buy and label with their destination in the US had been sent on ahead.

Joy's arms were aching and she put the case down, in order to be able to hold Patty, who was nearly a year old, in both arms. She was not in the mood for talking at all, unlike some of the other excited GI brides and fiancées who had been on the train down from Birmingham. Some had laughed and chatted nineteen to the dozen all the way. Joy had sat with feet like blocks of ice, holding Patty on her lap and trying to contain the tight, sickening ache that filled her chest and constantly threatened to make her break down. But she did not want to seem unfriendly. She and these women were going to have to live and travel together for some time.

'Oh, Philadelphia,' she replied, turning to a pretty red-haired woman who was behind her.

The woman's freckly face broke into a smile. 'I dunno where that is. I don't even know where the place is that I'm going to live with my Ed! It's called Iowa.' Her brow crinkled for a second. 'I dunno if that's a town or what.'

Joy could not place her accent – everyone came from all over the place. She could see one woman, Doreen, who she recognized from the platform when she had left Birmingham. She felt cold and homesick and just wanted to be back in the kitchen at home, sitting at the table and chatting with Mom.

They spent what seemed an age in the reception offices filling in papers, accompanied by the chatter of women and crying of babies. Joy was glad she had brought some rusks to keep Patty occupied. She was a dear little girl, a happy soul most of the time, with a cap of brown hair and big blue eyes, like Hank's. But even she was feeling the strain of all this strangeness, and Joy had to work hard to keep the child happy and distracted.

'I'm afraid you're going to have to get used to this,' one of the officials told them. 'But I'm sure you're all familiar with queuing by now.'

At last they were told to line up and wait for the buses that would take them to their billets. As they stood out in the cold again, some men were walking along the line, offering to carry suitcases to the buses. The one who bent and picked up Joy's case with a shy nod had the white letters POW painted on his uniform.

'They're Germans,' the redhead said, her lips close to Joy's ear. 'I've never seen one before, have you?'

Joy shook her head, repressing a sudden impulse to tell him not to touch her things. But he was already halfway to the bus with her case. And he was young and had been so polite, sweet almost. It gave her the strangest feeling, being so close to someone who had been their enemy for so long, and who looked so ordinary – nothing special or frightening at all.

Some of the women were taken to a place called Delhi Barracks. Joy and another bus-full were driven across the camp to rows of huts. Everything looked so cold and bleak that she felt like bursting into tears, even though some of the other women were cheering at finally getting to a place they could call home for a short time.

Joy sank down on to the metal bedstead they had each been allotted, with a thin biscuit mattress, amid the restless turmoil of women and children trying to get organized. If only she felt more friendly, instead of exhausted and scared. The redhead had disappeared into another hut, and now beside her was a sweet-looking woman with wavy honey-blonde hair and, once again, an accent she could not recognize. She had a little dark-skinned boy with her, who looked about eighteen months old. Joy couldn't help looking curiously at him, and the girl smiled shyly back at her.

'Yes, his father's a black man – everyone wants to know. It's hard, isn't it?' she said, taking garments out of her suit-case. Her eyes filled with tears. 'Leav'un home, I mean. My mother came to see me off and I was cry'un my eyes out and she said, "You marn't be doing that, girl – I don't want those eyes be'un my last sight of you . . ."'

Tears spilled down her cheeks. Joy was trying to keep up with all this, though from what she could make out, she felt exactly the same herself.

'I want to be with my Grant,' the girl went on. 'For him to see our little Davie here. But leav'un home, and my mother's break'un my heart.'

'I know,' Joy said, hardly able to speak, her throat so tight. 'It's not knowing if you'll ever seen them again – I can't even stand to think about it.'

The girl looked at her with interest.

'Where're you from then? That's a rum accent, if ever I 'eard one.'

They both laughed and introduced themselves. Joy started to feel a bit better. The girl's name was Susan, from Framlingham in Suffolk.

'You married already?' she asked and, when Joy shook her head, she went on, 'Grant and me are – after a fashion, anyhow. We got married on the telephone, but we said we'd do somethin' better once I get there. Here, want one of these? Your little girl might like a bit: there's cheese in 'em.'

She held out a wrinkled paper bag and, inside, Joy saw a number of scones.

'Ooh, thanks,' she said, taking one. 'Did your mom make them?'

'Yeah.' The girl sank on to the bed with a grin. She was a cheerful soul, Joy could see. 'Loves her cook'un, my mother.' She stared at the scone. 'This might be the last of it I ever eat.' And tears started to run down her face.

Thoughts like this had been plaguing Joy for weeks, ever since she received notification that it was time to set off, just before Christmas. Christmas itself had been a sweet agony. All she could think was, This might be the last time . . . Every little ritual tormented her: the Christmas crib service at St Francis's Church with her family, and seeing Norma there with Danny and Lizzie and little

Gary, who had been nine months old by Christmas, and her mom and dad; not to mention Joy's own parents and grandparents. How many more years would Margaret and Cyril live? Would she ever see them – or anyone in her family – again? Tears flowed down her face all the way through the service.

Broadcasts on the wireless, walks in their Bournville neighbourhood, people and shops and sights she had known all her life and had taken for granted – the Cadbury works, the carillon bells chiming from the school, Bournville Green with the snowdrops just peeping through the grass near the Rest House as she was leaving for ever – everything took on a glow of something always known and precious, about to be snatched away for all time.

Martin had managed to get home for Christmas. He looked so much older and stronger that it was almost as if he was a different person. But at least she was able to see him and say goodbye.

'I don't want to leave you all,' Joy sobbed one night to Mom in her bedroom. What on earth did she think she was doing, leaving everything to go and live on the other side of the world? 'I want to be with Hank, but I'm so scared. What if I don't like his family? What if I don't like *him* in the end? It's so far away – I don't know if I'm doing the wrong thing!'

'Patty's his little girl,' Mom said. 'And the three of you should be together.' Joy could hear her mother straining to say the right, encouraging thing, because she was in tears too and Joy knew how much none of them wanted her to leave, even if they wished the very best for her. 'I know I've got to let you go, love. But it's very hard, I can't say it isn't.'

As the date drew closer, Joy started to want to get it over with. The waiting to leave was awful. The feeling of *last this, last that* . . . Eventually the day they said goodbye to her at New Street was both harrowing and a relief. As she and Patty sat on the train as it pulled out, seeing her family receding as she craned to watch along the platform, everything felt almost unreal and Joy tried to keep control of her feelings, push them away. She was on her way, finally, to see Hank, her lovely Hank, Patty's father. She was to marry and become an American – that was what she had chosen, and that was what she must now turn her face towards.

Fifty-Five

The days at Tidworth were not idle.

'I'm start'un to feel like a beast got ready for market,' Susan said later that week.

The young women were quickly getting used to the routine. Lockers in the huts used by the US Army were swiftly converted into cots for the little ones, who slept snugly inside. There were fixed mealtimes in the mess hall, and most of the rest of the day was spent in the preparations necessary to process their immigration to the United States.

Joy knew what Susan meant, though. They had medical inspections and inoculations – both the adults and the children. The medic sat Patty on a little table and examined her eyes and her bones, gave her a vaccination and said that she was a lovely healthy child. They listened to Joy's chest, tested her eyes, ears and reflexes.

'What if we don't pass?' she said to Susan. 'Wouldn't they let us go?'

Susan shrugged, making a face. 'Send us to the knacker's yard, I s'pose,' she laughed. 'When he was do'un that test on my knees, I nigh-on gave 'im a kick where 'e wouldn't want one!'

There was endless queuing for passport inspection, papers to fill in, fingerprints to be taken – 'In case we go and rob a bank?' Susan asked. 'They've already gone through all our luggage as if we're smugglers!'

They were allowed to take £15 out of the country and they were able to exchange the money for US dollars.

When Joy handed over her English money, exchanged for 'greenbacks', as everyone jokingly called them, she felt a thrill of excitement and misgiving muddled up together. She had just surrendered one of the last things that made her British. She was now a full member of 'Operation Diapers', as the first delivery of women with GI husbands or fiancés to be despatched on a ship across the Atlantic was called. They were travelling on a vessel that had been a troopship, called the SS *Argentina*, and would be embarking from Southampton on 26 January.

Every evening in the huts they sat and talked. Those with children had to get them to sleep, and Joy was always glad she had Patty to care for. It gave her something, and someone else, to think about. The women all told stories about how they had met their 'boys' and compared destinations. Might it be that they would be near one another somewhere – a familiar face to come upon, amid all the strange newness of the life? It was peculiar enough being here, in this cold, bleak place so far from home, with German POWs wandering about. How much stranger was it going to feel over there?

But Joy had not yet spoken to anyone else who was heading for Philadelphia. They all looked at the huge map on the wall in the building where they were being processed. Some of the girls were stunned to find out quite how much more travelling they would have to do when they arrived.

Joy was relieved to see that Philadelphia looked very near New York, which was where they were sailing to. Whatever 'near' meant, on a map that size. Iowa, Susan's destination, looked a very long way away, near the middle of that enormous country.

'Well, I never,' Susan had said, standing just behind Joy. 'Me and my Davie're in for a long trip!'

'They said our boys were "overpaid, oversexed and over here",' one woman said behind Joy, as they stared at the great expanse of the USA. 'I wonder what they'll say about us?'

'I'm glad they brought us here for now,' Susan said, a couple of nights before they were due to leave for Southampton on the next leg of their journey. 'It makes it easier to say goodbye – as if we've already started on our way.'

'Well, we have,' one of the other women said. 'I ain't looking forward to going on that boat, though. I know I'm going to get seasick.'

Joy was doing her best not to feel anything now, if possible. It was no good looking back; she had made her decision. She kept reading and rereading Hank's last letter. He was back home now – just – and wrote saying that his father and mother, whom he called his 'folks', were looking forward to seeing his 'gal'. Joy wondered what they would think of her, a woman who had had a child out of wedlock – even if it was their first grandchild!

But Hank's letter was loving, and she clung to the memory of him. He was a nice man. He got along with his parents and had a good professional job. He'd be able to keep her and Patty, and he wrote of looking forward to them setting up house. She only felt a wrinkle of resentment at the way no one had any thought except that she should go and live in her husband's country, close to his parents, when she felt she needed her own mother so much – especially now that she had had her first child. But that was the way of things; it was what was expected.

'Can't wait to hold you in my arms, darling,' Hank had finished his letter.

The letter was lovely – Joy could not complain about that, although he never said anything about Patty. She found this odd and hurtful. His little daughter, and he never asked anything about her at all. Joy told herself that of course it was difficult for Hank – he had not seen her pregnant, had never seen Patty yet. When he saw Patty, he would fall in love with her straight away. How could he not! Joy read and reread the letter and sometimes, in her better moods, this all felt like an adventure and she felt a real tingle of excitement about seeing him, and about all that was to come.

It was their last day at Tidworth. It was terribly cold, with an icy wind blasting between the huts, and the young women all huddled inside.

'Listen to that!' Susan said, as the wind buffeted the roof. 'That'll be com'un off if it blows any harder.'

'What's it going to be like on a ship?' Joy said, rolling her eyes.

It felt as if it was going to be a long day. Most of the registration and checks for immigration were now completed. They were ready to go, and the waiting felt long and pointless. On all their minds was the next leg of the journey, and for now they just had to get through the day.

Patty was on the floor, playing with Susan's little boy, Davie, and another child. They had put a rug down on the bare floorboards for them to sit on.

The door of the hut opened suddenly, with a great gust of freezing air, and they all shrieked in protest. One of the POWs put his head around the door.

'A Miss Gilby?'

Joy looked up. 'Yes, that's me?'

'Come.' He beckoned. 'Please, now.'

'It's OK – leave her here with us,' Susan said. Patty was happily absorbed in her game, and Joy smiled a thank you as she got up, with some of the other women making larky jokes about who wanted her and what for.

She pulled on her coat and followed the POW outside, to cries of 'Shut that door!'

In broken English the young man said, 'A person wanting to see you. In ze reception office.' He pointed to the motorcycle he had ridden across on to deliver the message. 'You on get?'

For those few moments, speeding along the snow-lined road of the base, all Joy could think was, I'm on a motorbike with a German! It was only when she clambered off at the reception office, her feet already numb, that she started to be curious about what she was wanted for. No doubt one of the endless forms she had been required to fill in had something missing from it.

The German POW nodded in a military fashion and said, 'I wait.'

'Oh,' she replied. 'Yes. Thank you.'

She went inside the now-familiar building. There was no one around, except for a woman standing looking at the map of America on the wall. No doubt she was working out where the hell she was going to have to travel when she got there.

And then the woman turned round. Joy's breath caught. In that second she *knew*, her instincts taking over from her thoughts. Her blood quickened, thudding in her ears, and everything seemed laid out before her, though she would have been unable to put a single word of it into speech. Not then.

Because the woman dressed in a dark-grey coat and blue hat with a brim, whose strong features had turned towards her as soon as Joy came in and made her hurry to greet her, was Irene Bishop.

Joy stood there, unable to move or speak.

'I had to come,' Irene said quietly. 'I know you're going – over there. I know you've got your little girl, and that he's her father. And your mom said maybe I shouldn't – that you should be left alone . . .'

Joy stared at her, waiting; just waiting for the words.

'He's home. I mean, not home – not for a while yet. He's in hospital.' Irene's eyes filled and she looked really distressed. 'He's not in a good way. I went to see him two days ago. He hardly looks like our Alan. But he asked for you, Joy. He kept crying and asking for you, over and over again. It's all right, bab – I know it's a shock. Come on over here.'

Irene grabbed hold of Joy, as her shaking legs started to give way, and helped her on to a chair.

Fifty-Six

'They say the hospital's been moved here for the time being,' Irene said, looking up at the imposing, though neglected and smut-encrusted edifice of the Hospital for Tropical Diseases in Devonshire Street, London. 'Their other building was damaged in the Blitz.'

Joy felt sick. The past two days had been a whirl of bewildering activity, all so fast that she had had no time to catch up with what she had done. Things felt unreal. Irene's words, when they first met at Tidworth Camp, had pierced her soul. *He kept crying . . . Asking for you . . .*

It was as if something cracked in her mind; as if she had been forcing herself to live in a fragile glass globe in which her only future could lie with Hank, in going to America, in taking his daughter to meet him in Philadelphia. It was what everyone said she had to do, and she had not allowed herself to think of anything else. But Irene's few words broke open this shell that she had built around her thoughts, her hopes and fears. It was like crashing back to earth. There was fear and regret and worry – but amid all that, such a warm flood of relief. She didn't belong in Philadelphia. Here, at home in Birmingham, was where she belonged, where she wanted to be.

Joy took time only to pack her little bag with her things and Patty's. She went, with Irene, to convert her dollars back into pounds.

'I'm sorry,' she said curtly to the man handing her the currency – those familiar green Bank of England notes! 'I can't go. Can you cross me off the list? I've changed my mind.'

From her finger she slipped the brass wedding ring she had worn ever since she was heavily pregnant with Patty. She had never actually married Hank. It was bad enough carrying his child out of wedlock and now letting him down, without breaking marriage vows as well.

She was sure there were other official things she needed to do, but the rest of the arrangements would have to wait. She and Irene travelled back to Birmingham together and arranged to meet to take the train to London the following day.

'Alan's been in the country for a few weeks,' Irene told her on the way. 'They had him in hospital out there for quite a while, apparently, and they thought he was well enough to come home. But by the time they got him here – he said he flew into some air base or other – he'd collapsed.'

Joy tensed with misgiving. 'That sounds bad.'

Irene nodded. 'He's very weak. My mother hasn't seen him yet. I've told her things are better than they really are. Better if she sees him when he's well again.'

No wonder Joy's head was whirling as she stood, looking up at the hospital. From Tidworth and a quick goodbye to Susan and the other girls, via the shock, the confused dismay and happiness of Mom and the rest of the family, when she and Patty arrived back on their doorstep. And now to London – to see the man who, for so long, she had had to bury in her mind and never expected to see again. The man they had all forced themselves to lay to rest. The man she loved.

It was no good now asking herself whether she had done the right thing. Last night Mom had said, 'I suppose you could go on another ship later, if . . .' Her face was so full of anxiety that Joy could hardly bear it.

'I'm not going, Mom,' she said, looking down at her lap, trying to put all her confused feelings into words. 'Not to America. I don't like myself for letting Hank down. He's a good man – and I let myself start to fall in love with him because . . . I thought Alan was never coming back. But I owe it to Alan, Mom. He's the one I really love. I've got to stick by him.'

As they pushed open the doors of the ward they were met by a nurse in a crisp uniform, hair smoothed neatly under her cap, her eyes dark and serious.

'You have come to see . . .?'

'Alan Bishop,' Irene said. Joy could hardly even breathe.

The nurse's face softened. 'Yes, I remember now. You're his sister. And you? It's family only, I'm afraid.'

'This is Joy. She'd be his wife, if he'd not gone into the Army,' Irene said. 'Please – he's been so upset and begging me to bring her to see him.'

'Yes,' the nurse relented, hesitating. 'Joy. I have heard him mention your name a number of times. Look, perhaps I could have a word with you first.'

She indicated that they should step outside the ward once more, into a polished corridor where she spoke quietly and discreetly.

'Mr Bishop was deemed fit to be returned home. What seems to have happened is a flare-up of malaria, but also of various parasites that have taken up residence in his body.' Seeing Joy's alarmed expression, she smiled, very slightly. 'Both are very common, sadly. The tropics are teeming with such opportunists. If he were in better health generally, this would not lay him so low, but of course his system has been weakened by the conditions in the camps.'

They both stared at her.

'Did you not know?' The amazement showed on her face, despite her cool professionalism. 'Mr Bishop has been held in a camp run by the Japanese these past two and a half years. None of us know the full details, of course – we probably never shall. But the conditions were brutal. He is improving, but of course,' she finished carefully, 'the healing he needs is not only going to be in his body. You must not expect too much of him, my dear . . . Are you all right?'

Joy's sick feeling of dread had increased until she was starting to feel faint, but she did her best to nod. Seeing Alan after all this time felt strange enough. But who was it exactly that she was going to see? Lights flashed at the sides of her vision and she bent over for a moment, desperately trying to pull herself together. It was Alan who had been through who-knew-what, not her. A moment later she stood up cautiously.

'I'm all right now, thanks.' She gave the nurse a valiant smile.

'Third bed along the left,' the nurse said quietly as they went back in through the door. 'Just approach slowly and don't, whatever you do, take him by surprise. Let him realize someone is coming towards him.'

Bewildered, they obeyed. As they stepped along the polished floor, Joy was touched to feel Irene take her hand.

'It's all right,' she whispered. 'It's a bit of a shock, but he's still Alan, don't worry.'

Joy saw the outline of a thin body under the bedclothes, lying with his head slightly raised, a hollowed-out face, yellowish against the pillow, his eyes fixed on the ceiling. A kind of shock of recognition went through her – and, for an instant, of something more like horror. As they moved closer, it attracted his attention and his eyes swivelled towards them and stared, with a burning intensity. But there was nothing: no smile, no reaction.

'Hello, Alan,' Irene said softly. 'I've brought Joy to see you.'

For a second Joy felt like running away. It was as if Alan had no idea who either of them was. He seemed locked in a world of his own. And he was so emaciated she could hardly see that it was the vibrant lad she had said goodbye to in 1940, half a lifetime ago, as it seemed now.

Alan jerked upright suddenly with what seemed an angry violence, which made Joy think he was about to jump out of bed and come at her, and she stepped backwards in alarm. But there was little strength in him, and a second later she realized he was only trying to sit up, as if he had to find the force within him to launch himself into an upright position.

'It's all right, Alan – here, let's give you a hand,' Irene said, going to him and helping him.

But his eyes never left Joy's face.

'Come on,' Irene beckoned her gently. Joy could see tears in her eyes. 'Come and sit with him, Joy.'

Joy looked round nervously. She knew the rules in hospitals were very strict and she was probably not meant to sit on the bed. But it was too bad, and at that moment there was no one watching. She went and sat on the side of the mattress, her body trembling.

'Hello, Al,' she said.

His face crumpled immediately and his whole body began to shake with sobs. 'Joy. It's Joy. You're here . . .'

The sound of his voice tore at her: it had the high, reedy tone of someone weakened by hunger and sickness. Very gently she leaned forward and took him in her arms, sobs rising in her too as she felt the bones of him, the frail sickness of the man, reduced to a weeping shadow. Love rose within her, tender and fierce. This was where she had to be – whatever else. Here, with Alan.

'I'm here, my love,' she murmured, rocking him gently as she did Patty when she was tired or upset, as he kept sobbing out her name, over and over again like a prayer he had been saying, which had now reached its final Amen. She laid her hand softly on the back of his head, also as she often did with her little girl. 'It's all right. It's going to be OK, my darling. I'm here. I'm going to be here – always.'

Fifty-Seven

July

Ann turned as the bridal march struck up in St Francis's Church. Alan was waiting at the altar, seeming, in the shadowy light, a stooping stick-figure, someone almost without substance. Ann experienced the same wave of sorrow and pity for him that she had felt each time she had seen him since he came back. Poor lad, hollowed out and withdrawn – what in heaven's name had he been through?

Joy appeared, on Len's arm, the pair of them silhouetted against the bright sunlight outside. No veil and white cascades of lace for Joy. She had chosen to be married in an old but favourite dance dress, a diaphanous grey with an underskirt of plum satin and a dove-grey hat. The dress hung a little looser on her than when she was a curvaceous teenager before the war, but she still looked lovely, her dark eyes accentuated by eye-shadow, and her hair swept up and pinned prettily so that a few tendrils framed her cheeks under the hat.

'Look,' Ann whispered, 'there's your mummy.'

She was holding Patty, who was standing on the pew peering along the church, making sure the little girl didn't fall. Looking round, a couple of rows back Ann saw Hilda and the rest of the Baines family: Roy and their son John, now safely returned, and Norma and Danny and their kids. Beside them was Jeanette, and Ann returned their glad smiles. Gratitude filled her: here they were all together – well, almost all. Family and friends.

It might not have been like this. Joy might have been with her American on the other side of the world by now. Much as Ann had taken to Hank, she was so happy and relieved that Joy had, in the end, stayed.

Joy had shown her the letter she had written to Hank.

'It's one of the worst things I've ever had to do, Mom,' she said, holding it out to Ann to read, her eyes red from crying. 'The only thing that makes me feel a tiny bit better is . . .' and she started to cry again, 'he never even seemed that interested in Patty. Never asked or anything. Don't you think that's strange?'

'Well,' Ann said carefully, taking the letter, 'maybe none of it had really hit home to him? You weren't even expecting her when he left – well, not so far as he knew.'

'*Hank, I'm so, so sorry . . .*' Joy's letter began. '*I know you must think badly of me, but I can't come to America, and I can't marry you.*'

Over and over again she apologized from the depths of her heart and explained what had happened – Alan's return and all that came with it. She was honest with Hank, saying how sorry she was that she was depriving him of his daughter, how she could send pictures of Patty, if he would like, and maybe one day he might even meet her . . . And that Alan was prepared to be a father to Patty, and that she would be loved and taken care of.

She had sent the letter nearly six months ago and, to everyone's surprise, there had been no reply – not to date, at least. Whether Hank's silence was through hurt or anger, relief or indifference, it was impossible to know. Ann felt for the lad. But, she told herself, he had shown no interest in Patty, either previously or now. He was not offering to take any responsibility, it seemed.

'I suppose I was his little English fling,' Joy said sadly, after two months had passed. 'I just thought Hank might be better than that. The thing is, though, Mom . . .' She looked guiltily at Ann. 'Even when I was getting ready to go to America, I kept trying to see his face in my mind and I could hardly remember it. I wanted to love him and I really tried. But maybe he can't really remember me, either. As if I've sort of faded in his memory.'

Ann smiled sadly at her. 'There have been a lot of ships passing in the night during this war,' she said. 'And what with Alan and everything, you've had to make a choice that no one should have to make, love. Hank was a nice lad, but maybe it's for the best – for both of you.'

Joy nodded. 'I expect he'll find himself a nice American girl soon and she'll fit in better anyway.'

Ann put her arms round her daughter briefly, giving her a squeeze. 'Let's hope so.'

And now, she thought, her eyes filling as she swivelled to watch Len and Joy approaching Alan at the altar, nothing is ideal: Joy is with another man's child; Alan's sick and damaged, that is clear; and all the other changes and complications in her own family.

'Mommy!' Patty called, squirming in Ann's arms. Joy turned for a second to give her little girl a wave. Ann had been afraid the child might cry, but she just stared in fascination. At seventeen months, she took most things in.

'Mummy will be with you soon,' Ann whispered, kissing Patty's warm cheek. 'And we'll have our little party.'

And when had things ever been ideal? she wondered, looking along the pew to where Sheila was standing with Elaine and Robbie, and with Martin and Margaret and

Cyril. Sheila had heard from Kenneth that he expected to be despatched back to Britain and demobbed any day now. Soon everyone would be here. They were all alive. How very blessed they were, compared with so many others.

She cuddled Patty close, listening as Joy and Alan exchanged their vows. When Joy had come home from London that day, wrung out, she was so full of emotion that Ann had felt bound to ask. She had waited until she was alone with her daughter, side by side on the bed in her room.

'He looks terrible,' Joy wept. 'God alone knows what the Japanese did to him. Irene had seen him already, so it was less of a shock to her. But when I first saw Alan, I actually felt it go through me – like electricity.' She raised her face to Ann's, seeming ashamed. 'For a second I wanted to run away. He looked so terrible, like a complete stranger.'

Ann put her arm round Joy's shoulders. 'It must have been a shock for you.'

She nodded. 'He looked at us as if he'd never seen us before. And then he saw who I was and he was so—' Joy sobbed so hard she could not speak for a time. 'He was so . . . wretched. Sort of pathetic. I could never've imagined him being like that. But then he spoke to me and I knew it was Alan, and I started to get used to him. But he was so upset.'

'Did you tell him, about Patty?'

'I did – in the end. He was crying and he just kept saying my name and that he had been thinking about me all this time, through all of it . . . He said I was what had made him stay alive.' Again she looked at Ann. 'That's a bit frightening. I worry that he's expecting too much, as if he doesn't remember who I really am. And I thought, he's got to know: now, before it's too late.'

She pulled away and sat upright on the flowery eiderdown.

'I said, "Alan, there's something you need to know." He was clinging to me and he was in such a state that I was worried he wouldn't take anything in. "You must listen," I said. "Because I need to tell you something very serious." I could feel him tense up. I suppose he thought I had married someone else long ago or something. So I said, "I'm not married, Alan, it's not that. But you've been away a long time and I didn't hear a word from you. I thought . . . well, I thought I'd never see you again." I was trying not to cry, because I knew I had to say it. "I've got a baby daughter. She's called Patty."

'Alan pulled back then and looked at me. He was calm, not how I'd expected. As if he'd really heard what I said. It sort of cut through me. And he said, "Are you going to marry him – the father?" I said no, I wasn't, and he wasn't even in this country; and that if Alan could bear it, I wanted to be with him.' Joy's face contorted with emotion.

'And then Irene said, "Joy was just about to go to America, Alan – until she heard you were back."

'And Alan said, "A little girl." He didn't look angry or smile, or anything, he just took it in. And then he held my hand and said, "D'you think, after all this, a little girl is going to make any difference to anything? I want us to have a house full of little girls and boys. I've been to hell and back, and I want life, Joy – and I want you. That's all I need in the world."'

Alan, though still very thin, had grown stronger over the past five months as he convalesced, and they had set the wedding to take place on what turned out to be this lovely summer morning. Ann watched the two of them. She knew things were going to be far from easy. Joy had already told her that Alan's moods were very unpredictable. He had finally left hospital a month ago and gone to stay with his parents, and Irene confided in her mother that he was withdrawn most of the time, but sometimes burst out in a violent temper.

All this was going to take time to settle down, Ann thought, trying to quell her misgivings. Alan was a good lad and, for today, they would enjoy the celebration and put aside any fears for the future.

The couple processed out to *'Love divine, all loves excelling'* and everyone followed, singing and showering them with a scant amount of rice and confetti. The moment was frozen in time as the photographer pictured the whole family outside the church: 20 July 1946 – Joy, head back and smiling, her lips meeting Alan's, with all her family and his grouped around them, set for ever in the family history, on paper in black and white.

Ann had made sandwiches for them all back at the house. It was only a step away and was easy for everyone. She, Margaret, Jeanette and Irene had pooled their rations and at least managed an iced sponge as a wedding cake. Joy said she was not keen on fruitcake in any case.

The children whirled about the garden, full of excitement, and the adults settled down to enjoy a bite to eat and the celebration in general. Alan's father came in for a drink, looking very uncomfortable, and took himself off quite soon afterwards. But Irene and Ivy stayed, and Ann saw Jeanette talking gently with Ivy Bishop. Martin had come home with his friend Jack, both still Bevin Boys and big, solid lads.

'When are they going to let you out of there then?' Roy asked Martin. 'I've got to hand it to you, lad, I'd never've seen you doing a job like that, but you seem to be making a go of it.'

'We don't know.' Martin smiled at Jack. 'It was our war effort, and now it seems to be our National Service. I'll be glad when it's over – but it's not too bad. It's taught me all sorts of things I'd never've found out by staying in a classroom.'

'Such as?' Sheila teased.

'Ah,' Martin winked, 'wouldn't you like to know?'

Ann was in the kitchen, putting together another plate of tinned-salmon sandwiches, when Len came in. He looked shy of her almost, bashful.

'Good spread. I think it went off all right.'

'It did.' She smiled at him. She didn't want to say, 'I do hope they're going to be all right' or mention any of those misgivings, not today. It was their day to be proud parents. 'Well, that's two you've given away!'

Len was quiet, his fingers gently running along the edge of the kitchen table, looking down at it. He turned suddenly and pushed the door closed, then said, gently, 'Just you to go now, I suppose?'

Ann froze and looked up at him, then walked round the table and stood in front of him, this husband of hers. They could hear the happy laughter from the front room.

'I didn't expect us to be saying this, right at this moment.' She smiled, tears rising in her eyes. 'I suppose we have to give each other away, don't we, Len?'

They moved closer and put their arms around each other, holding one another close and tender, as old and good friends. After a few seconds Ann felt a tremor go through him and realized Len was crying as well. They stayed for a few moments in each other's arms, before drawing back.

'Look at the state of us!' Ann laughed, blowing her nose. Len was mopping his face and he attempted a watery smile. 'Come on, we've got to pull ourselves together – we've got a wedding to celebrate!'

Fifty-Eight

Ann stood on the platform at New Street, amid the cigarette smoke of strangers and the mellow warmth of late summer. It was a beautiful September day and a pale straw hat shaded her eyes. In the shadows of the dingy, war-wounded station she pulled her cardigan closer around her, tinglingly aware of every second of her life *at this moment*, of a sense of fate. She knew this was a day she would never, ever forget.

She was early, but she was too full of nervous energy to sit down even if there had been a seat free, so she strolled along the platform, shivery with expectation. These last few weeks had been an extraordinary time of change, of cleaving together and letting go.

For a start, Kenneth had arrived home. Ann had come back from work to find a tall, strong man – seemingly taller and stronger than she ever remembered – in a wide-lapelled demob suit, his tanned face beaming at her as she came in, and Sheila's beaming even more.

'Hello, Mom,' he said, getting up.

'Oh!' Ann put her bag down and flung her arms around her son-in-law. 'You should have warned us, Kenneth – we'd have put the flags out!'

'I don't need flags,' Kenneth said easily, letting go of her. 'All I need is my wife and kids. And I wanted to give Sheila a surprise.'

'I was just on my way out to fetch the kids from school,'

Sheila said, looking radiant. 'And there he was, walking along the street!'

'Oh, I'm so glad,' Ann cried. 'It's wonderful to have you home, Kenneth.'

'That's my daddy,' Elaine instructed her, as if Ann might not have this information.

'It is.' Ann took her hand. 'And you can be a good girl and come and help me make us all a nice cup of tea.'

She and Len had had long conversations in their room at night. There had been talks with Margaret and Cyril – dreaded by Ann, but in the end nothing like as bad as the first time. Everyone would be nearby somewhere, in the end. They would not be losing their family.

'We love all of you – you know that, don't you?' Margaret said eventually, when they had talked everything through. 'I never thought I'd hear the word "divorce" uttered in this family. But . . .' She shook her head. 'Well, we're not taking sides; what's the good of that?'

'It's odd to think how your mom's altered, looking back, isn't it?' Ann said to Len that night.

'Yeah.' He was sitting on his side of the bed and Ann was lying back against the pillows. 'Haven't we all, though? The war, I s'pose, partly. Changed a lot of things, hasn't it?'

'And the last one did.'

Len nodded. 'I'll say.'

'Certainly made it hard for all these young 'uns to find somewhere to live, hasn't it?'

Sheila and Kenneth and Joy and Alan would be waiting for housing for ages to come, it seemed. So many houses had been lost in the bombing or were slated for demolition. It felt as if the city was altering its shape.

'At least Marianne's got somewhere,' she went on.

Marianne was in fact doing rather well for herself. She

had worked hard and was being promoted at Boots the Chemist. And she had moved from her lodgings into a couple of rooms and had been able to take George back to live with her. She had found a shy young woman who seemed very well cut out to look after the boy when he needed it. After all, he was at school now, so a lot of the time things were easier. It was agreed that he would come and stay with his father for the occasional weekend and holiday.

Len was still not saying much. Ann leaned over and poked him in the side.

'You and all your women.'

He flinched, turning to her with a rueful look. 'Don't say that. Makes me sound terrible.'

'What're we going to do?' Suddenly she was deadly serious. 'It's going to be – well, not nice for a while, isn't it? Divorce and that . . .'

'I'm not even sure where to start.' Len shrugged, but then said hesitantly, 'At least Jeanette's got a place of her own.' Jeanette lived in her mother's terraced house in Maryvale Road. 'You could have our house – you and him.' He still could not quite say Tom's name without flinching.

Ann's mind was working fast.

'In the long run, yes. Thanks,' she said. 'But for the moment, I think the kids should live here. Sheila and family, and Joy and Alan. Alan's got to get away from his father, by all accounts, and the house is like a sardine can . . .'

Tom's words from the last time they had spoken echoed insistently in her mind: *I've got a ridiculous amount of space here. I'm rattling about on my own now. And I've still got to finalize things with the business. Once it's sold, at least I'll have some money available.*

And so the goodbyes this time had only been temporary: Ann giving notice at Cadbury's and settling the two couples into their house, and Len being about to move into the next street. All of them were still trying to take it in.

She put her case down now and turned, hearing the immense beast of a locomotive drawing closer, and watched it slide in alongside the platform, with its fierce, smoky breaths and glowing smuts. Ann climbed into the carriage, stowed her case and sat down. She breathed out, for what seemed a long time.

She stepped out of the carriage at Southampton, feeling as if she had entered a dream – a strangeness that was set to continue.

He was waiting, a figure emerging once more from the smoke, older but always the same, a little lopsided-looking in a brown jacket with its empty sleeve, the eye-patch behind his spectacles, the brown trilby. Him: her Tom, the same.

Thirty years to the day, almost, since she had parted from him as he left the hospital in Selly Oak, there was Tom, smiling, still loving her as she had loved him, all this time. And one day, after all this time, they too might be able to marry – as well as Len and Jeanette.

As their eyes met, he raised his hat and his smile broadened. She went to him, putting her case down, and they stood for a moment, looking into each other's eyes, still half in disbelief.

'Hello, Ann,' Tom said, his face – that beloved face – full of a tender joy that she had remembered and loved for so long.

'Hello, my love,' she said. And they stepped into each other's arms.

Acknowledgements

My thanks for particular details for this book go to: The Cadbury Library at Birmingham University for access to the *Bournville Works Magazine* for this period; to Sarah Foden at the Cadbury (Mondelez) archive and to Pat Hayward.

Among many books I consulted were: *Chocolate Wars* by Deborah Cadbury; *A History of Cadbury* by Diane Wordsworth; *The RAF Air-Sea Rescue Service in the Second World War* by Norman Franks; *Shot Down and in the Drink* by Graham Pitchfork; *Joyce's War* by Joyce Storey; *Called Up and Sent Down: The Bevin Boys' War* by Tom Hickman; *Over Here* by Juliet Gardiner; *Desert Rats* by Roger Fogg; and *A Cruel Captivity: Prisoners of the Japanese, Their Ordeal and The Legacy* by Ellie Taylor.

**Statistical Power Analysis
for the Behavioral Sciences**

Second Edition

Statistical Power Analysis
for the Behavioral Sciences

Second Edition

Jacob Cohen

Department of Psychology
New York University
New York, New York

LEA LAWRENCE ERLBAUM ASSOCIATES, PUBLISHERS
1988   Hillsdale, New Jersey   Hove and London

Lawrence Erlbaum Associates, Inc., Publishers
365 Broadway
Hillsdale, New Jersey 07642

First edition published 1969.
Revised edition published 1977.

Library of Congress Cataloging in Publication Data

Cohen, Jacob, 1923–
      Statistical power analysis for the behavioral sciences / Jacob
   Cohen. — 2nd ed.
            p.   cm.
      Bibliography: p.
      Includes index.
      ISBN 0-8058-0283-5
      1. Social sciences — Statistical methods.   2. Probabilities.
   I. Title.
   HA29.C66   1988   88-12110
   300′.1′5195 — dc19   CIP

PRINTED IN THE UNITED STATES OF AMERICA

10

to Marcia and Aviva